The Sugar Daughter

Also by Sharon Maas:

Of Marriageable Age
The Small Fortune of Dorothea Q
The Secret Life of Winnie Cox

middle of the crowd, a commotion, and a man started talking and shouting some sort of gibberish. He then threw himself to the ground, stood on his head and danced around on his head. It was a quiet man, Mr Gibb, a coach driver, who had never behaved strangely before. Somebody threw a bucket of water over him, which made him fall on his back. A few minutes later he got up and couldn't remember a thing. And everybody said afterwards he'd been possessed by an evil spirit from Le Repentir cemetery. That's the kind of place I was taking my Winnie to.

We lived on Butcher Street, which was one of the richer streets, with separate cottages in big yards full of fruit trees. It was probably named after Mr Khan, who had his butcher shop up near the north. Other streets in Albouystown were full of long buildings called ranges, tenements where several families lived together sharing the space. So we were actually lucky. But when I took Winnie there I didn't feel lucky. I felt ashamed.

Everyone here was struggling, and everyone here was coloured, either African or Indian. Except my bride. She would be the only white lady in the whole of Albouystown. People would stare. They would shun her. They would be afraid of her, just like they were afraid of all white people. I don't want to say it, because saying things sometimes makes them happen, but there were people in Albouystown who might wish her ill. Who might do her wrong. But when I told that to Winnie, she only stroked my cheek and smiled and said, 'George, George, don't worry about a thing. I can take care of myself.' And she did.

* * *

Winnie, if you are reading this – do you remember those first days, weeks? After the wedding, when I brought you home? I carried you over the threshold into that cottage. I felt bad about that, because I did not have a house of my own to offer you, but only a bedroom in my parents' home. But you said you did not mind, and maybe you really didn't. You laughed when I swept you up into my arms and carried you over the threshold; your veil caught on a nail in the door and because the veil was attached to your hairdo, all your hair was pulled away and it hung loose and when I set you down it was all over your shoulders, and you were laughing, laughing; and then you changed out of your wedding gown and we went off on our honeymoon, and then I brought you back home to Albouystown and our married life began in earnest.

Ma and Pa were in awe of her; all they saw was her skin, and in spite of what Ma had said, about white women stabbing you in the back, the truth was her upbringing reneged on all that and awe overcame suspicion. And now she was their daughter-in-law. White people had to be catered to, but you don't cater to a daughter-in-law, do you? You're supposed to be in authority, as her elder; they didn't know what to do.

* * *

I put Winnie down, careful that she should land on her own two feet. She was still laughing, grabbing her loose hair and pulling it back, and she stumbled, knocking over the little hall table. Ma heard the commotion and came out of the kitchen, drying her hands on her apron. She saw Winnie, and *curtsied*. I couldn't believe it. Ma curtsied! It was terrible, but Winnie handled it with grace; she opened her arms to Ma and gathered her into an embrace that was as genuine as it was touching, so that it looked as if there had been no curtsy at all; it looked as if Winnie had not noticed, even though she had.

'Where's Pa?' I asked. I was still dying of embarrassment because of that curtsy and I had to do something to distract from it, though of course Winnie already had, and in fact, Ma was still in Winnie's arms and Winnie was smiling at her and Ma was smiling back. But I still asked, 'Where's Pa?'

'Where you think? At Bernie's.'

And again I almost died of embarrassment.

'On my wedding day?' How could Pa go off to Bernie's, today of all days? Just an hour ago he was at the reception in the church hall. Just a small reception, the same people who had been at the wedding. But of course Albouystown folk were curious. They had gathered on the road outside trying to get a glimpse of the bride. Winnie must have been the only white lady who had ever stepped into Albouystown, and word had spread and people wanted to get a glimpse of her. You can't blame them. Everyone loves a wedding, a bride, and especially such an unusual one. I didn't blame them at all, for standing outside the church and then the church hall to ogle my Winnie.

But I was embarrassed, for her. But what did she do? She waved! You waved at them, Winnie, and you smiled, that innocent smile of yours. But they did not wave back. They simply stood and stared, and that's when I knew there was going to be trouble. And yet I knew: it would be good. In the end it would be good. Winnie would win them over, just as she had won Ma over, in the end. Winnie was like that. She would make everything good. And she was still only nineteen years old. Not yet twenty, not yet of age, and already she knew the wisdom of the heart: that everyone deep inside wants only to be loved, but that to love is greater than to be loved. And without even knowing these strangers, she was loving them with just a wave and a smile. They might not love her back, as yet, but they would.

But now that was over and here we were in that cramped little front hall and Winnie picking up the table she had knocked over. I should have done that but my awkwardness had lamed me and all I could think of was Pa's rudeness in not being at home to welcome my bride. Ma and Pa had not stayed long at the reception and they knew I would be bringing her home and the least Pa could do was be there when she came. But Pa didn't think that far. Pa had only one love, one obsession, and that was at

Bernie's. I knew what Pa would be doing. He would be sitting at Bernie's desk poring over a stamp album. Because that was what Pa loved most in the world: stamps. Postage stamps. And Bernie, who lived in Kingston and had a big house, had the best stamp collection in the whole of Georgetown and Bernie's was where Pa could be found whenever you were looking for him. So even on my wedding day, that was where Pa was to be found and I burned with shame. But I couldn't say anything, not in front of Winnie. So I just frowned at Ma to let her know I disapproved, and I turned to my bride and said, 'I'll show you our room. Would you like to rest? Or take a bath?'

She laughed. 'Rest? On my wedding day? Gracious me, no, of course not! I just want to get this dress off and put on some comfortable clothes. And I want to be off on our honeymoon!'

'You got to eat first!' said Ma. All Ma ever thought of was cooking and baking and feeding people, and wonderful smells were wafting their way out of the kitchen, and Ma came to her senses in that moment because she exclaimed, 'Oh Laus! Me pine tarts!' and she ran back into the kitchen.

I wasn't hungry, not in the least, so I said to Winnie again, 'Come.'

And I took her hand and led her into that bedroom.

Winnie and I occupied a double room. It was just a little bit bigger than the bed, which was jammed into a corner. On the other side of the bed there was a wardrobe. The doors in the wardrobe could not open properly, because the space between the wardrobe and the bed was too narrow. I was ashamed of these cramped quarters, but Winnie never complained. She pretended not to mind; she turned her back to me and asked me to unbutton her dress, which I did, and then I turned away to give her some privacy while she changed her clothes. Her little suitcase lay on the bed. We had had it sent there in advance. It was all she had brought into our marriage, though she had much more, of course. But Winnie knew she couldn't bring all her clothes. She knew that all there was room for was what fitted into this one suitcase. And I left her to change and went out to talk to Ma.

'Ma,' I said when I got to the kitchen, 'You can't do that. You can't curtsy to your daughter-in-law!'

'Don't give me no eye-pass!' she retorted. 'Who is the child and who is the parent? Just because you got a white-skin wife you think you could order me around, tell me what I can do and can't do?'

And she was of course right – a son shouldn't be reprimanding his mother – but the truth was, I was completely mortified by this situation, bringing Winnie home to such a place, and that was why I was rude to my own mother, giving her eye-pass.

Ma was bent over the oven, removing a tray of pine tarts. Ma's pine tarts were the best in all of Albouystown. The best in Georgetown. The best in the world! And even though I was still full from all the food we'd had at the reception – food that Ma had cooked – I couldn't resist; I stretched out my hand, forgetting that they were straight out of the oven and scalding hot. I soon found out; I cried out and Ma laughed, and all was forgiven.

So now I was Winnie's husband, the happiest man in the world, and the luckiest. I must put away this shame and this awe and just be myself, be the man Winnie knew, the man she had married, because she loved him. She did not want my awe.

'I don't have much to give you,' I said as I put her down.

'All I want is your heart.'

Winnie: the romantic. The trouble is, when she said these things she meant them, and she lived them. She did give me her heart. But I did not take good care of it.

I wanted so much to be strong for her. A man; manly. Her hero. To protect her and provide for her and our children, all while adoring her with every fibre of my being. Instead, I stabbed her in the back.

Winnie: what can I do to earn your forgiveness?

Chapter Two

Yoyo

I wore a hat to Winnie's wedding – and *such* a hat! That hat was the talk of the town, afterwards, as I knew it would be. It was the most beautiful, and widest-rimmed, hat ever worn in British Guiana. I had it made especially for the wedding. Winnie's wedding dress was rather plain, just as she is, so I knew that my hat would be what the ladies admired, more than her dress. The brim was almost a foot wide. It was trimmed with frothy lace and real red roses – my hat was a work of art, and that's the way it should be. Everyone I spoke to commented on my hat. It was a complete success.

Now, why would I be talking about a hat, a mere hat, so soon after my sister's wedding? You'd have to know what went before to fully understand. This wedding should never have taken place. It was an abomination. I could not believe that my sister, my shy, soft-spoken big sister, she who had always deferred to me, would actually go through with it, but she did. I had given her my opinion on this farce of a wedding but she did not heed me, and rather than create a scandal, with my opposition to it out in the open, and make my family the laughing stock of British Guiana society, I played along, pretending to have been swayed by her never-ending love for her so charming darkie groom.

I've never believed in romance. I'm as romantic as an old potato. Romance is a silly notion that infects most women, the silliest kind of women. I'm a married woman myself, and I know what men want, and it's not romance. I know what makes them fall to their knees before a woman, what can sway even the strongest man. That is the weakness of men, and all Winnie did was find a man who was easy to conquer. It was unbelievable. You don't marry a man for *that!*

Of course, there's no dearth of single English males hungry for wives in the colony, but hardly any of them are marriageable. Either they are Booker men – whom a Cox girl may not marry, for political reasons; or else they are ageing, or else they are, well, simply horrid. Yet does a lady need to stoop *that* low? As the elder of us, Winnie could have had the cream of the cake: my Clarence. Yet she rejected Clarence in favour of this George, this darkie postboy, and so Clarence is mine.

* * *

I married him soon after my father's trial; a small, inconspicuous wedding. I married him for two reasons:

One: So that I could take over management of the estate. Even as a sixteen-year-old I correctly assessed him as weak of character, and easy for a woman to control.

Two: to produce sons.

Promised Land must remain stable and strong far into the future, and the only way is to raise young men whose hearts and blood are wedded to the plantation – young men with sugar in the blood, young men whose hearts would race at the pungent smell of the burning of the trash, young men who can walk through the towering canes and know: this is my home. I will protect it with my last breath.

I don't care much for babies and young children but I suppose you can't have young men without them. Anyway, there are servants to deal with that problem.

And so, after my wedding all my energies went towards, firstly, training Clarence to know that I was the power behind the throne and, secondly, him impregnating me as soon as possible.

The first of those goals came easily enough; with my striking looks and even more striking character I soon held him in the palm of my hand. He is a foppish fellow, completely unsuited to plantation life; that he is here at all was the result of negotiations between Papa, or rather, Papa's solicitor in London, and Clarence's father Lord Smedley, who was anxious to see him removed from the dissolute life he was leading in London. So Clarence was imported to the colony by Papa, a surrogate son. He was supposed to invest in our struggling plantation, inherit it and marry one of the daughters, and as the elder sister remaining (our eldest, Kathleen, had left us for England years before), Winnie was the allotted one. But she rejected his advances, and so he turned to me. I was still only sixteen at the time, and needed Papa's permission, which he readily gave. After all, Clarence was now to manage the plantation, and we needed him firmly attached to the family by way of marriage.

Clarence, of course, was rejected by his own father, who got rid of him by sending him to us with a small fortune. He was a spoilt lounge lizard with a penchant for loose women, drink and gambling. Easy enough to braid into my hair; I needed him only for the position and the sons to come. And so Clarence was installed as heir to Plantation Promised Land, and in return invested the much-needed money for a sugar processing factory. Thrown into the deal, a Cox daughter as his wife – me. In this way Lord Smedley was able to wash his hands of this troublesome stain on the family name, and we got – well, we got Clarence.

He had – and still has – no knowledge of plantation business and no inclination to learn, whereas I have been absorbing the spirit of sugar and the rhythm of its seasons all my life. Learning the business side of it was easy for anyone with a quick brain, even a female. We didn't really need a Clarence, since I was there – but Papa had never heard of a woman running an estate, and

on rickety stilts, and little Indian children, some naked, who ran out to shout and wave at the car. They did not see many motor-cars, so we were decidedly a novelty. I waved back at them. *The next time I make this trip,* I resolved, *I will buy sweets and distribute them.*

Children! I smiled to myself. *Soon, very soon, George and I will have our own.*

I wanted many. A whole cricket team: lots of delightful girls and boys. I smiled to myself and then drifted off to sleep, leaning against the car door, my shawl bundled into a pillow.

* * *

We both awoke when we reached the ferry, and Mama and I straightened our clothes and hair and stepped out of the car to stretch our legs. The Berbice River is not as wide as the Demerara, but the water is just as brown – like the Atlantic. Our governess, Miss Wright, had told us that it was brown due to the waters of the Amazon River, several miles down the coast in Brazil, which poured thousands of gallons of muddy water into the Atlantic every hour. That's why our water is not as clear and blue as the Caribbean Sea, though we are so near.

Chapter Four

George

The first day of our married life, I got up early, as usual, to go to work. Winnie rose with me.

'George,' she said, 'What am I to do today?'

I was nonplussed. What a strange question!

'Whatever you like, my love!' I said, and drew her into my arms, and kissed her a thousand times on her cheeks. She giggled, but then pulled away.

'No, but really. You are off to work, and I am alone here with your parents… What shall I do?'

'Well, you can talk to them. Get to know them. Ma will be cleaning the house and shopping and cooking – you can help her if you like.'

I immediately realised my mistake. I was talking to my wife as if she were one of us – a girl from Albouystown. I had forgotten that she was white, and white people don't clean or cook. I had to put that right immediately.

'No, of course you don't have to help Mama! As I said, you can do as you like.'

I was proud to be able to offer my wife leisure time, in keeping with her former life. I would not have her toiling in the kitchen.

'Well, I would like to come with you! Can I do that?'

I chuckled. 'I'm going to work, my darling. What would you do?'

And then I saw the tears in her eyes, and stopped laughing.

'What's the matter, my sweetheart?'

'I just – I'm just a little afraid of your mother. She's – she's so stern! I don't think she likes me!'

'Well, she will love you, just as I do. Who would not love you? And I'll tell you a secret…'

I whispered into her ear. 'Ma's a bit afraid of *you!* That's why she seems so unfriendly. She isn't really. Just be yourself and you'll be fine.'

'What – what shall I call her?'

'Just call her Ma.'

We had breakfast together, all four of us – Ma served us a boiled egg each, and some bread with butter and guava jelly, and coffee. And then I bid Winnie goodbye, and she came with me down the front stairs and I unlocked my bicycle and snapped on my bicycle clips.

'I'm going to miss you awfully!' she said, and I hugged and kissed her one last time. I wheeled my bicycle on to the road. She stood at the gate, watching, and as I sailed off she still watched; and as I reached the corner I looked back and she was still watching, and I waved, and she waved back. I prayed to God that she would settle down soon. Ma could be formidable when she wanted to be. But Winnie could be formidable too. This uncharacteristic shyness: it would pass. Winnie was fearless. She had proven it to me over the last two years. Fearless and stubborn, and yet soft and feminine – what a mighty combination! I had no doubt that Winnie would win my mother over. It was in her name: Winnie was a winner. A winner of hearts and minds.

* * *

When I returned home that afternoon I saw immediately that I had been right. The first thing I noticed on entering the cottage was the aroma – the mouth-watering smell of baking. It lured me on, and following the trail I came to the kitchen door, and at once I saw that Winnie had indeed won Ma's heart. The two of them were standing at the stove making rotis for dinner; Ma was teaching her how to toss the just-roasted rotis in the air, and clap them in mid-air. Both were white with the flying flour, and laughing. They didn't see me standing in the doorway, so intent they were on their work, and I stood watching, smiling, for a while.

'Don't be afraid!' Ma cried. 'Pick it up and throw it! Throw it!' Winnie kept touching the roti as it baked on the roti pan on the fire, and then pulling her fingers away.

'Ouch!' she cried, laughing. 'It's hot! Scalding hot!'

'Never mind it hot! Just grab it and toss it up! Like this!'

And Ma reached out, grasped the roti at its edge and nimbly tossed it a few feet into the air. 'Quick! Quick! Now clap! Clap it quick before it fall!'

Poor Winnie! The roti spun in the air and she reached out for it, trying to clap it, to puff it out, but she clapped thin air and the roti fell exhausted back on to the pan.

'Oh no!' cried Winnie.

'Try again quick! Before it burn!'

This time Winnie managed to grab the roti and toss it as quickly as Ma had, and when she clapped it she caught it right between her palms and gave it three swift claps, and it fell back as a perfectly formed roti.

I applauded, and they both swung round.

'George!' cried my wife, and flung herself at me, laughing, covered in flour as she was. At first I drew back, but then I couldn't help it – how could I reject Winnie's embrace? I let those floury arms close around me, and I let that floury face nudge mine, and I felt her lips on my cheek, and I knew heaven.

'I love your ma, George! We've had a lovely day! I met so many people and we went to Bourda Market and bought tons of provisions and she's teaching me to cook!'

'As I just saw!' I said.

'Come! Look!'

She pulled me into the tiny space we called a kitchen – there was just about standing room for the three of us. On the second burner of the stove stood a big black pot, covered. Winnie picked up a dishcloth, folded it to make a pad and lifted the cover. A cloud of heavenly-scented steam rose from the innards of the pot.

'Chicken curry!' said Winnie, and I could hear the pride in her voice. 'I made it all by myself – every bit of it! I skinned the chicken and boned and quartered it and chopped the vegetables and everything! I can cook! I can't believe I can cook!'

'She need more practice wit' dem rotis, though!' said Ma, and though she was pretending to grumble I could hear the approval in her voice. Everything was going to be fine.

Chapter Five

Yoyo

I should have been pleased to see Mama, but I wasn't. Not really. Mama had deserted us: sailed away to Europe, leaving us in Papa's care. She stayed away for years, never writing to us, wallowing in some kind of gloom that stripped her of every motherly emotion. Now, apparently, she was healed. Winnie lured her back from Austria, met her at the harbour and brought her back to Promised Land with all sorts of radical ideas about how to run a plantation. All these people who know nothing, nothing, about the business, breathing down my neck! It was enough to send a sane girl to the madhouse. But I must keep my sanity, for the sake of Promised Land.

I love my home. I love the Corentyne Coast, the land so flat it seems to last for ever, the ocean lapping at our northern border, the vast sky. Most of all, I love the house.

* * *

Our house in Promised Land is a palace, a fairytale castle made of wooden lace. It's constructed of sturdy greenheart in the Dutch Colonial style, just like those magnificent mansions in Georgetown's Main Street. It sparkles white in the sunlight. Its filigree fretwork, the lattices on the outside walls, the curlicues on the jutting Demerara windows let in the cool Atlantic breeze, which flows throughout the house, up and down stairs, over the walls and through the windows, so that it is never hot.

I know that Winnie, too, loves this house, this land. How can anyone who grew up here ever leave? We have sugar in our blood, we girls. And Winnie has destroyed it all. Or tried to.

How are the mighty fallen! Our father, he who now languishes in a prison, was once a sugar king. Kathleen, Winnie and I were raised as sugar princesses. Our realm is magical: a sunlit, wind-blown bubble of sweetness. Sugar is our livelihood, sugar establishes the seasons, sugar is our world. We grew up basking in sweetness and light.

The rhythm of sugar dictates this world, and any child growing up here knows each season by the sights, sounds and smells of the sugar cycle. Full growth, when the canes are high and wave against the sky, the greenness stretching for miles. Then the burning of the trash, when fire and smoke consume the fields and the air smells of scalded, syrupy, smoky cane juice, intoxicating in its pungency. At harvest, half-naked coolies wielding cutlasses swarm the fields, shouting and swearing as they slash their way through the canes, felling those giant scorched denuded canes. Then comes the time to load the punts. Those same cane-cutters, their bodies now smudged black with soot, ash and cane juice, bent low with the weight of the bundles on their backs, carrying the canes to the navigation canals. The mules, several of them chained together, pulling the loaded punts to the factory. Then the grinding season, when the factory groans and chugs day and night, a dark lurking monster turning the once-green canes to gold. Sugar is our gold. Corentyne gold, we call it. Corentyne gold, Essequibo gold, Demerara gold. Each county in British Guiana produces its own version of sugar wealth. After the harvest the once-glorious fields remain behind, denuded, ugly, disfigured by endless miles of hacked-off stumps black from the burning. But then comes the flood-fallowing and new life, when the young green shoots, the *ratoons,* grow out from fields now glistening with water, and the coolie women bend low in the water as they weed. And every few years, the planting of new canes.

This was our world: sweet, romantic, magnificent. Yes, I know there is a dark side to it, and I know that Winnie saw herself as some kind of heroine, taking the side of the sugar-workers. And I know that Papa, my beloved Papa, had done wrong. But surely blood is thicker than water! In choosing the wrong side Winnie has betrayed us all, and it is left to me to save our kingdom.

* * *

The absurd thing is that, after Papa's trial and conviction, Winnie got some notion into her head that Clarence and I were not enough; that *she*, as the elder sister, was needed to direct the business. That I was too young, and needed help, her help. She, whose head was filled with nothing but fluff!

Well, perhaps I shouldn't say that. By the time of the trial Winnie had started to fancy herself as some kind of a revolutionary, the romantic bubbles in her head replaced by dissident fervour and communist ideas. But of course it was only to impress George and the other darkies and our coolie labourers. Apparently she was now their heroine, and tried to establish herself as such on the plantation.

How circumstances can change! She and I had once been the best of friends but now – now we were tottering towards outright enmity. We agreed on nothing. The first thing Winnie wanted to do was build new homes for the coolies. It's not that I did not want to do that – after all, building new homes, replacing that dreadful shantytown the labourers called home, squalid logies in stinking mud lanes, had been *my* aim too, right from the beginning. We agreed in principle. But Rome wasn't built in a day, and once I understood the economics of plantation running, I realised that there were other priorities. Just for the time being, of course. Charity could come later.

Winnie was rather emotional about the whole thing.

Tears in her eyes, she pleaded with me: 'Yoyo,' she said, 'remember Nanny! How could you forget Nanny?'

'Of course I haven't forgotten Nanny!' How unfair of her to bring up the question of Nanny! Nanny, my beloved nurse, who had spent her last days in the squalor of the logies. It was in fact Nanny's predicament that had catapulted the two of us into this whole sordid affair. We had lived in a dream world of frocks and parties before then. 'Don't bother your pretty little heads,' Papa had told us, 'enjoy your lives, and leave the estate to me.' And we obeyed. But then we found out how Nanny lived. How could I not care? How could I close my heart to the misery of Nanny's living quarters? I had vowed to change it all; but once I took charge I understood a little better that change would take time, and anyway, it was far too late to benefit Nanny herself, and frankly, my interest had waned. There was time for everything, lots of time. Winnie, however, now that Papa was in prison, wanted change *now*. Immediately.

And that is why I did not want her back on the plantation; but she came anyway, sticking her nose into matters that didn't concern her.

'Let me see the account books,' she said that day. 'I'm sure there must be money left over to build new homes for the coolies. There's certainly land enough – those fallow fields beyond the back-dam, for instance.'

'Those fallow fields,' I retorted, 'are not going to be fallow for much longer. There's a new strain of sugar cane we're going to plant there; with almost twice the yield!'

She said nothing to that, but only stared at me.

'You've changed, Yoyo,' she said mildly after a while. 'Very well then. If not that field then another, after the harvest. We'll just clear one of the present fields and build houses on it.'

She refused to understand, but it wasn't just the impracticality of her proposals that strained our relationship; there was that undercurrent of mistrust. How could I ever trust my sister again, she who had betrayed us all and dragged the Cox name through the mud? And so, though we argued about housing, the real issue was another, and sooner or later it was bound to come out, and it did.

'Why did you come back here at all?' I said after an hour of futile arguing, that first day. 'You're not wanted on Promised Land. Go and stay with your darkie lover!'

'You know I can't do that,' she said. 'We're not married. And this is my home as well as yours. I have every right to be here. And my opinion on the running of it is as valid as yours.'

'That's where you're wrong! Clarence is the estate manager and *he* has the last word, and I'm his fiancée. And besides – everyone hates you up here.'

'Including you?' She reached out her hands to me then, in a gesture of supplication. Winnie could not abide such ugly emotions as hatred; but she should have thought about that earlier. Yet I could not use the word hate towards her. She was still my sister. But not the sister I had grown up with, the one I once knew so well. She was now a stranger.

'I'm furious with you and you know why!' If my eyes could have shot poison darts, they would have. Already my voice was raised to an unladylike level – as Papa would have called it – and I longed to let go; to scream at her, to tear out her hair, to scratch that calmly smiling face of hers that refused to reflect my rage. But I held back. She would find out, one way or another, that I'm not the kind of person who takes kindly to betrayal. If not for Winnie's witness statement Papa would have left the court a free man. I still could not believe what she had done. Betrayed not only her own father, her whole family, but the entire English community. She would always be a pariah now.

'I did the right thing, Yoyo,' is all she said. 'I had to do it. And if you will only let me I can help you with the running of the plantation. I know I don't know much about business. But

I know about people. I know the workers, and what they need. They trust me. Now is the time to really change things; we could work *with* the labourers, instead of against them!'

See, that was just the kind of romantic notion Winnie was wont to entertain; always this talk of appeasement and goodwill, but you can't run a plantation on love and peace, and that was why I thought she should go. But she stayed, a thorn in my side, constantly nagging me about this and that, and though that first argument fizzled out more arguments followed and by the time Mama arrived I was ready to throw Winnie out – on her backside, to put it crudely. But I didn't need to, because she married her little darkie lover George.

* * *

The worst of it is that Mama has taken Winnie's side. The two of them, against me! By the time Mama returned from Austria, Winnie and I had each dug our heels in on our respective positions. Luckily for me, Papa passed power of attorney on to Clarence, not Winnie, and so I was on the winning side; nothing need be done. But Winnie seemed to think herself the voice of conscience; she placed herself clearly on the side of the coolies and they, of course, rallied behind her and got up to all kinds of mischief, such as refusing to work, or working slowly – that kind of thing. And that crazy fellow, that Mad Jim Booker, who Winnie referred to as 'Uncle Jim', the white man with a coolie wife – it didn't help that he was behind the whole thing. Always had been. How naïve I had been, not to have known about the plotting and the planning that had driven us into this position!

Winnie, and Mad Jim, and now Mama: it was all their fault. The coolies were helpless without support, and I found it abominable that white people, English people, should so forget their roots as to harness their indisputable authority to the so-called underdog, giving them a false sense of power. It has always been my position, even as a young girl of fourteen, that change must come from above. It must be *granted,* and we must be the ones to grant it, and in our own time: carefully planned, and in accordance with the economic needs of the plantation.

I won't say that I wasn't happy at Mama's return. It was a surprise, indeed; and initially a happy one. She had been away so long, I had almost forgotten her, and anyway, I'd hardly known her before she left, sunk as she was in her melancholy. I was happy to get my mother back; but she had changed, for her melancholy had left her, and she came full of vigour and fervour and before long she had ganged up with Winnie and Mad Jim against myself and Clarence. Thus the stalemate.

So when Winnie married her darkie George soon after Mama's arrival, I breathed a sigh of relief. It left me alone with Mama on the plantation, true enough: but it also removed Winnie and her constant nagging, and that's why I went to the wedding, abominable as it was. But I wore that hat to show her, to show everyone, that I am now in charge.

Chapter Six

Winnie

The following morning I took Mama to visit Uncle Jim. We went by bicycle, and as we walked over to the bicycle shed they all came out, the servants Mama had known in the years gone by. First Bobby, the yard-boy, now a grown man. Once I had called him simply 'Boy'; now I knew his name, and I whispered to Mama: 'His name is Bobby.' She nodded, understanding. He came up to me shyly, smiling somewhat hesitantly – but Mama stopped in her tracks and held out both her hands for his, and that wavering smile turned into a fully fledged grin.

'Ma'am,' he said, 'so good to see you back again!'

'Oh Bobby, how you've grown!' she exclaimed. Then came Doreen, the washerwoman, also waiting to greet her, and Patch, the gateman, who had left his post at the gate to approach, and others. People who had known us since I was a spoilt little brat, floating in an unreal bubble of light and beauty, oblivious to the trials and tribulations of the common folk. Mama remembered them all; she had always been good to the servants, and they welcomed her back with joy.

As for me: that spoilt little girl was long gone. I was a grown woman now. These people I had once treated as servants; I now understood that their inferior roles in life were just that, roles, roles as in a theatre play; and beneath the roles they were as worthy of respect, and even love, as we who play more elevated roles. And just as the actor is not identified only by the role he is playing, so too I knew that we are all on this earth as equals. Shakespeare's words sprang into my mind: *All the world's a stage, and all the men and women merely players.*

Mama spoke with them all for a few minutes, asking after their families, but then she took her leave and we continued to the bicycle shed and set off for Uncle Jim's.

* * *

I was curious to see how they would greet one another, former lovers as they were; Mama had insisted that she felt nothing but friendship for him, but would this change when she actually saw him? And what about his lovely wife, Bhoomie? How would *she* feel? Did she even know? Was it perhaps inappropriate, that Mama should come to visit at his home? But she had insisted, and here we were.

My concern proved to be unwarranted. Uncle Jim and Mama greeted each other as old acquaintances, with not an unsuitable word, gesture or glance: as dear to each as I and Uncle Jim were, yet with no undercurrent of romance. Bhoomie, too, greeted Mama with warmth and affection, and if she knew of their past liaison, well, she displayed no hint of that knowledge, much less the least trace of jealousy. She welcomed us into her home, and once we were seated in the gallery served us juice and biscuits and insisted we stay for lunch – an invitation we gladly accepted.

For lunch, Bhoomie served us curry and roti. Mama's eyes lit up when she saw the soft folded rotis, the steaming dish of chicken curry. 'Oh my!' she said to Bhoomie, 'I'd completely forgotten the food! The best food in the world! How could I!'

And she tore off a piece of the roti, wrapped it round a chunk of chicken and popped it into her mouth with an expression of utter and complete bliss.

Later, as we mopped our plates clean with the last of the rotis, Uncle Jim said: 'Would you like to have a rest now? I have a spare room with a double bed.'

A full and delicious meal in the hot midday sun is always exhausting. We agreed to a short rest, after which we returned home.

* * *

Yoyo was waiting for us.

'You've been away ages!' she complained. 'I've been waiting for you since lunchtime! Why didn't you say you wouldn't be back? I do think it was rude of you, Mama!'

'I told Matilda not to cook for us,' said Mama mildly. 'Didn't she tell you? I prefer just to have a little fruit in the middle of the day.'

Yoyo frowned and wrinkled her nose. 'Well – yes, she did. But still! I heard you went out to visit that Mad Jim Booker! I can't believe it! How could you be hobnobbing with someone like that? Don't you know he's a sworn enemy of Promised Land? A communist!'

Mama only shook her head. 'You shouldn't use words you don't fully understand, Yoyo,' she replied. 'Jim is not against *us*. He is for the workers. He wants to see the workers treated fairly. He believes that is better for all of us.'

'What nonsense!' cried Yoyo. 'I don't believe a word of it. But anyway, I don't want to discuss it now. Mama, you said yesterday you wanted to see the factory. I thought we could do that now. What about you, Winnie? Won't you be bored?'

Mama and I looked at each other. I had little interest in the business of sugar production, and had only visited the factory once before, when it was newly built a few years ago. I really had no need to see it again, loud and ugly as it was. But if Mama was going I didn't want to be left out, and so of course I nodded too.

The factory was about two miles away from Promised Land. It sat on the edge of the plantation, and when in operation, as now at harvest time, it would chug and groan all day and night, a great hulking beast devouring the prey the workers fed it. It was too far to walk in the hot post-midday sun, so Yoyo ordered one of the horses to be hitched to a wagon and we all climbed in. The groom took up the reins, flicked them, cried out 'Giddyap!' and off we went, the horse trotting along a dusty lane that cut through the cane fields, nude and bristly with the black stubble of cut cane.

In the old days, that is the days when we were growing up, we had been beholden to Bookers for the grinding of our sugar. As they owned the only processing factories in the colony – one here in the Corentyne, and one in Demerara – we had no choice, and the exorbitant, ever-increasing fees they charged us had been choking the life out of us. This was deliberate. Once we and the other privately owned plantations failed, Bookers could pluck us from the ground for a song and add us to their consortium of businesses. Thus Booker Brothers crawled the colony, scooping up struggling plantations so that they alone should survive, a monopoly.

Clarence's arrival changed all this. He had come with a small fortune, enough for us to build our own factory and thus be free from the grasping claws of Bookers. The price was that Clarence was made Papa's heir. Thus it had been so important for him to marry one of us. I as the elder of us had been the obvious sacrificial lamb, but I had chosen George. But luckily for Papa, Yoyo, sensing an opportunity for greatness, had willingly stepped into the void. Clarence, and the factory, had saved us from ruin.

At last we were there. A single navigation canal led up to the factory, and that was crammed with punts all loaded high with cut canes, waiting their turn in the queue.

Yoyo led the way up to the factory entrance, called out, and the factory manager Mr Piers opened the office door and approached to us, adjusting his tie as he came. Yoyo introduced us.

'They'd like to see the factory,' she said. 'Give them the tour, please.'

'My pleasure!' said Mr Piers. He wore a helmet and he was tall and thin, and white, of course. Nobody in authority on our plantation was anything but white, a detail that I had never noticed before, and which had never bothered me before; but now it did.

Mr Piers handed helmets to the three of us, and led us forward towards the canal.

The punts here were all jammed one against the other, waiting their turn at the factory entrance, slowly creeping forward. Behind them more punts, pulled by mules, made their slow way forward; the mules were unhitched and taken away, and Indian labourers pushed the punts forward towards the factory with long poles. As we watched, a huge metal claw descended from above, accompanied by much clanking and rattling of chains. The fingers of the claw closed around the entire bundle of canes on the first punt, and lifted it up, up, up and over to deposit them on to what seemed like a giant scale – which was exactly what it turned out to be.

'This is where we weigh the harvested cane,' explained Mr Piers. 'The labourers are paid according to how much they cut – each punt is served by a team of coolies and registered to that team. The more cane they harvest, the better they are paid.'

We watched as a conveyor belt moved the weighed canes along, shoving them into what seemed a great hungry mouth, and into the belly of the factory.

'Come along,' said Mr Piers, beckoning us inside.

'This is where the machines separate the wheat from the chaff, so to speak,' he went on, pointing to the enormous clump of black machinery into which the canes disappeared. A rather narrow conveyor belt carried what looked like straw away and up to the top of the factory.

'The bagasse,' he said, 'the chaff – the waste from the cane, but not really waste because it's going off to create steam, and the steam provides all the energy to keep the motors running.'

'How efficient!' commented Mama. 'So nothing at all goes to waste?'

'Nothing at all,' said Mr Piers. 'Now follow me.'

And that's what we did. We followed him right into the very gut of that factory, into the bowels of the beast. Every now and then he stopped, to point to some black hulk of rumbling, clanking machinery and explain what it was doing, his voice overpowered by the groaning and rumbling so that I could hear hardly a word. Up narrow metal ladders we climbed, and down again. Along metal grid walkways high above, precariously floating, it seemed, in the air, in the midst of chugging, clanking, moving metal wheels and turning cogs and sliding conveyor belts. We watched as the cane proceeded from one stage to the next, up and down, always accompanied by the deafening din of digestion. The only reasonably quiet place was the laboratory, where workers tested samples of the sugar and deemed it good or bad.

At the end of it all we stood on a narrow metal balcony and watched as the final machine poured out the finished product: sugar. It flowed in a constant stream from above into a cone-shaped mountain, pure golden crystals pouring out in a supple band, like an endless belt of cloth. Its fluidity fascinated; it seemed almost liquid as it gushed out, the soft, sweet and yielding end product of all that back-breaking labour.

For this, men had captured and enslaved other men, sent them chained and beaten across the ocean in the dark hulls of ships and sent them to toil in the broiling sun. For this, my forefathers had left their homeland and torn a new home from virgin territory. For this, innumerable men and women had lost their precious lives. For this, blood had been spilled right here on my father's land. I shuddered at the thought. I loved the sweetness of sugar; but the aftertaste, the realisation of the high price paid, was bitter indeed.

A final conveyor belt, this one smooth and fast-moving, carried the finished sugar out from the factory and straight into the next building, the packaging factory. Here, Mr Piers said, it would be packed into sacks of jute to be sent to Georgetown and out into the wider world.

'Corentyne gold. One day it will overtake Demerara; the best sugar in the world! The very best.'

Mama, who had not said a word throughout the tour, nodded and finally spoke.

'Very interesting,' she said. 'Thank you.'

Chapter Seven

George

The next day when I came home I found Winnie had been busy in a different way. Again, the house was filled with the aroma of cooking – but today it was a sweet, ambrosial fragrance, something like heaven. Again I followed the scent into the kitchen and there I saw it: a cloth like a hammock hanging from the rafter, bulging at the bottom; beneath it a large pot into which an amber liquid dripped. Winnie's back was to me, but she must have sensed my presence because she swung round as I stood in the doorway.

'George!' she cried, and pointed to the cloth. 'Guava jelly! My first batch! And the second batch is nearly finished!'

She stepped away from the stove and I saw another pot on the fire.

I smiled at her and opened my arms, and she rushed in.

'You've been busy!' I said.

'Oh, yes! Ma and I went out to the backyard to pick some guavas – George, you have my favourite variety, the white ones! And then I told her how much I loved guava jelly, and she told me she'd show me how to make it so we went to Bourda Market again and bought a whole bag of guavas – mostly the white ones – we got them much cheaper because we bought up Pansy's whole stock – Pansy is the name of the market lady – and then we came home and Ma showed me how to make the jelly.'

'Wonderful!' I said. 'I love guava jelly! But where's Ma?'

'She went to visit her friend Parvati,' said Winnie. 'She'll be back soon. They're cooking together and Ma will bring some dinner back – they seem to have some sort of an arrangement.' Indeed they did. Ma kept chickens and Parvati grew vegetables, and they had an exchange agreement – so that there would be no leftover chicken going to waste, Ma and Parvati would cook for two households and share, chicken one day and cook-up rice with vegetables the next, or fish-and-vegetable stew. Parvati's husband worked on the wharf at Stabroek Market and got free fish from a friend. This is how the people of Albouystown, the poor of Georgetown, survived. We all helped one another when and where we could.

As it happened, Pa came home before Ma. Pa's job, at the post office in Cummingsburg, was quite a long way across town and he had to walk as he did not have a bicycle. He mumbled a hello as he entered, and plonked himself down on the Berbice chair in the gallery.

'Where's Ma?' he asked, echoing my own question, but he didn't wait for an answer. He pulled a copy of the *Argosy* out of his satchel and opened it. That was Pa all over: not a sociable man. He didn't like to talk, so his job, in the back room of the post office, suited him well. I don't think he had exchanged more than three words with his new daughter-in-law. It wasn't rudeness – he just didn't know what to say to people. There are people who can chat about anything for hours on end – Pa wasn't one of them. He was just as taciturn to his two sons-in-law. He preferred stamps to people; and books, and newspapers.

Winnie had returned to her guava jelly; now she was pouring the steaming-hot boiled guava from its pot into another, which was lined with a muslin cloth.

'Let me help you,' I said, and held the cloth steady so that it didn't slip into the pot. Winnie scraped out the last drops of boiled guava from the pot, and then she took the cloth from my hands and knotted the ends together, after which she carefully, with both hands, lifted the bulging bag of fruit out of the pot. She looked at me.

'I've cut the string already, George – hand it to me, will you?'

Indeed, there on the tabletop lay a length of string all ready to tie the bag with, which she did just below the knot. I was impressed by how quickly and efficiently she did this – as if she had been making guava jelly all her life. In fact, I asked her: 'Have you made guava jelly before?'

She laughed. 'No, of course not! We girls at Promised Land were kept out of the kitchen. This is my first time.'

'Well, you look as if you've been doing it all your life.'

She laughed again. 'I was thinking, George – we're going to have so many jars of guava jelly after this, we could sell the extra jars in the shop!'

We had a family shop in Albouystown, which Ma had managed until recently and where we, the children, had all helped out now and again. Just last year, though, my sister Magda's husband John had taken over the running of the shop. It sold everything, in small quantities, from soap and matches and various other provisions – and maybe, in the future, guava jelly.

'That way I won't be a burden on you,' said Winnie.

'You're not a burden,' I said, 'you're my wife.'

'Still – I'm an extra mouth to feed. This way I can contribute.'

And I knew that was exactly what she would do. My Winnie was the most resourceful white woman I had ever met. Not that I knew many white women – in fact, only two, Winnie and her sister Yoyo – but I had always heard that they were lazy and self-indulgent and only liked to be served. Ma had told me so many stories about the white ladies she had once worked for, all in the run-up to my wedding, trying to dissuade me from an inappropriate alliance. I was happy to see Winnie proving her wrong. But that was Winnie all over. She had taught herself Morse code and learned it so well that she'd been the fastest telegraph operator in Barbados when she was exiled there last year. I was so proud of her.

Watching her now, as she tied the bundle of guava jelly to the rafter, I knew, for the first time, really, that just as she had taught herself Morse code and how to pluck a chicken and how to make guava jelly, Winnie would learn how to live in Albouystown.

Chapter Eight

Yoyo

'So Mama, it's just me and you now, running the estate.'

It was the day after the wedding; Mama and I had spent the night in the Park Hotel, and then Poole drove us to Promised Land. Tom, the new houseboy, came down to fetch our bags and Mama and I walked up the stairs, she before me. She had not been long in the colony, and was still getting used to it all after her time in Europe.

Mama, of course, had never felt at home here: not on the plantation, not in the colony. Her real home is among the snow-capped mountains of Austria. She tried to make a marriage and failed; her deep melancholia drove her back to Salzburg. Now here she is again, at her second attempt; this time as a mother more than as a wife. It is just us: two women, now that Winnie has gone. We both know that Clarence is just a figurehead; in fact we all know that, Clarence included.

'We can do it,' Mama said that day. 'You're young, but I'm so impressed, Yoyo, with your business sense.'

'You can thank Miss Yorke for that!' I said.

Winnie and I had both attended Miss Yorke's Institute for Womanly Arts. Business, of course, did not count as a Womanly Art, but I had been able to live there while attending classes in economics, accounting and business at Government College. I was the only girl in the whole place.

It turned out that I had a certain skill for accounting; I enjoy looking over the books and making sure the figures are in order. What I don't like is dealing with people. Mr McInnes in particular.

How can I, a girl of only seventeen, control a man who considers himself the de facto head of operations, now that Papa is removed from us?

'He leers at me so!' I told Mama later that day, as we sat down on the verandah to relax after the long journey. Miranda, the housegirl, bustled in and set a coffee pot and a plate of ginger biscuits down on the table, curtsied and took her leave. It seemed to me that Miranda had put on a little weight recently – she had been a slim little thing when we first engaged her six months ago, and now her uniform was bulging at the seams.

'Mr McInnes is at the root of all our problems,' said Mama. 'I saw it immediately when I first came here as a bride – he had already caught your father in his snare by then. I did try to free him, but you know what your father is like. "Women have no idea," and all that nonsense. But I know what you mean about the leering. He did it to me too.'

'It makes me hesitant to confront him. He looks at me as if I were a piece of meat, with no brain whatsoever.'

'Well, I haven't encountered him yet since I've been back. But we have to replace him. Immediately.'

'We can't, Mama. I've been looking for a replacement for months. There isn't anyone in BG, and until we can find someone on one of the islands and get him to come over we'll have to put up with him.'

Mama was silent then for a few minutes. She turned her face from me and gazed off into the distance – I thought she had simply accepted my last words and was thinking of something else, when suddenly she said, 'I know of someone.'

'You do?'

'Yes. He might take some persuading, and he hasn't done the work for many years, but he's just the man we need.'

'But – is he available? Will he want to move here and work for us? What is he doing now? Where is he?'

Mama laughed. 'He's not far away at all,' she said. 'And yes, he's available. I'm just not sure if he will care to do the work. But he can. And I can perhaps persuade him.'

'Who is he, Mama?'

'His name is James Booker.'

'James Booker? A Booker? Mama, are you mad?' I cried. The Booker clan and their Booker Brothers Company is the huge conglomerate that owns practically all of British Guiana: almost all of the sugar estates, all of the shipping, and most of the shops. They are our rivals, eager and willing to take us over, an evil spider ready to pounce. How could Mama even *think* of bringing one of them into the fold?

'You must be mad,' I repeated, calmer now. Mama had raised my hopes only to dash them again; we were back to the beginning.

Mama only chuckled. She took a sip of her coffee before she spoke again. 'I'm not mad, but they say that *he* is,' she said. 'You might know him better as Mad Jim.'

My jaw fell open; Mad Jim Booker! Mama must really be out of her mind.

Mad Jim lives on the edge of Promised Land; he owns a big house there, and has a coolie wife, and all the coolies run to him with their troubles. Rumour has it that he is the brains behind all the labourer bother we have been having. That he masterminds the uprisings; that he instigates the protests and strikes that have plagued us the last few years. Mama's suggestion was in fact to put the wolf in charge of the herd! It was preposterous. I said as much. Mama only laughed again.

'Hear me out,' she said. 'Jim's good. In his young days he was trained in estate management, so he knows the ropes. He grew up on Estate Prosperity, in the Essequibo – one of the most success-ful of the Booker estates. He's a renegade, it's true – he had too much empathy for the workers for the company's liking, refused to push them to their limits. But what he is now – as I've heard from Winnie, who knows him well – is a man who the labourers trust. They'll work for him.'

'But Mama – you can't run an estate on kindness! Mr McInnes is a brute but we can't go in the opposite direction! We need someone moderate – not a nigger-lover.'

The word slipped out before I could check it. I think I was as shocked as Mama. She sprang to her feet and strode towards the door.

'Never let me ever hear you say that word again in my presence!' she exclaimed, and she was gone.

* * *

The second part of my plan for Clarence – my impregnation – is proving rather more difficult than the first. It's said that men who drink rum are more easily excited by the ladies, but rum seems to have the opposite effect on my Clarence. It's rather frustrating. In the four months we have been married we have had only had conjugal relations three times. It's certainly not my fault. Once we are in our chamber I do all I can to charm and seduce him, but he simply flops and sleeps. How will I produce a son at this rate?

I have taken to reducing his rum intake at the evening meal, which is harder than it sounds. Some time ago he took to inviting his friends from the senior staff quarters, Mr McInnes, Mr Hodgkin, Mr Frith and so on, to join him for after-dinner drinks and conversation on the verandah, just as Papa had done in the past, and of course drinks are always served.

What an unpleasant, raucous lot those men are! I do not remember this level of noise when Papa was head of the household. Mr McInnes especially. Winnie and I had always loathed this man and had vowed to dismiss him the moment we had the power to do so, which unfortunately proved to be easier said than done; we can only let him go once we have a replacement, and that is proving more difficult than anticipated. Qualified estate managers simply aren't running around free in British Guiana looking for work.

We will have to look further afield; to the islands of the Caribbean. I sent a telegram to our relatives in Barbados, and they are spreading the word among their acquaintances on other islands; but till we find the right man we are stuck with Mr McInnes, whose main off-plantation strength seems to be telling bawdy jokes and guffawing heartily once he has told them – fuelled, of course, by our rum. Not in my company, of course – he isn't *that* uncouth – but I make a point of listening behind doors and curtains, and tough though I am even I blush at some of the filth coming out of that man's mouth. His daughter Margaret is my best friend and I cannot believe the things he says about her, his own blood! It is almost as if – but no, I cannot possibly harbour such a thought. But I will speak to Margaret about it, or rather, drop hints so as to find out more. Mr McInnes would never have dared to speak this way in Papa's presence! Yes, things are decidedly slipping downhill, and there is little I can do. In the end I am just a girl, hardly more than seventeen. Winnie wasn't much of a help when she was here, as all she could think of was her approaching wedding and the arrival of Mama.

But then Mama came, Winnie got married and everything changed.

Chapter Nine

Winnie

I quickly adapted to life in our Albouystown cottage. So many people had told me I wouldn't: I had to prove them wrong, and I did, and it wasn't even that difficult. Yes, the bathroom was in the yard and all it was was a roofless cabin next to the rainwater vat, with a bucket of water and a ladle. And the lavatory – well, it might not be ladylike to speak about that, so I'll just say it was a hole in the ground with a wooden seat built over it. But I'm not here to compare my old life with the new one. I had chosen the new one, and that was that. I would do it.

Winning over Ma's heart had been relatively easy. That hardness she had first displayed was little more than a shell. Once it was cracked she opened up, and treated and loved me like a daughter. And as I got to know her better she earned all my respect. Our house might have been small but Ma treated it like a palace; meticulously clean and tidy it was. Once a week Ma would bundle her long cotton skirts between her legs, get down on hands and knees and scrub the kitchen floor and the back and front steps. She used a scraper, a kind of wide knife-blade, and some kind of white soap. And she polished all the inside floors so that they glowed the colour of honey. And she cleaned all the windows with vinegar and newspaper so that not a streak, not a fly's footprint, remained.

There was a standpipe in the front yard from which we schlepped water for use in the house, for drinking and cooking and washing wares and, later, for bathing small children. Ma washed the household's clothes each Monday in a wooden tub next to the rainwater vat, using a beater, scrubbing board, Rickett's Crown Blue, salt soap and starch. The Blue was to keep the mens' Sunday white shirts white, and the starch to keep them crisp. Downstairs she kept a coal pot and three cold irons; once the clothes were dry she'd light the coal in the pot and, once they were red hot, she would place the irons upon them. She'd carefully lay a blanket and a folded sheet on the dinner table, which then became an ironing board; she used beef suet to grease the iron before use. Ma did not allow me to help with the washing, but the ironing became my weekly task, and I learned to enjoy seeing the mountain of rumpled clothes removed from the washing lines converted into neat folded piles to be returned to the cupboards.

Ma was meticulous about her own appearance, too. She never left the house without splashing herself with Evening of Paris perfume, and dusting her face with powder, and her body with Mim's Talcum Powder.

She had an acerbic tongue sometimes, but I soon learned that her bark was worse than her bite, and once I knew her ways we became a team, and she taught me the art of living in a very small space. One by one my spoilt English ways dropped away.

Adapting to Albouystown itself – well, that was not so easy. I am not a town girl. Growing up on Promised Land spoiled me for anything less than paradise. I missed the garden: the orchard that brought forth fruit of every imaginable variety, every month a different and more delicious kind; especially the mango tree with its low-slung branches inviting us to climb into its leafy canopy. The towering bougainvillea that climbed our porticos and porches, huge bunches of purple, pink and vermillion hanging low. Hibiscus and frangipani and oleander, and the rose fragrance wafting through it all, carried on the wings of a cool sea breeze. In

Promised Land, stepping out of the front door was like stepping into a Garden of Eden, framed by birdsong – the sweet fluting of the kiskadee, the whirr of the hummingbird flitting from flower to flower. The flutter of butterflies, their sun-filtered wings like artists' palettes.

How different were the narrow streets of Albouystown! Our cottage was just one in a row of similar ones, although surely the best-maintained. The cottage next door to the east – well, it was little more than a hovel, and the one to the west hardly better. And so it was all along Butcher Street, lines of cottages in various stages of dilapidation. They seemed to totter on their stilts, like falling birds. The staircases leading up to the front doors had missing treads and gaps in the balusters. The windowpanes were cracked; shutters were falling off their hinges. The street itself, potholed and cracking apart, had gutters on either side bridged by planks of all shapes and sizes, some rotting, so that one had to step precariously across them.

But all of that I swallowed easily. I'd seen similar in Kitty, when I'd stayed with Aunty Dolly. It was the *people* who upset me the most, to be quite honest. I had expected neighbourliness, friendliness. What I got was mistrust, rebuffs, rejection.

It started on my very first day, the very first time I left the house with Ma, on my very first expedition to Bourda Market. The lady from the cottage next door happened to be in her front garden (if one could call the patch of unkempt green between front stairs and front gate a garden!) She was bent over, seemingly picking peppers from a bush. She straightened up and glanced over as we proceeded to the bridge. She and Ma exchanged a short greeting, then her gaze turned to me. I smiled, waved and called out: 'Good morning! How are you? I'm Winnie Quint, your new neighbour!'

I expected her to smile and wave back, call out a return greeting, introduce herself. Instead, she stared a minute, did not re-

spond to my friendly greeting and bent back down to her pepper
bush.

I blushed – it seemed I had made a huge faux pas. Obviously,
I should have waited for Ma to introduce us; but Ma had walked
ahead of me, saying nothing.

'Ma,' I said once we were on the street and past the house,
'who is that lady? Why did she not return my greeting?'

'What you expect? You, a white lady, calling out like that?'

'I was just being friendly!'

'People here don't want white-people friends.'

'Oh! Really? Why not? I would have thought…'

George had warned me of this but I had not believed him.
After the trial I had been something of a heroine. The poor of
British Guiana, whether of African or Indian origin, knew I was
on their side; how they had cheered me after the trial! They knew
that I supported them, that I held no racial prejudice. I thought
of all people as equal, and my decision to marry George and live
with him here in his own community was proof of that.

I was rather proud of myself, in fact. I loathed the snobbery
most people of my race display towards those of dark skin, and
I had made up my mind to be different, to demonstrate by my
own actions, my own life, that we were not all of that ilk. That
we could be better. That some of us knew what it really means
to be a Christian. And I thought my sense of equality would be
immediately reciprocated by those abused by our terrible system.
That very first day I learned my lesson: it was not to be so easy.

Ma and I strolled down to the market, baskets slung over our
arms. We passed several other pedestrians. Ma seemed to know
most of them; she greeted them, sometimes by name, and they
greeted her back. And then dark eyes would alight on me, and
smiles would fade, and lips that had called out a greeting turned
silent, and faces grew blank, sullen even. In the shops, too, shop-

keepers ignored me, or served me with closed faces, never returning my smiles or my friendly words.

And so it continued, day after day. I was the only white person in Albouystown. When I walked the streets people stared, and animosity was written in their faces. When I went to the market the stall-women served me stony-faced and would not look me in the eye, whereas they served others with warmth and joviality. I could not understand it. I was embarrassed, hurt.

I understood well why white skin was not well-regarded by BG's black and Indian majority. For decades we, the Europeans, had ruled this country with an iron fist. We had brought slaves from Africa and indentured servants from China, Portugal and India, and treated them appallingly. We had exploited them, flogged them, abused them; our men had raped their women. We kept them poor, and we flaunted our wealth, and we behaved as if we were the lords of the earth and they lived only to serve us. But I was different. They knew I was different. Why then this cold treatment?

'George,' I said one evening after such a rebuff, 'it's just not fair, to judge me by my skin! You all complain about racial prejudice – this is just the same in reverse!'

But George shook his head.

'No,' he said, 'it's not at all the same. See – white against black prejudice comes from an ingrained belief of one's own superiority, and the inferiority of the other race. Black against white prejudice has a different cause altogether. It is derived from a history of abuse. People are wary because of their own experience. In their hearts burns anger; wounds are bleeding deep inside. They do not reject you because of your skin colour, but because of what your people have done to them.'

'But it's not fair! I'm different! I have not abused anyone! Why should I pay the price, just because of my colour?'

'People are wary,' George said again. 'You will need to show them that you are different. You must win them over. You won Ma over, didn't you? You must do it again. In time, you will show them that not all white ladies are evil.'

And so it was that once again, George opened my eyes to realities I had been blind to, hidden away as I was in my bubble of privilege. I had much to learn, and George, and Albouystown, would teach me.

* * *

In those early days he seemed shy and ashamed of the conditions he had placed me in, but once I had convinced him that I *really* wasn't going to look down on him and his family, once he knew I was really his for ever, for better or for worse, in sickness and in health, for richer, for poorer, the old George returned: the George I had fallen in love with, the George who had won me over with his enthusiasm for life and his commitment to The Cause.

What a discovery that had been – finding out that George, my George, the George I was already head over heels in love with, was Theo X, the young and charismatic rebel, one of the leaders in the movement to disrupt the industry, to demand humane conditions for the workers, to put more power into labourer hands!

'I'm going to a rally tonight,' he told me that first Saturday.

'Are you going to be speaking?'

'Well, yes – I am.'

'Then I'm coming too!' His face fell, as I knew it would. We had spoken of this before. George wanted me to stay away from his political rallies, the People for Justice rallies where he would drop his George Theodore Quint persona, and appear only as Theo X. Of course, many people, especially among our neighbours in Albouystown, knew who Theo X really was – Georgetown was such a small capital city that it wouldn't be possible to keep a secret like that for long. Still, Theo X's identity was officially a secret; the British, we assumed, did not know. If they found out, he would surely lose his job.

As Theo X, George came alive. It was at one of those rallies, which I had attended in secret as a runaway sixteen-year-old, that I had finally seen the real George and recognised how much bigger this thing was than a teenage infatuation. When George spoke, and in particular when George *sang,* he swelled into the giant he really was: larger than life, eloquent, passionate, on fire. He set hearts alight – certainly mine. That day, he became not just my sweetheart but my hero. I heard him speak to the crowds, and was mesmerised. I heard him sing to them, songs of motivation and revolution, and was transfixed. Not just a simple postboy, my George: he was a leader, a man of the future. And I loved him all the more for it.

* * *

That was the day I moved on from the frothy sentimentality of First Love to wade into the ocean that is True Love. That ocean is shallow at first, as all oceans are when they lap upon the beach; just so, it lapped upon my personality, enticing me to trust it and wade in deeper, to swim at last and trust the depths. I took the plunge, and then I was there, swimming; love was solid beneath and within and all around me. I trusted it. It was real. And finally it placed me here, in Albouystown, where it would be tested again and again, day after day.

* * *

Now George frowned and looked concerned, the way he always did when I spoke of being at his side throughout his mission, be-ing his other half, fighting side by side with him.

'Winnie – I don't want you to come. It's not safe. And when my people see us together they'll...'

It wasn't the first time George had revealed such fears.

'I don't understand it,' I said to him, not for the first time. 'After the trial I was such a heroine among your people. And, in fact, I wish you'd stop talking about *my* people and *your* people – aren't we just all people?'

George sighed, and took me in his arms. I struggled to free myself. I didn't want to be comforted with his love – I wanted to *know.*

'Tell me why!' I insisted, glaring at him with mock anger. 'Why won't they accept us as a couple?'

'We're not all one people,' he said. 'And we won't be for a long, long time. That's just wishful thinking, Winnie. It's one thing for you to openly stand up for the underdog and speak the truth. It's admirable for you to turn against your own people—'

I opened my mouth to protest. There was that phrase again – *your people* – how I hated it. But George held up his hand before I could speak.

'Let me finish. Standing up for truth is one thing, Winnie. But actually *marrying* one of us, or me marrying one of you – that's a different matter. It's breaking the code.'

'What code? I didn't know you had a code. You never told me about a *code.*'

'It's an unspoken code – it's like a – a betrayal. *Are our women not good enough for him?* people will ask. Our women will feel slighted – *why didn't he pick one of us?* And men—'

He stopped. 'What about men?' I prompted.

He didn't want to speak. 'Tell me!' I said.

'Men – well, men might disrespect you for marrying me,' he finally said. 'And resent me for aiming too high, above my station, when they have no such choice. Begrudge us both not knowing our place.'

'What is my place? George, I wish you wouldn't speak this way. It makes me feel that you too see a division that we can't cross. I thought we agreed: love is the way to cross the abyss between black and white. And our love has crossed it! We're just two people, a man and a woman, who love each other. What does it matter what colour our skin is?'

'But others won't see it that way,' George said. 'That's all I'm saying. People in Albouystown know we married and it's slowly trickling out to the rest of Georgetown. To people who don't know I'm Theo X. If they see Theo X with you the secret will be out.'

'They won't see us together,' I said. 'I'll wear a veil, like I did last time, and stay in the crowd. Quite a few people wore veils at that rally – people who don't want to be recognised. Why can't I? I just want to be a part of it all.'

'You *are* a part of it all, no matter what. Even if you stay at home, you're a part: I feel you behind me, in spirit. But that's not the point. Didn't you hear what I said? It could be dangerous. Sometimes the police come and break up the meetings. Sometimes they shoot – not to kill, but they did once kill a man, by mistake. I'm your husband. I've promised to protect you. I don't want you in that crowd. I want you safe.'

I laughed. 'George, you should know me better than that! When have I ever played it safe? Did you think I would change once I became your wife? I'm coming, and that's that!'

Who would ever have thought that I, Winnie Cox, middle daughter of the Honourable Archie Cox, would end up as the scandal of Georgetown! Growing up I had been the quiet, romantic one, given to poetry and Bach and flowers; I stayed out of trouble, was always polite and obedient. The old ladies would say, what a *sweet* little thing she is! Growing up, it was Yoyo who was the adventurer, Yoyo the renegade, Yoyo most likely to rock society's steady boat. Yet it turned out to have been me.

Papa's trial had brought out all the latent defiance that had built up in me over the years. My conscience, till then just a distant squeak, had roared out loud, to everyone's amazement –

including my own – and BG's English society had fallen flat on its back in shock.

Now, here I was, a citizen of Albouystown, the poorest and most run-down area, making a life for myself as the husband of the youngest and most hot-headed of the generation of rebel leaders spawned by the deplorable conditions on the sugar estates, in the factories, on the docks of Georgetown. Marriage for me was more than marriage to a man. It was marriage to a mission, a cause. It would be a fight, side by side with my beloved. Hand in hand we would struggle for change. I was fired by the spirit of revolution; young and passionate as we both were individually, I knew that together we were stronger. Together we would rock this complacent boat till it capsized, and we would be there to build a new, more equitable, more just society. That spirit of fight is what I loved most about George. I was at his side, and I would prove myself. There was no way I would be staying home that night.

George was putty in my hands. Not that he was weak – no one who had seen George in action would call him that – but once I had made a decision I stuck to it with all my might. Sometimes, in the past, they had been silly decisions, and the consequent tumbles had opened my eyes and drummed sense into me. But to be turned back by the fear of risk? No – that was not Winnie Cox's way, and it would never be Winnie Quint's way. Now, having informed George that I would not be obeying him – in spite of my marriage vows – I softened the blow by giving him my biggest smile and opening my arms to him, and of course he fell into my embrace. This is how, as a woman, I had learned the art of triumph; I fought for truth, calmly and stubbornly, and when I won I disarmed my man. This method worked well with George. I suspect it works with other men too. Men are basically powerless against us women, their ostentatious strength a mere shadow of our quieter power. I was a quick learner. And I would go to that rally.

Chapter Ten

George

In a way I was glad that Winnie had come to the rally. It was best that she heard the news from Theo X, the revolutionary, not from George Quint, her husband.

Winnie loved the latter, but she revered the former, and that had been bothering me for some time now. In solid, caring, reliable George lived the daring, dashing rebel she longed to emulate – but our lives had changed and the time for rebellion was over. That dual personality was inconsistent with marriage, which must be solid and strong and unified. Winnie did not yet understand. Youthful exuberance burned in her heart; the risks she had taken to be with me, the courage that had set her apart from her people and her race, they were like waves rising in the ocean and crashing on the shore: they were exciting, but limited. The ocean itself is still and deep. It carries the waves, but inevitably the waves fall back into it. Our marriage must be like the ocean, not the crashing waves. We must move on.

Theo X must die.

That night, though, Theo X was on fire as never before.

'Brothers and sisters,' I began, and even at those non-committal words the crowd broke into a frenzy. It was a larger crowd than ever before – over the years word had spread, and with each full moon the gathering swelled just a little more. Now, it clapped and cheered and people rose to their feet and called my name and chanted: *Theo X! Theo X! Theo X!*

Somewhere in that crowd was my Winnie. Knowing Winnie, she would be more enchanted than ever: proud of her Theo X, filled with revolutionary fervour, probably clapping and chanting herself.

'I want to be at your side, fighting for justice with you!' she had said earlier, and later tonight I would have to tell her it was all a dream. We were not going to be *that* revolutionary couple. She was married not to Theo X but to reliable, solid George Quint.

When the cheering died down, I began to speak. I never wrote my speeches in advance. They came spontaneously. It was like magic: the moment I opened my mouth the words would pour forth, as if recited from a script written in my soul. Words of inspiration, words of fire, words of truth:

'Never believe, not for one moment, that the colour of your skin makes of you a lesser man, a lesser woman, than the man and woman of white skin! Never believe that you are a lackey, a servant, a serf – even if you play those roles in your everyday life! In each of your hearts burns an ember, and it is the ember of true identity! Cling to that ember, cling to that knowledge, cling to that faith: you are precious, you are golden, you are a child of God! Let that ember lend you dignity, even if your outer life is one of servitude and toil. Let that ember keep your chin raised up, even if your back is bent under the weight of your burden! The ember might be tiny, so small you can hardly see it, hardly feel it, but I assure you it is there and in times of despair, in times of devastation, may you remember that spark of life and may it infuse you again and again with new strength, new courage, new hope. Change will happen, my brothers and sisters. It will. But whether that change comes slowly or soon, you must never let go of that truth: you are precious, you are golden, you are a child of God!'

Gradually over the last two years my speeches had taken that turn into personal motivation. I had not planned it; it was not a conscious thing. I did not resolve to do this. The words came not from me, but through me, and I was as surprised by them as anyone in the crowd. Tonight, they even took on a religious bent – where did this child of God business come from? I was not a religious man – why then did I say such things? Yes, it was time to stop.

The leaders of People for Justice were already in two minds about me. On the one hand, I drew the crowds. Of all of their speakers, I was the one who had people cheering and clapping. The speakers who had gone before me tonight had drawn little reaction with their words: basically, we had all heard the same things before. *Resist the white man. We shall overcome. Fight for justice.* Words that had become clichés over time, because how are you going to resist when you have to earn a living to put bread on the table; when your overseer is behind you on a horse and carrying a whip (even if he is not allowed to use that whip) or when the lady of the house commanded you to scrub floors on your hands and knees and the pittance she paid you would put crumbs of bread in your child's mouth? They were all empty words, and they had drawn little reaction from the crowd because we had all heard the same words before, from the same speakers.

But right now, words were pouring from my mouth and I had no way of stopping them. Where did they come from? Why was I speaking them? They scared me – and yet I could not stop.

'There is a light within you – cling to that light throughout the darkness! Believe in that light – know that it is always there, even when the darkness is closing in and you cannot see, cannot even breathe! Brothers and sisters, you are precious! Each one of you! Know that! You are diamonds in the dust! Keep the faith!'

It was as if the crowd arose with one single heart to accept my words, to bathe in them; the cheering was louder than ever before and it was several minutes before I could speak my last words, words that would burst the bubble.

'Brothers and sisters, thank you, thank you, thank you. I can feel your love and I know we are all joined in that love. But I must tell you one more thing. As of tonight, Theo X is no more. For personal reasons I have decided to retire from People for Justice. Please understand, please forgive me, and most of all: *keep the faith.*'

* * *

Utter silence descended on the gathering. For a moment it was as if the crowd was stunned, too shocked to react. But then they did react, and the concerted wail that rose almost coaxed me back to the dais. As I walked away a few people ran up behind me, grabbed my arms, tried to call me back. I shook them off. I could not go back. In fact, I was in tears. There was no return.

While speaking I had been transported away from reality, a mere mouthpiece for words I had not created, that came from who knows where. Now that it was over the stark reality burst in upon me: I was no more a part of the revolution. The realisation tore me apart.

I had thought I was making this decision for Winnie: to protect her and my family-to-be. I had seen myself as a rebel, a radical, a revolutionary, a fighter for Truth and Justice – both written with large letters. I was the one who would avenge Bhim's death – my closest friend, killed in cold blood by my future father-in-law. I was the one who would keep Bhim's memory alive, and work from my gut outwards to keep his mission alive.

But as I walked from that dais I knew I was none of these things. It was as if I had been struck down from on high. Smitten by a sword. *You are nothing,* said a voice from within, *you are but a grain of dust.* I walked on, weeping, a sense of disintegration, of cracking apart, tearing at my being. Now I was sobbing out loud, sobbing for a dream I could never fulfil: *Theo X was dead!* How I had revelled in that name, in that image! How I had basked in the sense of my own significance! How I had delighted in the adulation of others! And as Theo X crumbled into dust I wept.

I walked northwards, and so inevitably I arrived at the Sea Wall. I hoisted myself on to it and stood there, the breeze whipping my clothes and wiping dry my face. I opened my arms to the Atlantic, to the sky and the universe, and screamed, *What then? Why now? Who am I?* I screamed the words out loud and the wind tore them from my lips. And I closed my eyes and beat my chest as if I would beat the living heart out of myself… and the ocean beat against the shore in indifference, and the full moon sailed above in a vast and starless sky, and clouds drifted past in the pale moonlight, and I felt the pulse of the earth and my smallness in the grand scheme of things and a voice rose up in me, a voice so small it was near silent, and it said: *You are. That is all. Be Here Now.*

And with that voice came calmness, and no more tears, only a deep intake of breath as I settled into a renewed sense of simply being alive, and filled with joy and purpose and—

Purpose! My purpose was right here, where I was, and right now, and I was neglecting it! *Winnie! She* was my purpose, and I had left her behind, in that confused and floundering crowd! I turned and ran.

Chapter Eleven

Winnie

In order to keep the meetings truly secret, the People for Justice group met at a different place each Saturday night, that place only revealed through word of mouth on the Saturday morning. Tonight the meeting place was on one of the playing fields near the Sea Wall.

I couldn't help the colour of my skin, but I had to prove that I was not of a different ilk, and I had to take the distrust and sometimes blatant dislike I attracted as part of my heritage. I had to earn first their trust and then, if that went well, perhaps also their respect and their affection. And so, attending that first rally after my marriage, I went in disguise; I wore a black veil that hid my pale face, and kept my hands concealed.

George and I went together; I rode on the crossbar of his bicycle, and he let me down when we were near the field so that I could walk the remaining short distance. George himself wore a mask; just a half-hood that covered the top part of his face, with slits for his eyes. His work was becoming more and more dangerous, and it was vital that his identity be kept secret. Theo X had committed no crime that was in the book; but he was working to destabilise the colony's government, and that, in the eyes of the British, was indeed a crime.

I arrived in good time, and quietly merged with the crowd and found a place to sit on the hard ground. All around me, others took their seats; mostly men, some couples, but no other women alone as I was. But I spotted a group of three young women, sitting near me. I longed to be part of such a group; to have a friend, another female, who thought as I did, felt as I did! Someone to share my hopes and aspirations with! I had had few friends back on the plantation; Emily Stewart, in fact, was the only girl I could regard as a true friend, but I had lost touch with her since my engagement. What a shock that must have been to her! And so I was on my own here in Georgetown. But I must be patient; one day, I would find friends.

Meanwhile, I edged nearer to those three ladies. As a single woman in that crowd of mostly men I was an anomaly, and I noticed that I was indeed drawing attention. Heads turned to look at me; the fact that I was wearing a veil made me a mystery woman, and I understood their curiosity. How I wished I could tear away that veil, and sit there open-faced as did the three women in that group!

They put their heads together, and one of them glanced back at me: they were talking about me! I had attracted their attention, just as they had attracted mine. In that moment I made a bold decision: I stood up, walked over to the little group and sat down.

'Hello!' I said. 'May I sit with you?'

One of them giggled, and they shuffled to make room for me. 'Yes of course – sit down,' said the girl who had giggled.

Another said, 'Why you wearin' a veil?'

I looked around to make sure we were not being watched – we weren't; it seemed the fact that I was now part of a group had assuaged people's curiosity – and gestured for them to gather closer. Once they had shuffled near to me I lifted my veil, and quickly dropped it again. They all gasped.

My face was well known. During the trial – less than six months ago – it had been splashed all across the newspapers, on the front pages. I was as much a public figure as my father had been: he the villain of that story, I the heroine. That was the very reason I had to keep my presence here a secret, the reason George feared for my safety.

'Winnie Cox?' said one of the ladies at last, as if she couldn't believe her eyes.

'I am she,' I said. 'But I'm now Winnie Quint.'

One of the ladies held out her hand for me to shake. 'So pleased to meet you,' she said. 'My name is Kitty – Kitty MacGonigal.'

'I'm Eliza Woodcock,' said another, and I shook her hand too.

'Matilda Barnett,' said the third. 'Call me Tilly. You are very brave to come here!'

'You were very brave to do what you did,' said Eliza. 'At the trial, I mean.'

I shrugged. I didn't want to resurrect the past, and so I changed the subject. 'Do you go to all the PFJ meetings?'

'Most of them,' said Kitty. 'If we can all three get away, we come. We would never come alone, like you did.'

'Sssh!' said Tilly. 'They've arrived.'

The buzz of chatter that had been hovering over the field hushed into an expectant silence; one or two people clapped, but apparently this was frowned upon for they were isolated, and no one joined in. Three men walked to the front of the field and climbed up on what must have been a low dais, although I couldn't see it from my spot on the ground. Now their heads were all visible – all masked, but for those who knew them, still easily identifiable. My new friends craned their necks to see better.

'The one on the right,' Eliza whispered to me, 'that's Theo X – the youngest.'

'And the handsomest!' giggled Kitty.

'How you know that?' Eliza scolded, 'you ever see him without the mask?'

'No – but I got a sixth sense for handsome men!'

'Oh, you! Is time you got married!'

I smiled to myself. I longed to tell them the truth – that yes indeed, Theo X was very handsome; and that I shared his table, his bed, his home. I was his wife! My heart swelled with pride. One day, I would share my secret with these ladies. They would be my first friends in my new life. Kitty, Tilly and Eliza.

Tilly turned to me. 'Are you married?'

I nodded. 'Yes,' I said.

'And your husband allowed you to come? All by yourself?'

'He – he couldn't come himself,' I said. 'But he supports the cause.'

'A white man supports the cause? That don't make sense! You – we know about you and why you did it.'

'You weren't married then!' said Eliza 'I remember! You were Miss Cox.'

'It's true – I only married recently.'

'So then, you're not Winnie Cox any more!' said Eliza. 'What's your name now?'

'Quint,' I said. 'Winnie Quint.'

I began to sweat. I was getting dangerously close to breaking my promise to George.

Kitty wrinkled her forehead. 'Quint? I know a Miss Bernice Quint. She brings clothes for my mother to sew. My mother's a seamstress,' she added for my benefit. 'Bernice – she lives in Lacytown, near Bourda Market. A coloured woman. Any relation to your husband?'

All three ladies stared at me, curiosity in their eyes, but also accusation. The truth was, I had indeed heard George mention Aunty Bernice. I thought she was a cousin of his mother. I hadn't met her yet; she hadn't come to the wedding. And I still found it hard to lie.

I was saved by the megaphone.

'Ladies and gentlemen!' a voice boomed out above our heads, 'thank you all for coming. We shall begin.'

Chapter Twelve

George

I had told Winnie I would pick her up after the meeting; to meet me at the entrance to the sports pavilion. I would pick her up and take her home the way I had brought her, on the crossbar of my bicycle. I prayed she had waited for me. At least thirty minutes had passed since I had fled the stage, and people would have started heading for home immediately – my talk was always the last on the programme, the finishing touch. I was the one the crowds came for, my leaders had told me. *We want you to speak last, so that they will stay.*

I ran to the pavilion and, indeed, there was Winnie, just as we had agreed, waiting for me. The panic in my heart subsided.

She was not alone. Three women stood with her. I stopped running and strode up to her, my hands stretched out.

'Where were you?' she asked. 'I've been waiting ages!'

'I'm sorry – I'm so sorry! I'll explain!'

I would – but not in front of these strangers. Who were they?

'These are my new friends,' said Winnie, and one by one she introduced them: 'Kitty MacGonigal. Eliza Woodcock. Tilly Barnett.'

'You need to take better care of your wife, Mr Theo X!' said Tilly as I shook her hand.

'How you could leave her out here in the dark? You forget she or what?' That was Eliza.

'Is a good thing she got friends. Bad men out there you know!' Kitty said.

'I know, I know, I'm sorry. Winnie, you coming? Let's go home!'

I practically prised Winnie away from those women. Of course they were right, but I certainly wasn't going to explain myself to them in the middle of the night. I grabbed Winnie's hand and turned to go. Winnie, though, was reluctant. She turned back to the women.

'Tomorrow, then? Two o'clock?'

'Yes! You can find the house?'

'I'll find it,' Winnie called back, and then she turned to me. 'What's going on, George? Where did you run off to? What happened? Why did you—'

'I'll explain. I promise. Let's just find my bicycle.'

We found it, leaning against the fence where I had left it. Winnie eased herself onto the crossbar and I rode off, towards Albouystown. Annoyance was practically oozing from her body, and with good reason. What I had done was unforgivable – but she would forgive me, I thought. Surely she would forgive me when she knew.

But would she? Winnie revered Theo X. He was one of the reasons she had married me. Tonight I had discarded the persona of Theo X. He was no more – a skin I had cast off. Underneath that skin was me – plain old George. Would she love me just as much? It was a test we should have done before our wedding. But how could I have known? Theo X had not pre-announced his demise. He had simply dropped dead.

* * *

We quarrelled all the way home – our first quarrel. She was vexed with me for killing Theo X, and for being late, and, most of all, for not telling her of my plan; for Winnie loved Theo X. And that was precisely why I had killed him.

'But why – why? Theo was – he is – magnificent! Everybody loves Theo! I love Theo!'

'Exactly!' I said. 'You love Theo, not George. Winnie – Theo isn't a real person. He's a construction. I don't want you to love him. I want you to love me!'

'But I do – I do! Theo is part of you, part of what I so love about you – that passion, that resolve! Remember what you told me once? It's not about you and me, it's bigger than us – it's about the movement! The people!'

'I changed my mind – there are more ways than one to serve the people. My family comes first. You come first. If you are in love with this made-up revolutionary called Theo the two of us can't have a marriage. I want a real marriage, a good marriage.'

'How can we have a good marriage when you forget my existence and leave me to wait hours for you to come and pick me up – in the night? How?'

She was right. I should not have forgotten her.

'I'm sorry, all right? It was wrong. I admit it. It won't ever happen again.'

'It better not, George Quint! I won't forgive you so quickly next time!'

I should have left it at that – after all, she said she had forgiven me. But I had to have my say: I was vexed with her for revealing to those ladies that I was Theo X, and told her so.

'Well, what does it matter, if Theo X is finished anyway!'

'It's still confidential. What if the British find out that I used to be him? I'd lose my job. You women don't know how to keep a secret!'

'What? I was the one who spied in my father's house for two whole years. Keeping you a secret and keeping the whole worker rebellion a secret. Uncle Jim said I was the most discreet person he'd ever known, man *or* woman!'

She was right about that. Winnie had worked for us, secretly; listening at doors, rummaging in her father's desk for news, and reporting it all to Uncle Jim. All while pretending to be a sweet naïve planter's daughter who wouldn't hurt a fly. Winnie had kept her lips tight for the longest time. But still: 'You can't just go blurting out my identity to any stranger you meet on the road!'

'They aren't some strangers I met on the road! They're my friends!'

'You only just met them!'

'I make friends quickly. I'm friendly! And – and… George, I'm lonely!'

When she said that my heart just burst. I pulled on the brake handles so sharply the bicycle jolted and she almost fell off, but I leapt off the seat and caught her in time, and I held on to her, squeezed her to me, kissed her cheeks.

'Oh Winnie, Winnie – I'm sorry. I'm so sorry. I should have thought . All alone in that house, with my mother, no friends. I'm sorry my darling. You can have as many friends as you want. Go and visit them – or bring them home. I want you to be happy. If that's what makes you happy.'

'You make me happy,' she murmured into my collar, and squeezed my waist.

It was such a relief to make up with her. Loving Winnie felt like a clear sun-drenched sky with not a single cloud. Quarrelling with her was as if a heavy black raincloud had drifted across that sky, covering it completely, so that all the light was gone. Unbearable! Now, it was as if a black cloud fled from my mind. That, I realised, was marriage: noticing when the clouds came and returning to the original love, the original clear sky. Because the clear sky was real – the clouds weren't. The clouds were alien things – dark emotions that separated us into two so that we no longer shared the infinite expanse of Love. I harboured that thought so that I could share it with her later, when we lay in bed, wrapped in each other's arms, breathing in each other's substance. Winnie would like that idea, that imagery. It was something she might have come up with herself. Winnie – so sensitive, so aware of the movements of the heart, so wise for her age. I squeezed her again, lifted her back on to the crossbar, and we wheeled away.

That was the night I learned what it meant to return to Love. Love is an act, a conscious decision, a constant call back to itself. I put aside the clamour and vexation of my own little self, and here I was, happy again. Home again.

* * *

Months passed, and more and more Winnie adapted to life in Albouystown. I was away at work all day, so I didn't see much of the process, but I did see the results. The biggest result was Ma's complete turnaround regarding her daughter-in-law. She who had rejected Winnie sight unseen, now loved her with a startling and unconditional love – and it was all Winnie's doing. Winnie had decided that she loved to cook, and that Ma was the best teacher on earth. She threw herself into the daily task, and Pa and I were the beneficiaries, for every evening we came home to some new creation concocted by the two of them. Cow-heel soup, pepperpot, cook-up rice – all these delicacies served up at the end of a long day, and everyone happy and satisfied afterwards. Ma and Pa always went to bed soon after dinner. Winnie and I would wash the wares by the light of the kerosene lamp, and then we would sit in the gallery and play cards and chat about the past day until we too felt the urge for bed.

Winnie soon began to expand her talents. Little side dishes would appear on the table: mango chutney, lime pickle, pepper sauce. 'To spice things up,' Winnie said, and they were good, so good. After she had perfected her recipes Winnie began to make larger quantities and, just as she had done with the guava jelly, fill up jars and sell it in the shop. Once a week she made coconut oil. She'd buy a donkey cart full of mature coconuts, dumped in the front garden. Crack them open with a cutlass – Winnie could wield a cutlass as well as any water-coconut vendor. Remove the hard white coconut meat, grate it, squeeze it to produce the milk, let it stand for a day, then scoop away the curd to reveal the oil. Bottle the oil, and sell it in the market.

And she had won over the people of Albouystown. Winnie has a natural charm, a winning smile and a warmth that others, once they open up just a crack, cannot resist. It all happened so naturally. The cottages in Albouytoun might be small, but the yards they stood in were spacious and verdant, full of trees and bushes. Winnie would peer over the fences and, if what she saw looked promising, she would enter the yard, climb the stairs to the front door and ask the woman of the house if she had anything to sell. Guavas, mangoes, peppers, limes: Winnie took all that was on offer, and paid a good price. She would chat to the lady, ask after her children, talk about cooking and husbands and mothers-in-law. She would walk with the women into the back-yard and they would point to whatever they had that was beyond their own needs, and Winnie would buy it. Before long she knew the first names of all the women in the street. By the end of the first month they were smiling at her when they passed her on the street, waving to her from their front windows, calling out to her as she passed by. Mistrust melted, Albouystown opened its arms and Winnie stepped into them.

* * *

But the biggest change of all came after only four months.

After dinner she and I sat ourselves down in the gallery as usual, and I opened the top drawer in the gallery table to remove the cards, but Winnie placed a hand on mine.

'Not tonight, George,' she said. I looked up in surprise. Winnie's face, caught in the flickering light of the lamp, beamed back at me. Her eyes sparkled, and her smile was the most radiant I had ever seen.

'George – we're going to have a baby!' she said.

Chapter Thirteen

Yoyo

Winnie wrote to say they were coming to visit, she and George. I couldn't imagine what for – the last time I had seen Winnie, we had parted on less than cordial terms. But I supposed she wanted to see her mother. I almost wrote back to say she should come, but not to bring George. It was going to be most awkward. George, who was once our postboy on the estate, now living in the house as part of the family! Most inappropriate. It's not that I was a snob. I just felt it would lead to disrespect – not only on his part, but on the part of the servants.

Mama, of course, was delighted that they were coming. It was scandalous, how openly she showed her preference for Winnie. Though most of Mama's behaviour was scandalous anyway. Mama thought nothing of fraternising not only with the house servants but with the labourers as well. She was wielding far too much power around the plantation – I should never have taken her advice and employed that Mad Jim Booker as estate manager. Yes, it had been necessary to dismiss Mr McInnes, but we should have waited until we found an appropriate replacement.

Mr Booker was anything *but* appropriate, the way he ran around with that bushy beard and those faded old clothes! I had to admit, though, that he was a good manager; the coolies worked well for him – better, even, than under Mr McInnes – even though he was far too gentle with them. But perhaps it was indeed true what he said – the carrot was better than the stick.

I just didn't like the way he and Mama were undermining my authority. It's not that I necessarily disagreed with this approach – if it increased production, who was I to protest – but they needed to know who was actually running the plantation, and that was I. But the fact remained that I was better at figures than at people, and they were the ones out there giving directions whereas I was the one bent over the books. This was confusing for the coolies.

Coolies are simple people, like children, really, and they would never understand that in the end everything came down to me. That I was the boss. It was I who approved the plan to build new lodgings for them on the back-dam. We would have to sacrifice an entire cane field for this – would the coolies be able to grasp the significance of that? No! Of course not. They would think of us as soft, as giving in to their demands.

I had always said that change had to come from above – that was the only way to maintain authority. We could not be seen as having caved in as a result of their strikes and protests – but that was exactly what would happen. Once you gave them a hand they would take the whole arm – what would be the next demand? But it was not the coolies now who were making demands – it was that Mad Jim, hand-in-glove with Mama. Better pay, shorter hours, more free days, schools for the coolie children, a dispensary with a resident nurse, maternity leave, old age pensions – what would be next?

There was a time when I too had dreamt such unrealistic dreams. But I was only fourteen at the time, my heart softened by witnessing the atrocious conditions my beloved Nanny had lived and died in. I saw myself, back then, as some kind of saviour – a benefactress, bestowing blessings on my underlings. It wasn't a bad thing to be. Doing good makes one feel good. I understood that much. But now I had a plantation to run and you can't do that on kindliness and generosity. So I had to harden my heart and make myself more like a man. Rough and tough. That's the only way I could succeed.

Mama didn't understand that – she was all woman, kind and caring, and she had no business mixing herself into plantation business. Papa always said that women didn't have the head for business, and I could see that with Mama. Too kind by far. And now Winnie was coming. With George. Frankly, it was a catastrophe.

* * *

They arrived the following week; I had offered to send Poole down with the car to fetch them from Georgetown, but Winnie sent a cable back saying no, they preferred to come by train, but that we could send Poole to New Amsterdam to collect them.

They arrived in time for dinner. Mama, of course, flew at the car and flung her arms round both Winnie and George. I gave them a more circumspect greeting – I hugged Winnie, of course, and I gave George a polite and reserved handshake. It was an awkward thing, and once again I was reminded how very inappropriate this marriage was. This time, as I was at home, I didn't have a big hat to wear to show my disapproval, but I would wear a frown and a distant demeanour. Brother-in-law or not, George needed to know his place inside my home.

I sent them up to their room to change out of their limp and bedraggled travelling clothes, and sent the boy up behind them with their luggage. Their room. The biggest travesty of all. My sister, sharing a bed with the black postboy. It was beyond disgusting.

They came down again all washed and tidy. I couldn't help noticing that, although Winnie's clothes were clean, they were rather plain. As a young girl Winnie had loved fashionable attire – how could she bear living in Albouystown with a poor husband who couldn't afford to keep her in beautiful frocks? I was curious, and over the next few days I hoped to prise all the details out of her. A white lady in Albouystown! It was actually quite intriguing. And this husband of hers. Well, I intended to thoroughly size him up – discreetly, of course. What on earth did she see in him? She had pursued him relentlessly, running away at least twice to meet him secretly, when she could have had her pick of any number of appropriate young suitors.

According to Uncle Don, Papa's younger brother with an estate in Barbados, she actually turned down just such a young man on the island. And of course she could have had my Clarence, and been mistress of Promised Land. Yet she chose the darkie postboy, this George. It was extraordinary. I mean, I knew that George wasn't an ordinary darkie. He was quite clever, for a start, and I suddenly remembered the first time we had met him – I had been quite impressed at his knowledge of telegraphy and Morse code, and indeed I had found him rather interesting, for a darkie.

But Winnie, it seemed, had been completely captivated from the start. 'Love at first sight', she called it. Baloney! There's no such thing. But Winnie latched on to him like a leech, pursued him, betrayed her family for him, and this is what we ended up with: the family dragged through the ugliness of a public trial, our father a convict, and a Cox princess married to a darkie postboy from Albouystown. No wonder she and I quarrelled incessantly when she moved back to Promised Land after the trial! I could not forgive her, and I was glad when that cursed wedding was finally over and done with and I could get down to my work managing the plantation.

I hadn't reckoned on Mama being every bit as stubborn as Winnie when it came to making changes and, backed by Mad Jim Booker, overriding my objections.

And now here we were: the new housing almost finished, the coolies excited and rallying around their new manager; me in a subordinate position, reduced to mere accountant, and Winnie and George due to arrive at any minute.

So yes, I was angry. But I couldn't show it. Not blatantly, anyway. On the outside I would be as cordial as a sister can be; on the inside, seething. I would play my cards subtly, and cleverly. I was in no hurry.

* * *

We took our seats at the dining table and I glanced at George. He had changed into a rather smart suit with a white shirt and a bow tie, and actually looked quite dapper, if one looked past the colour of his skin. George could be charming when he wanted to be, and obviously, this evening he did want to be – after all, he had to impress his mother-in-law. Though he didn't have to work hard for that; it was quite obvious that Mama was completely taken in by George and fully approved of Winnie's choice. That, to me, was inexcusable. To her right sat Clarence, but it had been plain from the start that Mama and Clarence were like fire and water and, having lived with him for several months by this time, she had not the least compunction in ignoring him completely and giving all her attention to George.

The table was set for five, with Mama at the head, Clarence at her right and Winnie at her left. George sat next to Winnie, and I sat on Clarence's right, opposite George. Pansy brought out the steaming bowl of mulligatawny soup. I had engaged a male Indian cook from Georgetown – Rupnarine was his name – and I had expressly requested this soup, as it was his *pièce de resistance*. The very aroma of it was enough to make even the most dedicated ascetic swoon, and George, not being an ascetic, immediately commented on it.

'That smells delicious!' he said, making an exaggerated gesture of breathing it deep into his lungs. 'Mulligatawny is my favourite!'

'His mother makes it too,' chirped Winnie, smiling at Mama. This was her strategy, it seemed: to be constantly drawing attention to points in her new family's favour. 'And she's taught me to cook it!'

And, I might add, boasting of her newly found accomplishments in her new life. She never let me forget the fact that she was, apparently, an expert Morse technician and had even worked in the telegraphy office in Barbados – as if working in a public institution was anything to boast about! Perhaps she had forgotten one of the many German aphorisms Mama had taught us as children: *Eigenlob stinkt* – self-praise stinks. She had been far more modest before this affair with George; when we were growing up Winnie was the one who never seemed to believe in herself, and I was the star, the one everyone admired and praised. Yet here now was Winnie putting on airs, passing herself off as some kind of a gourmet cook.

'She's good, too!' said George, beholding her with shining eyes as if she were an angel with spreading wings floating above us all. Winnie beamed at the sycophancy.

'I like cooking,' she said. 'I never thought I would – I was never very practical as a girl – do you remember, Mama? You always said I had two left thumbs when it came to sewing and embroidery!'

'Tell her about your guava jelly,' said George, in between sips at his soup. He held the soup spoon completely wrong, slurping out of the front of the spoon instead of nipping at the side. It was obvious he had not been brought up with any kind of table etiquette whatsoever, and that Winnie had not bothered to teach him either. A drop of mulligatawny soup fell on to his shirt, and I couldn't help but titter. Clarence, too, noticed this, and we exchanged a secret smile.

Winnie, of course, did not notice – she would probably never see any fault in her George – and now she took his encouragement as a cue for yet more bragging. Oh Winnie, Winnie – where did you leave your modesty?

'Yes, Mama – you see, we have two guava trees in the backyard and they bear the most delicious, huge, white guavas. They are far tastier than the pink ones – quite a delicacy! Well, on my first day as a married woman George's mother – who can be quite formidable when she wants to be – taught me how to make guava jelly. And since then I've been going around Albouystown buying those white guavas from anyone who has a tree. I walk from door to door with a basket and I pay good prices. That way I also made a few friends among the women. And then I make the jelly, and sell it. You see, Yoyo – you're not the only businesswoman among us!'

I smiled and bowed my head in acknowledgement, but inwardly I fumed. How dare she compare guava jelly to a sugar estate? How dare she compare *us*? How dare she!

'And you know what?' said George. 'Now people have started calling the white guavas "White Lady Guavas". Not just in the neighbourhood – the name has stuck even in Bourda Market.'

Winnie had the grace to blush.

'How lovely!' I said, and caught George's eye. He frowned, and I suspected he had read my sarcasm, but Winnie hadn't – she was far too naïve to mistrust any praise I offered, possibly because it was so rare. She simpered and said, bubbling over with enthusiasm: 'I've brought you some jars, Yoyo, so you can try it. And some pepper sauce, and tamarind chutney, and mango pickle! I brought them in the trunk of the car. Has Poole brought them up to the kitchen yet? I've been trying out all these wonderful recipes George's mother taught me, and it's such fun – I never knew I'd be good in the kitchen!'

There she was again, fishing for compliments, and of course Mama took the bait this time.

'Yes – Winnie was always more of a dreamer, a musician. Do you still play, Winnie?'

Winnie's face fell. 'No, Mama. In fact I left my violin here – we don't really have room for it at George's place. But anyway, I'm so busy.'

'Well, you shouldn't let your talent go to waste. We'll have to do something about that one of these days – I'd love to play a duet with you again.'

And so the conversation turned to music, of which I know nothing. There it was again, the favouritism. It wasn't my fault that I didn't have a musical bone in my body, and that Winnie and Mama could get so carried away by Beethoven and all those boring German composers. Mozart of course was Austrian, and it didn't help that Mama came from Salzburg, his birthplace. I supposed we would all be subjected to after-dinner symphonies from now on.

Mama and Winnie, of course, had always been avid musicians. I remembered well those days when we were children, how the two of them would play duets: Mama at the piano, Winnie with her violin. I had stifled my yawns and survived those evenings. But now they were beyond eager to play again, and, it turned out, Clarence had learned to play the cello, and he was a musical aficionado, and he could keep up with the tedious talk. They did try to engage George in the conversation – apparently he played the banjo, and had a nice singing voice – but Mama and Winnie and Clarence, of course, played at a higher musical level than George and, with their talk of Mozart and Bach and concertos and symphonies and chamber music and major and minor keys and so on, soon left him behind.

I wondered how George would take to this side of Winnie. Of course, as a darkie he lacked that culture, that refinement of taste, and that was one thing he and I might have in common. Mama always used to say I wore armour over my heart because I didn't appreciate the subtleties of good music. But it just came down to taste, and music was just one way for Mama to dismiss me as a philistine and prefer Winnie. And now I didn't have Papa, for whom I could do no wrong.

It was clear that not even Clarence would stand up for me. Now the three of them launched into a deep discussion about Russian composers and all I could do was wrinkle my nose to show my boredom. Again I glanced at George; he was pretending to follow the musical conversation and show deep interest in the nuances of Tchaikovsky, but I would have bet anything that he was just as uninterested as I was. I managed to catch his gaze, and rolled my eyes. He understood my meaning immediately, because the ghost of a smile touched his lips and though he looked away again I knew I had found an accomplice of sorts.

Covertly, I inspected him, and I had to admit he was not a bad-looking fellow. He was tall and rangy, and had a certain awkward charm and grace of movement, though at the moment he was struggling with the cutlery. His eyes were fixed on Winnie, who was secretly showing him which knives and forks to use – I wondered if she had tried to cue him with the soup and he had missed it. Now he was almost dainty in the way he cut his meat and pushed it on to his fork. He had a long neck, slightly prominent cheekbones and a high forehead, and mossy black hair clipped close to his head like a cap, curving around his face in what the Germans called *Geheimratsecken* – a word that literally and rather poetically means 'secret councillor corners' but translates to the rather mundane 'receding hairline' – his high forehead going deep into his skull on the left and the right, giving him an air of intellectuality. I did remember him saying he had once won a scholarship to Queen's College, the best boys' school in the colony, which hardly ever admitted darkies. He had then had to leave to earn money, and had become a postboy. So I suppose there was more to him than his low status indicated. I wondered briefly if darkies had the mental capacity to become doctors, lawyers, statesmen, and if all they lacked was education and opportunity? I supposed it was all rather unfair, but that wasn't my problem. It was the luck of the draw: some of us were born this way, some that, and who was I to question a status quo from which I profited? I knew that Winnie did – which was why she had ended up in a ramshackle cottage in Albouystown – but Winnie had a touch of the martyr to her, and I can't stand martyrs. They all have this air of complacent self-aggrandisement that they hide behind a facade of modesty – it is all for show, and behind that facade they are just as proud of themselves as anyone else – proud of their martyrdom, their humility. Winnie didn't fool me in the least. We all want applause, and she wanted it for her great sacrifice – giving up her privilege for the sake of the underdog. I wasn't at all fooled. But Mama was. Winnie would always be her shining star.

The musical discussion seemed to have come to an end, and after a rather pregnant pause – I chose that adjective deliberately – Mama said, 'Well now Winnie, so what is this news you mentioned in your letter? You seem to be doing everything in your power to delay the announcement, but I won't let you wriggle away again!'

'Oh Mama!' said Winnie and turned quite scarlet.

'I think I can guess!' said Mama, beaming, and all of a sudden the penny dropped in my brain and I knew what it was and I couldn't help it – I dropped my knife and it clattered to the floor and there was a flurry of activity as Pansy, who had been hovering in the background, rushed forward to pick it up and I scraped back my chair to allow her room to retrieve it. But this little incident allowed me time to gather the chaos of thoughts and emotions I had been catapulted into.

Of course! Why hadn't I realised it right away! I was normally far more astute – I had of course noticed that Winnie had gained weight but I had put it down to the feeding-up she was getting from her mother-in-law – these people eat mountains of rice with little meat or fish to go with it, and of course everyone knows that rice settles on the hips and waist. But how perfectly idiotic of me to put two and two together and get five!

Now Winnie seemed to have lost her tongue, and while I carefully arranged the contours of my face to disguise my true feelings and not reveal even a trace of vexation, she hemmed and hawed

and simpered like the perfect fool she was. I don't think I have
ever hated Winnie more than in that moment. There. I said the
word. I hated her, even before she finally put away her false coy-
ness and said the fatal words:

'Oh Mama! You have guessed it, haven't you? George and I are
going to have a baby!'

She glanced at me then, and I saw the triumph in her gleam-
ing eyes. 'I beat you to it!' they said, though her lips stayed closed.
I seethed. But I smiled.

* * *

I wanted sons. I *needed* sons. Soon after Papa's conviction I had
discovered among his papers the deeds to some lands up in the
Essequibo region, and more land in the Corentyne, to the east,
near Skeldon. Land, lying fallow! What we could do with that
land! I needed a team of strong young men to develop that land,
to rule it and make this family great again.

But I can hardly be expected to deliver a son when my husband refuses to plant one in my womb.

Perhaps that is wrongly expressed. It was not so much that he
refused to plant the son; it was more that he refused to partake
of the very act of planting. It wasn't the *son* he didn't want – he
didn't want me. It seemed, in that respect, that any little coolie
girl running around on the plantation was preferable to me. It
was the insult to end all insults – but the more I rebuked him
for his refusal to oblige, the more he refused. Perhaps, though,
he had no choice in the matter – it wasn't so much an actual
refusal, more a failure, of which he actually seemed ashamed. I
had, as mentioned, tried cutting down his rum intake, but to
no effect.

He swore to me that he was faithful, that he had given up his
liaisons with labourer women since our wedding. I had wondered
for a while if he was one of those fairies, but his dalliances with

labourer women were well-known so it couldn't be that. But what else could account for such unmanliness?

I was inexperienced in such matters, of course, but everything I had heard about the subject indicated that it is the natural inclination of a man to do this rather disgusting thing – and yes, it does require a certain willing suspension of disgust on the part of the woman, but of course I was willing to suspend! I wanted to do it. I wanted sons, many sons, and if this was required of me then, very well, I would do it. I was not the least bit squeamish in that respect. I would do what it takes.

And now here was Winnie gloating and simpering and basking in Mama's attention and George's devoted gaze, and even Clarence had the gall to congratulate her, seemingly without the least bit of shame. But then they all looked at me and I realised I had said nothing congratulatory yet. So I arranged my face into the appropriate expression of required delight (hopefully none of my previous dismay had revealed itself), stretched and curved my lips into the requisite smile, and spoke the words they were all waiting for: 'Oh, how wonderful! A baby! A sweet little baby! I'm going to be an aunt!'

They seemed satisfied with that and mercifully left me alone to wallow in my distress. I clenched my hands in my lap to prevent me reaching across the table to dig out my sister's eyes. The violence of my reaction surprised even me, even though I know that I am, deep inside, not quite as ladylike as society requires and that I do have violent tendencies. I manage to disguise them well, as appropriate for my position. But now – oh, how I raged. My nails dug into the palms of my hands as I tightened those hidden fists. I took some deep breaths, which helped to calm me, but still, I almost shook with rage.

So intent was I on controlling my feelings I missed most of the sycophantic conversation swirling around Winnie. Mama, of course, was beside herself with joy: her favourite daughter was about to have a baby! Winnie's child would not be her first grand-child; our elder sister Kathleen, who had moved to England years ago, had already produced two daughters – but it would be the first she would see and hold and generally spend all her frustrated nurturing tendencies on. Mama had fallen into a deep melancholy when her last child, the much-longed-for heir to Promised Land, had died soon after birth. She had sunk so deep into that Darkness – as we all called it – that she had to be sent back to Austria, where a certain Dr Freud treated her – with some success, it seemed, since she had returned to us completely herself again.

Be that as it may, Winnie's condition now threw her into an ecstasy of projected commotion.

'I'm going to start sewing some clothes right away! You must come with me to New Amsterdam tomorrow to buy some fabrics, and embroidery threads, and patterns!'

I decided to throw a little cold water on her euphoria.

'A pity we no longer have Edward John's little things – those were exquisite!' I smiled at her in pretended sympathy. Mama had filled a trunk with beautifully handmade clothes for our poor little dead brother. Turning to Mama, I said, 'I gave it all away to a church group that cares for the Poor Unfortunates of New Amsterdam. That's what you would have wanted, isn't it?'

This, of course, was the first Mama had heard of that act of generosity, and a cloud passed over her features. I looked brightly from her to Winnie and back again.

'But I'm sure Winnie would not have wanted a dead child's leftovers – they would probably have brought bad luck. Isn't it so, Winnie?'

An awkward silence descended over the table as they all drank in my words. I did feel a tinge of conscience – perhaps it *was* slightly tactless, cruel even, to raise the ghost of Edward John precisely at this happy moment, and maybe I had not adequately disguised that cruelty – I had smiled sympathetically at Mama while speaking, but Mama did have the talent of reading people's eyes, and perhaps, just perhaps, I should have been more circumspect. However, it was Mama who broke the awkwardness.

'I shall make new clothes!' she said firmly. 'Winnie's baby shall have only the best!'

I smiled; I beamed at Winnie, so that she should have no inkling of my resentment. I even smiled at George, openly, for the first time.

* * *

But of course, behind the happy smile, I was devastated. Until, finally, the realisation dawned on me: Winnie's son would be a half-caste, and thus could never take over the plantation. And, of course, the baby might even be a daughter. The first was a certainty, the second a hope. I could not allow Winnie to have sons, when I couldn't produce them. That would be the ultimate slap in my face.

But their child would definitely be coloured. Papa would never allow a coloured heir to take possession of Promised Land. But how much say did Papa have in the matter now he was in prison? What about Clarence? Clarence's rights? If Winnie produced a male heir before Clarence and I did, would Clarence be deposed? I could not let that happen. I frowned in concentration. I really should have taken more interest in the contracts Papa and Clarence had drawn up, but I had not looked into the details. I would have to make sure that under no circumstances could a son of Winnie and George be instated as heir. Perhaps I could persuade Papa to disinherit Winnie and her issue completely. I would write him immediately – we should have thought of this long ago, at the time of her wedding. How negligent of us! And tomorrow I would have to go through the papers, just to make sure. How typical of Winnie to come from behind and upset the apple cart. Although I supposed it was to be expected. I could well imagine that she and George would breed like rabbits – it's said that coloured men are extremely potent. In contrast to my Clarence.

I caught Clarence's eye, and held it. I tried to put as much accusation as I could into that glance, and he flinched – he understood my displeasure all too well. I made sure my stare was as icy as could be – with some luck that would goad him into trying harder. I had to conceive a son! Many sons! How could Clarence fail me in this one essential matter, when in all other matters he bowed entirely to my will? I could not understand it.

They were all still chatting about babies. Clarence managed to pull his gaze away from mine and turn his attention to the general conversation – an act of subtle insurrection for which I would have to chide him later on. He even spoke a word or two, something about being an uncle and looking forward to cricket, or some such thing. I couldn't say a word; I let the chatter pass over my head. I was far too busy calculating. Perhaps I, too, could conceive in the next few days – I had heard that there were days in the month particularly conducive to conception, but I didn't know the details. Perhaps Mildred, my lady's maid, would know, or could find out – her sister was a midwife in the village. And perhaps – I went back to the comforting thought – Winnie's child would be a girl. If Clarence tried harder he could still fulfil his duty.

Thankfully, the talk once again turned to music, and again George was left out of the conversation, as was I.

In the midst of all this chatter my gaze somehow met George's, and read the boredom there.

I winked.

I couldn't help it. It happened quite spontaneously – a substitute for a yawn, perhaps, or a need to express my ennui.

George immediately looked away – but he blushed.

You might very well say that a person of George's dark hue cannot blush. But he did.

His facial skin turned a distinct shade darker. I had embarrassed him.

I liked the idea. I smiled to myself. What fun!

George of course had impeccable manners – doubtless he had picked them up from Winnie, who had surely coached him in the way to behave in an Englishman's house. He had done quite well in the use of cutlery (apart from that business with the soup spoon), following her lead, and he never spoke unless spoken to. He was humble, as behoved someone of his station who had risen in life, and courteous. I had caught him out, read his thoughts, seen his inner lack of comprehension and displayed my acknowledgement of our mutual discontent. And that, of course, was what embarrassed him. I had caught him out in a discourtesy towards his hosts. Never mind that I was the hostess – I had caught him out.

It amused me no end.

I realised right then that here was an opportunity. George was like a little house-pet – it would be amusing to tease him a little. I spoke up.

'Mama, why don't you and Winnie entertain us a little? The piano is still in the music room, you know, and Winnie, you can play your violin.'

Winnie had not taken her precious instrument with her to Albouystown. She said there was no room for it there. I could not imagine how small her home must be, that it lacked room for a thing as small as a violin case!

'Oh – but the piano is doubtless out of tune, if no one has played it for all these years. And in this climate!'

Mama once had filled the house with music, but since her return had not played so much as a scale. There had been talk of bringing in a piano-tuner from Georgetown, but she had not in the end acted on it.

'And *I* am out of tune!' Winnie laughed. 'I haven't touched my violin for at least a year.'

'A travesty!' I cried, now full of enthusiasm. 'Mama, never mind if the piano is slightly out of tune – no one will hear it but you.'

'And Winnie, and Clarence.'

'It would be fun, Mama,' said Winnie.

'I'd love to hear you play,' said Clarence, 'and I'll make allowances, if a few notes are off-key – I do miss music, out here in the wilderness.'

And so we all coaxed Mama into compliance, and we all stood up from the table and moved to the music room, which was at the back of the house, the south side, protected from sun and damp. For once, I thought, I will be amused by music.

George, Clarence and I took our seats on three of the stiff-backed chairs in the music room. I don't know why Papa never bothered to furnish this room with more comfortable seating accommodation; a few comfortable Berbice chairs would have been nice, allowing the bored listener to subtly fall asleep while pretending to be soaking in the music with closed eyes; Berbice chairs are wonderful for that. Well, the place was virtually mine now, and that was one thing I could do. Mama wouldn't try to intervene, seeing as she would always rather be a performer than a listener.

It was a large room with a colourful carpet covering the honey-coloured floorboards. When we were children the servants would roll back the carpets and Mama and Papa would dance to music while Mama sang – Viennese waltzes that would have us girls clapping and jumping up and joining in, with genuine glee. Mama was so gay, back then. So full of verve. What happened? Something did. Winnie, I suspected, knew more than I did, close as she was to Mama.

Now, the carpet stayed on the floor and we the audience of three took our seats. Mama lifted the cover of the piano and gently ran her fingers over the keys before pressing a few and tilting her head, leaning forward the better to listen.

'Yes,' she said sadly. 'It needs tuning. I don't know if I can bear—'

'Oh, Mama!' I interrupted, 'do go on! Just once, for old times' sake.'

Winnie, meanwhile, had opened her violin case and removed the instrument, and was stroking its smooth surface with infinite tenderness. Really, you'd think her violin were her baby; it would be interesting to see if she would hold a real baby with such tenderness. She tightened the strings of her bow, adjusted the keys of the violin, played a few notes, tightened, listened, stroked and, finally, satisfied, she looked up at Mama with glowing eyes.

'I'm ready!' she said, 'what shall we play?'

'What about…' Well, I don't remember what Mama suggested; it's all the same to me, but Winnie nodded and they played.

I can't say if they were good or not; I have no ear for music. I watched them for a while, then turned my eyes to George, who was listening with rapt attention. The boredom he had exhibited during the musical conversation had vanished; he now seemed genuinely captivated by the music. His eyes were fixed on Winnie, who stood with her violin under her chin and her bow arm swinging as she played, swaying, moving to the music, her eyes lowered, her body fully one with the body of sound emerging from her instrument.

I was seated just opposite him, and so it was possible to observe him while pretending to watch Winnie, as both were in my natural view. I did not at all like what I saw.

Most of the English population of British Guiana, not just myself, had of course been violently against this match. Winnie, everyone agreed, had disgraced our entire side by stooping so low, and as for George, he was obviously a social climber; having seen an opportunity to better himself, he grasped it with both hands. It was all about climbing the hierarchy – and, in the end, money. Winnie, besotted as she was, could not see that, but everyone else did.

Now, watching him watch her, I was not so sure.

I had never pretended to be anything other than an old potato where romance is concerned. I didn't believe in marrying for love; surely marriage was a contract undertaken to join two people for their mutual benefit, and to produce children. As for love at first sight, as Winnie had talked about this evening – what rubbish! I had always scoffed at the love stories Winnie devoured, Jane Austen and others of her ilk, and as for love poetry and love songs – well, they left me cold. Papa used to say I had a heart of stone, unusually for a girl emerging into womanhood. But I simply did not see the point.

Now, though, as I observed George, an unpleasant feeling overtook me.

What was that, shining in his eyes, if not love? That rapt attention, that sense of him drinking her in, absorbing her as she played; as if, in watching her, her soul became his, music and all. As if, through his eyes, her very being entered him – such softness, such happiness, such love!

One thing was certain: Clarence, my husband, had never looked at me that way. I had never expected him to. He never would, I was sure.

A great sadness enveloped me. Had I been wrong? Was there such a thing as love, and was it as precious as they said? Was it something vital, essential to one's internal well-being – and had I lacked it all my life, without even knowing?

For right now, watching George watch Winnie, I felt that lack.

A great yawning emptiness opened within me. A vacuum; a yearning for something I could not have; something I wanted without knowing I wanted it, caught up as I was in so many other, lesser, wants. All my ambitions, all my plans, all my striving for the top, crumbled in the face of what I saw in George's face. Crumbled into dust. I felt empty, forlorn, small – feelings I had never known in all my life, for I was a girl who had always known what she wanted and almost always got it. A girl with not a fingertip of doubt in her soul. Strong, they said, and cocksure. That was Johanna Penelope Cox through and through. Admired and applauded. But right now, she was nothing.

I could even put a name on that unpleasant feeling. It all narrowed down to one thing, one word, one emotion.

Jealousy.

While George sat absorbed by Winnie and her music, I sat absorbed in self-recognition, something previously alien to my nature. If a lovely woman, a woman celebrated for her great outstanding beauty and charm, had sat to regard herself in her boudoir mirror and saw nothing but an ugly old hag, she could not have been more shocked than I was at that moment.

I did not even notice when the music stopped.

'Why, Yoyo, you're crying! I've never seen you moved by music before!' That was Mama, of course, snapping me out of my spell.

Chapter Fourteen

Winnie

'Yoyo seems to have warmed towards you,' I said to George on our way home. 'I'm so glad. I couldn't bear her enmity. She was almost rude to you at the wedding, but tonight she even spoke a few words to you, and not unkindly. I knew you'd win her over, George!'

Though of course, Yoyo had known George right from the beginning; we met him together, at the post office, and she had liked him well enough then; it was more the fact that I had decided to marry him that had aroused her ire. But now, no doubt she had accepted that he was indeed a member of our family, and that wasn't going to change. She seemed truly delighted at the prospect of becoming an aunt. This baby, I thought to myself, will heal all wounds.

I missed my sister, and the closeness we had once enjoyed. Choosing George above my family had been a heart-wrenching decision, but now at last the broken bridges could be repaired, and this tiny creature growing within me would fuse us all into one again. We would be real sisters. I was even growing fonder of Clarence – I felt I had to make an effort to like him, since I wanted Yoyo to like George. I do believe that at heart every person is likeable – one must only strive to find the common spark that binds us all, that basic thread of humanity, and love *that* rather than be distracted by unpleasant qualities. And so I tried, and indeed much of my dislike put itself to rest. I would never exactly love Clarence, but I was growing to somewhat like him. The fact that he was musical helped. Music does bring people together; but more than music, the baby. Our baby. Our first!

*   *   *

George seemed to think that he, personally, was piecing that baby together inside my body. He was the proudest father-to-be who ever walked the earth, and he was going to be the best father in the world – I could tell! I never thought I could love him more than I had before, but now our love seemed to grow by the day, by the hour, almost. There is no limit to love, I discovered; there is just a limit to the obstructions we place before it, and the more those obstructions melt, the more love spreads, and the more it spreads, the more those obstructions melt. It's a self-propagating phenomenon.

This love, now, was so different to the euphoric swings that catapulted me into the stars when I first fell for George as a young and naïve girl: it was deep, rather than high, rooted rather than free-floating in the heavenly spheres, silent rather than shouting for joy. A touch of his glance, or of his fingers, was enough to pull me into it. His eyes could speak and, I'm sure, so did mine. It was a melting away of the hard-bound selves that we were, into a common Self that was greater than the sum of its two parts. Our single secret Self.

*   *   *

At first, nothing changed at home. I made my rounds as usual, collecting ripe guavas and peppers, mangoes and limes from our suppliers, and a farmer continued to deposit a cartful of mature coconuts in our yard at regular intervals. I continued to make my jelly, my pepper sauce, my lime pickles and mango chutney, my coconut oil. More and more shops agreed to sell my concoctions; the shop owners, sceptical at first, turned enthusiastic. Even in

Stabroek Market, also called Big Market, I was able to win over a few shopkeepers. My products sold!

I kept the profit in a Cow & Gate tin in the wardrobe. We could use it, one day, soon enough.

'By the time the baby is born,' I told George, 'we will have enough to extend the house – add a room at the back!'

'A room for each child!' George said, pulling me close.

I giggled. 'How many shall we have?'

'As many as God gives us,' he said. 'A house teeming with boys and girls! I can't wait to meet them all!'

'Well, let's start with one,' I said.

'What shall we call him, or her?'

'If it's a girl I'd like to name her after my mother – Ruth.'

'And a boy after my father, Theodore.'

'But your sister's son is Theodore!' I objected. 'We can't have two Theodore cousins – it would be so confusing!'

'One could be Theodore and the other Theo?'

'No,' I said decisively. 'I want him to have his very own name, not share one with a cousin. We can't call him Archibald – Father and I have too much strife between us. Besides, I'd like to leave Archibald for Yoyo's son, when she has one. She and Papa were very close – I'm sure she'd like to honour him in that way.' I thought for a while. 'We could call him after my maternal grandfather, Johannes – but that's too German. What's your grandfather's name?'

'Humphrey,' said George.

'Shall we call him Humphrey, then?'

'Yes! Humphrey for a boy, Ruth for a girl. I hope she's a girl. Both my sisters have had boys – we need a girl in the family.'

'Well – we'll find out in November. I don't care, as long as the baby is healthy.' I took a deep breath and reached for him. 'Oh, George – I can hardly believe it. You and I, parents!'

My pregnancy proceeded with no complications. I went to see a Dr van Sertima, supposed to be the best doctor for confinement

and birth in the colony. We could afford it – we had my Cow &
Gate savings, which was what I called my profit, growing in the
wardrobe. Dr van Sertima said I had the perfect body for child-
bearing; that all was in order; that I would have perfect children,
and many of them.

A month before I was due to give birth, we added a little room
to the back of the house, and an indoor bathroom and lavatory. The
extension could only be accessed through the kitchen, and it gave
the cottage a rather odd layout, but it was exciting to prepare for a
new family member, and nobody cared about the layout. Ma and
Pa, it was decided, would move into the new room, George and I
would move into their old bedroom and our room would be for the
baby. We considered ourselves privileged – not many new parents in
Albouystown had such a large dwelling as ours! Most families lived
four or five to a room. Yes, we were privileged, and we knew it, and
we counted our blessings – and the Cow& Gate money.

By this time my belly was bursting out of my clothes, and I
had long ceased to do my rounds buying fruit and selling jars.
Instead I employed a young boy to go from house to house buying the necessary supplies. Demand was growing, week by week.
Now shopkeepers in Bourda Market, Stabroek Market and even
in the affluent Downtown were placing the jars of jelly and sauce
and bottles of oil on their counters; even William Fogarty's, where
the English shopped. My friend Kitty MacGonigal helped by taking the finished products to market., and promised to help even
more once the baby was born.

I still cooked the products myself, though, and jarred them.
I prided myself on a secret ingredient that added just that subtle
touch of *deliciousness*. People were asking for more and more of
them. They were still calling them the White Lady jelly, or pickle,
or sauce, and I decided I had to give my products a name. White
Lady would not do. So once again George and I found ourselves
agonising over a name.

'Winnie's – something,' I said. I mean, I could call them Winnie's Guava Jelly and Winnie's Pepper Sauce and so on – but I prefer a name that would cover them all.'

'What about Winnie's Wonder?' said George.

'Hmmm,' I said. 'Not really.'

And then it hit me. 'Quintessentials!' I cried. That's exactly it!'

'I prefer Winnie's Wonder,' said George, 'but Quintessentials will do.'

'I'll get labels made, and Quintessentials will be in everyone's kitchen!'

But then all production stopped. Because my baby, my first child, decided to make a somewhat early appearance, at two on a Sunday morning.

* * *

My waters broke. I screamed at George: 'Go, George, fetch Dr van Sertima!'

'But he said to bring you to his clinic when the time comes!'

'Well, the time has come, and I'm not going anywhere!'

George's eyes opened wide in panic. 'What – what shall we do?'

'Call Ma!'

But Ma had heard the commotion through the open ceiling and was already at the door issuing instructions.

'Go to Deirdre Barrow house on Lime Street,' she commanded George, 'and tell she to come at once.'

She turned to me. 'Deirdre Barrow is a midwife – best midwife in Albouystown. In the whole of Georgetown. Everything goin' to be all right. Don't worry. Calm down. Breathe easy.'

George returned with Deirdre Barrow. Ma ordered him to put on a pot of water to boil. I could feel the baby pressing down, pushing its way into the world. An hour went by, two, with Ma and Deirdre ministering to me. Finally I let out a long cry of agony, and then it was there, sliding out on to the bed.

'A boy!' cried Ma.

'Give him to me! Let me hold him!'

'Just a minute.'

Ma and Deirdre exchanged a look. I saw something in that look that I didn't want to see. Why weren't they laughing with joy? What did the frown on Mama's forehead mean? I sat up in bed and reached out for my baby.

'What's the matter? Give him to me! Give him to me now.'

Deirdre smiled comfortingly. 'Leh' me wrap him up in a cloth first.' She was doing something to my baby, and my panic only grew.

'What are you doing? Give him to me! What's wrong? Ma, what's wrong with my baby? Give him to me, now! Ma! What's wrong? Is he all right?'

Chapter Fifteen

George

Winnie is so unlike her sister. I was not happy during our visit to Promised Land plantation. At first Yoyo ignored me completely, and then she started to stare at me. At first I thought it was just my imagination, but after a while I couldn't help but notice it. Her eyes seemed always settled on me. And not in a friendly way. In a calculating way. Once, during dinner, she smiled – it was during the conversation on music, which I was trying hard, but unsuccessfully, to follow. Winnie and her mother know a different kind of music to mine – my little banjo and the simple folk songs I sing can hardly compare with the great music of Europe – and so I perked my ears hoping to educate myself, and that was the first time our eyes met.

She gave me that smile so full of disdain. She has always disdained me. The very first time we met – I remember so well, since it was the day I met Winnie – it was Yoyo who told me to go to the back door to deliver my letter. It wasn't so much her words but her voice – all high and mighty.

We met again, later, at the post office and she seemed less haughty, perhaps because I demonstrated the sending of telegrams, which seemed to fascinate her.

But the moment she learned that her sister wanted to marry me she turned to ice. I could not be colder at the North Pole than in Yoyo's company. It was as if I did not even exist. I would have preferred downright hostility to such frigidity. And now, suddenly, this change.

While we listened to the musicians after dinner Yoyo fixed her gaze on me and left it there. As we were sitting on opposite sides of the piano, it might have appeared that she was watching her mother, but I knew better. Those eyes rested on me, and it made me squirm. I tried not to look back at her – I kept my own gaze on my mother-in-law – but how could I not see past to that stony face with its rigid gaze? What was going on behind that unmoving countenance? What was that clever brain thinking? What did she have in mind? Right then and there I decided to avoid Yoyo in future, and for the rest of that trip I did. It was with great relief that Winnie and I got into the car the next day for our return to Georgetown.

But the unpleasantness with Yoyo could not in any way cloud my joy at the prospect of becoming a father. I could almost leap for joy! My love for Winnie increased a hundredfold. I wanted to wrap my arms round her and protect her from every little mishap. When she was ill I rushed to fetch the basin and hold it for her. When she had been on her feet too long I encouraged her to lie down. When she frowned, I worried.

She stopped going on her rounds, collecting fruit and peppers, and I was thankful for that – but could she not stop cooking, as well, and just rest? No. My Winnie continued to make her guava jelly and pepper sauce, and would not take a rest.

'I'm not a delicate flower!' she laughed, pouring the steaming sauce into a jar.

'I know – but be careful! Don't burn yourself! Let me help you!'

But she would not let me. She shooed me out of the kitchen, telling me that I was making a nuisance of myself, and maybe I was. But I felt so helpless! Nature is unkind to fathers – there is nothing we can contribute while the woman is gestating; we can only watch and worry, and wonder and worship. It seemed such a miracle, such an impossibility! A small human being, growing in my wife's body! Yes, it happens a million times each day, all over the world, since the beginning of human history; and yet each time it is still a miracle, and I lived in a daze of wonder and amazement that this miracle should be happening to us. I felt so grateful, so privileged. I thanked God every day, and prayed for a safe delivery and a healthy child.

I had kept my resolve to retreat from politics. Now that I was to become a father this was even more necessary – I would need to provide for my little family, and could not afford to be arrested, as so many of our brothers were. Thrown into prison, and left to languish, for no other reason than stirring up trouble. I attended the occasional Saturday meeting, but only as an observer; and more and more the risk to the speakers became plain. Once, the meeting was broken up by the mounted police, and the speakers escaped arrest by only a hair's breadth.

The reasons I had retired from public speaking – and singing – were manifold and complex, and cowardice played no part. It was just that I felt a different stirring, a different calling in my heart. Yes, I wanted the equality of all races and justice for the oppressed of the factories and fields. Yes, my blood boiled at the treatment of sugar labourers and factory workers. Yes, rage still boiled in my heart when I remembered my friend Bhim, who had fought for our rights only to be mowed down by no lesser man than Winnie's own father. And yes, I had a gift for speaking, and for singing. Charisma, some people called it. But something had changed, and I didn't fully understand it.

Something I had been aware of for some time while I was still Theo X, the revolutionary. I was supposed to stir the crowds, and I did, but not in the way I was supposed to.

I only know that whenever I opened my mouth, it was not words of rage that emerged, but words of peace. No matter how much I tried, I could not whip the crowds into the frenzy needed for revolution. That was why I had given up Theo X. I was no longer that man of revolution. It was as if another being took hold of me and I spoke to individual hearts rather than to crowds; and there was nothing in the world I could do to stop it. And now, as simple George, people still loved my words, whether they were spoken or sung, and called for me to speak and sing to them. And over the months I found myself speaking at smaller gatherings all over town, invited into the homes of those who knew of my identity; and I spoke to them, and I sang.

This went on for some time. I didn't want to go, but I couldn't refuse. People called me, and I went. How can you not go, if you are called? But then came the night when all this came to an end.

* * *

'George! George, wake up! Something's happening'

For a moment I was dazed, but only a moment. I shot up in bed.

'Winnie! What's happening? Is it the baby?'

'Yes, George, yes! Everything's wet! The whole bed! My waters have broken!'

I didn't know what that meant, waters breaking. But it sounded dangerous. Anything breaking sounds dangerous.

'What shall I do?'

'Go, George, fetch Dr van Sertima!'

'But – but Winnie, he said to bring you to the clinic! He never said…'

Dr van Sertima was a fancy white doctor. How could I bring him here, to Albouystown? Would he even come? But how could I get Winnie to the clinic?

'Winnie – it's too early! The baby's due next month!'

The panic rose as bile in my gorge. It felt like the end of the world.

'Oh George, you're hopeless. Fetch Ma!'

Ma appeared at the door and she took matters in hand. She sent me to get Aunty Deirdre from Lime Street. Everyone in Albouystown knew Aunty Deirdre. Aunty Deirdre brought half of us into the world. She brought me into the world. I pedalled frantically through the streets till I came to her house and I hammered at her door, yelling for her to come.

She was there in a trice. She stood there glaring at me.

'Oh – is fancy boy George Quint. Wha' goin' on?'

'Winnie – Winnie! Her baby's coming! It's too early! Come, please come!'

'Oho! I thought you had a fancy white doctor?'

'It's Sunday – night-time! He said to bring her to hospital! How to get her to hospital this time of night? Please come, Aunty Deirdre.'

'I not good enough for the likes of you.'

I was in tears by now.

'Aunty Deirdre! Is one month too early. She gon' die, and the baby gon' die!'

'No white lady gon' want me fumblin' in she pumpum.'

I wept. I sank to my knees and buried my face in her nightie.

'Please, Aunty Deirdre! Please!'

Seeing me on my knees seemed to break something in her, because from that moment on she was all speed and business.

'George, go back home immediately and start to boil some hot water. I need clean towels – you have? Sheets? I'll be right behind you.'

And she was. I sped home and put the water on to boil and she was there at the door and then she was in the bedroom with Winnie and Mama and there was I, walking up and down the little passage outside biting my nails and pulling out what little hair I had. Winnie's moans and groans were as loud as if I were in the room, because there was no ceiling, and I longed to rush in and hold her hand but this was women's business and all I could do was pace the corridor and bite my nails and pull out my hair. And I prayed. Oh how I prayed!

'Oh Lord don't let her die. Please don't let her die. Please save her and the baby. I will do anything for you Lord, anything, just save her life!'

I prayed aloud, begging God, pleading with him. Winnie let out a blood-curdling scream and I fell to my knees, and prostrated myself, and begged again. It was as if my whole being was just that, a plea for her life.

And then I fell silent, and a great peace descended on me, and I sat back on my heels and held my hands on my knees with the palms upwards and the serenity that washed through me was more than I could bear. And all in me was silence. And in that silence I felt it.

And I knew in that moment that all was well. I knew it right down to my bones. I knew it in my blood and in my being – a sense of deepest peace flooding through every inch of my body and soul. And then the wail of a newborn child split the air and I wept once more, tears of relief and gratitude and love and dedication and promise. I knelt there weeping for several minutes and then I got up and knocked at the door.

'Can I come in?' I called.

'Just a minute – wait!' they called back.

And then Winnie's panicked cry: 'What's wrong? What's wrong with my baby?'

I could wait no more. I pressed the handle and flew through the door into the room.

Winnie was sitting up in bed, her hair dishevelled, her arms stretched out to the women in the corner, her face distorted by an agony that leapt right into my heart, banishing my new-found peace. Aunty Deirdre and Ma were standing aside, holding a bundle and whispering together. They turned round at my anguished cry.

'What's wrong? Give me the baby! What's wrong with the baby?'

Aunty Deirdre smiled, but it was a false smile. She walked towards me, holding the bundle, holding it out towards me.

'Your son, George. He's fine – a lovely healthy boy!'

I held out my hands for the bundle and she placed it in my arms and I looked down into the most beautiful face I had ever seen and my heart broke for the umpteenth time that night, and I fell in love for the second time in my life. A love like a hurricane, it was, sweeping through me and blowing away every fear and every doubt I had harboured.

'Why, he's perfect!' I said.

'Give him to me! Give me!'

Winnie was struggling to get out of bed, so I turned and held out the baby to her and placed him in her outstretched arms.

'It's all right, darling – he's fine! He's perfect!' I spoke soothingly, because she was so upset. I couldn't imagine what the problem had been but it was cast aside – our boy was wonderful, a little miracle.

'No – something's wrong! I know it! I just know it!'

She placed him on the bed before her and was busy unwrapping the blanket he was swaddled in. At last he lay there naked.

'Oh!' she gasped, and I stepped forward to look.

Aunty Deirdre stepped away to make room for me, and Ma sat down on the bed behind Winnie and stroked her back.

'He got a clubfoot,' said Aunty Deirdre. 'But apart from that he perfect! Congratulations, Miss Winnie, George – y'all got a son!'

Chapter Sixteen

Yoyo

It was as I had feared all along – Winnie gave birth to a son. Not that a son was any danger to me – though he was Papa's first grandson, Clarence was still the anointed heir and our son would be next in line. It was all there in writing – I had now checked it. Clarence's father and Papa had it all worked out. What worried me was that we might never have a son at all, the way Clarence was behaving. I had so hoped Winnie's child would be a girl.

The business of reproduction is horribly frustrating. One has no control whatsoever over the results. As a woman who likes every detail planned out in advance, I was pulled by this complete lack of power into a condition of emotional disorder that I did my best to hide, for it threatens my authority to be revealed as mentally weak. And authority was the one thing I could not lose. What in heaven's name was wrong with Clarence? Why couldn't he do his duty, as any man does with the greatest of ease? I let him know of my displeasure in no veiled terms, but my anger only seemed to aggravate the situation.

And so, while feigning joy at the birth of my nephew, I inwardly seethed. Winnie had sent a telegram bearing the good news: SON BORN HEALTHY STOP ALL DELIGHTED STOP. Mama was sickeningly elated at the dinner table, and Clarence smirked. He really did. It was as if he knew my 'Oh, how lovely!' was false; as if he took actual pleasure in denying me exactly that which Winnie now had, through no effort of her own. This is what happens when one marries a man who is not a real man.

Mama's pleasure overflowed – it was sickening!

'I shall go down to Georgetown tomorrow!' she declared. 'He's come three weeks early, so I haven't finished embroidering that last little jacket, but it's no matter – it's a size too big for him anyway, but he'll grow into it – all the tiniest garments are finished and waiting. I can't wait to see him! I do wish I had been there with them, but as we weren't expecting the birth yet...'

On and on she gushed. You would think this was the first child ever born on the face of the earth. I nodded and smiled, and finally managed to get a word in, but unfortunately I spoiled it all with my second sentence.

'How delightful,' I murmured. 'But what a pity he is a half-caste.'

'What? What did you say?' Mama turned to me, and she was no longer smiling.

'Oh, nothing,' I said, giving her my most gracious smile. 'Just that I'm delighted. Clarence, would you pass the potatoes, please?'

'Johanna, I heard what you said. There's always been a strain of spite in your nature. You might want to curb it. The child may be a half-caste, as you say, but he is as much valued and as loved as any white child that might be born into this family. Including your own, I might add, which seem to be taking their own good time.'

I looked up at her in fury. It wasn't like Mama to make such sarcastic digs.

'It's not my fault I don't have a child!' I cried. I pointed to Clarence. 'Ask him!'

Clarence merely bowed his head and pushed another fork of food into his mouth. He wasn't even capable of admitting his own ineptitude. I suppose it *was* rather too intimate a subject for the dinner table, but really. He might have spoken up for me in some way.

'This is not about you, Johanna. It's about your disrespect towards Winnie's son. I want you to know that in no way is he to be treated as a lowly half-caste. As you put it.'

'Oh, I certainly won't treat him as a lowly half-caste, as *you* put it. Indeed not! But you'll find, Mama, that others in the colony won't be as tactful as myself. Respectable society will shun him, just as they now shun Winnie. What school will he be able to attend? Certainly not the best English schools in Georgetown. Who will be his friends? Whatever it was I said, it was not due to "the strain of spite" in my nature, as you so kindly put it. It was out of commiseration for that poor child, and the unhappy future that awaits him. Half-caste, outcast. I was merely acknowledging the reality of his position. But you wouldn't care, would you? Everything Winnie does is perfect, and I suppose this child is perfect in spite of his obvious handicap, which you refuse to acknowledge. You have always favoured Winnie.'

There. It was out. The smouldering resentment, the rage I had tried so hard to hide, out in the open and placed on the dinner table for all to acknowledge. It all came spilling out, and though I knew I was losing control by allowing those words to be said, it was as if they had a life of their own, and said themselves, and I could no more withdraw them than I could change the colour of my eyes. Just as I could not prevent the outrage I felt from showing in my eyes. I knew it was there. I felt it. Mama would see it, and know. It was a damned thing, to lose control!

'Johanna,' said Mama calmly. She always called me Johanna when she was displeased with me. One of the reasons why I still let myself be called by the baby name of Yoyo was for that very reason – the name Johanna was tainted with rebuke and disappointment. Yoyo was a name of joy and childlike innocence, and though it no longer suited me, I clung to it. Perhaps, somewhere inside myself, I longed for those lost qualities.

'Johanna – you have always been jealous of Winnie. No, don't deny it. You needn't shake your head. I am your mother, and I know it. A mother sees these things. It's ugly, Johanna, and you need to look at yourself more critically and put yourself right. That is all I am saying. Do not let this jealousy overcome your soul. Look it in the face, and banish it. I am leaving you with those words of advice. I am now going upstairs to pack for my trip to Georgetown tomorrow. You are welcome to come with me. But only if you promise to behave yourself.'

* * *

I couldn't help it. The temptation was too great. However much I resented the birth of this child, however much I envied the birth of a son (for yes, I now acknowledged the name of that emotion burning me up) I could not stay away. And so it was that the next day Mama and I departed for Georgetown, leaving the running of Promised Land in the tolerably incapable hands of Clarence. At least Mad Jim Booker would be there to ensure that no disaster occurred in our absence.

And so here we were, on our way to Georgetown.

Neither Mama nor I, it seemed, wanted to prolong our argument; it came too near to touching on matters we both preferred not to explore, to tearing apart the treasured myth that a mother's love is impartial. We both knew it wasn't. Winnie had always been her darling. Perhaps that's why, now, she made an effort to be motherly towards me.

'Yoyo,' she said, 'what you said at dinner last night – about your childlessness—'

She stopped. 'Yes?' I prompted.

'You can talk to me about it, if you like. You are so young, and perhaps you need to confide in someone? I'm your mother, and you need not be ashamed to speak of such topics with me. We can discuss it, if you like. You said it's Clarence's fault?'

Her voice trailed off and she gazed off to the north, to the horizon. In spite of her words, I knew she was too embarrassed to speak of these things. But she was making an effort to be motherly. At least that. And at least she had called me Yoyo again. It was almost embarrassing, how much I clung to that childish name, a name so unfitting of my character! But spoken now, it meant that Mama had forgiven me my outburst at the dinner table last night; that, in spite of my bringing up yet another taboo subject, she was determined not to let the conversation escalate into quarrelsomeness. And so I replied in kind; suppressing my anger, I tried a more humble approach. There was no way I could speak to Mama about my little bedroom problem, and so I deflected her attempt to help.

'Thank you, Mama, but it's all right,' I said. 'I was just angry when I said that. I do apologise. I know I was spiteful – it's a fault I am aware of and will try to overcome. I'm sure that soon, I, too will have a son you can sew things for. Some women take longer with these things.'

'Very well, and you are right. Sometimes it does take longer. Be patient, Yoyo.'

The relief in her voice was palpable.

She reached into the bag at her feet, removed a handkerchief and wiped her forehead. It was indeed hot in the car, in spite of the open windows that let in the cool sea breeze. We had left Rosignol by now, and were heading westwards down the coastal road towards the capital. Poole drove at a tolerably swift speed along the sanded road, and rice fields moved slowly past us, along with now and again a village with its lowly shops and cottages and, very occasionally, to our left a glimpse of the Atlantic, with fishermen wading in the tide and boats upturned and women picking fish out of nets. How I loved this landscape! So did Winnie. It was the one thing we had in common: love for this beautiful country, our homeland.

Chapter Seventeen

Winnie

Yes, my son, our son, had a clubfoot. Yet still he was perfect. I held him in my arms and wept because he was so perfect. Little limbs awkwardly flailing, eyes shut tight, tiny lips moving as if searching for food – how could I not be in love?

George looked down on us and the wonder in his moist eyes was palpable – he leaned in and touched our baby's little hand, stroked his little cheek, and our eyes met and no words came, because no words were equal to the joy I felt, and my joy was George's, a quiet joy that wrapped us into one.

Deirdre bent over us with arms stretched out to take him from me. I did not want to give him up. But she took him and wrapped him in a towel and, laughing at my stricken face, said, 'Don't worry, I gon' bring he back jus' now. Just goin' to weigh him and clean he up a lil'.'

I watched as she placed him in a sling and held the scale aloft.

'Five pounds and a half,' she said. 'Not too bad considering he a month early. You got a name for he?'

'Humphrey,' said George, 'after my granddaddy.'

'Dat's a good strong name,' said Deirdre as she left the room with my son in her arms.

'Where are you going? Come back!' I called, and struggled to get up.

'Gone to clean he up on the dining table,' Deirdre called back. 'Don't worry. I not gon' teef he.'

Well, I knew she wouldn't steal him but not having my baby in my arms was a pain so intense it was physical; as if a limb had been amputated from me, and I wept.

For the first time, Ma spoke. 'Is alright, don't cry,' she said, bundling the wet and bloody bedclothes into a heap and straightening the sheet beneath me. 'Plenty chirren get born wit' crippled foot.'

I glared at her, and for a brief moment anger outweighed my pain.

'It's not his *foot* I'm crying about! I don't care about his damned foot!'

'Well, you should care! If you don't care who else gon' care! This whole mattress wet. You gon' have to move so I could put it outside to dry. You shoulda place old newspapers under you before you waters break!'

'Thanks for reminding me,' I said, but she didn't notice the sarcasm in my tone, and I was glad of it because that biting tongue was new to me – I had never spoken to her that way before.

'It's a clubfoot,' George said to me quietly. 'It's all right. I had a friend with a clubfoot when I was small. Other than that he is perfect.'

'He's perfect as he is,' I said defiantly.

* * *

George sent a telegram, and Mama and Yoyo came the next evening. Yoyo didn't think he was perfect, and neither did Mama, though she was more tactful about it than Yoyo, who actually wrinkled her nose when she saw the twisted foot.

'This can be corrected,' Mama said. 'What you need is a good doctor.'

'Oh, Mama! Is that all you have to say! Cannot you just love him as he is?'

'I do,' said Mama, 'but you might as well face facts. That foot will be a handicap and you should put it right.'

'I don't want to think about that,' I said, and looked down at my baby, who was wholeheartedly drinking at my breast. His face was perfect, his lips were perfect; that tiny hand resting on my breast, with the perfect nails – all I cared to do was drink in that perfection, swallow it whole so that it was a part of me. Why should I think about a slightly unshapely foot?

But Mama folded back the towel he was wrapped in and held the foot in her hand, stroked it lovingly.

'Poor little mite!' she said. 'We'll put you right. Just wait and see.'

* * *

The next day Mama and I took little Humphrey to Dr van Sertima, and he repeated what Mama had said. Yoyo had gone off to visit some of her Georgetown friends. She had lost interest in Humphrey almost immediately; after frowning at his foot – as if that was what defined him! She had fidgeted while Mama and I discussed baby matters, and then excused herself and returned to the Park Hotel. I had not seen her at all today, whereas Mama had spent the day with me, and insisted we see the doctor.

'There are specialists who can fix this,' said Dr Van Sertima, 'though none, unfortunately, in BG. I will send off a few telegrams tomorrow and see who can help. You will have to travel, though, Mrs Quint, and spend some time abroad. It can't be helped. And it will be quite costly.'

'We will spare no expense!' said Mama.

'Mama…' I began, a warning in my voice. We had argued about this already. I had some savings, but they were for the new rooms we would be adding to the house. I could not afford specialist care abroad.

'Ssshhh, Winnie!' Mama said to me, and turned back to Dr van Sertima. 'Where will she have to go? And Winnie, of course I will go with you!'

'Europe will be best,' said Dr van Sertima. 'England, or—'

'Germany! Austria!' cried Mama. 'That would be perfect. Winnie, I would take you home to Salzburg, to Vienna. Get the very best doctor to put him right. You will meet Father, your grandfather, and your uncles!'

'Mama – I can't possibly travel to Europe. I don't want to go anywhere! Can't we just…'

Can't we just accept him as he is, I thought. I couldn't bear the thought of putting this child through the torture of medical treatment – for whatever it was that could be done, it was clear to me that it would be painful, and a little baby cannot understand why his mother would put him through pain.

'Or can't we wait till he is older?'

'It needn't be done right away,' said Dr van Sertima. 'Still, the sooner the better, while the bones are soft and pliable.'

Soft and pliable! I cringed at those words. They wanted to bend and bow my baby into some perfect shape, and hurt him! I cuddled him close, and tears pooled in my eyes.

'No, no, I will not allow it!' I said.

'She will do it,' said Mama firmly to Dr van Sertima. 'And I will pay for it. Please find the best doctor in the world for what needs to be done.'

Chapter Eighteen

Yoyo

Alleluia! It seems there really is something like divine intervention after all, because all the prayers I would have said, had I been the kind of person who said prayers, have come true. It's far from my nature to gloat, but Winnie delivering a crippled baby has played right into my plans. The thing I was dreading the most was Winnie lording it over me, making fun of my inability to bear a son – when it is not my fault at all. It's all Clarence's fault. But I cannot let that be known without disclosing the intimate secrets of my marriage, and that wouldn't do at all.

So this has taken Winnie down a peg or two. She claims she does not care, that she loves this child just the same – but why then is she crying all the time? That's according to Mama, who has extended her stay in Georgetown.

So have I. It was not actually planned, but on my first evening here I paid a visit to my old friend Margaret McInnes, who is now Margaret Smythe-Collingsworth, having married Matthew of the same name shortly after my own marriage to Clarence. The Smythe-Collingsworths are Booker people, and everyone knows what *that* means: a manager of Booker Brothers, the ravenous monster company that's slowly devouring the colony, one shop, one shipyard, one sugar plantation at a time. Bookers now owns almost the entire Corentyne Coast, Promised Land being one of only three plantations not in Booker claws. Without Clarence's (or rather, his father's) investment we, too, would inevitably have been swallowed up.

Mr Smythe-Collinsworth, Margaret's father-in-law, manages a shipyard and Margaret and Matthew are staying at their house in Main Street just until they can find suitable accommodation of their own. Mrs Smythe-Collingsworth the elder is a very fine lady and invited me to stay for a week, and I accepted the invitation. I do so miss the excitement of town – I feel so locked away on the plantation, much as I love it!

So I sent a telegram to Clarence informing him of the delay. He and Mad Jim will just have to run the place for a while, and I dare say they will manage, though not without some strife. Mama too is staying on for a week. She is quite distressed about the baby, though she is putting on a brave face.

She says she cannot yet leave Winnie on her own, which is another example of favouritism. Had it been me she would not have hesitated to leave me in the care of my in-laws. Be that as it may, I am staying in town, and so is Mama. And I do intend to enjoy myself while here. Margaret has always been great fun, and she knows how to cheer me up. She intends to throw a party for me – how jolly!

* * *

A very interesting thing happened this morning. Margaret and I were sitting in the gallery of her house drinking tea and chatting, when the dog began barking; that in itself was not a problem, as the dog is tied to his kennel in the yard – but Margaret got up to see who had entered the gate, and she said, 'Oh – it's the postman.'

She was about to take her seat again when her face broke into a smile and she said, 'I almost forgot – he's your brother-in-law, isn't he?'

'It's George? Really?' I got up and went to the window, where I saw George walking down the garden path towards the house, several envelopes in his hand.

'He must have something for us to sign,' said Margaret. 'The postbox is attached to the front gate, and he only enters if it's a telegram or a registered letter.'

That's when I had an idea.

'Do you mind if I invite him in for a few minutes? Would your mother mind?'

'Well – she's not at home, is she? She need never know. What dastardly plan do you have up your sleeve, Yoyo? I know you – it's not the kindness of your heart speaking there!'

I grinned at her, and winked. She did indeed know me well. And I did have a plan, though calling it dastardly was perhaps an exaggeration. I just intended to have a bit of entertainment with George. He is so easily embarrassed, and this was a perfect opportunity.

I openly admit that I had been cold towards George in the past, and it was time for that to change. I had made a beginning the last time he and Winnie had come to visit us at Promised Land, and here was a perfect opportunity to show him the more pleasing side of my nature.

George was such easy prey – but no, that's the wrong word. My intentions with him were in no way malicious; I just enjoyed seeing him squirm, which he did, whenever I spoke to him. I suppose it had to do with his innate reverence towards the white race – all darkies have that, it's in their blood – and me being his sister-in-law; and added to that, my indisputable feminine charms. Many a young man has fallen victim to *those* in the past, and why not George? So yes, now I think of it more, *prey* is indeed the right word. What young woman doesn't enjoy seeing a young man reduced to jelly simply by dint of a suitably fluttered eyelash? Harmless fun – and I intended to have it.

So when George knocked on the front door it was I who got up to open it, and Margaret who accompanied me, shooing away the servant who hurried forth from the kitchen.

I flung the door open.

'Hello, George!' I said, offering him my widest and most welcoming smile.

Poor George! He actually jumped when he saw me, just as if he'd seen a ghost, and stepped backwards, stumbling on the porch.

'Careful!' I said, reaching out to help him find his feet. I took his hand till he found his balance, and I didn't let go once he had.

'George!' I said, 'Margaret and I saw you coming up the path and we wondered if you'd drink a cup of tea with us?'

He actually turned a shade of pale – difficult for a man of such dark complexion, but I swear it happened. He stuttered as he spoke.

'M-m-m-miss…' How darling! He still wanted to call me Miss Cox, even though he had every right to call me Yoyo!

'Yoyo,' I said firmly, 'Do call me Yoyo. I was so sorry to have missed you last night when I came to see your lovely baby – you must come in now. Margaret, get the maid to make a new pot.'

'Um, I-I-I can't, I'm working,' he said, patting the bulging postbag that hung over his shoulder.

'Oh nonsense. No one will notice. Just for a few minutes. I insist!'

And I pulled him inside the house and shut the door.

The poor chap! I swear there was panic in his eyes, like a trapped animal. I could hear Margaret behind me, tittering, and I too found it hard to suppress a giggle. What fun this was going to be! Still not letting go of his hand, I practically dragged him into the gallery, chattering all the time – some nonsense about how much I missed Winnie and how happy I was for her and how we sisters had to catch up while I was in town. Margaret meanwhile had scampered away to order the tea and I led George over to one of the Morris chairs and bid him sit. Which he did. I did let go of his hand now, for he was almost trembling with trepidation.

I sat down in the chair next to him and tilted my head prettily for his benefit. I discreetly pulled a strand of hair from behind my hair and twirled it round my finger while gazing intently into his eyes, which proved harder than I imagined as his were lowered.

'George,' I said, hoping that my silky voice would encourage him to raise his gaze. I had practised that voice with Clarence, on whom it had no effect whatsoever, but, after all, Clarence was an anomaly among men. Most men melt when a woman lures him with her softness. It's the antidote to their hardness. I discovered this as a young girl, at all the balls we girls were taken to. There is a dearth of white girls in the colony and a superfluity of men, and that's how I learned the ways of men. Even a young girl of four-teen can have adult men grovelling at her feet. These tough men, accustomed to the brutality of plantation life, were as dough in our hands; they pine for our gentleness. And even a married man, even a happily married man, which I assumed George was, cannot resist. It's instinct, and I learned this at a very early age – perhaps that is *our* instinct, as women. Thus it is that women are ultimately the stronger sex; we just must know how to apply that strength. Coupled with crafty intelligence and a plan, it cannot be defeated. The trouble with Winnie is that though she has that softness she lacks both intelligence and a plan. She is without wile, unlike me.

Indeed, George looked up and I saw the capitulation in his eyes. I smiled in triumph and reached out my hand to him again. Since he did not take it, I took his, placing my fingers gently round it as it lay on the armrest of the chair. Immediately he stiffened, and pulled away – I allowed him to. It wouldn't do to scare him too much on this first day. I returned to curling that stray lock of hair with my finger, and gave him my most beautiful smile, even while turning my head in a way I knew was charm-ing, exposing my long neck. He was palpably frightened – that wouldn't do. I thought it would relax him if I spoke about Win-nie, with whom he was still besotted, so I did.

'Tell me, George – what's this I hear about Winnie going into serious business with her guava jam and pepper sauce? Is it really true that she's even selling it at Fogarty's?'

He nodded. 'Yes, ma'am.'

Ma'am! He actually called me ma'am! Obviously an attempt by him to distance himself as far as possible! Which meant that, deep inside, my strategy was working. I decided to ignore the ma'am. I chuckled.

'Goodness gracious! So she *is* a businesswoman. Dear me – I *am* impressed. Winnie didn't know how to even boil a kettle of water as a girl! How droll to think of her in the kitchen with all the pots and pans, cooking up gallons of guava, selling them all!'

'It's very good,' he said, defending his wife as a good husband should.

'Oh, I know! Up at Promised Land we finished the first jar of guava jelly you brought us in no time, and we are now halfway through the second. And the pepper sauce has its place on the dining table – a little too hot for my taste, but I do try a little now and then.'

Margaret returned, and shortly after that the servant appeared with a tray on which stood a teapot and a cup and saucer, as well as a sugar bowl and a little jug of milk. I kept up the chatter as she poured George's tea.

'Oh! I'm so sorry – I didn't introduce you to my friend, Margaret Smythe-Collingsworth. Previously Margaret McInnes – you know the McInnes family, of course – you used to deliver their letters.'

Margaret giggled at that, and I caught her eye and winked. She knew full well what I was doing, and was richly enjoying the game. Just as I was. George was such an easy prey. It pleased me to see, once again, how much power I could have over a man, seeing as how I had failed with Clarence. It pleased me to see George's discomfort. It was all so harmless, at this stage; a little game that gave me infinite pleasure even as it pleased me to see this unwanted addition to our family in discomfort. A little act of revenge, one might say.

'I'm sure Margaret would love a jar of the guava jelly, and the pepper sauce!' I continued. 'Do you like it hot, Margaret?'

She shook her head, unable to speak as she was almost bursting with unspent giggles. I, on the other hand, managed to keep a straight face as I said, 'Well, I'm sure your husband does! George, you must bring a jar of each round tomorrow when you deliver your letters. I'm sure they'd fit in your letter-bag. You must make sure, though, that the lids are on tightly. We can't allow the pepper sauce to leak all over your letters – now *that* would be a catastrophe!'

It was a joke, and so both Margaret and I were permitted to laugh out loud, which was a relief – one can only keep a straight face so long! Poor George. He didn't see the joke. I'm afraid the poor boy entirely lacks a sense of humour. I believe all darkies do – one never hears them laughing and joking among themselves.

Instead, he sipped hastily at his tea; it must have been far too hot, but he didn't seem to care. Perhaps it's true that they are insensitive to pain. He sipped again and then downed the rest of the cup in a few gulps, extremely rudely, of course, and with a complete lack of etiquette. Which just goes to show how shallow were the manners he had displayed during that ghastly visit to Promised Land. At heart he was crude. Having emptied the cup, he stood up.

'I got to go,' he said, picking up the postbag.

I would have loved to keep him longer, but I decided to let him go.

'We must see more of each other, George!' I said as we walked to the front door. 'After all, we're family now! I'll make sure you and Winnie are invited to a party I'll be attending later this week.'

That was a lie, of course. There was no possibility of a fellow of his ilk being invited to a society party. But getting his hopes up was all part of my ploy. A cat and mouse game – that's what it was.

I had to admit that, were it not for the colour of his skin, George would have been a decidedly attractive man. He had a certain appeal to him, a certain innocent charm, which most of our own men lacked. Perhaps it was his lack of male posturing and self-aggrandisement, which can be so very tiring. I know I had initially rejected him, but I could now understand a little why Winnie had been so completely gaga for him. I wondered: if I had seen that appeal before her, would I have fallen as strongly for him as she did? Would I have cast caution to the wind, and given up all for him? I did not believe in romantic love, not at all – but a certain magnetic pull cannot be denied. That day at Promised Land, when George had first squirmed under my gaze, I had noticed the pleasure it gave me to see his discomfort. And today, that pleasure was so much more. Clarence's rejection of me had given me such doubts – a little harmless game with George was enough to restore my faith in myself as a woman. Just a little harmless game. It was so easy to tease him.

Poor George almost fled down the front stairs, his postbag banging against his hip.

Margaret collapsed against me in giggles.

'Oh Yoyo, you're such a coquette! That was simply – simply tremendous! Your finger in your hair! Your pout!'

'Yes, I am rather a tease, aren't I? I never knew it was such fun. Or that I could be so good at it.'

'I have to say – he is rather nice-looking, if one looks past his colour.'

'He is, isn't he? And not really black, either. More a delicious cocoa-brown.'

She giggled again. 'Cocoa-brown! Oh, Yoyo, that sounds as if you'd like to *eat* him!'

'Well, I could, of course, if I wanted to. Those darkies would cut off their limbs to get a white woman in their bed. *Any* white woman, but someone like me, a high society beauty, well. I could just snap my fingers and he'd come running.'

'Oh, but not *George!* Everyone says he absolutely *adores* Winnie.'

'Nonsense, Margaret. It's all just lust. *She* adores *him*, so she was just the easiest white woman he could get. I could easily win him off her. If I wanted to, that is. There's no such thing as fidelity when a man is tempted.'

'But you wouldn't tempt him, would you? Not seriously!'

'It would be rather fun, wouldn't it? Just to show him how silly this love nonsense is. He doesn't really love her. A serious temptation, from another white woman, and this whole notion of love would fly out the window.'

'But you *wouldn't,* would you? Not seriously. You couldn't. Not with a *darkie!*'

'Well – that whole aspect of married life is so dreadful anyway. There's that rumour that black men can be quite enjoyable. I am slightly curious, you know! Can an act so utterly disgusting be actually *enjoyable?* I wonder…'

'*Yoyo!* You wouldn't!'

I didn't answer. I merely smiled, a secretive smile. An interesting little thought had occurred to me, and I didn't know whether to dismiss or entertain it.

'Yoyo! You have that naughty twinkle in your eye! You're up to something again!'

'You and I – we always had those bets, didn't we, Margaret? Dares. And I never turned down a challenge, did I?'

Margaret burst into uncontrollable giggles, her hands over her mouth. Me, I simply smiled.

Chapter Nineteen

George

My sister-in-law is a strange being indeed. Cold as a fish at first, she one day suddenly showed great interest in me, and even artificial warmth. It had started during our visit to the plantation, but now it was even worse. I suppose it is a result of the baby – everyone loves a baby, and no doubt the birth has encouraged her to accept me as a family member. But her lack of sensitivity is alarming. She interrupted my postal rounds by inviting me into her friend's home – she didn't give me a chance to refuse, and did not understand that I had no leisure time to sit around in a gallery drinking tea, and certainly no time for a chat.

I managed to break off the unnecessary delay by simply rising to my feet and leaving. It may have appeared rude but frankly at that juncture I didn't care. I should have been that firm right from the beginning, but she took me by surprise. In future, I swear, I shall be wary of this woman. She is unpredictable. I finished my rounds without further disruption, did some letter-sorting work in the afternoon and then in the evening returned home to my wife and child – the high point of my day.

For now, Mama has returned to Promised Land, and, to my relief, Yoyo went with her. I was glad of that. Every day on my rounds she has attempted to waylay me again but, forewarned, I have been able to avoid her. I never entered the Smythe-Collingsworth house again.

* * *

When I hold him in my arms the love I feel for that child sweeps through me like a hurricane. I have never known anything like it – different from my love for Winnie, it is; the love of a father is a protective love, infused with a sense that this scrap of humanity is more precious than diamonds; that nothing on earth can ever diffuse or dilute that love; that it can never grow stronger, for it is perfect from the first moment and onwards, perfect and full and fulfilling. In it is power, for in love is all the power of God, and it sweeps through every tiny particle of body and soul. Winnie and I were joined in that complete love. We needed no words; a glance, a smile, a touch told me that this was the consummation of all that had been before.

Humphrey's tiny left foot is twisted so that the sole turns sideways. It does not seem a serious disfiguration to me. Babies, after all, are not shaped like small adults. He is not a miniature man. Surely it will grow out?

But apparently not. Mama – as my mother-in-law insists I call her – swept him off to Dr van Sertima and now there is talk of treatment abroad – perhaps even as far away as Europe. I am strictly against it.

'He will never be able to walk without a limp,' Mama said when she and Winnie came back from the doctor's. 'Never run like other boys, and jump. He will not be invited to join the cricket team, if you do not operate.'

'Well, maybe he will be a quiet boy, one who loves reading and – and postage stamps, like his grandfather! Not all boys like to play cricket.' I cradled him in my arms, rocked him to and fro, placed my finger on his palm. His little fingers closed around mine in a vice-like grip, and I smiled fondly.

'He will have no friends, for the boys will tease him and make fun of him. He will be lonely and unhappy, for he will be left out. He will suffer!'

The thought of my boy suffering caused me to suffer. A lump rose in my throat, and I pulled him closer to me. I said nothing, for words stuck in my throat. Winnie, who had been in the kitchen preparing warm water for his bath, came into the gallery and stood behind me, her hands on my shoulders.

'It is for him, George. For his future. I don't want to go at all, but it is the best thing to do.'

'But – where will you take him? How long will you be gone?'

'Dr van Sertima has taken some photographs of the foot and is writing a letter to a specialist in London. We must wait for a reply. There are good hospitals in London and Germany and Austria. I may have to go there.'

'We cannot afford a trip to Europe, and to pay for expensive doctors!'

'I will pay,' said Mama. 'My grandfather died last year and left me a good deal of money. I can afford it. I will pay.'

'I cannot accept—'

'We can accept, George. I didn't want to at first either, but the doctor and Mama have persuaded me otherwise. It is best for him. We want him to be healthy and happy, don't we?'

What could I say to that?

* * *

Weeks passed, and at last we had a reply. Yes, said Dr van Sertima's specialist friend, there were excellent doctors in Europe – but why travel all that distance?

'Dr Garcia is one of the world's greatest surgeons in paediatric orthopaedic surgery,' said the letter, 'and he is based in Caracas, Venezuela. Isn't that near to where you are? I have taken the liberty of sending your details, as well as the photographs, to Dr Garcia. I am sure he can help. You should be hearing from him shortly. Should you, on the other hand, insist on coming to London, I am willing to accept poor little Humphrey as a patient. I just thought it would spare you the trouble of a long sea journey.'

And so it was planned: Winnie and Humphrey shall go to Venezuela, and I must wait for them at home. They will stay for as long as is necessary. I don't know how I will bear it; but it is for Humphrey's sake, and so I must. Winnie's friend Kitty MacGonigal shall take over the running of Quintessentials.

Mama will go with them, see them settled, and then return. They are likely to stay several months. They will go when Humphrey is eight months old.

Chapter Twenty

Winnie

My baby became my world, caring for his needs my mission in life. He filled me up, raised me up – just looking at him filled me with delight, and every task I did for him I did gladly, my limbs moved by love. It was, indeed, a delirium of love.

Yet I did not forget George. George felt exactly the same towards Humphrey, though his task of love was a different one: that of providing for us, that our little home be safe and secure. The annexe was now finished and Ma and Pa had moved into it, leaving the bigger bedroom for George and me. The bedroom we had once shared became my workroom, the place where I made my jellies and sauces and stored them. I now had less time for the making of them, and none for the delivery – but the income from sales was enough to employ Harold, the son of one of our neighbours, who made the deliveries for me.

My life was perfect, but it was not to be for long. Mama had made all the arrangements for the trip to Caracas, where Humphrey was to be treated by Dr Garcia. I know nothing about banking, but somehow she had arranged for money to be transferred from her bank in Salzburg to Dr Garcia's account, advance payment for the treatment – a lump sum, I was told, which included my board and lodging on hospital property. Everything was in place. Mama and I would move to Caracas in a few months' time; once I was settled, Mama would return to BG and I would stay for however long it took to get Humphrey's foot repaired. I knew it was an ongoing task – that he would be wearing a leg brace for years to come, and would always walk with a limp. But he would be a loved child, a healthy child, and that was what mattered.

Everyone loved Humphrey! He was a good-natured little chap, and though I suppose all mothers think that of their children, he had the sweetest baby-face I had ever seen. But I wasn't the only one to think that. My friends Kitty, Eliza and Tilly visited me frequently, and they all confirmed what I knew – that Humphrey was the sweetest baby alive.

I sensed, though, that George was unhappy. It started, really, the day before Mama and Yoyo were due to return to Promised Land. It was a Sunday, and they came round to say goodbye. Now Sunday is the one day George and I can be together the entire day, and I understand that he was irritated that he would have to share that one day with my relatives. But surely they are *his* relatives too? Surely he could welcome them, and share his son with his grandmother and aunt? But no. The evening before, sitting in the gallery enjoying the night air, we had a little quarrel – more of a lovers' spat, really.

'I thought you liked Mama!'

'I do. It's just…' He shook his head.

'George! Don't turn away. If you like Mama… it's Yoyo you don't like, then?'

He hesitated just a fraction of a second too long before replying: 'Yoyo…she—'

'You don't like her! George, how could you? I mean, I know she was rude to you at first, when we announced our engagement. But she has made such an effort. It's not easy for her, you know. She's still a part of English society and people might shun her just because of us. I mean, *I* don't care about being shunned but it's hard for Yoyo – *she* isn't the one who married you, after all. And you have to admit she has made an effort. She was so kind to you when we were at Promised Land, and the fact that she came to town to see Humphrey, it shows that she is now willing to accept us, accept you. You could be a bit kinder, and more forgiving.'

He said nothing and I know he was not listening. He had hardened his heart against her.

'George, she's my sister! I love her. I want you to love her too – or at least, be friendly towards her, when she is making such an effort. I insist – they're coming, and I want you to be at home and agreeable to both.'

George again did not respond. He stood up, glass in hand, and walked out of the gallery. I would even say he stamped his feet a little while walking, like a petulant child. I sighed, and got up to follow him. But Ma, who had been sitting silently in her rocking chair all this time, grabbed my hand as I swept past. The gallery was so narrow – there was hardly room for the three of us to sit at ease. Pa was already in bed.

I looked down at Ma.

'What's the matter?'

'Don't nag him about that girl.'

'About Yoyo? But she's my sister. I don't understand why he's so disagreeable towards her. And he refuses to talk about it!'

'That girl is trouble.'

'Oh, Ma! I know she isn't the friendliest person; I know she's a little bit snobbish, and she may have slighted you when she was here. But you must make allowances. She has never been in a cottage like this before, never set foot in Albouystown. She has never hobnobbed with our kind before. She—'

'Your mama also never knew people like we before. But she was all gracious and kind when she was here, and did not look down she nose at we.'

'Yes, but Yoyo—'

'Yoyo think she better than we. She got malice in she heart.'

'Malice? Oh Ma, what a horrible thing to say! I agree that Yoyo can be chilly and dismissive of others at times but she isn't malicious. You are doing her wrong. I promise that in her heart she's a good person, and would never do anyone any deliberate wrong. I *know* her!'

Ma sighed, and let go of my hand. 'Winnie, you is too simple-hearted. You think everyone is like you. Is not true. One day you gon' see into the hearts of people and you gon' see the nasty things brewing there.'

That hurt me. Simple-hearted! As if that was all I was, after what I had been through! I had seen the evil nestling in my own father's heart, and had wrestled with my conscience, and won – how could she dismiss me as simple? And to be so suspicious about my Yoyo…

'You have no right to call my sister nasty, Ma.' I said it with as much dignity as I could. 'Yes, I *do* prefer to see the good in others. And what of it? I thought you were a Christian – going to church and praying for others. Yet you say such things. Is it because she is white? Well, remember how you were suspicious of *me* at first? How your suspicions meant you formed an undeserved bad opinion of me? Just because I am white? Well, this is *exactly* the same. Yoyo is my sister. I know it's your house and if you don't want her to come here I will let her know and I will meet her elsewhere. But I—'

'Let she come. I don't care. All I sayin' is, watch she like an eagle. Now go an' make up wit' George. Is not good for husban' an' wife to go to bed on a quarrel.'

I stood for a moment, looking down at her as she gently rocked in the chair, eyes closed now, humming gently to herself as if she had completely dismissed our conversation. I wanted to continue it, to convince her that she was wrong. But I thought the better of it. I could smell the sweet-acrid scent of the mosquito coil George had lit in our room, and I was anxious, as Ma had said, to make up with him. She was so right about not going to bed on a quarrel. What did it matter what she thought of Yoyo? In time she would change her opinion, as would George. I had to give them time. Yoyo would show them her true colours, all in her own time.

'George!' I called. 'I'm coming.' And I almost ran from the gallery, and plunged through the doorway and into his waiting arms.

'I'm sorry,' he murmured into my hair. 'Of course your sister can come tomorrow. I'll be friendly to her. I promise.'

'I'm sorry too,' I said. 'I was so horrible to you. I'm a horrible person.'

'You, horrible!' George's voice held a smile. 'You're too decent for your own good, Winnie. Your goodness shines in your eyes. But you need to be wary in this world.'

'I know, George, I know. I am a bit naïve, sometimes. But I know Yoyo. I'm the closest person to her and I want us to be friends again. Give her a chance. Please! Isn't that what you preach? To see the best in everyone? To learn to love? Why not practise with Yoyo?'

'I will. I promise.'

And so we closed the day in peace and harmony.

* * *

And he kept his promise. When Yoyo and Mama came the next day my George was the perfect host. He greeted them both warmly, and I was happy to see how amiable Yoyo had become. Her initial hostility towards him had vanished completely, and it was so rewarding to see that she now appreciated his qualities: his warmth, his kindness, his charm. And she responded in kind.

'You will miss Winnie when she has gone to Venezuela,' she said. 'You must come to Promised Land whenever you want. It is your home too.'

'Unfortunately,' said George, 'I will not be able to come very often. It's such a long journey – a day trip there, and a day trip back. I work six days a week and it is not easy to get a day off.'

'Well then, I will have to come to Georgetown more often,' Yoyo replied. She turned to me.

'Margaret is expecting her first child soon. You and she should get together. You can perhaps offer her some advice – it's time, Winnie, that you found your way back into society. You have been punished enough.'

Hearing such words from Yoyo was sheer music. My heart leapt in joy – but at the fact that she spoke them at all, not at the words themselves. For I had no intention of finding my way back into society. Marriage to George and life in Albouystown had altered me so much that I knew I could never again be a part of that world, with its affectations and vanities and its snobbishness. I had never much liked Margaret McInnes, and I doubted I would like Margaret Smythe-Collingsworth, much less make friends with her. I had become a different person in a matter of months, at home in my new surroundings and voluntarily isolated from the values I was reared with.

So who am I, exactly? Well, I am a work under construction, like a building whose blueprint is not quite finished in the architect's eye. A wife, a mother, in the first instance, those roles which provided me with the fountain of love that would form the foundation of the woman I would one day become. But they are just that – roles. Roles that every day teach me more about myself, my strengths, my weaknesses; roles that will help me to find my feet in the world I have adopted. And even Humphrey's problems, serious though they are, provide an opportunity for me to be strong, and decisive; it is as if skin after skin, layer after layer of the old me falls away even as the new me emerges from the dead skin of the old.

* * *

Kitty, Eliza and Tilly have become my firm friends, even though since Humphrey's birth I see somewhat less of them. I like them, and enjoy their company, but, as George explained, as members of the in-between layer of society, wedged between the dark-skinned labouring class and the ruling upper class, they firmly strive upwards, and I can't get rid of the sense that at least part of their friendship is rooted more in where I come from than in who I am. They are all three single, and I can easily pick up their hints. They are hoping I might have access to some eligible white bachelors.

It is dispiriting, how much the colour of one's skin, the quality of one's hair, the thickness of lips and hair determines one's place in this society. The girls, as I think of them, speak quite openly of it. Eliza, for instance, spoke disparagingly of a young man who raised his hat to her after church.

'With his Negro features, who does he think he is?' she sneered.

'He's not very dark, though,' said Kitty. 'And quite handsome. And he has a good job at the Hand-in-Hand Insurance Company.'

But Eliza shook her head. 'No. Not for me.' She turned to me. 'Winnie, dear – I'm thinking of throwing a big party for my twenty-first birthday. Don't you know some nice young men from the plantation – you know, from the senior staff, I mean – who might like to come?'

All three of them looked eagerly at me, and I knew at once that this one thing had been the reason for today's gathering. Eliza had asked me round for afternoon tea – not unusual in itself, but I had been surprised to see not only my other two friends but Eliza's mother and her aunt, hovering at the tea table and offering me a variety of cakes and pastries, wearing smiles that did not reach their eyes.

'I hardly ever see them any more,' I said. 'Some of them moved to England, and the others – well, we don't move in the same circles. They have jobs now – a few of them in town, but—'

'That's *exactly* the kind of fellow we mean,' said Tilly in excitement. 'Well educated, and working in management in businesses around town. Young single men! There is a positive dearth of such young men in our circles.'

'Surely you know of a few?' Eliza pleaded. 'All you need to do is ask. The worst they can do is refuse.'

'I haven't kept in touch,' I argued. 'I don't even know where they are working. I'm not really a part of that society any more.'

'But you can find out!' said Eliza. 'Surely you can! You must know their names, and you can ask your sister, and—'

'Oh Winnie, please do try!' Tilly joined in. 'We are all getting on in years and it's so hard to find a suitable husband in this colony. Please try!'

'Please!'

How could I refuse? 'Well,' I conceded, 'I suppose I could make investigations – my old friend Emily is living in Kingston and she might know—'

'Yes! Yes! Just ask her – and of course she can come too, if she wants to— Oh!'

Tilly jumped and cried out in pain and I realised what was going on. Eliza had kicked her under the table. Eliza clearly didn't want any English young ladies invited to her party. I smiled. I understood exactly.

'I'll go and see Emily in the next few days,' I promised. What harm could it do?

'And you'll come too, won't you? To the party? Surely you will?'

I thought about it. Since Humphrey's birth, and the concern about his foot, I had felt little inclination to attend parties, and George and I had declined all invitations from our friends – *his* friends, really – in Albouystown, or else George had gone alone. This was different, though. These were *my* friends, *my* invitation, and that nuance suddenly felt important.

Yes, I knew very well that in *this* particular stratum of George-town society I was something of a status-symbol friend. That much I had learned of the intricacies of the town's racial hierarchy, the complexity of which I had been completely oblivious to while basking in the fool's paradise of the white upper class. The coloured middle class was upwardly striving, ambitious, and even more colour-discerning, unlikely though that may seem, than the former. But I did, though, feel that Kitty, Tilly and Eliza liked me for myself as well, that their concern for me and interest in my life was genuine. The invitation to a 'young man from the plantation' might be calculated; the invitation to me, though, was from the heart. And I wanted to go. What fun, to leave little Humphrey with Ma for just one evening and meet some new people of my own age! And there was a way, I thought, to use the opportunity to make a silent statement.

'George and I would love to come,' I said.

* * *

I had not seen my old friend Emily Stewart since long before my marriage. In fact, I realized, not since before Papa's trial. Since then I had caused so much scandal, so much upheaval, I could not even begin to guess at how she felt about me. She had not contacted me, not sent a Christmas card. But then, neither had I. She had not been invited to the small ceremony of my wedding, as it had been just close family, and there had been no public announcement of Humphrey's birth in the newspapers – I was, after all, no longer society. She had probably forgotten me entirely, having her own life and her own events to care about. I had heard of her wedding through Yoyo, and I knew she lived in Kingston. Having a postman as a husband has its advantages – it was easy to find out the address of the Whittington family, because even though George did not deliver in Kingston, he knew who did. That information acquired, I sent her a little note asking if I might drop by, and the following day I received the reply – yes, of course!

Thus it was that a few days later I stepped out of a coach right before Emily's house in Parade Street, Humphrey bundled in my arms. I entered through the gate, which released a volley of bell chimes, and a moment later Emily appeared at the open window, cooing and calling and waving.

I climbed the stairs to the front door, which opened even before I reached the landing. There she stood in the doorway, arms open to receive me. The once slim, slight Emily had gained weight since I'd last seen her, and her freckled face was now round, her body soft and chubby. But when she clasped me to her in an effusion of joy I realised that her bulk was more than fat, for she was not all soft.

'Emily!' I cried. 'You're going to have a baby!'

'I am. And I'm so excited! And this is your little one! I heard you'd had a little boy – oh, he's so sweet! Let me hold him – what's his name?'

I passed Humphrey to her as I entered the house, and removed my bonnet, which I hung on the hatstand near the door. I told her his name, and she ushered me into the gallery, cooing to Humphrey and chattering with me all at the same time.

'I can't tell you how happy I am to see you again! Do you know, I don't have a single friend in Georgetown – everyone has married and gone to live on some plantation or other in New Amsterdam. I'm frightfully lonely – Andrew is a dear of course but a girl needs lady friends, doesn't she, and a brother doesn't quite cut it. How can a man ever understand our trials and tribulations!' She giggled, but then turned suddenly serious, perhaps as the last words she had spoken took root.

'Oh! Oh dear Winnie, I'm so sorry. I didn't mean to rub your nose in it. You have had an appalling time of it, haven't you? People can be nasty – but you know I have always defended you, always! And your troubles haven't stopped, have they? I've heard about poor little Humphrey and his foot. How devastating for you!'

'No!' I interrupted at once. 'It's not devastating at all. I love him just the same and to me he's perfect.'

'But – a cripple, Winnie. It can't be easy.'

Red-hot lava rose up in me and must have coloured my face.

'He's not a cripple, Emily, and if you call him that I must leave at once.'

'Oh, Winnie, I'm so sorry, please forgive me! Come, sit down and tell me everything. Mildred will bring tea and cakes. There you go. I'm so sorry, and he's so sweet. Now tell me all about him.'

I immediately forgave her, of course, and very soon we were immersed in the kind of conversation I assume all young mothers and mothers-to-be engage in all over the world and have done in all the ages past. It was extremely edifying. I was so glad I had found Emily again.

Eventually, however, a change of subject was called for and I brought the conversation round to the purpose of my visit.

'So,' I said. 'What has become of everyone? Where did they all end up? You must tell me all the gossip!'

Emily gladly complied. She told me all the gossip. And that is how Emily's brother Andrew, and his friends Stanley Grieves and John Eccles, single white young men living and working in Georgetown, came to be invited to Eliza Woodcock's twenty-first birthday party. One, hopefully, for each of my coloured friends.

Chapter Twenty-One

Yoyo

Running a sugar plantation is not as easy as I thought, especially with uncooperative advisers. Those would be my mother and her right hand, Mad Jim Booker. In actual fact, we all know that he is not mad, simply eccentric. Eccentric meaning that he had the temerity to marry first an African woman – who died in a fire – and then an Indian, and produce not one but *two* litters of half-breed children. The first lot, of course, were by now grown up and going about their adult lives. The second batch was small but growing – a toddler, a baby and a third one on the way. So though he is not technically mad, he has his own version of madness – why would a white man, a Booker no less, possessing all the usual attributes of the privileged class, choose to live this way? Isn't it a form of madness to voluntarily lower oneself? And so I continue to call him Mad Jim – though always only to myself or to those who understand. Never to Mama.

Mama and Mad Jim were hand-in-glove from the start. From the beginning they made it known that our very first project would be the razing of the labourer huts – the logies – and the building of adequate accommodation for our coolies. Now, in principle I was not opposed to such a measure. After all, as a young girl I too had been appalled by the squalid conditions in which the coolies lived, and in fact Winnie and I had been naïve enough to think that we could cajole Papa into making improvements. Now that I am an adult and a businesswoman I can appreciate Papa's arguments. It was all about money, Papa said, and now I saw that for myself.

I keep the account books. I had learned accounting at business school in Georgetown – the only girl in a class of fifteen – and I have always been good with figures anyway. Papa used to say that women should concern themselves only with the serious business of winning a suitable husband, running a household and raising well-behaved children. I believe in my heart that it is possible to fulfil all these duties and yet still be good at sums, but my hands are well and truly tied. I have, certainly, acquired the said husband and I run the household like clockwork; and if I am not yet raising the required children and the sums fail to add up it is hardly my fault. But I am good at sums, and I could clearly see that a plantation is not a charity.

Building what my mother called 'suitable accommodation' had been costly, and I feared there would be no return on it, apart from happier coolies. But the happiness of coolies is not the aim of a sugar plantation. That is what Winnie and I failed to understand as girls. We had no inkling of the notion of profit. Now I understand.

How could we pour a small fortune into the building of what would essentially be a village, row upon row of cottages with suitable plumbing and drainage and paved roads, and still expect to balance the books?

'We are not a charity!' I cried when Mama presented me with the blueprint she and Mad Jim had come up with.

'In time it will work out to our advantage,' she replied calmly. 'Happy labourers will be more productive. You will see. Trust Jim.'

But I could no more trust Mad Jim than I could trust one of the invisible *baccoos* said to haunt the logies. If it weren't for Mad Jim, the disaster that ended with Papa in prison would probably never have happened. But I won't go into that now. What's done is done, and we cannot go back in time. Yet I hold Mad Jim responsible, and I do not like him, and will never trust him. He does not have our best interests at heart, but only those of the coolies.

Mama and I finally arrived at a compromise. We built the new village on the back-dam, but instead of cottages we built rows of attached shacks, ranges, each spacious enough to house a family and each with a small kitchen area, with outdoor lavatories and bathing rooms for groups of homes. That would have to do, and that was the situation at the time when Winnie went off to Venezuela.

And to my surprise, Mama and Mad Jim seem to be right, for the time being. Production is up. Better workers are undoubtedly better for business; but can it be true that happier coolies make better workers? The figures seem to be telling me exactly that.

* * *

With the plantation running so smoothly, I found I had more time for playful fantasies, and they included George. The last time I had seen him – the day before Mama and I returned to the plantation – he had been decidedly more affable towards me than in the past. I think that my teasing of him had terrified the poor boy, and during that visit I made a concerted effort to be kind. And he too was not just polite. It was almost as if he had made up his mind to turn over a new leaf. I put this down to the fact that he was finally being honest with himself regarding his relationship with me. His blanket rejection of me had not been honest – it was a defence. Now, he was quite changed, and to my delight he even initiated a conversation on one of my visits to town.

'Are you enjoying being the mistress of Promised Land?' he asked me. Not a particularly insightful question to ask, and such ambiguous vocabulary, but since Winnie was present I supposed our talk would have to run along established lines. George, Winnie and I were enjoying a walk on the Sea Wall promenade; Mama had volunteered to look after Humphrey for Winnie and it was good to get away and take an afternoon stroll in the invigorating sea breeze.

'Indeed!' I said. 'I am discovering that a woman can fulfil many roles at once, and enjoy them all.'

'Oh, that's so true!' said Winnie, inserting herself unasked into the conversation. 'I'm discovering just how much I can do and I really love it!'

'How nice,' I said to her, and turned back to George. 'Though I hope to soon follow Winnie's example and be a mother, I do find there are certain advantages to *not* having a child. More time to oneself, for instance. More freedom to pursue one's own interests, and friendships, without the burden of a baby to look after. The plantation is almost running itself these days, and I am certainly enjoying my leisure time!'

There! Those words, coupled with the languid look I passed him, should be hint enough. The attraction that came from him was so visceral I could almost touch it, cut it with a knife. I was almost afraid that Winnie would notice, but of course she was far too innocent-minded to pick up such a subtle intimation. And walking on the other side of George, of course she could not see my face, read my eyes. George, though, regarding me as I spoke, could. However, Winnie was quick to interrupt yet again.

'Oh, but little Humph isn't a burden! He is a joy! I love every moment with him, and I would not exchange him for buckets-full of leisure!'

Oh, the smug little prig! I should have known she'd say something like that, just to put me in my place. How could I ever find a retort to that? I did my best, however.

'Well, motherhood is no doubt a joy still to come to me, but in the meantime I am certainly enjoying my life as it is. Especially when I am in Georgetown.'

Just at that moment a strong gust of wind swept the promenade and blew away my bonnet. I had deliberately left the ribbons untied as I thought it looked more charming that way, but I had forgotten about the breeze. George immediately ran after it and recovered it. I thanked him.

'I'll have to be careful I don't blow away myself!' I added. 'But George can hold on to me, can't you? Won't you offer your sister-in-law an elbow?'

Not waiting for an answer, I hooked my left arm round his elbow. That might have been just a bit too forward; embarrassment flickered for a moment in George's eyes. But Winnie was her usual unsuspecting and unworldly self, and said, 'He can hold on to us both!' and she grabbed his other arm, and so we strolled on for a while in silence, George between us. A few people threw us curious looks – a black man between two white ladies was a very unusual spectacle in BG – but I have never worried about what people say or think. I care only for my own plans and desires.

The silence gave my mind the space to concoct a new plan. It was fairly simple, and so I went on to express it.

'So, Winnie, I take it that you will be leaving for Venezuela in September? For half a year, or longer?'

'Unfortunately, yes,' she replied. 'We don't know how long it will take as yet – that will depend on how well Humphrey's little bones respond to the treatment.'

'So you will be gone for Christmas! What a shame! Or will you come back for the celebration?'

Everything depended now on her response. But I need not have worried.

'No,' she said. 'Much as I'd love to, it's not worth interrupting the treatment for the time it will take me to come here and return. I will spend Christmas in Venezuela.'

'Then, George, you must come to Promised Land and celebrate with us! Yes, I insist!'

'Oh, Yoyo, how kind of you. That's a wonderful idea. George, you must go! You will have two days of holiday anyway – Christmas Day and Boxing Day – and added to the Sunday, perhaps you can take a day or two of unpaid leave, and make a real holiday of it all.'

George was silent for a while, and then he said, 'If I do take unpaid leave I would rather join you in Venezuela.'

'Oh!' said Winnie, and reddened as she considered this tempting option. I suppose George *had* to say that, to deflect any suspicion she might have, but it was a risk. Suppose she accepted his proposition? But then she spoke, and relief flooded me.

'No, George,' she said. 'You would have to take almost a week off just to account for travelling to and from Caracas. That's too much. Just two days off to visit the family is far more reasonable. We must be sensible. Not that I wouldn't love you to come – but I'll sacrifice that joy. We shall have so many more Christmases together – let's not worry about this one.'

And so it was decided. I looked up at George in triumph, but his face was turned away, towards his wife. I suppose that after such a noble self-sacrificing speech he had to show his appreciation. How droll, the way she played right into our hands!

Chapter Twenty-Two

Winnie

They arrived late; I think the girls had almost given up hope. But then the bell by the door chimed one more time, and Eliza's face lit up and she rushed to the door. Once there she stopped, brushed her hands over her hair, straightened her skirts, glanced back at us all and swept open the door. The three fellows marched in, hats in hand. A collective signal swept through the room, emitted by the ladies. Eliza had chosen her guests carefully; she had planned the party entirely around these three male guests of honour. There were about twenty guests in all – men and women; but the only single women were my three young marriage-hungry friends. All the other women were there with their husbands. Perhaps this observation of mine is a bit mean: perhaps Eliza's only single friends *were* Tilly and Kitty. But I rather thought not. There were one or two single men: Kitty's brother Harold and a friend, whose name I've forgotten. But it was strikingly obvious that these newcomers would have a limited choice of female company.

'How wonderful of you to come!' Eliza managed to say with great charm and dignity. I knew that she was excited beyond words, but from her demeanour one would think she did this every day – hobnobbed with highly eligible young white men. And these young men were indeed catches. Andrew, Emily's elder brother, was a lawyer, just returned from his studies in England. Once upon a time Emily's mother had hoped to see him married to me, but George had put an end to that plan. Now here he was, a handsome young man just starting out on his promising career. Further enhancing his appeal, he was handsome, the best-looking of the three.

Emily, quickly scanning the three newcomers, must have taken note of this, for she chose Andrew to hook by the elbow – casually, again as if she did this every day – and lead over to our little group. George and I were seated with Kitty and Tilly in gallery chairs, glasses of mauby in our hands. George had been reluctant to come at first, and had been extremely reticent at the start of the party, but my three enchanting friends had managed to penetrate his reserve and now he was entirely relaxed and chatting with us all with his usual easy charm. I was proud of him.

Eliza tonight was simply beautiful. She wore a lovely dress of pale mauve satin that exposed her exquisitely bronzed shoulders just enough, and displayed her slim waist and full bosom to great advantage. Her face was alight with natural joy; her eyes shone, her face glowed, and when she smiled her teeth gleamed white in perfect contrast to the smooth brown of her skin. Her hair was coiffed into an elaborate style involving plaits and ribbons. She was without doubt the most striking female at the gathering, which was entirely fitting, it being her party.

It was obvious from the start that Andrew was not at all oblivious to all these charms. Though he greeted me politely – we were, of course, old friends – and made an effort on introduction to Tilly, Kitty and George, during the ensuing conversation his eyes returned again and again to Eliza. As did those of his two friends. And I realised then and there: Eliza, too, was a catch, and all that she had lacked to date was the opportunity to meet a man of higher standing. Though it hurts me to use such vocabulary, I must be honest: in the mating game, a good man can be the turning point in a woman's life. Eliza, being beautiful, was in high demand, and could take her choice; but she had held out for an opportunity like this one, and her success was immediate. We had all seen it: that spark of mutual frisson that leapt between her and Andrew. These two were meant for one another, and to have played a part in their meeting filled me with great satisfaction.

The other two chaps tried their best. They talked about cars – one of them was importing one from Britain – and cricket – the other was in the national team. The girls were suitably impressed, and gasped and giggled at the appropriate places in conversation. Both were relieved not to be in England right now, 'considering that there's going to be a war.'

'We'd probably both be killed, and what good would that be to anyone?'

'It's true then?' asked Tilly politely. 'There's going to be a war in Europe?'

We all read the papers and followed the goings-on in Europe – but it was all so far away, and those of us born and bred in BG with no family ties at all to Britain felt it was really not our business; that we were lucky to be an ocean away. But these young men were English through and through; they may also have been born and bred here, but their lives were nevertheless rooted in that small island on the other side of the ocean. They had uncles, grandparents, sisters, aunts, cousins over there. That was the great difference between them and us. The war, to them, was the news of the day. They were involved, as we weren't.

'Oh yes, there'll be a war all right!' said one of them.

'But without us,' said the other.

'Just a little scrap, most likely. A little tussle.'

The other disagreed. He thought it was going to be huge, with all the countries in Europe at each other's necks, and possibly America joining in as well. They argued for some time. Tilly and Kitty yawned, and not too discreetly, but the men didn't notice, so intent were they on their war talk. Andrew leaned forward to whisper in Eliza's ear and she giggled, her hand over her mouth. A few moments later the two of them stood up and excused themselves to go off to chat on their own in a far corner of the gallery. That seemed to snap the two other fellows to attention. They brazenly looked at their watches and declared they had to go. Tilly looked disappointed; Kitty relieved. But we were all happy for Eliza. It was her birthday, and she deserved the best.

Just a month later Eliza and Andrew announced their engagement. According to Emily – whom I now saw regularly – this prompted no end of spiteful talk among the ladies of high society. How dare Andrew – one of the most eligible bachelors in town – choose a coloured girl over them!

'But who cares!' said Emily to me. 'I think she's delightful, and they're so in love. Doesn't everyone love a bit of romance? And now I have a sister, and a new friend. Life is good.'

'My good deed of the month,' I said. 'And now it's off to Caracas.'

Chapter Twenty-Three

George

I missed them so much, but it was all for the best. Winnie wrote to me every day, and sent me long letters like diaries once a week, documenting Humphrey's treatment every step of the way. She was pleased with the way it was all going. And as happy as she could be under the circumstances. Once her mother had seen her settled, she returned to Promised Land; Winnie was invited to stay at the home of one of the nurses who were looking after Humph, and she enthused over Gabriella's kindness and the warmth of her family. She was learning Spanish; she was learning about life. She wrote me all sorts of things.

'George, I do admire so the dedication of all the nurses and doctors here in the hospital! And do you know, if I could live my life over again, I think I would become a nurse – or even a doctor! It's so strange that Papa never gave me the option of finding out what I could do with my life, besides getting married. Not that I for one instant regret my marriage to you, George! It is as it is, and as odd as my life is, I think I have made the most of what was possible for me. It's just that... well, there's no point whatsoever in regretting what never could have happened, is there!'

'I'm so glad to hear that Kitty is enjoying the running of the business. She is a good cook and her guava jelly is every bit as good as mine. And her pepper sauce as hot. And she has the time, as I do not. And space: her home is much bigger than mine, living alone with her mother as she is. I think we have come to a good compromise as regards profit-sharing; she does need the income.'

'George! I'll give you three guesses! No I won't because you'd never guess right. We are going to have another baby! Somehow in all the hullabaloo of getting Humph over here and his treatment I completely ignored my body, but actually the signs have been there for some time and now it has been confirmed. She will be born soon after I return home with a much more able-bodied Humph. I say "she" because I feel in my bones that it's a girl. A boy and a girl – how lovely! I know you would love a daughter!'

Once Winnie had written to me that she was expecting another child I became almost delirious with loneliness. I longed to hold her in my arms, stroke her belly, cuddle Humph and talk and talk and talk about our future. Our daughter! What would we call her? Automatically my mind began to go through lists of girls' names. I thought a flower name would be lovely: Rose, Marigold, Daisy… but when I wrote to Winnie with my suggestions she immediately dismissed them.

'No flower names, George! Please! That is so obvious! Let's find something beautiful in itself. I love the name Charlotte. Or Sibille, after my friend in Barbados. But do you know what I would love? Gabriella, after my best friend here in Caracas! Isn't that a wonderful name? Of course, we have to be open to the fact that it might be a boy, so let's think of boys' names too. One never can tell, can one! But, fingers crossed for a girl!'

I had to agree with Winnie – Gabriella was indeed a lovely name; and so it was settled. 'Gabriella Rose!' I wrote back, and Winnie agreed. Our daughter – if the baby was indeed a daughter – already had a name. She was almost a real person! I loved her already.

The one thing I worried about was the size of our cottage. Ma and Pa were doing well in the annexe, but we only had the two bedrooms in the main part of the building. My two sisters and I had all grown up squeezed together, and I knew it could be awkward, girls and boys sharing a room. Of course it doesn't matter when they are small, but later on it would have been better to separate us. I know that thinking this way is getting above my station – after all, who else in Albouystown has the luxury of separate bedrooms for girls and boys! But I am ambitious for Winnie's sake. She deserves better. She deserves a proper house with a lovely garden, and enough rooms and a big kitchen and even a balcony. I have the ambition to offer this to her.

I have not told her yet, but I have applied for the position of telegraph clerk. They are expanding the department and a new post has been advertised. I am certain I can get it – and then there will be a raise in salary. It comes with training – but of course I don't need much training! I taught myself the Morse code, I built my own Morse machines when I was younger. Morse is my second language! I know that there will be applicants from young men of good families, but surely none of them will be as qualified as I am? Their fathers will pull strings, no doubt, and utilise connections – but I am determined to win this position through talent alone. I have sent in my application. And I made it original – after the usual details as to my education and work history, I rewrote everything – in Morse. Just so they know what I am capable of.

Even if I get the job, it will still be a long time before we can afford a new house. But already I am dreaming. As I ride through town on my bicycle I look at the nicer homes – not the Main Street mansions of course; I do know my limits – and imagine Winnie living in one of them, our children playing in the garden. Winnie at the window, waving to me as I wheel my bicycle through the gate, home from work in my white shirt and tie. No more postman's uniform for me! A boy and a girl leaping at me as I walk up the stairs, calling out 'Papa! Papa! Papa!' And Winnie with a baby in her arms, smiling for me as I walk through the door, falling into my embrace. I am determined to make this happen.

But that is in the far distant future. The telegraph job is to start on the first of January. I still have December, and the dreadful Christmas season, to endure. Not that the Christmas season is dreadful in itself, but it will be dreadful without Winnie. But most of all, it will be dreadful because I must spend it at Promised Land. Yes – I dread Christmas week as I have dreaded nothing in my life. My instinct tells me nothing good can come of it. But Winnie insists, and I have promised her I will go.

Christmas and Boxing Day, both public holidays, happen to fall on a Friday and Saturday, so I have only taken one unpaid day's holiday on the Thursday, Christmas Eve, for travelling up, and will return home on Sunday. That is ordeal enough.

* * *

I was called for an interview in mid-November. Interviewing me was the head of the telegraph department, Mr Talbot, a white man, though I would call him more ruddy than white. He possessed a large white handkerchief, with which he kept wiping the sweat from his face – he did seem to have a lot of it. Some of the English never adjust to our climate, and I wondered what kept them here. However, Mr Talbot didn't give me much time to wonder, for he plunged right into the core of the matter.

'I liked what you did,' he said. 'Wrote out the whole application in dits and dots. Original thinking, that! Your application stood out from the rest – shows initiative. You say you taught yourself Morse?'

'Yes, sir!' I said, 'and I built myself a Morse machine – I've brought it along – here it is.' I plunged my hand into the cloth bag I had brought with me and removed the little wooden apparatus I had made myself, at the age of nineteen. It was a primitive thing, of course, consisting of levers and springs I had salvaged from various discarded machines and things, with a small wooden base. But it worked, and I was immensely proud of it. I placed it on the table and tapped out a quick SOS.

Mr Talbot leaned forward and took my machine in his hands, turned it round, tapped out a few words himself.

'My goodness!' he said. 'I would say this is almost a work of genius, for a young man of limited means. You say you made this all by yourself? How did you…'

'Well, I was at Queen's College and we were learning about telegraphy and we had a picture of a real Morse key, and so I just – well, I just figured it out myself. And then I kept practising and practising until I could send messages with my eyes shut. Look!'

I shut my eyes then, and tapped out a quick message:

PLEASE GIVE ME THE JOB STOP I AM THE MAN YOU ARE LOOKING FOR STOP

Mr Talbot threw back his head and roared with laughter.

'Well, Mr Quint, you have certainly made an impression – I like you! We do have a few more applicants to interview – the job is in demand – but if it were up to me… well, it's not my decision to make. I have to consult with the board. We will let you know in a week or two.'

My heart sank to my shoes. I knew what those words meant. There were bound to be a few coloured middle class chaps who had applied, and even English chaps whose fathers knew how to pull strings. I knew I had won over Mr Talbot himself, but what about this mysterious board? Why would they accept me, a humble postman? I had walked in to that office with my head high, confident and smiling. I walked out with a slump. I knew what would happen. It was hard for a fellow of my standing and my colour to rise up in the world.

* * *

And yet, just as Mr Talbot had said, a week later an official-looking letter arrived. I tore open the envelope and scanned the single page, and at the very first words my heart leapt up to the heavens: *We are delighted to inform you that…* It was signed by Mr Talbot. Somehow, he had won over the board, and around town there would be several coloured middle class and maybe even one or two English boys wondering what had happened, and why the strings they had pulled had snapped. The job was mine! I hastened to write to Winnie with the good news. This would mean a significant rise in salary – we could start saving for a new house. A home of our very own. Now there was just the ordeal of Christmas to put behind me.

* * *

I should have trusted my instincts, which had told me quite clearly that Christmas at Promised Land would be a mistake. That instinct was confirmed almost the moment I walked in the door. Yes, it was true that Yoyo's attitude towards me had changed enormously in the past year – ever since our last visit, before Humph's birth, in fact – but this time she was practically fawning over me. I was not the only house-guest – her friend Margaret Smythe-Collingsworth and her husband had been invited for the week – but I was the only one treated as if I were guest of honour. It was downright embarrassing, her *George Darling* this, and *Darling George* that. I wanted to tell her to stop – but how, without making an ass of myself, and earning not only a rebuke but perhaps even a tantrum? Everyone knew that to upset Yoyo, to contravene her plans or contradict her in any way, was to play with fire. And anyway, I had promised Winnie to do my best. To be nice. And so I acquiesced, accepted her graciousness with an awkward smile and walked directly into her trap.

She showed me up to my room herself. This was properly the task of a servant but no, Yoyo had to take my hand and lead, almost drag, me up the stairs. I threw my mother-in-law a desperate glance over my shoulder – a call for help – but she only shrugged and made a gesture of helplessness with her hands.

Yoyo led me to the same room I had shared with Winnie on my last visit – it had once been Winnie's own room, I understood – with its two east-facing sash windows. The bed was a four-poster, with a mosquito net bundled over the top.

'Mavis will come in to tuck in the net before dinner,' said Yoyo. 'I think you'll be very comfortable here.'

She winked at me. I took a step back.

'If there's anything at all you want – anything – just give me a call,' she said. 'I sleep in the room next door. Alone. Clarence has his own room across the hallway.'

Why was she telling me this?

She winked again.

There was something sly, something lustful even, in her eyes. I hoped I was mistaken. I hoped against hope that what I was seeing was my own too-vivid imagination. I hoped – no, it could not be! But I hoped this sense of dread, this hollowness in my belly, was based on nothing real, nothing emanating from her. Because, if it were real, how would I deal with it? I only wanted to run. Run back to New Amsterdam, cross the Berbice River, grab the train and run home to Albouystown. I ached for Winnie to be there. But, of course, she wasn't.

* * *

Yoyo left me so that I could change for dinner. I stayed in my room until the gong rang out, and then cautiously descended the stairs. I had hoped that Margaret and her husband would absorb Yoyo's attention during the meal, and allow me to engage with my mother-in-law, but, of course, no such luck. Yoyo seemed determined to make sure I was a part of every single conversation she held with her friend – quite the opposite of her treatment of me a year ago. Then, she had rudely ignored me, sometimes even turning away when etiquette called for a polite greeting. Now, she turned to me after almost every sentence. Her eyes held a gleam, and when they landed on me I instinctively recoiled. Hopefully it did not show; I could not afford to anger Yoyo, and instinct told me that rejection would anger her.

'Margaret, George has such wonderful news – he is to be congratulated on two counts!' were her very first words as we took our seats.

'Oh, really? Do tell, George!' Mrs Smythe-Collingsworth turned beady eyes on me. She was in an advanced stage of pregnancy by this time, and had gained so much weight all round that her eyes seemed hidden deep within her face. There was something mocking in her voice, and in her stare. In her presence I always felt like a museum exhibit, or a rabbit to be experimented on. I did not like her even a little bit. But then, I had not liked her father, Mr McInnes, the cruellest estate manager on the Corentyne Coast. No one did. I wondered how Yoyo had managed to maintain the friendship with his daughter after dismissing the father; but it was not my business.

I did not answer right away. I did not care to talk of personal matters with virtual strangers; but Yoyo had simply plunged in and put me forward as an object of interest.

'Go on George!' she prompted after a moment of my silence. 'Tell her!'

Her prompt only made me hesitate further. I shook my head vaguely and looked up at Mavis, at my side, placing a leg of roast chicken on my plate. I felt grateful for her presence. In this house

I felt more comfortable among the servants than among the masters. Yoyo would say I knew my place. And still she enjoyed her little pinpricks of provocation. And, as always, her goads were more in the *way* she said something than in *what* she said.

'Well, since his tongue seems to be tied, I will tell you myself. He is to be a father again! And furthermore, he has received a promotion. Winnie has told us all about it.'

'Oh, well done, George!' said Mrs Smythe-Collingsworth. 'Another baby! What fun our little ones shall have together. Won't they, Yoyo?'

'They are hoping for a girl this time,' said Yoyo. 'And they have even chosen a name! Gabriella Rose.'

I definitely wasn't imagining things – there was a jeer in that voice. The way she said my precious daughter's name! A shudder of annoyance went through me, not at Yoyo – who after all was just being Yoyo – but at Winnie, for divulging such private matters to her sister. Really, Winnie needed to learn discretion, especially where Yoyo was concerned.

'What a pretty name!' said her friend. 'We of course are hoping for a boy. A boy should always come first, don't you agree, Yoyo? And don't worry – *yours* will come in due time!'

Yoyo scowled slightly at those last words; any reference to her childlessness invariably evoked annoyance, and sometimes a sharp reprimand. Winnie and I no longer mentioned it, but we did know that she wanted children, but for some reason they were not forthcoming. Could the separate bedrooms she had referred to earlier be the problem? The chill that seemed to hover between her and her husband? But of course it was none of my business to speculate, and Yoyo made sure it would not become a topic by deftly turning the conversation back to my affairs.

'I should think the main concern is that the child is healthy, whether it is a boy or a girl,' she said. 'What a shame about little Humphrey.'

'Yes – but he is being treated, surely.'

Yoyo shook her head sadly.

'But he will always be a cripple.'

At that word I had to speak up.

'Humphrey is *not* a cripple!' I said, my voice somewhat louder than table manners dictated. 'He is a perfectly healthy child. Don't call him that.'

'Ssshhh, George, no need to shout! Nobody here is deaf. All right, I won't call him a cripple again – but still, let's all hope that the next child has no such deformities – I mean, *problems*. I mean, it's not just the foot, is it? He's also a half-caste. A half-caste crip— oh, sorry. But let's face it; the poor child is twice cursed. Poor little thing. I feel so sorry for it.'

She laughed, and her eyes narrowed in mockery. I seethed. I wanted to say something, but no words came and anyway, I feared anything I said would come out wrong. I'm not a good speaker – not when I am agitated. I knew she was waiting for me to react and that it amused her. So I kept silent, and after a while Yoyo continued to speak.

'I do hope Winnie will be able to cope. She's such a little kitten, isn't she? Sweet and tame. A little too tame, I fear.'

My blood boiled. But I managed to keep the rage to myself and said as mildly as I could:

'Winnie is by no means a *kitten!*'

I wanted to say more but I was afraid of saying too much. Yoyo had no such fears. She laughed.

'Oh, I know she fancies herself as a bit of a revolutionary. A communist or something like that – running around with the underdogs, defending them in court, that sort of thing. And of course running off to marry one of them. But be honest, George – she's not really up to it, is she? Winnie is as mild as... as a gentle mountain brook. Whereas I'm a wild-water river. Have you ever seen one of those, George? Papa once took us on a boat trip up the Essequibo River, where the water tumbles over rocks, white and rushing. That's me. But I suppose your taste is more for the gentle brook? Some people can't handle the white-water wildness.'

She turned to her guest. 'George is so charmingly protective of his family, isn't he? He's so sweet!' And she placed a hand on my wrist, and squeezed it, and looked up at me with wide open eyes, and pressed her reddened lips forward into a pout. I glanced at her, then away, and my eyes met Mama's across the table.

Mama was so different from Yoyo. I truly had grown to love her, but I wished she were more dominant in this household. She spoke so little, and allowed Yoyo to hold the reins of conversation. Now, as her eyes caught mine, I saw sympathy there, and understanding. She could read me in an instant. She knew exactly what was going on, yet said nothing. She knew her daughter well. Did I read a warning in her gaze? Beyond sympathy it was hard to tell what went on in her mind. She was an enigma. But I knew she was on my side, and that helped.

Yoyo now deftly turned the conversation around to speak about my promotion, and then about our living conditions, and if we would all fit into the cottage, and how, each question more embarrassing than the last. It was excruciating.

* * *

After dinner we all retired to the gallery, where Mavis served us our rum-laced Moonlight Mixes. All the windows were open and the sea breeze swept through, cool and soothing. The choir of night creatures screeched out their cacophonous symphony, and light thrown from the flickering lanterns chased shadows on the walls and the floorboards. It would have been a relaxing end to the day if not for the discomfort Yoyo's presence made me feel. Yet now she was curiously silent, allowing Margaret Smythe-Collingsworth to take centre stage with various stories of her friends and relations in Georgetown – gossip, for the most part, and I suppose amusing, though not so to me. Her husband and Clarence guffawed now and then, as they knew the persons concerned, and provided some anecdotes of their own. I listened with only half an ear, glad that Yoyo's attention was no longer on me.

The Christmas weekend stretched before me as a chore to be accomplished. I would have to avoid Yoyo as much as possible, and my thoughts jumped to Uncle Jim. I would certainly visit him, and some of my old friends from the village. I had not seen them since long before the wedding; at the trial, as a matter of fact. I wondered how my friends would react to me; I had after all changed sides to become a part of the Cox family. The sugar kings were generally hated – but of course Winnie was different, and so was her mother.

Uncle Jim, of course, would be the same as ever. I had last seen him at the trial: he had stood on the street with us protestors, holding a placard and chanting with the rest of us. Now he was an estate manager, in a position of authority over the very labourers with whom he had once plotted and marched. How times changed! Uncle Jim may have superficially changed sides, just as I had, but his heart would have stayed firmly anchored in solidarity. Uncle Jim was not a man who whipped with the wind, out only for his own advantage. Of that I could be certain.

I determined to visit him early the next day, and spend as much of the weekend with him as politely possible. Uncle Jim would advise me, as well, on how to deal with Yoyo and her extraordinary behaviour. He knew women better than I did; he was much older and wiser than I was, and been married twice; and he worked with Yoyo day after day and certainly knew her well. Relief flooded through me as I thought about it. Yes, Uncle Jim would help me find my footing in the precarious territory I walked through.

I was glad when, after only about fifteen minutes, Yoyo rose to her feet and placed her glass on the central table.

'I have rather a bad headache,' she said. 'I'm off to bed. I'll see you all in the morning.'

'Toodle-oo, darling!' said Margaret. 'Hope you feel better tomorrow! It's Christmas after all – we can't have you ill in bed!'

'No, I'll be fine,' Yoyo assured her friend. 'It's just the excitement, I suppose. I just need some sleep.'

Everyone said good night and she swept past me towards the stairs. She did not glance at me, and I took this as a sign of waning interest. Everyone knew of Yoyo's moods – she could move from hot to cold in the wink of an eye. Once she had gone I could relax, and my breathing, which I now realised had been stiff and shallow, returned to normal.

The conversation, led now by the men, turned to cricket, and this time I was able to join in. At Queen's College I had been in the cricket team and, though I hadn't played myself for several years, I often attended the local matches, and I knew the players they now mentioned. They, of course, had places in the pavilions of the Georgetown Cricket Club in Queenstown, whereas I stood with the crowds behind the barrier downstairs. Which was somewhat better than the free seats on the trees outside the grounds, invariably filled with young boys who could not afford a ticket. Once, I had been one of those boys. Yes, I had moved up in the world – but not very far. I would never enter the pavilion. The only coloured men in there were those in white uniforms serving rum and cucumber sandwiches. But here tonight we – the men at least – all loved cricket and that united us, and so the rest of the evening was spent pleasantly, and when we all said our final good nights and retired to our rooms my mood – so nervous at the start of the night – had been restored to normal and I looked forward to my bed and sleep and the coming day, which I would spend, hopefully, with Uncle Jim.

* * *

Mavis handed out lanterns at the foot of the stairs, and we marched up in single file. My room – or rather, Winnie's – was at the end of the top landing, and I pushed open the door and entered, closing the door behind me. The flame in the lantern was not yet quite steady, and in the light it gave out I did not see her at once. But I heard her.

'I thought you would *never* come, darling George!'

I froze. Everything within me turned to solid ice. I almost dropped the lantern in shock at that voice. My instinct was to flee, but instead my body froze while my mind raced. Run! It said! Run! Flee! But where would I flee to? What would I do, where would I go? I was in a strange house, trapped. With her. The light, now steady at last, threw its glow towards the bed. The mosquito net was down, but as a veil it did not hide much.

My sister-in-law lay stretched out on the bed, stark naked. And even as I registered this, she sat up, raised the net, ducked under it and stood up. She held out her arms in invitation. She smiled as she slowly walked towards me. She spoke as she walked.

'You look shocked, George. Don't be. This is me. Here I am, all yours. I know you want me, but you think you can't have me, don't you? I'm here to tell you that you *can*. This will be our little secret. Come, George darling. Forbidden fruit is the sweetest on earth.'

She walked slowly, so slowly, and that was my window of escape. This time my body did not freeze. I ran. Plunged to the door, opened it, stopped for just a second to pull it closed behind me. Had there been a key I would have turned it. I fled along the landing, down the stairs. The lantern swung precariously as I ran. Across the drawing room, to the front door. Down the outside stairs. And only then did I stop, my heart racing. The guard dogs broke into a volley of barking. Joseph the watchman appeared from out of the shadows.

My heart pounded. My thoughts raced. My breath so ragged I could speak only in staccato, I managed to stutter a few words.

'The-bicycle-shed… can you-open it-for me?'

Somehow in my mad flight from that cursed house I had known what I would do, where I would go.

Joseph led me to the shed. I easily recognised Winnie's bike – the only red one. I grabbed it, wheeled it out. Joseph walked with me down the drive to the main gate. He was obviously bursting with curiosity, and goodness knew what the servants would say the next day – Christmas! – but I did not care. I spoke not a word more. By the time I reached the gate my breath and my heartbeat had returned to normal, and a glorious sense of freedom washed through me. It was as if a curse had lifted.

Once outside the compound I mounted the bicycle and sailed away, pedalling at full speed as if chased by a fire-breathing monster.

Twenty minutes later I stood outside a familiar gate ringing my bicycle bell. Dogs barked. A light went on in the windows of the large white house before me. A man stood at the window.

'Uncle Jim!' I called. 'It's me, George! Come down and open!'

In a zigzag, roundabout way I had come back home.

Part 2

All Boys Town
FIVE YEARS LATER: 1918

Chapter Twenty-Four

Winnie

'It's her, this time, George. I feel it. I know it.'

I felt like a parrot; I had said those words, or similar, so often over the years. And yet, never had the certainty been stronger. In the past it had been mere wishful thinking – how I longed for Gabriella Rose! And that wish had translated into a feeling, with every pregnancy, that she was on her way to me. This time, I knew it. I really did.

But George did not believe me. True, he nodded and smiled and agreed with me, as he always did, but in his heart he had given up. Five boys already. He had grown used to boys. His mind was made up. I was afraid that that closed mind was what prevented her from coming in the first place – what if she was a soul, hovering in the background of our lives, longing to come, but convinced that George no longer wanted her? It sounds ridiculous, I know – I would never say such things aloud to George, who is so very *scientific* – but what if?

Even the boys did not believe it. Humphrey, my strong silent eldest, would only nod sagely when I spoke of his future sister, but I could see the disbelief in his eyes. Humphrey would never contradict me. He would never say anything that might hurt or disappoint me. Out of my five boys, he was the rock. As the eldest, he assumed a responsibility beyond his years – what would I have done without him? Humphrey was used to boys, and Humphrey could not begin to imagine a sister; but he would never tell me so to my face. He kept the myth of Gabriella Rose alive, for my sake. He said what I wanted to hear: that a sister was on her way. I loved him so!

Gordon at five, had no such compunctions. Gordon said what he thought, the words tact and empathy foreign to him. He could not grasp their meanings, much less practise them.

'We live in All Boys Town,' he would say. 'Ma, why would a girl want to come to All Boys Town?'

Patiently I explained to him the difference.

'Yes, dear, it sounds like All Boys Town. But it's not written that way.' I picked up his school slate and wrote down the proper spelling of Albouystown and then All Boys Town beneath it, to show him the difference. But he would only shake his head.

'There's no difference,' he said. 'I don't hear no difference. It's all the same. All Boys Town.'

I went to the trouble of investigating the source of the name Albouystown, for his sake. I had to get that troublesome idea out of his head before it infected us all, made us believe in it. Albouystown was called that for a reason, and it was disrespectful to distort that meaning. But Gordon only shook his head.

'All Boys Town. You're going to have all boys. And it's better so. I don't want a sister. Girls are silly.'

'Lots of girls are born and live in Albouystown,' said Humphrey. Humphrey would always stand up for me, support me, even if he didn't quite believe me. 'Look at Mrs Murray across the road. She has three daughters!'

'But this is us and we are going to have all boys. I want more boys. Ten boys!'

When he said that I almost fainted. What if it were true! Ten boys! No! It could not be. A girl was on her way, Gabriella Rose.

William, four and always eager to learn something new, took the slate and slate-pencil from my hand and began to copy the words All Boys Town beneath my own writing.

Gordon looked at Will's writing and laughed. 'You write like crabfoot!' he said, and burst into song: 'Crabfoot marching in the burial ground, tek a big stick and knock 'um down.'

'You forgot the apostrophe,' said Humphrey, taking the slate-pencil from him and adding the little mark. Humphrey had taught himself to read and write at the age of three. He was meticulous and careful; his cleverness was of the slow, introspective but rather pedantic kind rather than the quick and sometimes slapdash, extrovert and very vocal intelligence of Gordon. It was Humphrey, not Gordon, who had penetrated the brooding silence of Pa, merely by showing an interest, and then an equal passion, for the dull pursuit of philately. Humphrey could sit for hours on Pa's lap learning the intricacies of stamp-collecting. Humphrey had an eagle's eye for errors in perforation; he knew the history of certain famous stamps, and he could handle stamp tongs and magnifying glass like an expert; and all that at the age of six.

'What's an apos trophy?'

'Apostrophe. It's that little mark. It means the possessive of boys. It's to show—'

'It's stupid. It makes no difference. It's still All Boys Town, isn't it?'

'Yes, but—'

'Well then. They don't need no trophy.'

'That's a double negative. You can't say that.'

'I can too! I just did!'

'Ma! A double negative is wrong, isn't it?'

I had turned away to run behind Charles, three years old had found the Cow & Gate powdered-milk tin and was trying to prise it open with a knife. I took the knife away from Charles and gave him an empty tin to play with, placing the full one back in the cupboard he had quietly opened. Absent-mindedly I said, 'Yes, dear, it certainly is.'

'What's a double negative?'

'It's what you just did,' Humphrey broke in. 'You can either say they don't need a trophy, or they need no trophy. If you use both at the same time it means the very opposite.'

I smiled to myself at Humphrey's explanation. I had taught him that particular grammar rule. Living in Albouystown, the boys were obviously going to pick up the local speech, which did not care about such niceties as double negatives. I made sure they learned and spoke correct English at home, at least. Indeed, a local boy would have said *they ain't need no trophy*, so I could be at least grateful for Gordon's *don't*. But of my two oldest boys, Humphrey was the one who would always strive to speak King's English. Gordon, I knew already, would not care. He would grow up to speak like a local, at least outside our home.

Their very looks confirmed that difference. Humphrey was fair, his skin a shade of dark cream, his hair black, crinkly, but soft. Gordon was a very dark shade of bronze, the image of his father, and his hair a close-fitting cap of kinks, a helmet of black moss. Visually, he fitted in perfectly in Albouystown. Humphrey, like me, would always stand out as different. Humphrey was quiet, refined; even at six years of age, he possessed an aura of maturity, wisdom beyond his years; but, paired as it was with his inherent kindness and humility, he would never be a snob. Humphrey crossed his t's and dotted his i's. Gordon never would.

Already Gordon was proving to be the most physical of them all; my bet was that he would be our sportsman. His favourite toy was the little cricket bat George had carved for him, and he was always to be found out on the street with much older boys, batting and bowling and running. Humphrey had been out of his brace for some time now, but he still walked and ran with a limp; never as wild as Gordon, he nevertheless loved outdoor games just as much, cricket especially. He was excellent at bowling, and never put a foot wrong when climbing trees, unlike Gordon, who would clamber and fall and get up again and try again. Will's main sport was the catching of guppies from the gutter running beside the road, and he was an avid tree-climber, with little Charles not far behind on the lower branches of the mango tree.

And Will was our musician: already he played the recorder better than both Gordon and Humphrey. I would soon be sending for my little half-violin, which was still packed away at Promised Land, and starting him with lessons.

I found it fascinating how each child had his very own character, his way of being, his strengths, his world. As their mother, it was my task to identify and know each little individual, and bring him to fruition. I was developing eyes in the back of my head, and as many hands and arms as a Hindu god. I saw the world through each child's eyes, new and miraculous every single day.

In the afternoons they would run out to play with some of the raggedy older boys down the road: cricket in the street, or catching creatures in the gutters, to keep in jam jars. Climbing trees, stealing fruit from neighbourhood gardens, coming home covered in mud or with faces smeared with overripe mango. Ripped shorts, buttons missing. Cuts, bruises, bumps, sprains, scratches, rashes. Ringworm, tummyaches and once a broken arm (Gordon). Earthworms, guppies, tadpoles. A pet scorpion. Black soles of bare feet to be scrubbed each night. Laughter and tears. Ants in sand-filled jam jars. Tree-branch swords and slingshots. Marbles and newspaper aeroplanes. Slugs and snails and puppydog tails. Boys, boys, boys.

When it rained, and it rained often, they stayed indoors playing word games: using an atlas, they learned to name all the countries in the world, continent by continent. They loved lists: all the fruit that grew in BG, for instance. If you paused longer than a count of three, the next one took over. Will, as the youngest of the three older ones, started: 'Orange, tangerine, lime, lemon, grapefruit, pawpaw, banana, mango, guava... is pineapple a fruit?'

'1-2-3 yes,' said Gordon and continued: 'Star-apple, golden-apple, custard apple, sugar apple, monkey apple, mamee apple, soursop, simatoo, sapodilla, gooseberry…' He paused too long, and Humphrey took over: 'Cherry, grapes, psidium, cashew, tomato—'

'Stop! Tomato isn't a fruit!'

'Yes it is!' said Humphrey. 'Fruits come from the ovary at the base of the flower. They contain the seeds of the plant. I read it in the encyclopedia.'

'Know-it-all!' said Gordon.

'…tamarind, plums, locust, pomegranate, jamoon, five-finger, whitey, cookerite, owara, corio, avocado—'

'Cheating! Avocado *definitely* isn't a fruit!'

'It is! It is! I'll read it to you from the encyclopedia!'

'I bet you can't even spell cycle-whatever it is!'

'Of course I can!' Humphrey did exactly that, and I confirmed it.

'But I can list all the fish in BG and you can't do that!'

'Go on then!'

They reeled off Gordon's tongue: 'Catfish, hardhead Thomas, kwakwarie, cuirass, kassee, bangamary, four-eye, queriman, gilbacker, basha, two-belly basha, butterfish, grouper, snapper, sea trout, silver fish, churi churi, sunfish, hassar, patwa, hoori, lukunani, hymara, luggalugga, dew fish, mullet, cuffum, snook, paccoo, morocut—'

He stopped. 'See! I can too! And I bet they aren't in your blasted cycle-book!'

Will piped up at once: 'Mammeeee! Gordon said a rude word!'

Humphrey sniffed, vanquished yet again by his younger brother. Gordon was our fisherman. The big boys taught him to fish in the Sussex Street trench for kassee, cuirass and hassar, and catch prawns in a rice bag seine. For that, Ma procured an iron barrel hoop, sewed it along the top of the bag, put flour and rice mixed with molasses along the sides and bottom and put leaves in it. Gordon would put a few stones in it to make it sink and stay

under water; he'd let it down with a cord to the bottom of the
trench, and there it would stay for an hour or so. When he pulled
it up it would be full of prawns. Ma would peel, wash and lime
the prawns that same night and the next day we'd have the most
delicious prawn curry.

And so my boys were becoming proper Albouystown boys,
learning the ways of the street and how to fend for themselves. I
was infinitely proud of them.

* * *

My babies, I called the two youngest ones, even though Charles
had more than outgrown his toddler legs, and was quite preco-
cious. He was bright and cheerful, good at everything he put his
hand to. Charles and Leopold were so close to each other in age
that I almost thought of them as one – feeding times, sleeping
times, play times: their lives seemed synchronised to the minute. When one cried the other was quick to join in. When one
vomited over my shoulder, so did the other, on the newly made
bed. When one child reached out for a cuddle, so did his brother,
demanding, needing, little parasites hungry for my lifeblood. Yet
they too were different. Charles, dreamy, artistic, sweet-natured.
Altruistic. Leo, brash, assertive. Always taking away Charles's toys
– although he'd have given them willingly enough – and even
those of the older boys. Screaming when he didn't get his way.
Charles was a giver; Leo was a taker.

My babies. Little people. Souls in my care, for me to mould
and guide and help to be who they were. It was, finally, a good
thing. In two or three years they would each show their calibre.

Sometimes, a few minutes of *nothing-to-do* opened up like a
green alpine valley newly minted from the hand of God and I
would throw myself across the bed or into the rocking chair and
close my eyes – but never for long. Exhaustion nipped constantly
at my heels. I was not born to this kind of life. I was not raised to

raise a horde of babies without maids and nannies. Sometimes a grumbling little voice nagged at the back of my mind. *Why? Why did you choose this life? You could have done better! You know you could have done better! Think of...* and a name, a face, *a lost alternative,* tried to edge itself into my consciousness. But it never did.

I learned to gag that little devil voice. *Get Thee behind me!* I would cry out in silence, mimicking our Lord in the desert, and that stern command was always enough for it to slink away, a dog with its tail between its legs. I lectured myself. *You chose this life because you loved George.* No, not *loved:* LOVE. Love placed you here. Love is your master, love your storeroom of strength. And I would sigh and rise to my feet and walk on, one step at a time. I thought of the other mothers of Albouystown; they too had broods of children, they too got through the day. And they had had no options, whereas I had chosen this life. So who was I to complain? I refused to be that white lady from the white mansions too good for practical work, too proud to raise her own children. No – I would be as good as any Albouystown mother, as strong and resilient and upright in my duties. I would keep going.

Yes, I admit, it was hard work, keeping up with my boys as well as managing their care. Ma helped, of course, but her day was filled with housework and most of it fell to me. I wouldn't have managed, I admit, without hired help – a girl called Cherry who helped in the kitchen, and Efna, who sometimes minded the youngest ones. Both of them were themselves dwellers of Albouystown. They should be working in the more affluent areas of Kingston or Cummingsburg, not for a neighbour. It made me feel privileged, a sense I had been trying to overcome ever since I first fell for George. I had determined to start at the bottom and work my way up. Doing the simple household tasks that kept a family going had brought me down from my fool's paradise of dresses and dances, made of the fluffy-minded dreamer a down-to-earth and practical woman, a mother with hands that knew what to do. But now, with five boys – well, I was grateful for the help. If only I wasn't white and they brown. The differences in our skin colour reinforced the tired old hierarchy of privilege, and that was what caused my guilt. Being an Albouystown resident made it all much worse.

But I was learning to love Albouystown. It was the residents who made the difference. None of this stiff-upper-lip business that characterised the British upper class. Albouystown folk were down to earth. They showed you what they felt. There was no pretence; they wore their hearts on their sleeves. When they were upset, they cried. When they were angry, they yelled. If they hated you, they showed it. And if they loved you – well, I was beginning to be loved by one or two, and it meant the world to me. It meant acceptance. I was beginning to forget the colour of my own skin, forget any difference. Yet I still had no close friends there. Many of the ladies I thought of as 'gate friends', since we only chatted over the garden gate when I came to collect fruit or peppers or tomatoes from their gardens. But a gate friend was good enough for me; after all, I had Kitty, Eliza, Tilly and Emily.

Though most Albouystown residents were of African descent, there were many Indians, too. The Africans came from former slaves from the sugar fields, the Indians from former indentured servants, all of whom had been freed or turned their backs on plantation life. I suppose my reputation as a rebel against plantation conditions went before me and helped to ease my path. But I was eager to know them better; who were these people who came from far away, who sweated and toiled in the broiling sun for a pittance, to make us British rich?

I learned that there were two kinds of Indians, Muslims and Hindus. You could tell by their names: Muslims had names like Khan and Hussein and Ali. Hindus had names like Ram and Persaud and Nataraj. Muslims did not eat pork; Hindus did not eat beef. It was easy to tell a Hindu home, as they would have clusters of tall thin poles at the front fence bearing raggedy red flags. I wondered at the meaning of these flags, and in conversation with a Hindu housewife, Basmattie, I finally found an answer: the flags are dedicated to the gods Hanuman and Shiva and the goddess Lakshmi. They are prepared at a Hindu prayer service called a jhandi.

Basmattie, in her eagerness to explain to me what they meant, arranged for me to be invited me to a jhandi prayer service at a friend's house. I was most excited at this invitation, for it meant a further step into the heart of my new community, a further opening of my own heart.

I arrived early in the morning, and found all the women of the household cooking in enormous pots in the yard over open fires. Basmattie and her friend were picking flowers and making garlands for the service, and invited me to help; I eagerly did, but my fingers were slow and clumsy and they laughed good-naturedly at my poor attempts at garland-making. They had been learning the art since they were little girls.

Later on the pandit arrived and we all went upstairs. A ceremony followed that I couldn't quite understand; prayers were chanted in a strange language that I later found out was Sanskrit. Various gods and goddesses were worshipped and the flags blessed in their honour, Hanuman receiving one more than Shiva and Lakshmi. Later, when I asked Basmattie about the many gods of Hinduism, she laughed. 'We have many gods,' she said, 'but only one God, with a capital G, just like you. And our God is the same as your God, and the Muslim Allah. We all pray and worship in different ways; our gods are our pathways to Him. Jesus is your pathway. But we all are going in the same direction: to love and peace.'

This made perfect sense to me, and I nodded.

At the end of the ceremony the pandit gave some teachings in English about right living. 'What you do is not important,' he said. 'No work is more worthwhile than another. It's not what you do that counts; it's how you do it. Do your work with right attitude, and it will be of benefit to you, even if it is lowly. Regard your work as service to God, and do it with dedication, no matter what it is. The motions of work are not important: it is the motions of mind that count. Happiness comes not from the pleasure you can abstract from your work or the world, but from the love you pour into your work and the world.'

I found that teaching most helpful for my life in Albouystown, and determined to try to live by it. And in that way I felt folded even closer into the heart and soul of Albouystown, and learned to live my life there. And I determined that my children would learn all about all religions, because all are meandering paths to a single truth. They were all baptised Catholic, but I hoped that they would grow up to understand that every religion is a pathway to God, and only that: a path, and not the whole truth; and that He favours no particular path, but sees only the sincerity with which it is walked.

* * *

There were ways not to have more children. Women spoke of such ways, and so did George, even though he was a Catholic and, officially at least, not allowed to inhibit conception.

'We have enough,' George said. 'Let's stop now.'

He said that after Will, and after Charles, and after Leo. It was I who refused.

'Gabriella Rose,' I said. 'She is next. Her soul is waiting. I know it, I feel it. One more, George. Just one more and then we'll stop. The next one will be Gabriella Rose.' But it never was. Until now. But this one, this little being beneath my swelling abdomen – this was she. I knew it with every fibre of my being. This was different. I could actually feel her this time – feel her as a companion, invisible but real, so real, beside me every minute of the day, and in my dreams. This had never been the case with any of the boys. This certainty! This *knowing!* This was her. I placed my hands on the tight skin of my belly and sighed, and smiled. Just a few months more, my little love. Just a little while longer.

* * *

George wanted desperately to get me out of Albouystown. He had worked so hard over the years, and it had paid off: he was now head of the telegraph office, the most senior non-white employee in the entire BG civil service. He had a good salary and, augmented as it was by the profits from Quintessentials, we were doing well financially. But he wasn't happy. George wanted a house. A lovely big family home in a nice location, to where he could transplant us all.

Most evenings after work he would bundle us all into a hired coach and we would drive to the Sea Wall for an afternoon airing. George would wear his Sunday best, a crisp white shirt and a striped tie. He cut a very dapper figure, straight and tall with me on his arm. Up and down the jetty we would stroll, arm in arm, and watch the children play – Humphrey in charge of the little ones digging in the sand, Gordon and Will playing cricket on the beach – and he would dream. A big yard, he wanted, with trees the boys could climb and a gutter of their own that they could fish in. A two-storey house in the middle of it, with a window-fronted gallery and four bedrooms; a lovely white wooden house with Demerara windows and jalousies painted green. Sometimes he rode up and down the desirable areas on his bicycle, looking for available plots. He scoured the city, sending out feelers for our perfect place. I would laugh at him.

'George, you seem to think the place is already there, with our name on it. Just waiting for you to turn up and identify it!'

He smiled rather sheepishly.

'That's a bit how I feel. I can almost picture it. I want a mansion, Winnie, not a cottage! You deserve the best.'

'Oh, stuff and nonsense. A ready-made house will do. Gabriella will need a room of her own – so at least four bedrooms. The boys can share two rooms. A kitchen, a bathroom, a gallery and drawing room – what more do we want?'

'I want it big. As big as the house you grew up in. Why should your children have less than you did?'

'Oh *George!* You're such a snob! As long as I have you and the boys and Gabriella I'd be happy living in a dog kennel! And as for the boys – they are happy here in Albouystown. They have their friends here. Why can't we buy a bigger house here, if it has to be?'

A bigger home was, in all honesty, my dream too – what mother does not want the most comfortable nest for her family – but I was too busy with my everyday challenges to think much about it. But it was all George thought about. Every extra penny went into the savings account he had opened for that very goal; and within a year, he said, we would have enough to make a deposit on a piece of land on which we would build our future. The very thought of moving home gave me a headache.

'The boys would be happy anywhere,' George said, 'and I want the very best for them. The best home and the best education, the best friends, so that they will go far.'

'You take care of it, then,' I said wearily. 'I don't care.'

I sighed and laid my head on his shoulder, hoping to silence him. I placed his hands on my belly, so that he could feel Gabriella Rose and stop thinking about that imaginary house. This house had haunted him ever since my return from Caracas. This idea that our home had to be as wonderful as Promised Land. It never would be – Promised Land was indeed special, but I had put it behind me for ever when I chose George. But George – he seemed haunted.

* * *

I had always thought my children would visit Promised Land, the family seat, frequently, but George adamantly refused to return there, and I could never manage to take them on my own. With each new child the possibility of showing them my old home faded more and more into the realms of the impossible. They would be almost adult before we could possibly make it as a family – and then it would be without George.

Something had happened on George's last visit to Promised Land. Some quarrel with Yoyo. A bad quarrel, bad enough for him to vow never to speak to her again, never to set foot in her home.

'But it's also my old home, George!' I had pleaded, but he was adamant. No.

'If you would just tell me what happened! I know that Yoyo can be very obnoxious, but surely there's a way to forgive her and start again – things were going so nicely between you. If you'd just tell me perhaps I can—'

'Yoyo,' he said, 'was insulting towards you. She called you a tame little kitten. You're anything *but* a little kitten.'

I only laughed. 'A kitten! I like that! So I suppose if I'm a kitten she's a tiger?'

'Don't you see how she's trying to insult you?'

'Oh, George! Yoyo is always calling me names. She always likes to tease me. It doesn't matter. If I'm not offended, why should you be on my behalf? I don't mind.'

'But *I* mind! I won't go back there until she apologises.'

'Oh, you silly boy! Yoyo will never apologise. She never has, in her whole life, not for anything, even when she was clearly in the wrong. It's totally beneath her dignity – she won't. That's just the way Yoyo is. It doesn't matter. We have to accept Yoyo just as she is, love her just as she is, with all her little foibles. I don't care, so why should you?'

'I won't speak to anyone who disrespects my wife. It's a point of honour with me.'

'No, George, it's just your pride. And what does the Church say about pride? Isn't it one of the seven deadly sins?'

'There's a difference between pride and dignity. I would feel less of a man if I allowed Yoyo to cast aspersions against you without protest. And since she will never take back her words, I cannot step foot in her house again. I'm sorry, Winnie. I just can't.'

'What about turning the other cheek, George? Forgiving those that trespass against us? It's really very un-Christian of you.'

'She insulted Humph. She called him a cripple and a half-caste.'

'Well, the words aren't very nice but it's all true in a way. Yoyo doesn't mince words. She doesn't have a tactful vein in her body. She speaks her mind – that's just the way it is.'

I sighed. George was so very stubborn. He didn't begin to understand Yoyo, wasn't even trying. There had to be more behind this: I suspected that Yoyo had made some disparaging comment about his race. She can be very blunt, and I'm afraid that she still thinks the white race superior, and sometimes says things to that effect. That would certainly have annoyed George – he's very sensitive about race – but I could imagine that he didn't want to tell me.

'Did she say anything about you, George? Make some racist comment? I know you hate that.' He didn't answer, but hung his head, and that's when I knew.

'Oh, George! She did, didn't she? Look, she doesn't mean it. She loved Nanny, who was Indian. Deep inside she's got a good heart – really.'

'Why don't you go by yourself, if you want to see her so badly?'

'But I want us to go as a *family*, George! With the baby! If I go alone it will look as if we have quarrelled and she will certainly ask questions, and then I'll have to explain that you're being stubborn, and then she'll laugh at you and then I'll be cross with her for insulting you, and then I'll be cross with you for being cross with her… and then it will all be so complicated. Why can't everyone just love each other and be nice to each other and forgive and forget? I will never understand it. Truly, never.'

He took my hand. And squeezed it.

'I'm sorry, darling, I really am. I know I'm being stubborn but…' He didn't finish the sentence. He just shook his head and looked infinitely sad. It was so tiresome.

But George remained adamant. He would not tell me, and he would not go. And she would not come. As a result I had not seen Yoyo for five whole years. And I missed her.

* * *

In the meantime Kitty, Eliza and Tilly had become my *ersatz-*sisters. Yes, in the beginning, they had used me as a ladder up Georgetown's social slopes. But by now it was more than that. With Kitty especially I felt a deep rapport – she had taken over entirely the running of Quintessentials, and she did it well. Profits were better than ever before, and she enjoyed the work. Enjoyed it so much, she said, that she definitely did not want children.

It was Kitty whose life was most dissimilar to mine. She was the only unmarried one of us. Eliza and Tilly were now both well settled: Tilly had married a prosperous up-and-coming business-man named Peter Sawyer, and had a daughter, and Eliza – well, Eliza had married Emily's brother Andrew, and so had achieved her end in 'catching' a white man. Though she didn't put it as crudely as that: she did love Andrew, and he her; but he was, for her, a trophy, a goal achieved, and her two children could 'pass for white', a term I heard many a time.

Kitty had suitors enough but had, up to now, held back. I had always wondered why, but Kitty did not readily speak of personal matters, and I felt it rude to ask. But now the information had come freely, and from her.

She had first let me into her big secret when Gordon was a baby. Kitty still lived with her mother, a widow, who had a big house and garden in Waterloo Street, and I often took the chil-dren there in the afternoon to let them play and run. And with them all in tow we would walk up to the Sea Wall and stroll along and let the children play in the sand.

On one of those days, Kitty told me her secret. I had dropped a little hint about her own future children, and she had replied, rather bluntly, 'No offence, Winnie – you're doing a marvellous job and I admire you no end – and I love being an aunty to yours. But I couldn't, and I won't.'

'You won't have children?'

'That's right.'

'But then – you won't marry?'

'Oh, maybe I'll marry one day,' she said. 'But it's going to be hard finding a suitable husband, isn't it? They all want children. That's the whole point of marriage, they all seem to think. I do make sure a man who wants to court me is informed right from the start, and they all back away when I tell them. So I don't let myself fall in love. It's that simple. Or that hard.'

'Oh Kitty, I'm so sorry! I hope you—'

'Don't worry, dear. Perhaps there's someone for me out there. It's finding him that is so hard.'

'I'm sure you will! Someone as nice as you shouldn't be alone in life.'

'Well – till then I've got Mama and Papa. And you. And Eliza and Tilly. I'm a lucky woman!'

'And we're lucky to have you.'

And I was. The isolation I felt in Albouystown evaporated when I was with my friends, and I was beginning to understand that my best efforts to penetrate the barriers made by my race and my class – the fact that it was actually a *former* class did not count – would always be in vain. Too deep and bloody were the wounds the white man had cut into the hearts of the slaves and their descendants, too near the surface the anger emanating from those wounds, too ready to explode. They were not ready to forgive my race, and I had no right to demand forgiveness. Even though it was not I who had made those wounds, I represented those who had, and must accept rejection as a stand-in for the truly guilty. I could be as friendly and warm and caring as I wanted, but I could not cross that divide. The best I could hope for was a polite wariness. Even Aunty Dolly, she who had taken pity on me so many years ago and helped me find George when I thought all was lost, would never be a real aunty. Our lives would always be separate.

But these three, Kitty, Eliza and Tilly, the result of irregular relationships between slave-owners and slaves far back in the past, were my friends. They had crossed the divide by dint of blood. Though the wounds of the slave-women once violated, raped, abused must have been as deep as a ravine, they had no doubt loved the children so produced, and so was born that class of cross-breeds, neither one nor the other, striving for upliftment, insecure because of their black blood but ambitious because of their white blood. I longed to argue that all blood is red, but I knew that those arguments were futile. I had been lonely for female friends, and now they were there for me. It was not my task to change them, or educate them, or teach them. I wanted only their friendship.

Emily played on the sidelines of our group. She had been my only friend back when I was Winnie Cox, the sugar planter's daughter. Emily had been my confidante when I first fell in love with George; Emily had helped me run away. Now, like me, she was a married woman; though her husband, of course, was an acceptable member of English society. Emily and Andrew had never been as snobbish as their parents, and as Eliza's sister-in-law she sometimes joined us mothers when, occasionally, we brought our children together to play. But she played with fire in maintaining a friendship with me.

Emily's mother, Mrs Stewart, once my sycophantic admirer, anxious to win my company for her daughter (and perhaps my hand for her son), had turned her coat and been at the forefront of white society's drive to cast me out. She had been furious when Andrew married Eliza, of course, and had blamed it all on me.

Somehow, she had heard of the party Andrew and his friends had been invited to, the party George had attended and at which Andrew and Eliza had met. It had been something of a scandal at the time, and of course it was all my fault.

* * *

Andrew and Eliza, too, had become outcasts; but later on, their children had proved to be a ragged path back to family peace. Eliza, light-skinned as she was, would find reluctant acceptance in white society. It helped that she had a winning personality, quick intelligence and genuine charm. She would make it, as I never would. While a coloured woman marrying a white man could rise into acceptance, it did not work the other way round. I had lowered myself to an irredeemable level in marrying George. Too low, in Emily's mother's eyes, to be her daughter's friend. Yes, we laughed and joked about it, but it hurt all the same. It hurt as did the rift in my own family.

'So are you still not speaking to Yoyo?' Emily asked one day.

I shook my head sadly. 'It's not that I'm not speaking to her. It's that I never see her. It's she who's keeping away from me. I would meet her in a wink – but how can I go to Promised Land with all the children, if George refuses to go? I can't drag five children, including two babies and a wild five-year-old, up there. They would all fall – or jump – off the ferry the moment my back was turned.'

'I still don't understand. Why does George refuse to go? Does Yoyo still reject him, even now?'

I shrugged in frustration.

'It's ridiculous, if you ask me. Yes, Yoyo rejected George at first, but then it seemed that she was making an effort to get to know him. But you know Yoyo – she can be quite rude when she wants to be, and that's what happened. When I was in Venezuela they had some kind of a falling-out. He won't tell me exactly what she said, and Mama – who was there – is quite vague about the whole thing. All she says is that Yoyo was rather condescending and insulting towards George and me. I suppose he took offence. But I think he should forgive and forget. Yoyo is just the way she is. We have to accept her with all her faults. She's still my sister, and I love her.'

'Can't your mother help, somehow?'

'Mama has said she will stay out of our affairs, and she's right to. Yoyo seems to harbour some kind of jealousy towards me and Mama doesn't want to appear to take sides.'

'It seems such a pity. You know, don't you, that Yoyo's in town right now?'

'She is?'

'Yes. My mother saw her at the Georgetown Club last night. She was there with that dreadful friend of hers – the McInnes girl.'

'Margaret Smythe-Collingsworth. Yes, they would be together.'

'Why don't you try to bring about a reconciliation? Try to meet her and talk to her about things?'

I sighed. 'I *have* tried. So many times. I've written to her and begged her to apologise to George for whatever it is she said, but she won't. The effort has to come from her, but she's too proud to make that effort, and George – well, George has his pride too. Until she sincerely apologises he won't forgive. I just wish I knew what happened, what she said.'

'Winnie, darling, you must bring them together. Somehow. It's not good to let a stupid quarrel seethe underground for years and years. It's unhealthy. You must do something. And now's your chance.'

I sighed again. I was so weary, and this tiresome family rift only added to my burden.

'Yes, I suppose I must,' I replied. 'And I suppose it is.'

'I have an idea,' said Emily after a short silence.

'Yes?'

'You know it's Andrew's thirtieth birthday next week, and we're having a big party for him – Eliza and I are organising it, and you and George are invited, of course.'

'We're not coming – I've told you so. What about the children?'

George and I never went to parties any more. With five rambunctious boys and a little girl on the way a party was the last thing on my mind, and of course George wouldn't go anywhere without me. I always gave 'the children' as my excuse not to attend these social affairs, but in all honesty, it was lack of interest.

But Emily only waved her hand in dismissal. 'Oh, the children! Your mother-in-law can take care of them for one night, and you can get one of the neighbourhood girls to help. You need to get out more without the children, Winnie. Really you must. Anyway, you and George will come to the party, and I'll invite Yoyo as well. Then she and George will be forced to at least be polite to each other. The rest will follow. Mark my words.'

'If George knows she'll be there he won't go.'

'But he doesn't have to know, does he? If you don't tell him he won't.'

I hesitated. Much as I longed for the family rift to be bridged, I wasn't sure if manipulating a meeting was the right path to follow. George was so adamant about not speaking to Yoyo – would he appreciate being manoeuvred into a meeting? Was it fair? Shouldn't I wait, and allow time to heal whatever quarrel they had with each other? Was I being a busybody, like Emma in my favourite Jane Austen novel? George was such an easy-going, good-natured fellow – it felt underhand to be plotting him into a situation he had tried so hard to avoid. These things could so easily go wrong – what if there was a huge flare-up between the two of them? With Yoyo, it was entirely possible. Her volatile nature needed only a tiny spark to explode.

'It's not a good idea,' I said finally. 'I want no part of it – not in this underhand way. I mean, I long for them to reconcile, and maybe I'll try to meet Yoyo while she's here, and talk to her again. Try to broker some kind of peace. But not like this – not with a trick.'

Emily's face fell. 'What a pity. All right then. I promise I won't invite Yoyo. But I do want you and George to come. You will, won't you? Just this once.'

I hesitated. I really didn't want to…

'Come on, Winnie. You can't hide away all your life just because you have children! You're young. It will be a change for you.'

…but perhaps I should. Perhaps I needed to go out a little more, meet people. It wasn't as if this would be one of those stiff, snobbish English affairs: Emily and Andrew had friends of all races and colours, and her party would be a lovely escape from the domesticity I had locked myself into. Once, I had loved dances and dresses – why not, just this once? Aunty Dolly could easily whip up a beautiful new frock for me, one that could accommodate my swelling belly. A spark of excitement shot through my body, and I looked up and smiled at Emily.

'Very well,' I said. 'We'll come.'

Chapter Twenty-Five

Ruth

Last week I found my old diary. The one I started when I first met Archie, and continued through all the happy years of our romance, and through the terrible years when everything fell apart. Right up to the moment that Archie discovered it, discovered my betrayal of him, and sent me away.

Somebody seems to have removed it from Archie's desk and hidden it at the back of Winnie's bookshelf, and that 'someone' can only be Winnie herself. That means she must have read it. I blush at the thought. Then Winnie knows! To her credit, she has never spoken a word of the matter to me. What a shock it must have been. But she has always been fond of Jim, so I expect she accepted it eventually. She must have wondered at least a little, though, about my presence here at Promised Land. She must have wondered whether, since my return, Jim and I—

Well, we haven't. That part of our lives is over. It was wild and passionate and necessary while it lasted – we both buried our troubles in the illusion of a Great Love – but that is decidedly over. It was over even before my return to BG. Jim had a new young family, and I had the plantation to sort out, and two daughters to make amends with.

With Winnie, that has already happened. When she summoned me back from exile, her cry for help was a shaft of light plunged into the darkness I had escaped into. It was so easy, finally! The darkness had been a huge black cloud hanging over my true spirit, and Winnie's telegram burst it open, like an abscess. I returned to the chaos waiting for me here, and for the most part it has all gone well. Winnie's growing family gives me great joy – though I wish she would recover from this Gabriella Rose obsession. She has five fine boys and another on the way. Yes, of course this one too will be a boy, but I can't tell her that. She will love him as she loves the others, and no harm done. She enjoys being a mother, and I enjoy being a grandmother, and a mother-in-law. George is a fine man, and he is working hard for his family.

It is Yoyo I worry about. Reading between the lines of that old diary, I realise how much I failed her as a mother. How little I was there for her, pawning her off on Nanny for so many years of her childhood, so that she was closer to Nanny than to me. It's true that Yoyo's nature was not as compatible with mine as was Winnie's; and I know now that she felt that I loved Winnie more. That is far from true. I love my children the same, just in different ways. Kathleen was always independent, and she sailed off to marry in England and she is happy there, closer to Archie's brother's family than she ever was to her own. I love her, but I let her go, as she wanted.

Winnie and I have always been close, apart from during the years of my Darkness. How she must have suffered! But she has forgiven me and those wounds have healed. Reading my diary must have helped her to understand, and so, in spite of my embarrassment, I am glad she knows.

Yoyo is the one to worry about. She is the one to watch. I must find a way back to her heart. There are shadows hiding within it, and she is nurturing those shadows. The shadows have grown darker over the years, and I worry.

* * *

Christmas, five years ago. I remember it so clearly. George was with us, and the Smythe-Collingsworths, and Yoyo was behaving atrociously, flirting openly with George, teasing him, trying to engage with him, provoking him deliberately – the very man she had only a year previously ostracised, rebuked, reviled. A married man. Her brother-in-law! After dinner I pulled her aside and tried to find out what her game was, but she would have none of it.

'I have a headache, Mama. I am going to bed.' And off she went. George looked relieved, but the next morning he was gone, and Yoyo was in a foul mood.

I had my suspicions, but no proof.

Later I discussed it with Jim. Jim and George had always been good friends: father and son, almost. I managed to find out that George had turned up at Jim's house late that night, spent Christmas Day there and gone home the following day. More, Jim would not tell me, though it was plain that he knew more; that George had confided in him.

My suspicions deepened, but I decided to let things rest and stay out of it. It was not my business, after all. Yoyo and George are adults and must know what they are doing. Yoyo can be a predator when she wants to be, but George seems capable of looking out for himself. And he loves Winnie above all else, and would never hurt her. In that I take my comfort.

Yoyo is a different story. She acts without thinking of who might get hurt – and she would hurt her sister without a second thought. She harbours such dark thoughts about Winnie! Once, when I again defended Winnie against an unjust accusation on Yoyo's part, she flew into a rage:

'You always preferred Winnie! Your darling little girl! Your favourite: goody-goody Winnie!'

It shocked me, frankly, but when I tried to argue her face hardened and she refused to speak.

I believe that Yoyo is carrying a deep wound in her heart; and that I am to blame. She was so small when my troubles with Archie started. And yes, I neglected her, and she turned to Nanny, and when I saw her growing closer to Nanny than she was to me I was glad of it! Instead of reassuring her, loving her, holding her, winning her back, I was glad she had found an anchor and I left her in Nanny's capable hands, too wrapped up in myself and my own problems to rescue my daughter's heart. And now we are all paying the price. Yoyo's pain has turned into something vicious, a thorn in her heart that now and then turns into a dagger that she will thrust at anyone who crosses her.

George crossed her that Christmas Eve so long ago. I am sure of it. She has seen neither him nor Winnie for five years; it's not by accident, either. George will not go back to Promised Land, Winnie tells me, and Yoyo, though she goes to Georgetown several times a year, has not made the effort to visit them. Not even at the births of their children. Does that not tell me everything? I am afraid even to put it into words, but Yoyo does not forgive or forget.

Whatever happened that Christmas Eve, it seems to be the night that Yoyo changed. She had been hard even before that, but after that night she became – well, heartless. Yoyo always had a basic kindness towards the labourers – a result of her love for Nanny – but that now turned into an indifference to their welfare. Jim and I had been working on several projects for the labourers: a health centre, a primary school, an old-folks care system. Yoyo had been grudgingly in favour – that is, agreeing in principle but holding back the money – before Christmas. Afterwards, though, she put her foot down and quashed it all. She quarrelled constantly with Jim, telling him he must drive the coolies harder. Jim had cut their work hours when he took over from McInnes; now, Yoyo said, he must once more insist on work from 6 a.m. to 6 p.m., with only a short break for lunch, seven days a week. Pregnant women, who had previously been given four months off before birth and one after, must now work right up to confinement and return three days after. Older workers, allowed to retire at the age of sixty under Jim, must now work until they fell. And so on. Jim is fighting a losing battle.

'If you don't like it you can go!' she screamed at him, and Jim, dear Jim, only replied, mildly, 'Happy workers work better, Yoyo. That is one thing you must learn.'

But she flounced off, and that was the end of that. Jim would have gone voluntarily; he did not need Yoyo's tantrums, and he did not need the job, being a man of independent means. But he was the only buffer between the workers and her. If he went who would come after? Another McInnes, or worse? He reluctantly complied with her new rules, did as she said, and stayed.

I feared that Yoyo was turning into her father. Archie: a good man turned bad.

As I write these words Yoyo is in Georgetown, staying with her friend Margaret. Margaret is McInnes's daughter, and I have never liked her. She has a sly streak to her, a false smile. But she and Yoyo have always been best friends, and Yoyo's trips to Georgetown are becoming longer and longer. It gives us breathing space at Promised Land, to be sure – it's like a holiday when she is gone – but sometimes I wonder what she is up to. Her marriage to Clarence seems to have broken down completely – Clarence, the putative heir of the estate, has re-established himself as the rake he was before coming to BG, drinking, running after dark-skinned maidens, peppering the estate with half-breed urchins. But he is here to stay, and under the terms of the agreement stay he must.

(But I mustn't complain. Clarence is very musical, and he has had his old cello shipped from England. Thus I now have someone to play duets with of an evening. This is heaven, and makes up for many a drunken silliness.)

Yoyo has sent a message from Georgetown to say that she will be staying another week. She and Margaret have been invited to a dinner party. I am glad. It means an extra week of easier breathing.

Chapter Twenty-Six

George

I have found just the property, but I'm not telling her yet; it will be a surprise. It is a large plot of land on Lamaha Street, near the train station. It has several old fruit trees growing on it: mango, and genip, and guava; and the rest of the yard is a bit of a jungle. It has a small one-bedroom house on it, which won't be of any use to us – but the house is in good condition, and we can add to it, make it big enough to fit us all. I am beyond excited, jumping for joy within, but I can't speak of it yet – I need to make sure it can really be ours before I get her hopes up only to dash them again. I have reached an agreement with the owner as to price. A little above our budget but we can do it. Tomorrow I have an appointment with the bank manager, and I pray with all my might. I have been saving so rigorously over the past five years… I worry only that he might think I am overstepping my boundaries. Cummingsburg is a high step up from Albouystown. This house will place us firmly in the domain of coloured middle class. The bank manager, being white, might not approve.

* * *

Oh joy! The loan has been approved! The conversation went something like this:

Him: *Mr Quint, your name seems familiar, somehow. Have we met before?*

Me: *No sir. Not as far as I can recall.*

There are, after all, very few occasions on which someone like me meets someone like him. We live in different worlds, different universes. I can count the white men I have ever spoken to on one hand, and Uncle Jim is one of them.

Him: *But that name, that name – George Quint. I know I've heard it before.*

My blood froze. I knew where he had heard that name before. Seven years ago, before the trial of Winnie's father, my face and my name were splashed all over the newspapers. Me, carrying a sign screaming for Justice – Justice, against a white man! White society rallied for their own, and I was the enemy… I knew then that I could say goodbye to the loan, to the house, to our future. I remained silent. I was not going to remind him. Let him remember on his own. Why should I aid and abet the crashing of all my dreams?

Then suddenly, he pounded the desk with his fist.

Him: *I know! I've got it! I remember!*

My heart crashes to the ground. This is it. The end.

Him: *Your wife! Is her name Winnie?*

Me (questioningly): *Yes?*

Him: *She makes a guava jelly called Quintessentials, doesn't she?*

Me: *Yes?*

Him: *She was here, many years ago, applying for a small loan so that she could expand. She brought me a jar of that jelly, and some other things too – pepper sauce – too hot for me – pickles and what-not. My wife – she was ecstatic! Your wife is a remarkable woman, you know! Such an easy charm, she has. She gave me the samples, told me to take them home and try them, and she'd be back a week later. She was, and she got her loan. Winnie Quint. How could I forget! A remarkable woman.*

Me: *She is.*

Him: *My wife told me a bit about her. Said she'd married a black man, a George Quint. That's how I remembered your name. My wife loved the jam but disapproved of the marriage, turned up her nose. Told me a bit about some murder trial – the usual gossip. You know what most women are like. Gossip, gossip, gossip, and bad-talking each other. Your wife is different. Me, I thought the marriage only confirmed what a remarkable woman she is. Shows bravery, it does. And you must be a remarkable man.*

Me: *Thank you, sir. I'm lucky to have her.*

Him: *Well, I can see how hard you've saved over the years, how well you've managed your money. And you want to buy a house for her, you say? I think you deserve each other. And you deserve to get your house. Yes, of course you can have the loan. I'll get the papers drawn up – come back next week.*

I walked out of that bank dazed and stumbling, as if drunk. I could hardly ride my bicycle. I wanted to sing and shout and dance! But all I did was ride down to the property and gaze at it in longing. It is ours – I know it is! It is perfect. Just a ten-minute walk up Camp Road to the Sea Wall. Round the corner are the beautiful Promenade Gardens. Queen's College, a five-minute bicycle ride away – all my boys will go there! They will all become doctors and lawyers. They will win scholarships, as I did, but do something with their education, as I didn't.

Round the other corner, a few blocks southwards and to the west, is Bishops' High School, the best girls' school in the country; round the other corner, a few blocks down, is St Rose's High School, Catholic. If we ever have a girl we must choose…

I can still hardly contain my joy, and it is the hardest thing not to burst out with it, to tell her. But still I must wait. There are some legal issues concerning the ownership of the property; the previous owner died a month ago and it is still under probate – a question about the will being contested. My heart is in my mouth. I fear it will all fall apart at the last moment, and I cannot let Winnie rejoice only to disappoint her again. No, I will wait until the last signature has been signed and the house is ours. A home for us all! I am even beginning to believe that the baby is a girl. That Winnie is right, this time. That Gabriella Rose is on her way to us.

* * *

I feel so bad that I have denied Winnie her visits to the home she loves so much, Promised Land. But I cannot go back there, ever. Not after that terrible Christmas Eve, when Yoyo showed her true colours. And it tears my heart apart that I must keep the truth of that visit a secret from my wife.

It has taken all my skill and all my wiles to deflect her from that truth. I invented a quarrel with Yoyo; that is, I exaggerated the little spat we had had that time over dinner, and made it into a conflagration, a fully-fledged quarrel, one that I could never overcome unless Yoyo apologised. I made her believe I was stubborn and unforgiving. I even allowed her to believe .that Yoyo had insulted me about my race. I didn't lie directly, but when she asked I hung my head and pretended to be too insulted to talk about it. I knew she'd jump to that conclusion. I'd let her believe anything rather than tell her the truth about what happened.

Because telling her the truth would destroy her inviolable trust in her sister. How could I shatter her illusions? Winnie holds Yoyo in such high estimation. Yoyo is everything Winnie is not: assertive where Winnie is accommodating, outspoken where Winnie is tactful, uninhibited where Winnie is discreet. Winnie admires her sister no end; yes, she knows that Yoyo has faults, but she minimises those faults and sees them only as minor flaws. How could I tear away that image of near perfection?

And so I allow her to believe that it is only my stubbornness that prevents reconciliation, and a visit to Promised Land. I foster this belief, make it the sole cause of my refusal to visit Yoyo, and we have never gone back, for five long years. Every year, especially around Christmas, we have this little argument, and every year there is one more little boy to complicate matters.

There is some risk in this strategy – what if Winnie approaches Yoyo and tries to get her to apologise? Yoyo might laugh and tell her the truth – that really it was just a short exchange of words, a few mild insults. What if she indeed apologises, laughs them off, mocks me for taking offence when none was intended? I'm fairly certain she won't tell Winnie what actually *did* happen – Yoyo certainly wouldn't want Winnie to know the extent of her betrayal. But – what if she lies? Winnie herself has told me that Yoyo is careless with the truth. What if Yoyo tells her that *I* tried to seduce *her*? Who would she believe?

These thoughts have plagued me all through the years. And the guilt, that Winnie is kept from the beautiful house that was once her home and must live in a cramped cottage. But all that is going to change. I shall build her a home as beautiful as Promised Land.

* * *

I came home later that afternoon, trying hard to wipe the grin from my face. For how could I explain it? Winnie can read me like a book – what would I do when she asked what was making me so happy? What would I say? And so, as solemn as could be, I wheeled my bicycle through the gate and into the shed. But Winnie was already halfway down the stairs.

'George, wherever have you been? You're so late! I've been waiting and waiting!'

I no longer had to try to be solemn. Her stern voice wiped the smile from my face.

'Sorry, dear, I-I was held up at work, and—'

'Oh, I don't want to hear the whole story – just hurry up now and get ready. We're running late!'

'Late? What for?'

'Oh *George*. So you *have* forgotten. It's Andrew's birthday party! Remember? I told you about it last week. It's tonight!'

The words wiped the last remnants of joy from my soul. Andrew's birthday party. Yes, she had told me last week and we had almost quarrelled, for I did not want to go. All those white people!

'Oh George! You always accuse the English of being racist but you're just as bad.'

Would she ever understand the difference? When the English reject us it's because they consider themselves better, us inferior. When we reject them, it's because we know this, and prefer to avoid their sneers. I'd explained this to her a thousand times but try as she might, she could not bridge the gap.

'You could at least *try!* And not everyone is going to be white. There's Eliza, and her friends. Kitty and Tilly will be there, and Tilly's husband – as dark as you. This is the most open-minded group of English in the whole colony – you could at least try. Nobody is going to look down on you. They're my friends, you know. I really want to go out a bit more. I need to – I need the change!'

And that's the argument that changed my mind. Winnie did need to go out more, by herself, without the children. Just the two of us. When was the last time we'd gone anywhere together, just us? I couldn't recall. And tonight it wouldn't be just us either – really, I would have preferred a quiet dinner somewhere, or a walk just with Winnie, rather than a party. But she needed this, and how could I have forgotten? All weekend she'd been excited about the dress. A dress that would flatter her while concealing her condition as much as possible. Aunty Dolly came and measured her – in the sixth month of pregnancy, Winnie of course had quite a bulge – and the two of them had spent hours bent over a women's magazine discussing styles and cuts and so on. Women's matters. Winnie purchased yards and yards of some shiny green material at Fogarty's, and it was to be her first new party dress since the wedding. I assumed it was finished now – I had not thought of it, or the party, for days. I had agreed to go, and promptly forgotten.

'Anyway, you're here now. So hurry up – you need to bathe! I've laid out your best clothes for you.'

'Where are the boys?'

Usually by this time the boys would be climbing all over me, screaming *daddydaddydaddy*, grabbing my hands, pulling me in four different directions. Today the house was quiet. No boys, no screaming babies.

'Oh George, I told you this morning! Don't shake your head – I did remind you. The big boys are with the Barrows and the babies are with Ma – she's taken them to a neighbour so they'll be out of our way. Now here's a towel – hurry up and bathe.'

She thrust a towel at me and I did as I was told. The bathroom was in the backyard – how Winnie would rejoice at the new house and its indoor plumbing! – and I took my time, washing off the sweat and the grime of the day under the cool spray, lathering the soap into a fragrant foam. I took my time – Winnie's vexation was shallow, that I knew, and there was still plenty of time. My happiness had returned. I thought of the house that was to be, and how delighted she would be when at last I broke the news. I closed my eyes and held my face up to the shower head, letting the water wash away the suds from my face. A silent prayer rose in my heart: *Thank you, Lord. Oh thank you thank you thank you.*

By the time I was bathed and dry, and back in the house with the towel wrapped round my hips, Winnie was dressed and Aunty Dolly had arrived to prepare Winnie's face and hair. Aunty Dolly had once worked for an elegant English lady and knew all about fixing the hair of white women.

There was plenty of time. It was a mystery why Winnie had been so frantic at my lateness. If only I could have told her the true reason! I dressed, poured myself a glass of lime juice from

the jug and settled down in the gallery with today's newspaper. I
read the news and then picked up a pencil to do the crossword.
I could hear Winnie and Aunty Dolly discussing hair styles and
lipstick colours over the partition walls to the bedrooms. I smiled
to myself at some of the conversation.

'That belly nice and round! And low! Is another boy, I tellin'
yuh, Miss Winnie!'

I could hear Winnie's confident smile in her response.

'Don't tease me, Aunty. You know as well as I do that *this* time
it's a girl!'

'Don't count you chickens before they hatch. Is not good to
get too cocky about the tings we want. When we get too cocky
the Lord does step in to make we humble again. Dorothy daughter was seven months gone and she start to bleed and lose the
pickney. Better not to—'

'Oh, Aunty, don't say things like that, please! You scare me!'

'All right darlin'. Sorry. But you'se a strong woman. A good
strong woman, and you done had five babies already with not a
problem. Everything gon' be all right. Here, take the mirror and
see if it all right at the back.'

'Oh Aunty, it's beautiful. Thank you so much! I must show
George. George! George, come!'

I sprang to my feet and hastened to the bedroom. I stood in
the threshold, speechless with wonder. Aunty Dolly had worked
magic on my wife. She stood there in her glistening green dress,
looking like a queen, radiant, exquisite, utterly and completely
glorious. Her lips, stained a subtle pink, bowed in a smile and her
eyes were like jewels. I wanted to rush forward and take her in my
arms. Instead I only gaped. She would surely be the most beautiful
woman at the party tonight – and that despite, or maybe because
of, the beautiful protruding roundness of her belly. I could hardly
believe that this was my wife. I was the luckiest man in the world.

Little did I know that I was just about to ruin everything.

* * *

The coach came and it was time to go. All of my worries had flown by this time; I was proud, so proud of my beautiful wife, proud of escorting her to the ball; tonight she was my queen, and I was in a fairytale, and it had all come true. I had married the princess. What had I done to deserve such luck? My misgivings at attending this white-people party had all fled; in the coach Winnie and I laughed and cuddled and flirted and then I placed my hands on the tight round swell of her belly and closed my eyes and she was still and it was the most perfect moment of my life; the three of us, Winnie and me and the soul of our unborn child united in a place where there were no bodies separating us, just a single blissful soul.

The Stewarts lived in Kingston, near the sea. Once Winnie and I had bought our property and built our house we would be just a stone's throw from them – walking distance. I had met Andrew once before, and of course I knew Eliza. They were good people, kind, like us a mixed-race couple, though reversed. Of course, it was much easier when the man was white and chose a coloured woman as his spouse. There would never be the accusation of *him* rising above *his* station; instead, he had lifted *her* up. Eliza would never have to face the revulsion and rejection Winnie had; by dint of her husband's skin colour, she would slowly but surely find her place in a higher echelon of society. It is the man who determines the woman's position. Andrew lifted Eliza up; I dragged Winnie down.

But all that was going to change. I realised now how selfish I had been refusing to socialise with these higher-positioned folk. Yes, their acceptance of me was hesitant and probably in some cases grudging: but if it was my aim to lift Winnie out of the squalor of Albouystown then I must accept the condescension that would inevitably accompany her movement upwards. And I do accept it. Tonight is the beginning.

* * *

Looking back on the events of that terrible night I can only say I was living in a fool's paradise, lost in wishful thinking that blinded me to the stark reality of who I was and where I stood. There is something in me that perhaps will always be lowly; something in me that knows my position and will always bow when the white man – or woman – passes by. That will always be in thrall to the command of a white voice. That will *come* when a white finger beckons. It is ingrained in me; it flows in my blood; the child in a slave-mother's womb feels her fear and absorbs it into his soul; and that fear is passed along from generation to generation.

But that night I thought no deep thoughts. I knew only pride as I stepped into that drawing room, Winnie on my arm; and that pride swelled yet more as heads turned and conversation hushed and faces lit up in admiration.

Eliza rushed forward, arms held out.

'Winnie! You came! Naughty girl, you're ten minutes late and I was beginning to worry. And George! Welcome, welcome. I'm so glad you made it!'

Then Andrew too, came forward, hand held out for mine, and smiling. He led us to the group of people standing at the back of the room and introduced them, one by one, and I could see right here how the rigid lines were softening. At least half of the guests were of mixed blood – mostly women, admittedly, and I was the darkest of them all – and as they all, every one of them, welcomed me with genuine warmth the last of my inhibitions fled. Georgetown society was changing. Could it be that one day there would be nothing remarkable in a mixed-race marriage? What a joyous time that would be!

Andrew looked at his watch. 'Four more guests to come, and then we'll move to the dining room,' he said, and turned to Winnie. 'Why, you know one of the guests, from back in the day. Remember how we all used to play together? Margaret McInnes, and her new husband, Jeremy Smythe-Collingsworth – I ran into them at a friend's house this week, and invited them on the spur of the moment. She asked if she could bring a friend along – she has a house-guest. I've no idea who it is, but—'

At just that moment the doorbell rang. The housegirl opened it, and in swanned Margaret Smythe-Collingsworth, followed by her husband and…

Yoyo had always known how to make an entrance and she did it now. She swept in, all wide flouncing skirts of rustling red satin, cast her cold dead eyes around the room, and, the moment they lit on Winnie, she strode forward with the smile of an imposter painted on her face.

'Winnie! How lovely to see you here! I haven't seen you – why, in donkey's years! And George! Dear George! What a surprise!'

In that moment I knew that this had all been planned. Rage rose within me – although against whom I did not know. Had Winnie planned it? No, that couldn't be. The anxiety with which she looked at me, the embarrassment in her stuttered response, the pain in her eyes – no, Winnie would never be party to such a trick.

Eliza? But she too looked flustered and abashed, as if she knew that something was wrong; that Yoyo and I are not supposed to be in the same room – ever. Nobody does know why as far as I'm concerned; except, of course, for Uncle Jim, and Yoyo herself. Had Yoyo told others? Surely not – surely she would not spread a scandalous tale that painted her in a bad light! But with Yoyo you never knew. Quite possibly she had told Margaret Smythe-Collingsworth . Yes, I was sure she had. That smug smile, that fevered excitement in Margaret's eyes as I glanced at her told me everything. She knew. This was planned. In that moment I knew that I was the prey tonight. Yoyo was out for revenge. What's that they say about a woman scorned?

* * *

I had sworn to myself never to set eyes on that woman again. Never to speak to her. Never to look again into those calculating ice-blue eyes. But she had other plans. She planted herself right in front of me and said, in that false, high-pitched voice of hers, 'Well, *hello*, George! We meet again!'

What could I do but smile? I avoided her eyes but still I felt the frozen dagger of her glare. I turned and walked away, and she cackled behind me. Glacial talons closed around my soul. If what we fear and what we loathe is what holds us bound – well, Yoyo was about to prove it. It was as if I had, right then, even though I walked away, a premonition of what was to come. That I could no more prevent it than I could prevent the sunrise the next morning. That I was doomed.

Yet as the night wore on I relaxed, for Yoyo kept away from me. I told myself that she had done her bit, and it was over; that she had seen my fear, and was satisfied. My senses were all alert and I heard her voice, loud and commanding, as she chatted with her table partner. I heard that distinguishing cackle again and again, but far from me, and as, later on, we stood to move to the drawing room for dancing, I was relieved to see that she had hooked her arm possessively into that of the gentleman she had arrived with – a tall thin white man I had been introduced to, but whose name I had forgotten.

The Stewarts had a new thing: it was called a gramophone, and with it one could play music on flat round discs called records. It was the newest invention from America, and it was miraculous, almost as miraculous as telegraphy. There were only a few of these gadgets in the colony; Andrew had procured his through a distant cousin in America. He turned out to be as fascinated as I was by the technology of it, and he and I struck up a conversation on the subject and stood next to it, talking excitedly.

Someone pressed a glass of rum punch into my hand. I took a sip and gasped at the strength of it, and Andrew laughed. I found him not only keen but genuinely friendly and I came to the conclusion that Uncle Jim was not the only white man I might trust. Perhaps tonight really was a breakthrough for Winnie and myself – perhaps we would one day find acceptance in a different, more tolerant set. I hoped so.

As I chatted with Andrew the music played and couples danced. Winnie, I saw, was enjoying herself. She did try to prise me away from Andrew, but half-heartedly; she knew I couldn't waltz. I had never danced in my life! Not this kind of European dancing. She seemed happy, anyway, dancing with the other gentlemen. From the corners of my eyes I could see her, laughing with abandon as she swirled past. Now and then I glimpsed the red shine of Yoyo's gown, flashing flags to alert me of distant danger. But the rum punch was delicious and as I finished the glass another full one appeared as if by magic in my hand, and I nipped at that too. I was not used to alcohol and I found the sense of light floating pleasant. How stupid I had been! How irrational my fears! A sort of relaxed excitement drifted through my body, warm and soothing. Andrew cracked a joke and I laughed loudly. I completely forgot that he was white and I was black. I told a few jokes of my own and he laughed too. We could be friends; we would be friends! Eliza and Winnie, Andrew and I. When our house was built we would invite them over. I was so happy I could not help it – I began to drop hints about our future house. My head was light; I was in love with the world. What was that, another full glass, my empty one vanished? I nipped at it in complete and utter satisfaction. Yes, that was the word. Satisfaction, deep and warm. Wanting for nothing.

After a while I felt a pressure in my groin and I discreetly asked Andrew the way to the bathroom. Upstairs, he said.

'Wait here – I'll be back!' I said and stepped away.

Up the stairs I went, found the lavatory and relieved myself. It felt so good. These people had electric lights in their house.

I was completely amazed. All one had to do was pull on a cord and the light went on, pull it again, and it went off. On, off, on, off. I laughed and played with it for some time. How technology was advancing! When we built our home we would have all the latest inventions. Radio and a telephone, and a gramophone so that Winnie could play European music and waltz as much as she wanted. She could teach me to waltz too – I would learn! And she would play the violin again. Electric lights. Of course, a motor-car! And we would have a dog. Five boys and a girl – the perfect family! We would walk out to the Sea Wall every afternoon.

I left the light on and walked over to the mirror. My head was spinning – I felt a little dizzy, and stumbled as I walked. I looked at myself in the mirror. I smiled at myself. I've never been vain – I always assumed I was ugly. But looking at my reflection now, I had to say: not a bad-looking chap I was. Giddy gladness swept through me. My body was relaxed, loose, free. I must go back to Andrew and ask him about the gadgetry in his house so that I knew how to put it in mine.

I opened the door, pulled the cord and switched off the light as I went out into the upstairs hallway. Strangely, it was in darkness. I could have sworn the light had been on when I came upstairs. Where would the switch be? I would need the bathroom light to be able to see. I opened the door again and pulled the cord. The light came on and shone out into the hallway. I stepped out into the half-light.

She was waiting for me, standing in the darkness. The red-ness of her dress glimmered in the half-light cast from the open doorway, but her face was in shadow. I didn't see the redness at first; I walked straight into her and stumbled. She cackled as she gripped and righted me.

'What on earth were you doing in there so long, George? I've been waiting ages!'

My entire body froze, including my brain. All my thoughts stopped and the dizziness fled. Breath stood still for those few moments of shock. I was an empty vessel, without thought and without will. Her body pressed into mine, forcing me against the wall. Her hands wandered up and down it. At last, words came.

'No – I—' But her mouth was on mine, her lips forcing mine apart. I shook my head but her hands moved up and held it steady. I could not help it – my body was reacting in a way I did not want but could not prevent. She moved her mouth away. Her hands busied themselves.

'No,' I moaned again, 'no. No.' She only laughed in glee.

'Yes,' she said. 'See, George – you want it. You know you do!'

And before I knew it she had pushed me along the wall and a door appeared at my back from nowhere; and then the door was open and then she turned the knob and pressed me through the threshold into the room and slowly backwards into the darkness, fumbling with my belt and the opening of my trousers, and though I kept moaning *no* I didn't know if I meant it or not, I only felt this power under whose sway I was; a helpless puppet and she was the puppeteer. And I was helpless. Weak. Completely and utterly subject to her will, a will that conjured reactions that my mind rejected but my body refused to accept. There was me and my body but my body was hers, not mine. And though my brain was awake and screaming *nonononono*, my body was not my own. It was hers and in her hands and we were on the bed and doing something I should not be doing but I could no more stop than I could stop a hurricane and it was sweet and terrible and tremendous and beyond my control and it was all dark and I could not see her face but then all of a sudden there was a sound and a light came on from outside and I jerked to a stop and looked up and there was Winnie standing in the doorway and though her face was in shadow I knew the horror on it for horror was in her scream.

And mine.

Yoyo looked up, turned her eyes to the door and laughed.

Chapter Twenty-Seven

Winnie

The nightmare will be with me for the rest of my life.

I didn't see much in the half-light. Just a tangle of red satin and black naked flesh I recognised as George. I had looked for him everywhere; someone suggested he might have been tired and gone to lie down. He had been drinking one glass of punch after the other, and George is not used to drink. So I had decided to look in the bedrooms. Andrew switched on the upstairs lights for me, and up the stairs I went, in my last moments of carefree innocence.

The black naked flesh I saw, legs and buttocks, from the back, was my husband's. The red satin was Yoyo's dress. The long white bare legs, hers.

* * *

I screamed and turned and fled. Down the hallway, to the top of the stairs. Down the stairs. But I had forgotten the folds of my beautiful new green dress and my feet caught in the petticoat halfway down and I missed my footing and screamed as I tumbled down the last ten steps.

My belly bounced against the edges of the stairs. Both hard, but only one yielding.

'My baby!' I moaned as my body bounced downwards, a ragdoll helpless against gravity.

'My baby!' I cried as I landed in a heap at the foot of the stairs.

'My baby! My baby!' My hands pressed against my belly to keep her safe, but already I knew.

They all gathered around me. Hands reached out to me. They called my name. Calls of 'Are you all right?' 'Are you hurt?' And all I could mumble was 'My baby!'

'I'll get the car!' Andrew's anxious voice, in the distance.

More voices.

'She needs to go to hospital. She might have broken something.'

'Andrew's getting the car.'

'At least she's alive!'

'My baby!' I moaned.

And suddenly in the chaos, his voice, his face, pleading, terrified, horrified; his hands reaching out too, but I slapped them away. 'Winnie, Winnie, Winnie!' he cried and he was weeping as I had never seen him weep before.

They lifted me up, very carefully, and as they carried me away I looked up and past George's face, and I saw, at the top of the stairs, her. My sister. Yoyo. Smiling triumphantly, a vision in red.

And then the world turned black.

* * *

When I came to I was in the hospital ward, giving birth.

'No!' I screamed when I realised what was happening. 'No, please, no!'

Doctors and nurses in white and blue uniforms busied themselves with my nether regions. One nurse looked me in the face and said, to the others, 'She's back,' and to me, 'It's all right, dear. You're in good hands.'

Her face was black and shiny and reminded me of Aunty Dolly. Her eyes were kind but filled with woe.

'My baby!' I wailed. 'Save my baby! Please, please, save my baby!'

'I'm sorry, dear,' is all the nurse said. She squeezed my hand.

'Here it comes,' said someone and I felt something slide easily from my body.

They held that something, passing from hand to hand. I caught a glimpse of it. It looked like a skinned rabbit.

'A girl,' said someone else.

'Poor little thing. What a pity!' murmured another voice.

I tried to sit up but 'Aunty Dolly' pushed me back. 'Be calm, dear. Be calm.'

I flung away her would-be comforting hands and reached out for my daughter. My Gabriella Rose. I fought away other hands trying to push me back down. I sat up and, moaning and wailing, stretched out my empty arms.

'Give her to me! Give her!'

'It's better not, dear. It's better not to—'

'I want her!' I screamed. 'Give her to me!'

They looked at each other and then they laid my poor little naked baby in my arms. My dead little girl. My dearly beloved daughter. I wrapped her in a sheet and cuddled her and wept and wailed and then they took her gently from me and thankfully I must have fainted because that's the last thing I remember, gentle hands taking my dead baby from me.

When I came to I was in another room and all cleaned up. A nurse was holding my wrist, taking my pulse. It was a private room, clean and airy, the wooden walls painted a cheerful yellow. I realised then that I was in Dr van Sluytman's private hospital. I had given birth in this hospital several times, recovered in this room. Another nurse entered.

'Ah, she's awake,' she said. 'Dear, your husband is outside, in the corridor. I'll go and call him in.'

'NO!' I cried. 'Keep him out! Don't let him near me! Ever!'

And that is all I can say of that night of nightmares. There are no words to describe what was going on in my soul. No words.

Words are feeble little things compared to the power of sheer devastation.

All that remains is tears. The moment I was alone again they exploded out of me, bursting through the membrane of polite pride that had held me together till now. Wailing sobbing heaving ugly brow-beating hair-pulling body-writhing screaming end-of-the-world tears.

Chapter Twenty-Eight

Ruth

Yoyo has caused the scandal of the young century with her behaviour – and she doesn't give a hoot. In fact she seems to be enjoying it all.

The news reached me the very next day, by telegram, sent by a desperate George. I hurried down to Georgetown with Poole. By that time all that was left of Winnie was a puddle of tears. Yoyo, I heard, had already left town and was on her way back to Promised Land. We must have passed each other on the way. In fact, I vaguely remember seeing a car just like hers racing past me towards Berbice, and shaking my head at the careless driving. That must have been her, running away from the mess.

First of all there were the boys to take care of. George's mother was doing the best she could but her relief was palpable as she opened the door to me. I was torn in four directions: George, Winnie, the children and, perhaps most of all, Yoyo: they all needed attention. One by one I dealt with them: Humphrey, bless his soul, was a great help with the older boys, and took them to a neighbour's house. That's how it works in Albouystown: neighbours help neighbours. I hired two girls to help Ma with the babies, and went to the hospital to see Winnie who was, at this time, beyond help and comfort and support.

I could understand that.

I too had lost a much-wanted unborn child. A little boy. My Edward John, never forgotten. That loss, and my reaction to it, might be at the root of all our troubles today. Edward John was today's Gabriella Rose. In those first few days – I remembered clearly – outside support would have been useless. The bereaved mother must go through that particular fire on her own. I could be of no help to Winnie.

But George. Back at the house, George told me his story amid sobs and breast-beating self-reproach. I believed his every word, because I knew Yoyo and had seen her behaviour at Promised Land and I remembered that Christmas, so many years ago. What had happened then had remained, a landmine between Yoyo and George. It was bound to go off one day. That it had happened so publicly was our bad luck. But Winnie knew nothing of Yoyo's behaviour that Christmas. We had all done our best to protect her from the truth, George, me and Yoyo herself. That kindness, as we had thought of it, would complicate matters now no end; Winnie still lived in blissful admiration of Yoyo and allowed no criticism of her sister. Yoyo could do no wrong in her eyes; Winnie actually believed that the silent war between her husband and her sister was all down to George's stubbornness and pride. Winnie believed in fairytale endings; for years she had longed for these two to be friends. How could we tell her now that Yoyo was the guilty party here, and George the innocent?

* * *

George. The story he told me was dreadful, but it rang with truth. I knew my youngest daughter. And I knew George. I reached out, took his hand, and said, *I believe you, George.*

I took him into my arms and he wept like a baby against my breast, and I comforted him like a baby. That was when the knock came at the door. The older boys were at a neighbour's and Ma had taken the troop of little ones to the gardens, so it was I who opened the door.

A policeman stood on the landing. When he saw me he removed his cap.

'Good day, ma'am. I'm here to see Mr George Quint.'

I straightened my back and glared at him.

'And why would you want to see Mr Quint?'

'Ma'am, I am not in a position to pass on information to third parties. Is Mr Quint at home?'

I made a quick decision. Opening the door wide, I said, 'Come in.'

I led him into the gallery where George still sat weeping in the Berbice chair.

'George,' I said, 'This gentleman would like a word with you.'

George looked up, his face tear-streaked. His eyes were still watery. I gestured to the officer to take a seat but he remained standing.

'Good morning, Mr Quint. I'm here in connection with an incident that occurred Saturday night last. A witness has reported an… an attack. Sir, you have been accused of indecently assaulting a young lady and I would like to question you.'

'What? Assault? *He's* supposed to have assaulted *her?* Who told you that rubbish? It was the other way round!'

'Ma'am, if you don't mind, please let the gentleman speak for himself.'

But I would not let this go. I needed to get my words on record. George was in no position to defend himself at this moment.

'Let me tell you this, young man! The lady in question – and I'm not sure if the description "lady" is even appropriate – is *my daughter* and I have every right to give my opinion as a character witness – is the guilty party here. Write it down right there on your little pad: this man is innocent.'

The officer chuckled and shook his head.

'Since when are women capable of raping men?'

He chuckled a little more, obviously amused by the very notion.

'So now this has changed from indecent assault to *rape?*' George howled in anguish as I said those words. I turned to him. 'Don't worry, George. It will be all right.'

'Ma'am, please let me ask this gentleman my questions.'

'No. This man is innocent and should not be subjected to such a ridiculous rigmarole. Don't think I don't know what is going on here. It's not only that a *woman* might be guilty of assaulting a man – it's that a *white woman* could never, ever, not in a thousand years, ever assault a black man. Is that not the problem here?'

'Ma'am—'

'Who reported this? Yoyo herself? A witness, you said? What witness? Who? Many people were at that party. But nobody was in the room with them.'

'Ma'am, I am not at liberty to say. If you would just allow me to—'

For the first time, George spoke up.

'Mama – let me talk to him. Please. I can explain it all.'

My fury fled immediately at his words. He sounded calm and in control. Very well, I would leave him to it. All he had to do was tell his story, just as he had told it to me. So I retrieved my hat from the hat-rack and went out. I decided to go to see Winnie again, and Poole drove me to the hospital.

* * *

'She's no better,' a nurse told me. 'We've given her tranquillisers, so she's asleep now, but the shock is deep and the moment they wear off and she remembers, it's the same. Hysterics no end.'

Since there was nothing I could do for Winnie I went to visit the Stewarts. I liked both Andrew and Eliza and I hoped they could give me a neutral report of what had happened.

To my delight that visit confirmed my own suspicions. Eliza was alone at home. When she heard about the police visit she immediately placed a telephone call (the Stewarts had all the latest inventions; I looked on in amazement) to her husband, who was, of course, I remembered, a lawyer; when she returned her face was drawn.

'This could be serious, Andrew says,' she said. 'George should not have spoken to the police without a solicitor present. Andrew is going to George's place right now to sort things out. And he'll get it sorted. Don't worry,' she went on when I opened my mouth to speak, 'He'll work for free; George is a friend.'

* * *

By midday the rumour was running wild in Georgetown's high society: George had raped Yoyo. It seemed, to some people, thoroughly impossible that a white woman would willingly have done what Yoyo is supposed to have done with a black man. No. He must have attacked her, forced her into submission.

Those who knew her, and those who had been present at the party, only laughed at that suggestion and shook their heads. But there was no proof, and as yet no accusation from Yoyo herself. A witness, the officer had said. Someone had reported a rape. But as yet there was no evidence of anything. They had only this: George, Yoyo and Winnie upstairs. Winnie running downstairs, tripping and falling. But that, it seemed, was enough fuel to fan the fire of rumour, and George's imaginary crime was on every white person's lips.

* * *

The next day George was hauled before a judge, a white judge. Andrew was with him, armed with witness statements. These, together with George's utter devastation, must have been convincing enough for, pending Yoyo's statement, he was not charged.

I wondered, for a moment, if she would go so far as to confirm rape. Had I raised such a monster? Or rather, had I NOT raised such a monster? I knew that a rape charge was the only way to save her reputation, whatever was left of it. She had stood laughing at the top of the stairs, witnesses from the party confirmed, and that, perhaps, is what convinced the judge that there might be some truth in George's story.

That evening a message arrived, special delivery, from the telegraph department. George had been suspended from duty pending the outcome of criminal investigations.

It was the last straw for George.

'How will I maintain my family? How will I find work? It's not true! It's not true! I didn't assault her, it was she, she who – what will Winnie say? What if they send me to prison, Ma? What if she lies, what if I am tried and convicted? Isn't that what she will want?'

'Shush, George, don't worry. We will all work to clear your name. Soon you'll be back at the job.'

I wondered, though. Once a man has such a rumour attached to his name – even if it is proven untrue – can he ever free himself from the cloud of doubt hanging over his head? There will always be whispers, rumours.

Then another outburst:

'The bank! The bank!' he cried out. 'I've lost everything! Everything! Our house!'

Bit by bit, the story came out. George had been saving for a down payment on a house, and had found just the place, on Lamaha Street. He had been just about to sign for a bank loan; it was to be his big surprise for Winnie, her birthday present next week.

'If I lose my job I can't get the loan,' he sobbed.

'Don't worry about the loan,' I said, stroking his hand. George had long slim hands; the hands of a pianist. He had a musical streak; with a few more advantages he would certainly have mastered more sophisticated instruments than the banjo. 'If the worst comes to the worst, I'll buy the house. You can pay me back at your leisure. But it won't come to that. I will speak to Yoyo. I won't let this happen, George. I promise. Yoyo is naughty but she's not a devil.'

He shook his head and said nothing, as if he disagreed with those last words. But then he looked up with eyes bleeding anguish and said, 'If you can help me save the house, Mama… if it comes to that – if I lose my job – if they try me and find me guilty – oh Mama! It's not just the house. It's everything. You can't save my marriage and that is a thousand times more than my job or the house. It's my all!'

I continued to stroke his hand, and all I could say was 'Shush, George, Shush. Winnie will calm down and when she hears the true story she will forgive you. She will. I know it.'

'But – the baby! The baby! It was all she wanted! She will never forgive me for that!'

That is indeed troublesome. That little girl lost. How will Winnie ever recover? Ever find it in her heart to forgive George for THAT loss? His faithlessness can be explained and forgiven; the consequences of this tragedy will remain for ever. I knew from my own loss that a mother can never recover fully from losing a child – and I knew that Winnie might well pin the blame on George.

But I am a mother, and a grandmother. Mothers contain a power in them, the power to put together the pieces of their child's heart. The power to heal. The power, sometimes, to pull out the weeds from a soul that is all a-tangle, weeds that have been allowed to grow; no, nurtured and nourished until they strangle every noble impulse in that child's heart. *Mother* is a not only a noun: it's a verb. An *active* verb. I had not done much mothering when my girls were growing. I had to do it now.

In my children's youth I had not been mother enough. I had failed them. For years I had been in withdrawal from my role in their lives. Winnie had weathered those years well enough, and grown into her own woman as a result. But Yoyo. Yoyo had pretended not to care but perhaps, deep inside, she did. Perhaps my neglect was the barren earth that had allowed these weeds in Yoyo's heart to grow; weeds that now strangle the truth of who she is, that have allowed this second Yoyo, this ugly parody of herself, to flourish. If my neglect was the root cause, so, perhaps, my care now can provide the balm that will heal.

I am Yoyo's mother. I must save her from the weeds that are smothering her. *Mother* is contained in *smother.* I must un-smother Yoyo, or die doing so.

* * *

The children are all taken care of. Winnie will still not speak to me, and I sense this will still be the case for days to come. When the time comes, as a mother who has known the ultimate grief myself I can hold Winnie's hand through the process of slow recovery. I had no one in my days of loss and grief; she will have me, and that will be the difference. Winnie will not fall into the abyss, as I did.

George is in the best of hands with Andrew.

I must hurry to the child who needs me the most – Yoyo. I must return to Promised Land.

Chapter Twenty-Nine

George

Winnie is forgiving by nature, but she will never forgive me for *that*. Those are the words I spoke to Mama, and in my heart I believe they are true. I think, in time, she can forgive my infidelity – once she knows, and believes, the truth. It was wrong to keep the truth from Winnie. I should have told her the true reason for my avoidance of Yoyo right from the start. Between a loving couple there must be no secrets – not even secrets that might hurt. I now became fully aware that in cultivating this fiction, I allowed Winnie her indulgence of Yoyo, allowed her to believe that it was only my stubbornness that prevented a reconciliation. I took the blame, exaggerating a small quarrel into something momentous.

In allowing her a false image of her sister I was not trusting my wife to be adult enough to cope with the truth. I was treating her like a child. I should have told her right from the start. But it's not too late for her to know the whole story, and one day – soon, I hope – she will be prepared to listen.

But the death of our daughter! How will she, will we, ever recover from that! The daughter we have dreamt of for years; the daughter Winnie had longed for with every fibre of her being. Now it is not Yoyo who needs forgiveness, but me. My weakness alone has caused this. Yoyo's disloyalty is nothing, nothing at all, compared to my own. And the result, the death of our daughter, is beyond forgiveness.

At the hospital I was permitted to see, and to hold, Gabriella Rose.

I wept over that cold little body. That perfect little dead thing. But these remains were not my daughter. My daughter had disappeared into the ether. I wept and laid her down, but then I was called to sign papers and I was given the body and told to take it; to bury it.

Still weeping, I went to a funeral parlour and they made arrangements for a burial. I signed some more papers. What hymns did I want? What prayers? But I could not think about hymns and prayers. How could I bury our daughter without Winnie at my side? What hymns, what prayers, would Winnie want? Could we not wait for Winnie to decide?

No, they said. Gabriella Rose must be buried immediately. Bodies decay very quickly in the tropics. She must be placed in the earth today, or tomorrow at the latest. I must choose a coffin and pay for it. I must bring clothes to dress the body. I must—

I chose a coffin, paid for it and for the burial costs, and turned away. This was not my daughter.

'Just bury her,' I said.

* * *

Andrew was magnificent. He rallied several people who had been guests at the party. He himself remembered talking to me immediately before the incident – as the terrible thing was now called – and others remembered Yoyo going upstairs a few minutes after me. What a good thing that Yoyo was such an eye-catching figure, a woman who captured and held people's attention! She had, apparently, been part of a small group chatting near the stairs. When I went upstairs, Andrew joined that group. And it was *after* he did so that Yoyo, suddenly silent, had excused herself and gone upstairs.

'And just about everyone remembers Yoyo afterwards, standing at the top of the stairs, looking down and laughing,' he said to me. 'She did not look like a woman who had just been raped.

She looked like a woman triumphant, George. Five people have given statements to that effect. Tomorrow you must go before the judge, but there is no evidence at all that anything untoward has happened. Nothing.'

'But who reported that I had assaulted Yoyo? Someone must have! Did Yoyo do so herself?'

'That report, unfortunately, is confidential. But I believe it was that friend of hers, Margaret Smythe-Collingsworth. Yoyo herself has not made a statement.'

'And what if she does? What if she lies to make it seem that I did what they are accusing me of? Andrew, there were no witnesses. It's her story against mine. Who will believe me, a black man? Who will believe that a white woman of high society would have seduced her sister's black husband? No one will believe me! No one!'

Panic gripped me, cold fingers tightening round my throat. I could hardly breathe, and my heart thumped so hard I was sure Andrew must be able to hear it.

'George, you must remain calm. We'll cross that bridge when we get to it. At present, Yoyo has not made a statement. She has not accused you of anything. She returned to Promised Land the next day and no doubt the police up there will question her. We must wait for whatever she has to say.'

'But she will accuse me. She will. That woman is evil! She is out to harm me, harm us. Of course she will accuse me. How else can she save her reputation?'

'Ha! From what they say about Yoyo, she's a woman who doesn't care a fig about her reputation. The things I've heard – rumours, of course, but still. No smoke without fire.'

'But if she's out to damage me, that's what she'll say. What she'll do. Andrew! I'm lost. My life is over. Everything I've worked for, everything I've cared for, I've lost.'

It was as if the whole world was crashing in against me. I would end up in prison, just like Winnie's father.

How could I? How could I have been so weak, so feeble? Why had I not pushed that woman away, struck at her groping hands? Escaped? Escaped just as I had at Promised Land that dreadful Christmas Eve? Knocked her down, if need be? But no – that would only have given her more ammunition. Had I been violent she would surely not have hesitated to accuse me of that dreadful crime – or at least, of attempting it.

But why had I been like putty in her hands? Why had my body reacted the way it did? The spirit is strong but the flesh is weak, the Bible says, or something like that. In Yoyo's hands, my body had had a life of its own. Surely, had my spirit been stronger, my *no* more genuine, my body could not have reacted that way? Was there some tiny spark in me that *wanted* what had happened?

What kind of a man am I, to do this to the wife I adore? What kind of a man am I, to be led not by his love but by his lust? Where is the strength of heart I once knew, the force that placed me at the forefront of a mighty battle for freedom? The George of old would not have succumbed in this way. The George of old was a man of substance; his head held high, he would have walked away from temptation. The George of old would not be a whimpering mass of tears and self-pity. Where has the spirit fled that had me side by side with the bravest man I ever knew, my friend Bhim; the George who had once told Winnie, 'This fight is bigger than us both, and bigger than our love?'

Where is my spine?

Chapter Thirty

Ruth

Yoyo's first words to me were cynical, her glare defiant.

'Well? How is my dear sister?'

I would have none of it. I saw through her as if she were made of glass. This is not the real Yoyo. She pretends to be strong and above it all. She's not. There was a telltale red rim to her eyes, so I knew she had been crying. There was a quiver in her voice. I knew she was about to lie. There was falsity in the role she projected, for that was all it was: a role. I refused to play her game.

'Johanna, stop it. Stop it at once.'

She wavered.

'Stop what'?

'You know very well what I mean. Stop this nonsense.'

'I don't know what you're talking about.'

'Don't give me that story. I can see through it at a glance. I can see through you. Johanna, tell me: how could you?'

'How could I *what?*'

That's when my own act collapsed. Fury took over.

'Don't play your silly little games with me! I am your mother – I know you inside out! Don't you dare pretend you don't know what you have done! Deliberately made a play for your sister's husband, deliberately trying to lure him into your web, deliberately playing on his weaknesses as a man! I saw you doing it when he was here, that Christmas years ago. Do you think that makes you strong? Do you think that because you turn heads you are some kind of a – a goddess, with the power to destroy hearts at the snap of your fingers? Hearts, and lives? How could you do it, Johanna? How could you!'

When I started my tirade Yoyo had been standing still as a statue; her gaze lowered, for her eyes could never have withstood the fire of my wrath. Halfway through, her bottom lip began to quiver. At that last word she let out a deep gasp, turned and fled. Out the front door, down the stairs to the garden.

I hadn't even told her yet of the trouble George was in.

I walked to the window but she was not in sight. Running away from the truth, as she always did. I stood at the window, waiting; I knew what would come next, and it did. Whenever Yoyo was upset as a young girl she would go riding. Sure enough, a few minutes later I heard the clatter of horse's hooves on the driveway leading from the stables. Yoyo came into sight, seated on her gelding Vitane. She was not dressed for riding, and her skirt was halfway up her legs, exposing her calves. The stirrup leathers would pinch her bare legs, and by the time she returned they would be red and painful. But that pain was nothing to that which I knew would be burning in her heart. I smiled to myself. My treatment was working.

It is not love to help those one loves to hide from the truth. It is not love to indulge them in their own illusions; and to remain silent is to indulge. Good sense might tell me I should have given my little lecture in a calm, collected manner. But letting my emotions, my rage, take over had been exactly right. Because that rage had definitely hit home, in a way calmness never could have. Had I been calm Yoyo would have kept on her mask and argued with me; my fury had given my words exactly the thrust they needed to puncture her at the core of her iniquity. And that was what was needed. A laceration. The lancing of an abscess.

I moved away from the window, satisfied. We would talk, but later.

* * *

The police arrived before Yoyo returned. Not a local policeman from New Amsterdam – they had sent one up from Georgetown, which was some indication of the seriousness of the case. When Yoyo finally walked in, her clothes dishevelled and limp with sweat, her face dusty and tear-streaked, her hair falling out of its bun, she stopped and stared and her face turned hard.

'What's *he* doing here?' she said, pointing with her chin, as she plopped her riding crop into the umbrella stand.

The officer, who had been seated on the bench in the front hall, rose to his feet and walked towards her. I had been talking casually with him; offered him some lime juice, and avoided the topic we both knew he was investigating.

'Ma'am, I came from Georgetown to discuss the alleged assault that took place Saturday night last.'

'Assault? *Assault?* Is that what they're saying now? Poor little Georgie-boy was *assaulted?* I'm telling you, he *wanted* it! He wanted it! How could it have happened if he didn't want it? I'm not saying a word without a solicitor!'

'Yoyo! Just hold your mouth for a second and let the officer speak!'

'Ma'am – It's not—'

But Yoyo had taken the bit between her teeth, and was running with it. In a way I was horrified, but on the other hand I rejoiced. With her own words Yoyo was throwing cold water on the case against George.

'All right – arrest me. Put me in handcuffs and drag me down to jail. Make a laughing stock of me. Who cares? Not me. My reputation is shot anyway. Go on, put on the handcuffs. I'm a terrible terrible person. I'm a slut and a harlot and whatever other names they can hurl at me. What do I care? Go on. Arrest me.'

She held out her hands to the officer, upturned wrists together, and at last she left enough silence for him to get a word in.

'Ma'am, I'm not here to arrest you,' he said very gently. 'No one is accusing *you* of anything. It's the other way round. The – er – gentleman concerned has been accused of violating you and I'm here to take your statement, to find out the truth of the matter. So that he can be charged with rape. If you wouldn't mind…'

Yoyo turned a whiter shade of pale. She stared at him, struck dumb for a moment.

'George – raped me?'

'Yes ma'am, that is the allegation. I would like to take a statement from you as to what occurred last Saturday night at the home of Mr Andrew Stewart, if you don't mind.'

She fell silent, and I watched her face as one emotion after another passed over it. Yoyo has always managed to keep a stony mien even under pressure, even as a child, and I had not always been able to read what went on behind that. But today the inner upheaval was visibly cracking the hard outer casement, and I could read her like a book: guilt, surprise, calculation, hostility, fear and, again and again, guilt. I realised, as she must have done, that Yoyo possessed now the power to twist everything to her advantage. To salvage her reputation, and bestow the final punishment on George and Winnie. She held an axe in her hand, and George's neck was on the chopping block. I held my breath, waiting for her next words. And I realised that Yoyo had reached a fork in her road. Her next words would determine which way she would go. What would she say?

She whispered one word. *'Margaret.'*

All at once the shifting emotions fled from her features. Her eyes turned hard as rock, and she spoke the words of absolution: 'I have nothing to say. You can put your notepad away.'

'But, ma'am—'

'Didn't you hear me? I said I have nothing to say. Nothing happened. Go back to Georgetown and tell them that nothing happened. Nothing.'

And for the second time that day she stormed off, this time up the stairs, two at a time.

And I let go of the breath I had been holding.

* * *

After the officer had left I walked upstairs and knocked on her bedroom door. When no answer came I walked in. Yoyo lay face down on the bed, sobbing her heart out.

I walked over and placed a hand on her heaving back.

'Dear,' I said. 'Would you like to talk?'

'What's there to say!' she spluttered between sobs. 'I'm just a horrible horrible person, a mean nasty horrible person. I'm bad, through and through bad. Everyone hates me, everyone, and I deserve it because I'm just so horrible, horrible, horrible!'

'No darling, you're not horrible. You just made some terrible mistakes, that's all. But we all make mistakes. The thing to do is, when we recognise that, go back and put things right.'

'How can I put things right?' She sat up and glared at me. 'How can I put it right! Winnie has lost her baby. How can I put it back into her womb, alive? It's all my fault but it's not what I wanted. It's not what I wanted at all! I'm sorry, so sorry, so sorry, Mama!'

She flung herself at me then, and howled into my breast, repeating again and again the words she had just said: words of regret and rue and repentance, words of sorrow and grief and com-passion for another. Words of healing. I held her then, and let her weep and bitterly sob, and as I held her I felt a tide of darkness leave her body and wash against my own heart. I felt a greater love for Yoyo at that moment than I had ever felt, greater even than the love I felt when she was first placed in my arms as a newborn. Love filled me through and through, and welcomed her darkness. Ab-sorbed it into itself. And after a while the sobs subsided and Yoyo simply lay in my arms, like a baby. It was an absolution – of sorts.

* * *

But it wasn't as easy as crying on Mama's shoulder; it wasn't over. Yoyo still had work to do. The next morning, after breakfast had been cleared away and Clarence had slipped off to work, Yoyo stood up to go. I reached out for her hand. 'No,' I said. 'Yoyo, please stay a moment. Let's talk.'

She hesitated, then sat down again, a quizzical look in her eyes. Contrition does not wear well with pride, and by the look in her eyes I could tell that some of the old Yoyo had reasserted herself.

'What is it?'

Defiance flared in her eyes, as if she knew what was coming, and already resisted. She had been subdued all through breakfast, but humility did not sit well with Yoyo. She liked to be on top; on top of everyone and everything. Which is exactly what had led to the present fiasco.

I hesitated. This might be difficult. The last thing I wanted was to provoke a Yoyo-rebellion. Even as a child, she had never liked to be *told* what to do; she liked to be led by suggestions; she liked a move to be offered mildly so that she felt she had a choice, so that it appeared to originate with her. She liked her pride protected, the reins of control firmly in her hands. As a parent, tact had been required. One had to say, soothingly, 'Yoyo, don't you think it would be a good idea to…' Anything else was likely to produce the very opposite of what was required; often a tantrum.

Now, I took a deep breath and the words emerged: quite different ones to the mild encouragement I had planned. Words with a life of their own, unplanned, and most direct.

'Yoyo: you must go to Winnie. You must confess. You must open your heart to her as you did to me last night. You must.'

She gasped. Her eyes opened wide. But it was not rebellion or pride I saw there, but panic; and I knew I had said the right thing. I had caught her while she was down; I had encountered the true Yoyo, the Yoyo unprotected by pride.

'Oh Mama! No! I can't! How can I face her? How can I tell her the things I've done?'

'I thought you were so strong, Yoyo? Then prove it. This is a strong thing to do. You must save what can be saved, and the first thing you can help save is Winnie's marriage. Neither she nor George deserve to live with the consequences of what you did. You must put it right.'

'I don't want—'

'It's time to stop doing what you want and start doing what is right. The two don't always go together.'

'But, Mama! She hates me already – she won't listen, she'll—'

'Johanna! Stop making excuses and just do it! You and I will return to town today. You will go to Winnie in hospital and you will tell her exactly what you told me last night. You must do this.'

'How can I look her in the eye?'

'You will. You must. That will make you truly strong. Your pride, your arrogance, is your weakness, Yoyo. Your honest confession will give you strength. It will make you clean.'

* * *

We drove to town in separate cars, for I intended to stay there longer; Winnie had hopefully moved on to the next stage of grief, or would soon. Sooner or later she would need me, and I wanted to be near her when that moment came. I was a veteran of grief, an expert. I knew it inside out. At my time of grieving there was no one at my side, no mother, only an unrepentant Archie long alienated from me. I had been alone; I had to make sure that Winnie wasn't.

Since Yoyo was heading for the hospital, I told Poole to drive me to Albouystown, to George. But George wasn't at home. He was back at work.

'Dey drop de investigation,' his mother told me, smiling broadly. 'Dey in't got no evidence and no proof.'

I sighed with relief. 'Thank goodness! Of course they have no proof because no rape happened.' I told her briefly of my conversation with Yoyo.

'It turns out the mysterious witness was Margaret Smythe-Collingsworth,' I said. 'Trying to protect her own reputation.'

Once Yoyo had explained, it all made perfect sense. Yoyo had been Margaret's guest; they were best friends. She had confessed a certain illicit attraction to George, and Margaret had goaded her on. She could never prise George away from Winnie, Margaret had taunted; George was far too devoted to his wife. Yoyo had taken up the challenge. She could. Of course she could! George would be a pushover. She had tried, and failed, that Christmas Eve so long ago. That failure had gnawed at her over the years. Then came Andrew's party, and a second chance. But it all went dreadfully wrong. After the disaster, Margaret saw it as her duty to rescue Yoyo, and herself, from an impossible predicament.

For Yoyo to have voluntarily dallied sexually with George, a black man, a *married* black man, a black man married to her own *sister*, would mean social ruin. Yoyo would never be able to hold her head up in society again. She was now a scarlet woman, a slut. That's what people would call her. And as her best friend, that ruin would reflect on Margaret herself. They would both become outcasts. When Yoyo went home to her that night Margaret had explained all this to her, but Yoyo didn't care; Margaret did, though. The Smythe-Collingsworths were BG's elite. Even knowing Yoyo was playing with fire for Margaret; this scandal would be catastrophic.

The only way for Margaret to save her own skin was for Yoyo to have been raped. She had tried to convince Yoyo to press charges before leaving town but Yoyo had brushed her off – *that* kind of a lie was anathema to her. She had rushed back to Promised Land the next day, leaving Margaret to pick up the pieces, never guessing what would come next.

Margaret had not wasted time: she made up a story of rape, and had run to the authorities to ensure that *that* was the fiction being spread in Georgetown, that *that* rumour should take root. Proving that she was every bit as vile as her father.

'She's a she-devil!' said Ma.

'Indeed!' I replied. 'But Yoyo refused to go along with it – she does have *some* integrity.'

'Hmmmph!' snorted Ma.

'She's gone to the hospital. She's going to talk to Winnie. Tell her what really happened.'

'Hmmmmph!'

'Hopefully, this will mend things between Winnie and George. Yoyo's explanation is better than George's.'

'Dat girl is a slut!'

I immediately withdrew my smile of goodwill.

'That girl is my daughter and I would thank you not to call her names. She has made a dreadful mistake and hopefully she can put things right.'

Mrs Quint sniffed and turned away. 'She can't bring back dat dead baby though!'

She was right, of course. I didn't want to quarrel with Mrs Quint, who was rightly appalled at what had happened. Yoyo's 'dreadful mistake' had led to the death of a much-wanted baby girl and of course she would not be easily forgiven by that baby's other grandmother. My tone had been haughty; my reprimand uncalled for. Ma was a mother too and had had to support George through this terrible time. Of course she was furious at Yoyo; of course she would call her names.

I hurried up to her.

'Mrs Quint!' I cried. 'I'm sorry for my tone just now. It was rude. And I'm here to help. How are the boys coping? How are *you* coping? How is George?'

She gave me a searching look, as if checking to see if I was sincere, and I must have passed muster because her features relaxed and she said, 'Everything all right. George took de boys to play cricket on de beach yesterday. And he helped with de babies too. Dem girls you engaged – dey a bit lazy. Dey don't know one thing about babies.'

'Well, I'm here now so we can dismiss them, and hopefully Winnie will be back from hospital soon. Yoyo's with her now.'

She looked at me, startled. 'Yoyo gone to Winnie?'

'Yes,' I said. 'She went to tell Winnie the whole story: to confess and say she's sorry. That won't bring back the baby, I know, but at least it might heal things between Winnie and George. If Winnie knows that George – well, George is only a man. Few men can resist a woman like Yoyo, if she turns on the seduction.'

That won a smile from Mrs Quint. 'Men!' she said, 'when de willy talk de mind gone. Men is slave to dey willy. No brain! An' still dey tink dey strong!'

'Oh, you can tell me that again! I can tell you a story or two…'

And I did; and she and I laughed and joked over men-stories as we cared for the babies and by the end of the morning we had found a new rapport; and then Yoyo's car drove up and a pale and visibly distraught Yoyo stood in the doorway.

'Mama,' she said, 'that was the hardest thing I've ever done in my life. But I did it.'

'How did Winnie take it? Did she accept your explanation? How is she?'

'What do you expect? She's still crying. She didn't want to see me. But I forced myself on her and I forced her to listen. I'm good at forcing people.'

I smiled at her irony. 'And sometimes it's the right thing to do,' I said. 'So she listened? Did she say anything?'

'Well, you can ask her yourself. She's coming home tomorrow. And I'm going home. I did what you wanted. It was the right thing to do. Now, I won't be back in town for a long time. Town does bad things to me.'

And she was off.

Chapter Thirty-One

Winnie

Those three days I refuse to relive. I won't speak of them.

But on the fourth day, Yoyo appeared at my bedside and forced me out of my hole.

'Go away.'

'No. I need to tell you something.'

'I don't want to hear it.'

'You must.'

How dare she! How dare she come to my bedside to stand there and gloat! I used to adore Yoyo, as everyone did. Though she was younger than me, she had been my idol: always so confident, so self-assured, so strong. Not just strong but *head*strong, it was true, and sometimes Yoyo had needed me, as a boring but sensible elder sister, to stop her from barging her way into situations only to make them worse. Yoyo could never see consequences; I could. It made me tiresome to her; she mocked me for it, looked down on me. Disrespected me.

Now she had barged her way into my life with her red dress and her perfume and her powers of seduction, the very ones I lacked. She was still young, and beautiful, her body unspoilt by childbirth, whereas I – well, after five births I lacked the flush of youth, and I was often so very tired at night. No wonder I couldn't keep hold of George.

How I had envied her, in the past! Boys, men, had always been charmed by Yoyo, and well she knew it. She could twist them round her little finger with a pursing of her lips, a tilting of her head, a wink, a word, a sway. Simply by breathing. They fell at her feet, and she so careless with their adoration. Now George, my George, had fallen too. Into her web. I could not bear to look at her. I no longer envied her. She repulsed me. I abhorred her. She made me sick.

'Go away!' I cried it out loud, I screamed it at her. 'Go away, go away, go away! What are you doing here!'

But she stood her ground. Yoyo always stood her ground. Or, to be precise, she sat her ground, drawing up a chair to my bedside and plonking herself down on it.

'Winnie, you must listen to me. Please! Just let me talk. Just listen!'

'I don't want to hear anything you say! I just want you to go!'

I reached for the bell-pull to call a nurse but she grabbed my wrist before I could get there.

'Let me go! How dare you!'

We wrestled for a moment; but I was weak and she was strong.

'I'm not going until you hear me out!'

'I hate you, I hate you, I hate you!'

'I know you do and I deserve it. Listen, Winnie: I hate me too!' Her voice was hesitant, as if it were a struggle to speak the words – but her eyes were steady, locking on mine, and pleading.

'No you don't. You're in love with yourself. Always have been. You don't care about anyone else.'

'I do and I came to say I'm sorry and – and to explain.'

'I don't want any explanation. I know what happened. I saw. And I saw your face afterwards. Laughing. You enjoyed it. You're not sorry, Yoyo.'

'I am now. I came to tell you that and to – to apologise.'

'I don't want your apology. It's not going to bring my baby back.'

At those words the howling started again. The abject, desperate howling that sometimes had overtaken me during the last three days. Howling like some pathetic animal that had been wounded and left to die. A wolf maybe, or a jaguar. Because I had been wounded to the death.

'Don't,' said Yoyo. 'Don't. Don't. Don't. Don't.'

And then the impossible happened. She too burst into tears.

Yoyo crying was so rare, so astonishing, that it immediately stopped my howling. I could only remember seeing her cry once in my life, and that was when Nanny had gone. She never even cried when Mama left us so long ago. And now here she was, bent forward so that her upper body rested on the bed, her face buried in the sheet, and sobbing as if her heart would break. Heaving and spluttering, her fingers grasping the sheet and the mattress like a drowning man grasping at flotsam.

I couldn't help it: I have a soft heart. I cannot bear to see another creature suffer. I reached out and placed a comforting hand on her back. Immediately she grabbed that hand and clung to it, and then looked up.

'I'm truly, truly sorry, Winnie. Let me confess. Please, let me confess.'

How could I remain hard?

'All right then,' I said. And I let her talk, and I listened. She told me everything. She did not spare herself. She did not sugar-coat her behaviour. She did not make excuses. It was all her fault, she said. George had said *no,* clearly and repeatedly, but she had been determined to overcome that no. She had – practically – forced him into compliance. George was a good, sweet man, she said. Too naïve for his own good. Unschooled in the wiles of women, the wiles she knew so well and had bombarded him with. George was innocent, even if his body was guilty. She had known how to make his body react the way it did, and she had used that knowledge. It's the power of a woman, our only power, perhaps, over a man. And she had used it, unashamedly. It was a power I knew little of; I had been a young girl when I met George, seduced only by the romance of it all.

'But *why*, Yoyo? Why did you do it? I don't understand *why*.'

'Because he loves you. He loves you so much. And nobody loves me.'

And she burst into tears again.

* * *

Yoyo stayed at my bedside all afternoon. We talked. It was the longest conversation we had ever had, and the deepest. It was a conversation that equalised us; she repentant, I forgiving, we reached out for each other in a way we had never done before. Because never had there been such necessity, never such pain between us, never such a mountain to climb. But we climbed it, hand in hand. Yoyo, I discovered, had depths I had never imagined; once she had left the shallow shores of personal pride and ventured into the risky waters of introspection and self-examination she began to find her feet and, even, to revel in honesty, and in confession.

'I envied you, Winnie. I did. You were always so mature and Mama loved you more.'

'Oh, but she didn't, Yoyo! She really didn't. She and I are very much alike but when you were small you were Mama's pride and joy – so clever, so quick, so pretty! I remember when I was about six and you were four how jealous I was of you because you could speak so quickly and so well, and I had to mull over every word, and I stuttered a bit, and you would make people laugh because you were so witty, and Mama used to delight in the things you said and nobody ever laughed at what I said – I was the boring one and you, everyone doted on you, including Mama!'

'But you could speak German, fluently, with Mama. You read German books with her, poetry and novels, and sang those boring Schubert *Lieder,* in German! And you played the violin and she loved that you were musical. And the two of you would play duets and it was as if you were one entity, lost in your music, and I didn't understand music and I was just about tone deaf—'

'Just like Papa! You were Papa's little girl and I envied you so much! Every girl wants to be Papa's darling and I wasn't, I definitely wasn't. You were prettier and wittier so he loved you more – I swear you learned to flirt with Papa!'

She blushed. 'Maybe I did,' she admitted. 'It's true I had Papa twisted round my little finger. But look where Papa ended up.' She stopped to reflect. 'And now it's Mama who has brought us together at last. It was touch and go, you know. I nearly didn't make it. My pride, Winnie. Pride is such a terrible thing. And envy. I envied you so much! You had everything I wanted. A husband who loves you. Sons. Those are the things I want. And up to now I always got what I wanted, but I couldn't get those. It made me so furious! I like to be in control, you know, and if I'm not I get angry and do stupid things. And for the first time in my life I wasn't in control. It was as if my pride was behind me with a whip, spurring me on to do things I knew were naughty, and I just didn't care. I wanted what I wanted and nothing else mattered. Pride is not a good master! It's led me into the most terrible messes in the past, but this is by far the worst.'

She chuckled. 'The seven deadly sins. Remember Pastor Pearson's sermons? How he used to go on about them! Vainglory is my worst, I think. Wrath. Envy.'

'Lust?' That seemed to me the most obvious in this case, but she shook her head. 'Not in my case. Actually, I used the lust of *others* to get my own way – so, greed more than lust.' She looked at me mournfully. 'I didn't really want George, Winnie. I didn't lust after him. It was more a game – more to see if I could win him, somehow. I so envied the way he loves you. I'm sorry.'

'I don't understand. You have Clarence. You have a husband of your own. Why don't you try to love him? Doesn't he love you?'

'Hah! Clarence? You must be joking, right? Don't you remember how we joked about Clarence when he first came to BG? And you thought I was mad to marry him. You don't really think there's love in my marriage, do you? It's a marriage of convenience. I told you that long ago.'

'I know. I'm just confused. You always said you didn't want love, you didn't believe in love; it's all romantic nonsense. And yet—'

'And yet, seeing the way George looks at you... well, it did something to me. It made me jealous. I couldn't help it. But – but what I did was unforgivable.'

'I – I think I can forgive you, Yoyo. You're my sister. Of course I can forgive you.'

'You must forgive him too, Winnie. You must go to him and tell him that he is forgiven. Please. Go to him.'

'I will.'

'Today?'

I nodded. 'You promise?'

I nodded again. Her voice was small and humble.

'Another thing, Winnie.' She stopped and started again. 'I know that the worst of it all is your baby and I can't bring her back and it's all my fault. I will always feel terrible about that. I know you can't ever forgive me.'

'But I do, Yoyo. I know you didn't mean for me to fall. It's – it's just a consequence; it wasn't deliberate. I don't think we should be pointing fingers of blame here. I'm not going to.'

'Still I want you to forgive me. Say it, Winnie.'

I wanted to tell her that she had to forgive herself. That she had lost herself for a while but now she had found her way back to who she truly was; that there was no value in looking backwards to that lost person but that she must stay here, in the present, the new Yoyo right here holding my hand and looking at me with pleading eyes, begging for absolution. I knew she wanted to hear certain words from me and so I spoke them, and I meant them with all my heart.

'Yes, Yoyo, I forgive you.'

She was silent for a while, and then: 'Thank you, Winnie.'

I opened my arms and she fell into them, and I lay back on my pillow and she lay with me, and so we lay together and I fell asleep, and when I woke up again she was gone, and I knew I had to go to George.

Chapter Thirty-Two

George

Winnie came back to me that night. We were having dinner in the cramped hallway at the cramped table, Ma and Pa and Mama and me and the bigger boys; and suddenly she was there, standing in the doorway. I leapt to my feet and rushed to her and only then I remembered, and stopped.

But she held out her arms to me.

'Winnie, I—' I began, but she put her fingers to her lips and she said, 'Shush, George,' and so I said nothing but only stepped into those arms and they closed around me.

'Yoyo told me everything,' she whispered into my ear, and if I had not known before that I had the best woman in the world, well, in that moment I knew it.

She let go of me and drew away and stooped down and held out her arms again and the boys rushed forward into them. Ma got up to fetch another plate and filled it with cook-up rice and chicken and we all sat down at the table again and it was as if nothing had happened, almost; and even the great sadness that hung over us all seemed banished for the evening.

But it wasn't. That night when the boys were in bed and Winnie and I were at last alone we wept together. We wept for our Gabriella Rose, the little girl who had hovered for a while at the periphery of our lives and then was swept away, it seemed, on the breath of God. She was gone, and in the vacuum left by her departure Winnie and I filled spaces in each other's souls, and in each other's bodies, and we were one as we had never been before.

Later, much later, I told her about the property in Lamaha Street and the house that would be our home.

'The vendors have sorted out their problems,' I told Winnie. 'The loan was approved. Today I signed the papers. The place is ours.'

'As long as we are together,' she whispered to me through the darkness, 'I don't care where we live.'

'How can you still love me, after all of this?' I still couldn't believe it. I did not deserve her love. How could she forgive the ultimate betrayal?

'George,' she said slowly then. 'I do love you and always will. But...'

'But what?'

'But – I don't know. I'm trying to find the words.'

In her hesitation I knew there was something serious she had to say; that she knew very well what she had to say, but was afraid to say it.

'What is it?'

'It's just – well. You've changed, George, over the years. You're no longer...'

She paused again. My heart pounded so hard I could feel it thumping away in there: thumpity thumpity thump. I feared what she would say next.

'No longer the George I fell in love with. The passionate strong fighter, the man who would change history. The man who wanted to avenge his best friend. Do you remember what you told me, George, after the trial?'

'I told you many things!'

'No, but those few words stuck with me. You said: *This is bigger than both of us, Winnie. Bigger than our little personal lives. Bigger than our love.* And you know, those are the words, more than anything else, that bound me to you. That made me give up all I had, to come to you. You were so strong, so determined! You were my hero.'

'But that was then, Winnie. Now we have children. Now we have to live in reality. I can't be that reckless revolutionary and still be a good father and husband. That's something for single men. I have to care for you. I can't—'

She hugged me, snuggled into me. 'You're the best husband any woman could want, the best father. It's just – perhaps a bit too much? You put me on a pedestal, George, and that's not right. When I came into your life you were so young and so full of drive for something marvellous – you were going to change history! You and all the others. And I loved and admired that – yes, I fell in love with you, the person, but there was something behind you, just like you say – something bigger than both of us and our little romance and that is what is missing in our lives. I remember that first rally I went to, on the Sea Wall – do you remember? When the police came afterwards and you didn't know I was there and you were so cross and swept me up into your arms and hid me in a boat and commanded me to stay put! Oh, that was marvellous, George! That was the real George! And I bet you, I bet you anything, that that George wouldn't have been seduced by Yoyo! You'd have sent her packing! Because it was big, George, so big! And when we first married it was the same. The Saturday rallies! The moment you began to speak, I'd feel a thrill all down my spine, and when you sang, oh, my heart melted! You had the gift of moving crowds, George. Inspiring people. You would leap into their hearts and make them want to do good things, brave things. And then you gave it all up because you wanted to be a good husband and father!'

'Being a good husband and father isn't wrong! It's important.'

'Of course it is! But I don't see why the one has to exclude the other. Look, when I committed to you I also committed to that, to your work. I told you, didn't I? I'd be right there at your side. It was bigger than both of us and we'd work together. It's what I wanted, George – it's what I still want!'

'You mean – I should go back? Go back to the rallies, go back to being Theo X?'

'Maybe not – maybe Theo X, that hot-headed young man, can be put to rest. But you can still inspire, George, and you should. It's your God-given gift. You shouldn't give it up for me. Maybe you can just be George – speak to them, sing to them. They need it!'

I'd never known Winnie to talk so much. I listened, and as she spoke something began to grow in my heart. Just a tiny sprout, or a flicker, of light – a spark. I watched that spark, and felt it grow in strength, like a tiny flame fanned. Every word she spoke was like a breath of air that fanned that little flame. I could feel it, deep inside, gaining strength and confidence. And as I watched it I knew that she was right. It was the thing I had lost, my essence. Lost it under the weight of responsibilities.   But it wasn't lost! There it was again, eager to grow, straining back into life. I took a deep breath. Yes! There it was again! Strong and full of courage and upright and invincible. The real me.

Chapter Thirty-Three

Ruth

I am no longer needed in Georgetown; tomorrow I return to Promised Land. Winnie's story is intriguing, and I must see for myself. Yoyo, contrite and confessing and begging for forgiveness? It seems an impossible thing, a miracle. Can a person change overnight, into the very opposite of her former self? But then, maybe it is not so much a change Yoyo must have gone through today at the hospital; rather a shedding of her not-self, a removal of a cloak of iniquity.

I do believe in the inherent goodness of all people. That we are all born good – are not all children sweet and innocent, until they learn the crooked ways of adults? Are we not drawn to that innocence in children, because we know that it is in ourselves as well? That we all wear cloaks of not-self, distorting that inherent goodness? Applied to Yoyo, this means that she was desperately unhappy because she saw and felt only her own dark cloak, a cloak of envy and selfishness, distorting her inherent goodness and blinding her to it. She has asked for forgiveness, and been granted it. Is this a new beginning? Will a new Yoyo await me when I go back to Promised Land? I hardly dare hope.

* * *

I need not have worried. The Yoyo who received me when I arrived home was a transformed person: a fresh-faced shiny-eyed angel of a daughter. Gone, the complaining grump finding fault with every little detail of plantation life. Even Jim noticed the change, and remarked on it. Jim, of course, knew the whole story, had seen it in its infant stages, and now that Yoyo had confessed, Winnie knew the truth and George was absolved, we were finally able to discuss it.

'That Christmas Eve, suddenly George was standing at my gate and asking for a bed,' Jim told me. 'He was trembling, a wreck, and he stammered out a story about Yoyo in his room, naked. Must have been a sight to behold! Poor George!'

I chuckled. 'Some men might say, *lucky* George! What a titbit placed in his hand!'

Jim laughed too, and his belly shook. 'Not our George! He must have leapt out of his skin and hightailed it over to me: "What shall I do, what shall I do?" Well, what could I say? "That girl is trouble, George!" I told him. "Better to stay away!"'

'And he did – for years,' I said. 'But I suppose it still bristled somewhere deep inside. The things we bury have a way of surfacing when we least expect it.'

'It'll have bristled in Yoyo too – she won't accept defeat. I bet she's planned this for years.'

'You think so, Jim? You think it wasn't just an opportunity she grasped? That it wasn't spontaneous, but planned?'

Even as I spoke the words I knew they were true. Yoyo was just not the type to humbly accept defeat. That's what made her such an excellent businesswoman, capable of seeing through even the most difficult decisions to the end. But socially, it made her hard and unyielding and, in this case, had led to disaster.

And now, as I write this down, I'm beginning to believe that disaster is just what she needed; that disaster was the only thing that could wake her up and bring about change. A warmer, softer Yoyo – I have seen that new side to her today, and I can only hope it lasts.

* * *

Three months later.

Rereading those last words I can say this much: Yes, it has lasted, more or less. Yoyo is making an enormous effort. She is kinder to the labourers, and she gets along with Jim at last. She tends to be as close-lipped as ever towards me, though – I think she has still not really forgiven me for deserting her as a child. That will take some more work; but I am hopeful. Of late especially she has been particularly gay, almost sparkling; and today I found out the reason.

This morning she drove off in the car, but didn't say where she was going. She was gone all morning; I wondered if she had gone to town – if so, it would be the first time since the hullabaloo with George. None of them have seen each other again, and rightly so. It will take some time before we can be a normal family again, even with the change in Yoyo and the peace she has made with Winnie.

As the sun reached its zenith and began to descend and Yoyo had still not returned, I began to worry. If she had indeed been going to town surely she would have told me? Perhaps she had gone only to New Amsterdam – but what business could she have there that would have taken so long? My great fear, of course, is always that she might have an accident. Yoyo drives too quickly, and she is reckless. A stray dog running into the street, a child chasing a ball, a donkey cart in her way – all kinds of hazards waited for her on the narrow coastal road.

But finally, at just past five, I heard the roar of the motor and the crunch of wheels on gravel and I breathed a sigh of relief – she was back. I watched from the window as she handed the car keys over for Harold to bring the car round to the garage, and walked towards the front stairs.

No, she didn't walk. She skipped, she danced, she twirled – this was a happy Yoyo coming up the stairs! I opened the front door for her and she leapt into my arms.

'Oh, Mama, Mama!' she cried, and tried to swing me round in a clumsy polka. 'Mama! At last, at last! Mama, I'm going to have a baby!'

I froze and stared, stunned into silence. It had been plain for years that marital relations between Yoyo and Clarence had ceased completely; it was there for all to see. Not just that they slept in separate rooms; it was their coldness to each other, and Clarence's blatant and undisguised preference for African and Indian labourers, his own employees. Girls he could master, and who bore his children. He had at least three such bastards; he acknowledged them and supported their mothers, and made no secret of it. Yoyo's baby had to be from George.

I can't say the thought had not occurred to me before – and obviously I had hoped that there would be no such consequences. But I assumed she had taken precautions, seeing as it was a planned encounter, and since she would certainly not risk bearing George's child. It seemed obvious. But this! This joy, this elation! It was a mockery of everything; a mockery of George, of Winnie, of her so-called confession, her so-called repentance.

'Well?' she said after a pause. 'Aren't you going to congratulate me? You know I've always wanted a son! Aren't you happy for me?'

'Happy? Happy? You expect me to be happy? What is it about you, Yoyo, that makes you love hurting your sister so much? What devil lives inside you?'

I turned and stormed away, sick to my stomach. But Yoyo ran behind me, grabbed my arm.

'Mama, Mama no! It's not – not what you think!'

I swung round. 'Don't tell me this is Clarence's child because I won't believe you!' I cried. 'And it's not something you'll be able to hide, is it! How far along are you?'

'The – the doctor says three months. But—'

'Well, there we have it. Three months. You couldn't get your husband into your bed so you get your brother-in-law to father a child. What a despicable thing, Yoyo! And don't tell me that wasn't your intention – if it were a mistake you'd be horrified, not joyful!'

I turned to walk away again, but she pulled me back.

'Mama, please just listen. You're adding two and two and getting five. I can explain it all but you have to listen! You see – you see…' She paused, as if struggling for words.

'I see nothing!'

'You see, Clarence and I – well, I always wanted children but it's hardly possible if your husband rejects your bed! Clarence is incapable of – of relations with me. Just with me! He seems to have no problems with other women, as we all know!'

She grimaced. It can't be easy for a woman like Yoyo, a woman every other man seemed to covet, to be rejected by her own husband, and to see him, at the same time, running after every young skirt on the plantation. Clarence is such a bastard! But we are stuck with him by the terms of the contract; he is de facto master of the plantation, even if Yoyo runs it herself.

'I'm too strong for him,' she continued. 'It puts him off. He prefers docile women. Well, he knows I want, I need, children and since he can't give them to me he agreed that I should be free to find another – shall we say – seed donor.'

She made another face. The subject was obviously distasteful to her, and no wonder. What woman likes to speak of these private matters, and especially to her own mother!

'And he agreed to pretend to be the father, give his name to the child and so on, so that it would all be perfectly respectable.'

'But why *George*, of all men? Your own brother-in-law! It will be so obvious! The child will be dark and the world will know – but mostly, Winnie and George will know. It's a slap in their faces!'

'I told you, Mama, the child is *not* George's! Why would I choose a darkie as father? Of course not! There was – someone else. I have a – companion in Georgetown. I have kept it very discreet – only Margaret knows. She arranged it, in fact. I go to town once a month to meet him, during my fertile phase. There is such a phase, you know, and a clever woman can time these things perfectly. Haven't you noticed that I run off to town for a few days each month? Well, it's for that. For baby-making. Just for that.'

'But then I understand even less why you should run after George, entrap him. What a risk! What if it turns out to be his baby, after all – it will be so obvious!'

'I told you – it's out of the question. For a start, if you remember, I stayed in town a week longer than usual that time. So I was past my fertile phase. And secondly, um, well, you see, George didn't finish. He didn't – well, you know. We were – interrupted. As well you know.'

She smiled then, as if to make a joke of it. I would have no such thing.

'But it was a risk you willingly took. And it's not as if you could pass George's child off as Clarence's. If it did turn out to be George's the world would know immediately.'

'Well. It won't happen. And you know, a few of George's boys are so fair you can't even tell!'

That's true: Humphrey, the eldest, is very light-skinned – but he has dark, very curly hair. The fourth son, Charles, though, is so fair he could very well have been fathered by a white man. It is certainly remarkable what nature will do with a man's seed!

Chapter Thirty-Four

Winnie

Losing that baby broke something within me. It broke my fruit-less obsession with having a daughter. It humbled me. I was able to stand back and see how totally I had poured myself into that one desire, making it the focal point of my whole life. How wrong that was! It blinded me to so much. To the five boys I already had, and their needs – yes, I had taken care of them, physically, as best I could, but there was something missing in that care, something essential. And it had blinded me to my husband, who had become basically a means to an end: a little girl.

My little girl's death rocked me to the foundations of my being. That Winnie, who thought day and night of that one goal: well, she cracked open. The initial devastation was complete. It destroyed me as nothing else could, leaving me ravaged as a country after a war, blind and deaf to those who cared for me and wanted to rescue me. I refused to see George; I rejected Mama's ministrations. To tell the truth, at the back of it all I was terrified. I knew very well what could happen. I had seen with my own eyes what the death of a longed-for baby can do to a mother. It had thrown Mama into a deep dark pit and torn her from her living children, and much as I was lost among the ruins of my self, somewhere within me was a spark of sanity, a little flame that warned me against following in her footsteps. And that's when Yoyo came and sat at my hospital bed, and refused to go until I heard her out.

In effect it was Yoyo who saved me from myself – or rather, the truth of Yoyo's story. When the old Winnie cracked open, a new Winnie was there, waiting in the wings. I saw then that I was composed of layers of self. That new Winnie was ready to forgive, to return to the children she had instead of wallowing in sorrow for the one she had lost. My grief would remain with me, but I could not allow it to overtake my life and destroy my family. With Mama's story as a lesson to me, I awoke from ruination to face a new day and a new life.

First of all, I had a marriage to save. In my obsession with Gabriella Rose I had neglected George – not just physically, but emotionally; and that, perhaps, had made him susceptible to Yoyo's charms. His regret, his guilt, was complete – how could I not forgive him? But had George himself not played a part in my neglect of him? George had tried to be the perfect husband and in doing so lost himself – that is, lost the vital spark in himself that had first drawn me to him and fanned my own love. He had become smaller in my eyes and in my heart. Without that charismatic force George was just a doting husband with no spirit of his own.

We needed to start again, from scratch; rebuild our marriage and our family, not from the debris of the present tragedy but from the memory of what we once had. We discussed this far into the night, and in the morning we overslept and, had not the babies woken me with their screams of hunger, George would have been late for work and the older boys late for school.

But we woke up smiling. Everything was new. We had made new decisions and new plans. My obsession with a daughter had disappeared overnight. Yes, we might have more children, but we would love and accept whatever came our way. We would build a house. George would return to his banjo and his calling as a speaker. Yoyo and I would be friends again. With Yoyo and George it was a different story, and that rift would take longer to close, but I would not try to force things. Our broken family would find healing. All would be well. The sun would shine brightly upon us. I was the inveterate optimist and I had faith. Faith in myself, faith in God. We went to church again that Sunday, and took all the boys. We were blessed, and would move forward as a family.

* * *

All went well for three months. Then Mama appeared on our doorstep one evening and announced that she had news for us. We all went into the gallery and sat down. Mama didn't look well. She had started to age; the rings beneath her eyes were puffy and her face had a distinct pallor that showed through the tan. Was she ill? I asked.

'No,' she replied. 'I'm not ill. I'm worried.' I reached out and took her hand. George appeared with a tray on which were balanced three glasses of lime juice. He set it down on the little table and handed Mama a glass. She took it and nipped at it.

'What's the matter, then, Mama?'

'George, do sit down. This is about you. *Maybe* about you. Yoyo is pregnant.'

I felt it then. The cold shadow of fear; fear that the good life we were rebuilding for ourselves was about to break apart once again, the destruction this time complete. In fact, George and I had spoken of this very possibility. George had shyly told me it was not possible. Now Mama was telling me the opposite.

'It's not possible!' he said right away, now.

'How do you know it's George's?' I said. 'She's married; surely that's enough explanation! Why don't you think it's Clarence's child?'

'Winnie, you're so naïve! If it were so easy for Yoyo to have children the normal way, with her husband, don't you think it would have happened long ago? Years ago? You know how much she longs for children.'

Yes, I did know. Even before she married Clarence, Yoyo had told me of the dynasty she intended to found. She had wanted sons, many of them, two or three at least, and a few daughters to break up the male monotony. She had had it all planned – but then, nothing. I had of course never asked why she remained childless, though it had seemed strange to me, knowing how in control of her life she generally was. What Yoyo wanted, Yoyo got, by hook or by crook.

In the twinkling of an eye the edifice of goodwill between myself and Yoyo crumbled. Suspicion and jealousy reared their ugly heads. But then again, if she had seduced George only to get pregnant – why him? Why a black man, who would give her a child she could not pass off as her husband's?

I looked at George. 'You said it wasn't possible, George! You assured me it couldn't happen!'

George had frozen. He simply sat there staring at Mama as if he hadn't quite grasped the words she'd spoken, hadn't heard my outcry. So I repeated it.

'George! You said it was not possible! You said…'

I was crying by now, and that seemed to bring him back to earth.

'It wasn't – I didn't—'

'I don't want to hear the details. I'm just – I'm just…'

I was just crying. Bent double in my chair and weeping. In that moment it all came back to me: my grief over my lost child; my jealousy of Yoyo; my anger at George. All mixed into one huge ball of despair. It hadn't disappeared. It had all just lingered beneath the surface, waiting for a trigger so it could leap back into view.

Mama's hand was on my back, her voice in my ear.

'Shush, dear. I'm sorry. I put it too dramatically. It's not certain that the child is George's. Yoyo is certain it *isn't*, in fact. There's another contender for a father, aside from Clarence. George is actually unlikely to be the father, according to Yoyo. Let's just hope she's right.'

'I'm not. I can't be,' George kept muttering. He knelt before me, put his arms round me, but I shook him off.

'Don't touch me!'

'Winnie darling—'

'George, leave me with her. It's best you stay out of this. I'll take care of her.'

'All right.'

I sensed rather than heard George's retreat. I felt sick to my stomach. I had heard Mama's explanation but the words had only flickered through my mind. To me, the possibility that George *could* be the baby's father made him *in fact* the baby's father, and that idea sickened me to the stomach. That there should be a living breathing consequence to George's infidelity! That his stupidity and weakness should emerge from Yoyo's body as wriggling, screaming evidence of his dalliance… it was too much to digest. I didn't care whether or not it was true. It was possible – even if George said it wasn't – and that made it something I could believe. How would I cope? What if the child looked like George? What if – what if it was a *girl?*

Mama continued to hold me and comfort me, but it was all rather futile. I was lost in an emotional breakdown that rivalled the one I'd only just recovered from. I heard Mama's words as from a distance. She now seemed determined to convince me that the child was definitely not George's. She told me of Yoyo's prolonged attempts to have a child, her extramarital arrangement – with Clarence's approval – and her monthly visits to Georgetown for exactly that purpose.

'Yoyo leaves nothing to chance. You know that, Winnie! She even has a chart – her doctor has explained to her the body's rhythm and she knows exactly on what days she is fertile. She was with George *afterwards*. She definitely was pregnant already.

There's nothing to worry about. Yoyo has it all planned out. She would never risk having a baby from George – it would be far too obvious, and she always intended to pass it off as Clarence's child. She told me this in confidence. I'm not even supposed to tell you. She wants to have a white child, Winnie. It will be the heir she has longed for, if it's a boy. She can't risk having a coloured baby. People would talk. The child would grow up in scandal, the butt of jokes. It would be a catastrophe! Yoyo knew exactly what she was doing, Winnie. She's happy about the child – would she be happy if she were not absolutely certain it could pass as Clarence's? No. She would be nervous in that case, and she isn't. She's sure. You can't let this come between you and George. You were doing so well! You were so strong – forgiving him. He's making such an effort. I'm so sorry, Winnie. It's all my fault. I was untactful, over-dramatic, announcing it like that. Come on, dear. All will be fine.'

On and on she rambled. I listened with only one ear, lost as I was in the ocean of grief washing over me. I let her talk, never responding; only crying. Drowning in my tears, allowing Mama's words to go in one ear and out the other.

Eventually, Mama grew tired of me. Suddenly she seized my shoulders and jolted me, so that my head flung back and my eyes opened wide, startled. She shook me, once, twice, so that my head wobbled.

'Winnie, snap out of it. That's enough. All you're doing now is wallowing in self-pity, indulging yourself with all this emotional nonsense. Wake up, daughter! Pull yourself together! I told you there's hardly a chance at all that George is the father – why don't you listen? Oh! I could slap you!'

And she did! She slapped me hard on the right cheek and then on the left, and that is what woke me out of my stupor.

'Oh!' I said, and placed my hands on my stinging cheeks.

'Yes, oh, indeed! Now, girl, stop being a baby yourself. Get up and go and find George. Tell him exactly what I told you. That poor boy is probably just as worried as you but he doesn't allow himself the luxury of a breakdown. Go and support him. That's what wives and husbands do for each other. That's marriage. Just go. I'm sick and tired of you.'

Mama's words worked like a bucket of cold water on fighting dogs. They brought me right back to my senses, and to reality. I saw that she was right. Mama, no-nonsense Mama, had once more worked her magic. I sniffed, and she produced a handkerchief. I wiped my eyes and my cheeks and said thank you.

Then I rose to my feet and went off in search of George.

Chapter Thirty-Five

Ruth

It was, perhaps, the happiest period in Yoyo's life since my return to BG. She was good at pregnancy; some women bloom, and she was one of them. Her skin glowed, her hair gleamed, her eyes shone; but most of all, she smiled. Yoyo's smile, when it was genuine, could light up a room. And I believed that at last she had truly found peace. Kind to everyone, and never cross – *This, I thought to myself, this is the real Yoyo.*

Though I could not approve of the *way* she had chosen to accomplish motherhood, I had to concede that under the circumstances it was perhaps the *only* way, and as long as Clarence agreed, then why not? After all, Clarence had his own share of extramarital flings, though obviously he could not keep the offspring from those for himself. The mother, after all, has priority – one of the few advantages a woman has in this lopsided world, in which everything else is heavily weighted in favour of men.

Yoyo's serenity helped to banish my last doubts as to the paternity of the child. Yoyo had, she let me know bit by bit over time, planned this down to the last detail – down to the colour of the potential father's eyes, his height, his hair. Her friend Margaret – and, it seemed, Margaret's husband – had played a major role in selecting the victim, approaching him, cautiously suggesting the role he was required to play. The successful candidate was a man called Richard – I never learned his surname – who worked as a minor clerk at Bookers Shipping and who, as required, bore the requisite shallow resemblance to Clarence. He was single, modest and discreet, a few years younger than Yoyo, and more than willing to fulfil the duties required of him. Which man wouldn't – Yoyo was a beauty, a woman who turned heads. With her handed to him on a platter, Richard complied admirably.

'How long has this been going on?' I asked.

'Just over a year,' said Yoyo. 'He's my second attempt. The first one – well, the less said of him, the better.'

'And it's taken you this long to get pregnant?' This was my last little remnant of worry raising its suspicious head. But Yoyo shook her head.

'Sadly, no. I've been expecting before. Twice before. Both times I had a miscarriage.'

'Oh! Maybe you got that from me – I had three miscarriages before Edward John's birth.'

'Really? Then it must be that. That's why I waited before I announced this pregnancy. I was so afraid I'd lose this baby, too. And look at me now!'

Yoyo was joyously pregnant, her bulging belly taut and big, like an oversized watermelon about to burst open. I laughed, and placed my hands on it. 'I can feel it kicking!' I said. 'Isn't that the most perfect feeling in the world?'

'Him,' corrected Yoyo. 'He's kicking. Only a boy would be kicking around so much. Oh Mama! I can hardly wait!'

'Have you chosen a name for him yet?'

'Yes – Ralph, Clarence's middle name. And Archibald, after Papa.'

'Papa will like that,' I said. 'I assume you've written to him with the good news?'

'Indeed I have, and he has written back. He is ecstatic – at last a grandson he can be proud of!'

That was rather a dig, and I reprimanded her.

'Winnie's sons are perfectly good children and your father should be ashamed of himself. They are his grandchildren just as much as this one. He has every reason to be proud of them!'

'But he isn't, is he?' she replied, gaily and matter-of-factly. 'Papa never wanted George as his son-in-law and being in prison hasn't changed that. Why mince words? Papa wanted an heir and he's going to get one – through me. Seeing as Kathleen has only produced daughters, like you!'

She was technically right, and so I held my tongue, but that truth hurt – the truth that Archie rejected completely Winnie's children, solely on the basis of their mixed race. It didn't seem fair. But it was a fact, and so I let it be.

* * *

And then the night of her confinement was upon us. The maid came knocking at my door in the middle of the night, and I was up in a trice.

'Is Miss Yoyo, ma'am!' she said, eyes wide with panic. 'She water break! De baby comin'!'

'Very well, Mabel. No need for panic. Woman have been having children for thousands of years. Now run along, find Poole, and tell him to drive to the village and fetch Nurse Prema.'

Nurse Prema was the Indian nurse-midwife who had moved to the village from Georgetown three years ago, and now ministered to all the births on the plantation, be they labourer birth or European, black, brown or white. I for my part rushed to Yoyo's room and then, establishing that she was comfortable, to the servants' quarters to wake Cooky, whom I instructed to boil water. It was going to be a long night.

But, it turned out, it wasn't. Yoyo, now that she had held on to a baby to full term, proved to be as much a natural at giving birth as she had been at pregnancy. Hardly had she let out her first protracted scream than the baby slipped out and into Nurse

Prema's competent hands. A strident wail filled the room, and the requisite tears my eyes.

'A girl!' cried Nurse Prema as she cut the cord.

'Oh! A girl!' Yoyo sounded stunned and just a little disappointed. 'I was so sure – oh, but never mind! Come. Give her to me!'

She held out her hands to receive the baby. Nurse Prema and I exchanged a knowledgeable glance. This wasn't going to be easy. Nurse Prema took the baby, wrapped now in a white sheet that brought out all the more the dark *teint* of her skin, and placed her in Yoyo's waiting arms.

Yoyo's smile vanished in an instant. She frowned.

'Oh, but…' She folded away the sheet to regard the baby in her full naked glory. 'But – how could – I didn't…'

And then the cry came: 'She's black!'

'She's perfect,' I said. 'She's just perfect.'

'Very healthy child,' said Nurse Prema by way of encouragement. 'Good lungs!'

The little bronze baby lay on the bed in front of Yoyo, naked, wriggling and screaming. I longed to take her in my arms, but this was Yoyo's child, Yoyo's task.

She didn't fulfil it. Instead, she turned away.

'Take it away,' she said, pointing to the baby. 'I don't want it. I don't care what you do with it. Just get rid of it. Give it to George.'

I tried. I really tried. Immediately after birth is not the time to make wise decisions.

'Yoyo,' I said, 'wait a few days. I know it's a shock, and a disappointment. But when you get used to the idea, maybe—'

'No!' she burst out. 'I know what I'm doing! Take that child away! I don't want it! I can't bear that screaming!'

She put her hands over her ears and pressed, her face an ugly grimace.

I handed the child to Nurse Prema, who simply said, 'I will take care of her. Some mothers need time.' She bundled the baby into her arms, kissed the tiny head and headed for the door.

'How could this happen!' Yoyo wept. 'How could it!'

Nurse Prema, the baby in her arms, turned round.

'Ma'am – you have intimate relations with a coloured man?'

'Yes, yes…but—'

'Then that's the reason. Nature in't picky.'

'But we stopped – he stopped – didn't finish…'

Nurse Prema chuckled. 'You mean, *coitus interruptus?* It never worked. You know how many ladies – and they husbands too – I had to warn, because they think not finishing goin' to stop a baby from gettin' born?'

'But it was late in the month – too late! I thought…'

'That method don't work either. You didn't use a French letter?'

'No, no, I thought, I thought…'

The thing is, Yoyo hadn't thought. She had seized the opportunity, and trapped poor George. She had thought she was safe because of the timing, and afterwards she had thought she was safe because he had not finished, as she always discreetly put it. But we all know that nature has a mind of its own. A woman might do all she can to conceive, but if nature says no, well, it's no. And she might do all she can to prevent conception, but if nature says yes, well, she's in big trouble if the man's not her husband. Not even French letters are perfectly safe; many a woman has told that tale. Yoyo took a big gamble and she lost. And this poor child would have to pay the price.

'Have a rest,' said Nurse Prema now, 'have a rest and when you feel better you will love this sweet li'l baby. Such a pretty baby! Soch a lovely li'l thing!' and she kissed the baby's head again and left the room.

But I knew my Yoyo. Stubborn as an ass. She would not change her mind. Yet still, I had to try.

'Yoyo, darling,' I said later, after she had rested. 'You have a little daughter. You are strong. Since when have you been afraid of scandal? Yes, people will talk but you are your own mistress. I'm sure Clarence will—'

'Mama, didn't you hear me? I said I don't want this child. You must give her to George. He's obviously the father. I don't know how it happened, some kind of a twisted miracle, because – well, surely it wasn't possible, considering how... But look at her! Black as sin! Give her to George. Didn't they want a daughter?'

'Yes. But—'

'There you are, then. A daughter for Winnie and George and they didn't even have to work for it. No pregnancy, no labour, no nothing. I did it all for them. It's my present to them. Tell them that.'

Yoyo has the sensitivity of a turtle, and that's an insult to the turtle. Can't she see how utterly impossible her proposition is? Winnie and George have recovered so nicely from the dramas and scandals of last year. They have rallied their forces, strengthened their marriage. Winnie has forgiven George; their new home is almost finished. Their family is complete, Winnie having found a new commitment to her boys. When I went down to spend Christmas with them she confided in me:

'Mama, my obsession with having a daughter blinded me to the boys. I neglected them. Not physically, of course; I looked after them as well as ever. But *emotionally.* I refused to really *see* them, to feel them, to comprehend them, take them into my heart and truly love them.'

It's as if George's infidelity and all the pain it caused has made her see her own blind spots. Cracked open the armour of her obsession, so that she can be herself again, find the loving-kindness that is her true nature. But most of all, it's the change in George that has healed them.

George has found a new lease of life in his music, his singing. What a voice that man has! I always thought I was an excellent musician, but my talent seems technical, acquired, stilted in comparison to George's. When he sings shudders run up and down my spine, my heart swells, I want to cry.

I'm not a very religious person – I converted to Christianity just to please my husband's family, and my initial enthusiasm has grown cold over the decades. But when that man sings – oh, I'm a believer all over again. He moves me to the marrow of my bones. To the core of my being. And that's his effect on everyone.

But he keeps it private. George could easily make a career out of singing if he wanted to. But he doesn't want to. He sings for private groups alone; every Saturday he is invited to this or that home and sings for that family and their friends. He will not accept money. He sings for the poor of Albouystown and the rich of Cummingsburg and Kingston alike.

And it is George's singing more than anything that has saved their marriage. It had grown dull; George had lost his fire, as had Winnie, mired as they both were in the responsibilities of raising a family of five rambunctious boys in cramped quarters. George's singing has brought life into their lives and now they sing together as a family every evening. It calms the boys, who are now each learning an instrument. Humphrey has a violin, and he is good at it – Winnie finds the time to teach him. Gordon and Will have recorders; Will is better than Gordon. The toddlers have their drums and bang away as toddlers do – with full enthusiasm. This is a happy family. The wound has been healed. The birth of this child was always going to crack it open again; and now Yoyo wants me to give the child to them? She is out of her mind.

The empathy of a turtle.

* * *

The child was born yesterday, a Good Friday child. I'm not sure of the significance of that but there must be some message. The poor little thing. Nurse Prema has taken her to a wet nurse in the village for the day and will bring her back later, to see if Yoyo has changed her mind. If not, I don't know what I will do.

Before she left, Nurse Prema said to me, 'Ma'am, I got to register the birth.'

'Well, then do so!'

'A lil problem, ma'am, with baby father name.'

'Ah – what do you do in such – uncertain – cases?'

'Mother's husband is always official father, ma'am.'

'Well then. What's the problem? The baby's father is Clarence Smedley.'

'What is the baby's name, ma'am?'

'Well, how should I know? Ask the mother.'

'Mother don't want to name the baby, ma'am.'

'Well then, let's ask the father. Mr Clarence.'

Clarence had dropped in to meet his latest child, and had been not in the least shocked at her appearance; I suppose he was used to it, having already sired several half-caste children in the village and on the estate. I have this to say for Clarence: whatever his other faults, he has not a bit of racial prejudice.

'Poor little mite!' he said when he saw his latest daughter. 'I should like to keep her. I wish we could.'

'Perhaps Yoyo will come to her senses in a day or two,' I said.

'It's not possible, though. What with the obvious – er – discrepancies. Paternity and whatnot.'

I was disappointed, though I suppose it was too much to have hoped for. It's one thing Clarence acknowledging a white child as his own – but a dark-skinned one? That was, I suppose, too much to ask.

'I think it's a good idea, to give her to George and Winnie to raise,' he said. 'They'll make excellent parents to her.'

I sighed. Neither he nor Yoyo, it seemed, sensed a problem there.

Now, Nurse Prema and I went to see Clarence, who was enjoying an early-morning celebratory drink on the verandah.

'Nurse Prema is going to register the birth,' I said. 'She will have to give your name as the father, as Yoyo's legal husband. Unless you object.'

'Object? Object? Why should I object? Nurse Prema has registered me as father on many a birth certificate. Not true, Nurse Prema?'

'Yes, sir. But this time...'

Clarence took a sip of his drink, licked his lips and said: 'One half-blood bastard is as good as the next. Who cares. Father, mother, it's all the same.'

'We need a name for her,' I said then. 'Yoyo refuses to name her.'

'Mary,' he said. 'Call her Mary, after my mother. A perfectly good English name. Poor little mite. Let me look at her once more.'

Nurse Prema bent over so that Clarence could behold his putative daughter. His eyes turned moist and for a moment I thought he was going to reach out for her. But he didn't.

'Poor little mite,' he said again. 'Poor little Mary. Give her to George. He's a better father than I am. Me, I'm just the sire of bastards. Poor little half-blood bastards.'

Chapter Thirty-Six

George

Easter Sunday – my favourite day of the year. Kite-flying day. Of course we all made our way to the Sea Wall. Humphrey and Gordon had made their kites themselves, with just a little help from me. I made Will's kite with just a little help from Will. Winnie made tiny kites for Charley and Leo: frameless paper pentagons in gaudy colours, with tails of twine decorated with raggedy bows; they'd never fly, but the babies loved them. Babies! Charley and Leo would always be our babies, though they were nearly four and nearly three, and growing a bit more each day.

After breakfast we rounded them up, laughing and running after the more rumbustious ones in order to get them out the house and down the road to meet the tram.

'You are the most boisterous children on earth!' I said. 'Leo! Come back! Leave that dog alone! Will, no, you can't have Humph's kite. You have your own!'

'Want big kite!' wailed Leo. Humphrey lifted his kite high above his head.

'No, it's mine! You got your own!'

'Winnie! Winnie, where are you? These boys are out of control!'

It was like rounding up a troop of monkeys; the moment one was ready to go the other found some new distraction. Now Gordon had spotted a ripe mango on the neighbour's tree and had slyly removed his slingshot from his trouser pocket and, silently

and stealthily, picked up a pebble and taken aim. You needed eyes
at the back of your head for that boy. I snatched the slingshot
from his hands at the very last moment. Mr Greer was protective
of his mangoes; he and Gordon were fighting an ongoing feud.

'I'm coming!' called Winnie. 'I forgot to pack the black pudding.'

'Of course we're boisterous!' said Gordon. 'We're boys and
we live in All Boys Town. We're the boisterous Boys of All Boys
Town!'

'That's good!' shouted Humphrey. 'The boisterous boys!'

'Of All Boys Town!' chorused Gordon and Charles.

'The boisterous boys of All Boys Town, of All Boys Town, of
All Boys Town... Pa, you must write a song for us!'

'Yes, yes, a song about us all! Please, Pa!'

'I will if you all get into line and stand still and stop being so
boisterous right now! Chop chop!'

'Are you going to chop off our heads if we don't?'

'I might!'

'No you won't!'

'Yes he will! With a carving knife like the lady in 'Three Blind
Mice'!'

'*Three Blind Mice, Three Blind Mice, see how they run, see how
they run, they all ran after the farmer's wife, she cut off their tails
with a carving knife...*' sang Charles on cue.

'Maybe Pa will cut off our tails and not our heads!' cried Gordon.

'But we don't have – oh!' That was Humph, who often took
words a little too literally.

They all burst into laughter. 'We have front tails!' cried Gordon, and immediately pulled down his trousers to demonstrate.
'And I need to use mine.' He ran to the fence and began to pass
water.

'Gordon! You don't do that outside! Go to the outhouse!'

'But we're ready to go – I'm just saving time!' said Gordon, who had already finished and now returned to the group, pulling up his trousers.

'Pa, I need a wee too!' cried Charley.

'Me, too!' said Humphrey.

'I thought you had all gone already?'

'Yes we did but—'

'Here I am!' called Winnie, bustling down the front stairs with a basket slung over her right arm and a big canvas bag over her shoulder. A picnic for five boys and two adults needed as much organisation as a huge formal dinner party.

'Ma, Pa's going to cut off all our willies!' cried Charles, who was obviously going to run with that joke all day long.

Finally we managed to herd them out of the front gate and down the road to the tram stop, Humph and Gordon holding hands, Will and Charles behind them refusing to hold hands, Winnie and I at the rear, Leo riding on my back. I held the basket and Winnie carried the bag over her shoulder. She looked pensive, and did not speak. I wondered if she was remembering, as I did, last year at this time: she had been pregnant, and just beginning to show, and looking forward to Gabriella Rose.

'A year from now,' she had said, 'our family will be complete. Gabriella Rose will be with us.'

I hoped she was thinking now, as I was, that our family *was* complete. I hoped she was as happy as I was, right at this moment. Yet she looked sad.

But if she had been sad at the start of our trip, by the time we reached the Sea Wall all trace of it had disappeared from her features. It was a beautiful sunny Easter Sunday and it seemed that every single Georgetown child had dragged their parents to the beach, kite in hand. Long before we arrived we could see from the tram window, the boys pointing and exclaiming, the heralds in the sky – spots of bright yellow and red, and green, sailing against the cobalt blue of the sky, swaying in the brisk Atlantic breeze, soaring up to the sun.

My heart soared too as we climbed out of the tram and mounted the wall. We walked along, single file, for about a hundred yards until we came to the promenade, and there we descended on to the beach. The tide was out, and the hard undulating sand reached out seemingly to the horizon.

Despite the morning's chaos we were early, but quite a few families were already there and their kites were the ones we had seen as we approached. But there was still space for the boys to run as they launched their kites, to scamper and scream and hop on one foot and fall over each other. There were kite-fights and kite-bombs and sometimes tears, and as the beach filled with yet more families and Easter Sunday blossomed into fullness I felt happier than I had for a long, long time. I gazed up to watch Gordon's kite, swaying leisurely from side to side in a mass of brilliant speckles. Winnie's hand slipped into mine, and I looked at her and smiled and knew that she, too, was happy. I let go of her hand and placed my arm round her shoulder, and drew her close.

'Our boys!' said Winnie.

'Aren't they wonderful?'

'The best!' she replied. 'And you know what, George? I just realised: I am a mother of boys. That's just – well, it's everything.'

I pressed her to me. Her head rested on my shoulder. I kissed the top of it.

'The best mother of boys,' I said.

She looked up at me and smiled mysteriously.

'What is it?'

She reached across for my other hand, placed it on her tummy.

'Guess what's brewing in here?'

'Winnie! No!'

'Oh, yes! Another one of them!' The smile was in her voice.

'Oh, Winnie!'

'We really need that house now, I suppose.'

'We do. Oh, Winnie!'

Words failed me then, and her too; she simply snuggled into me. The boys were happily at play. Humph had taken little Will under his wing and was helping him to fly his little miniature kite. Leo and Gordon were holding the string to Gordon's soaring kite together, Gordon bending down to Leo's level. Charley had made friends with another little boy and their two kites flew side by side.

Winnie and I both gazed upwards. The symbolism of it all struck me with a great force, taking my breath away and filling me with deep and quiet joy.

'The risen Christ,' I murmured, 'I feel Him in my heart. Do you?'

She squeezed my hand. 'Indeed I do! I remember Easter back at Promised Land. Mama would take us three girls to the church on the estate. But this is better.'

'Kite-flying is like praying,' I said. 'We lift up our hearts. Up there they are flying, soaring.'

'You should write a song about it,' Winnie said. 'An Easter song. A British Guiana Easter song. About kites. And flying. And soaring hearts. And resurrection.'

'I will,' I said. 'as well as a song about the Boisterous Boys of All Boys Town.'

I felt her arm round my waist.

'We did well, George!'

'Indeed we did.'

* * *

Later that day we returned home, satiated with joy, exhausted, sweaty. Winnie and I bundled the boys out to the bathhouse in the backyard and showered them down, one by one. Soon we would be doing this in our own home in Lamaha Street, the home taking more solid shape in our minds every day. Five bedrooms and a verandah and two inside bathrooms – what a luxury!

We bundled the younger boys into bed and they fell asleep the moment their heads touched the pillows. Someone knocked on the door.

'I'll get it!' I called to Winnie. I strode to the door and opened it. On the landing stood my mother-in-law. She held a bundle in her arms, which she held out to me.

'It's your daughter, George. Yoyo doesn't want her. So I brought her here.'

Chapter Thirty-Seven

Winnie

George had been gone for a while, so I picked up the tea towel and walked into the hall drying my hands.

'Who is it – *oh!*'

I stopped in my tracks. George and Mama were standing in front of the still-open door. George held something in his hands; it looked like a bundle of cloth. He gazed at me with huge pleading eyes and held the bundle out to me, saying nothing.

It seemed they were both holding their breath; neither spoke and only the bundle whimpered. Both of them just stared at me, waiting to see what I would do. The bundle wriggled and I looked at the little exposed face. I knew at once. How could I not know? A lump rose in my throat. I stared at that tiny brown face. The little lips parted; a kind of grunt emerged.

I have a visceral, animal instinct when it comes to babies, newborns in particular. I just can't help it. Nothing can hold back this eruption of caring, compassion, love, wonder, tenderness, devotion, awe, all bundled into one, that springs from somewhere in my depths and takes complete control of my thoughts and senses. It melts me completely. Melts me down to the bones. Every single time. I suppose that this is what they call the maternal instinct, but I don't care what it is called; I only know how powerful it is, how when it overtakes you there is nothing you can do against it.

I dropped the tea towel and took the bundle from George, hesitantly holding it against my breast, looking down into that tiny screwed-up face. George said, quietly, 'It's a girl.'

'Yoyo doesn't want her,' Mama added. 'She said I should give her to George.'

'We don't *have* to, Winnie!' George exclaimed. 'I'll understand if you – if you…'

'Oh, *George!* I could say no more. I turned away so they wouldn't see the tears in my eyes. My capitulation was a private thing, between myself and this little miracle. Just between us two. This warmth that flooded me from the tips of my toes to the top of my head, washing through body and mind as if I was nothing *but* that warmth, that intimacy, that knowledge. That unity. It was between her and me, us alone. It wasn't even George's to see. My eyes stung with unshed tears. I couldn't speak because a lump had stuck in my throat. Anyway, there was nothing more to say.

Part 3

The Golden Girl
Eighteen Months Later

Chapter Thirty-Eight

George

'Papa, Papa, Papa! Grace has started to walk!'

'Come and see, Papa! She took two steps and then she fell and then she stood up again and Mama held her hand and she walked like that and then Mama let go and she walked right across the room!'

'And now she can't stop walking, Papa! She's walking *everywhere!*'

There's nothing for a father like coming home – your very own home, built to the blueprint of your loftiest dreams – to a gaggle of excited boys all jumping up around you, each trying to grab your hands as if you had six instead of two, their shrill voices an incomprehensible tangle as they pull you up the front stairs to your own home. Their cries are the sweetest music to my ears – sweeter by far than anything I can sing myself. But then I walk through the front door and there she is, my queen. She folds me into her arms – every single day – and smiles at me and I am the happiest man on earth.

But that particular day – oh, it was a day of celebration! We had all been a little concerned about Grace's failure to start walking at the required time – all the boys had learned to walk around their first birthday, but Grace had taken her time. The twins Rudolph and Percy, born six months after Grace, could both walk steadily by now, but our Grace preferred to gambol about on all fours. I always said it was because the older boys – and of course

Winnie and I – spoiled her, carried her around too much, paid her far too much attention. Yes, our Grace was undeniably the star of our household. The boys adored her, and as for Winnie…

'I told you so!' she said now. 'I told you that some children need more time. Now you'll see – she'll be running and jumping and riding ponies in no time!'

And then, there they were, my youngest children, clamouring for me in the drawing room: Rudolph and Percy stumbling towards me on their stubby legs, and Grace, my darling Grace, sitting on the floor and reaching her fat little arms out for me. I gathered them, all three, into my arms at once. Yes: I was the happiest man on earth.

Chapter Thirty-Nine

Ruth

Why do I get this feeling that, in spite of appearances, all is not well? The past year has been such a delight. The moment Grace entered this family it was as if a halo of light descended on them all; a blessing. Yes, all had been going smoothly up to that moment, as I wrote in my last entry, almost two years ago, when Grace fell into the family; yet still, there was a sense of trying, trying hard, to overcome the shadows of the past. The sins of the father. All the good George did – it was to atone. Guilt was the driving force of his every effort, forgiveness the driving force of Winnie's responses. It worked, indeed; and then Grace came into their lives and with her sunshine, dispelling the last tendrils of darkness.

Despite her rocky first days in this world, Grace was a sunny child. She smiled early, and at everyone, and everyone smiled back. She was one of *those* babies: so irresistibly pretty strangers would stop and coo, and smile stupidly, and ask her name, and sometimes even to hold her. And Winnie was generous, grateful for the praise, eager to share her joy.

Grace's very skin glows with sunshine; sapodilla brown, they call that colour in BG, after the sweetest fruit that grows in this clime, dull brown on the outside, succulently golden on the inside. She was bald when she first entered the world, but her hair has now started to grow in soft black curls. Winnie gathers it up to the top of her head and decorates it with a little bow. If she was quick on all fours, she is even quicker on two feet and now she is everywhere, up and down and all around. Her older brothers adore her, watch over her, play with her, talk to her, entertain her, protect her. And even her younger brothers seem to be under her spell; the twins, born six months after Grace, willingly cede to her their right as the youngest to the most attention.

Grace might have grown up a brat with all this coddling; but she hasn't. Sunshine is her very nature. Pretty children, even at a very young age, can be manipulative and demanding – not so this child. It is as if all Winnie's accumulated hopes and dreams over the years have gathered into a single flow of blessings and entered Grace's soul.

I have been living with them in Georgetown ever since the house was completed. Frankly, I no longer saw the point of living with Yoyo at Promised Land. Yoyo's streak of self-critique and self-improvement ended soon after Grace's birth, and she reverted to type.

If Grace's birth has brought joy to Winnie's family, it brought disaster to Yoyo's. Hardly a month later Clarence, staggering home from some party or other, fell into an irrigation canal and drowned.

Yoyo undertook the requisite mourning, but I had the distinct feeling that Clarence's death came as rather a relief to her. The fact that he was the official estate owner-in-waiting, while knowing not one whit about the sugar business, had always irked her; now she spoke of an official instatement of herself as head of operations, and wrote Archie a long letter to that effect.

In the meantime she dismissed Jim, having recruited a new estate manager, a Mr Geoffrey Burton. Burton is a formidable chief. Jim's way of offering perks for better worker performance is not his style; quite the opposite. He punishes. Female labourers are now required to work through their entire pregnancies, and return to work one day after birth – Jim had given them the last few months of pregnancy off, as well as a month after birth. The sick are required to work unless they are practically carrying their head under their arm in the fields. Retirement age has been entirely abolished: now, a man or woman must work until they drop. No days off. An earlier start and a later end to the day. That is Burton's style.

Burton is American. He is from Louisiana, where he is the youngest son of a large and prosperous sugar estate owner – he knows the business, grew up with a sugar spoon in his mouth, like Yoyo. He came to BG hoping to research the sugar industry here and, I learned, to investigate the possibility of growing tobacco. He and Yoyo have reserved a fallow piece of land at the back of the estate and are experimenting with tobacco, and there are plans to develop the Essequibo lands for that purpose. Archie would have a fit if he were here.

Burton is single, and quite handsome, and it soon became clear to me what was going on between him and Yoyo. She makes no secret of it; I assume that, once again, she is trying for a son. I suppose she intends to marry Burton but is putting the cart before the horse, so to speak; calculating as ever. She is so set on having a son! Such things never end well; we saw that the last time she tried. But of course my opinion is of no consequence to Yoyo. As ever, she does what she wants. I dread to think what will happen if she marries Burton. He is not at all the type she can wrap round her finger; he is no Clarence. My guess is that he is just as calculating as she, and is playing a waiting game with her.

When Jim left so did I. So much pleasanter it is too, living with George and Winnie in their new home. From the first, George wanted it big, and big it is, with the drawing room occupying almost the entire ground floor and a lovely kitchen at the back, with stairs leading down into the backyard, which Winnie has left wild and wonderful for the boys; fruit trees to climb, a treehouse, a swing – everything a child could desire. The boys go fishing in the roadside rainwater gutters outside the house. They collect tadpoles and watch them grow. They ride their bicycles everywhere, and have made Waterloo Street, the quieter road round the corner, their own private bike-yard. They have a dog and are teaching him tricks.

* * *

As for me: I am busier than ever. I am giving violin lessons to neighbourhood children, and so is Winnie. Having taught Humphrey the instrument, she realised that she has a talent for teaching, and so has taken on two students, who she sees together once a week. She will have to give that up soon, though, when the new baby arrives. I have two classes, one of five for wealthier children whose parents pay, and another class of six for children of poor parents; this is free. I do enjoy it. I have been asked by the headmistress of Bishops' High School if I would like a job as music teacher there, and I am considering it.

George has been promoted once again. He was so happy to abandon his postman's uniform, and go to work in a shirt and tie! Now he never leaves the house without his new uniform – such a dapper fellow he is! He now has a motor-car, although he uses it rarely – he still goes to work on his trusty bicycle. And he has taught Winnie to drive – she does need a car to ferry the boys around town while George is at work, as she refuses to hire a chauffeur.

Last week we all went to the Botanic Gardens in the car – I don't know how we all fitted in, but we did, one practically on top of the other. There's a little zoo there, and the boys were fascinated by the caged wild animals. A real jaguar! Gordon stood watching it pacing for ages. I felt sad for it, though. Wild animals should be free. And there was a harpy eagle and all sorts of horrible snakes. When we had finished we went to see the manatee, in the pond outside the zoo. At first there was nothing to be seen, just a silvery-brown stretch of water reflecting the trees surrounding it. But the boys knew what to do. They picked grass and threw it on to the water and whistled, and slowly, slowly, ripples appeared and then the big black snout of the manatee as it rose from the depths and devoured the grass. The boys screamed and pointed and jumped up and down, and I looked at them and marvelled at their beauty and their joy.

On Saturdays the family packs itself into the car and George drives them to special places up the coast and down the Demerara. On Sundays, they all go for a walk to the Sea Wall, and occasionally I go with them. We walk along the Promenade greeting other families. We go down to the beach and the boys play cricket in their Sunday best. We walk towards the mouth of the Demerara and out along the jutting promontory of the groyne, watching the ships come in and go out, and we talk of far-off lands, and I tell them about Europe, England and Austria and particularly Salzburg, and they are eager to see the world out there. Gordon says he will fly an aeroplane one day, into the backlands of this wild country, to places no one has ever been before.

It is all so perfect. Perhaps it is too perfect. Perhaps this very perfection is the cause of my unease. A sense of foreboding, almost.

Chapter Forty

Winnie

'So, whose turn is it to push the pram?'

'Mine!' yelled Gordon and Charley together.

'You will have to take it in turns, then. Gordon first, then Charley. Humph, are you all right carrying Grace?'

'Of course!' said my eldest son. I expected nothing less; of all the boys, Humphrey was the quietest, but the most dependable, the most trustworthy, the most likely to complete a boring task without complaint. Not that carrying Grace to the Sea Wall was boring; but, at just over two, she was getting too heavy for the younger boys. I have heard that there are sitting-prams for toddlers on sale in England now; I shall send for one. Her little legs are strong, but not strong enough for walks like the one to the Sea Wall – a long way for her as yet. A little push-pram so she can sit and look around when she is tired would be ideal.

We gathered the boys and the pram – Freddy was just two months old – and off we went, George and I and our little horde, on our Sunday outing to the promenade. We were well organised, as ever. First walked whoever was pushing the pram – Gordon today – with Freddy. Then came whoever *wasn't* pushing the pram, Charley for now, hand in hand with both Leo and Will, one on either side. Then came Humph, carrying Grace. George and I brought up the rear, each of us carrying a twin. Passers-by coming down from the wall invariably smiled and greeted us as they walked by, men raising their hats and women waving at Grace, who always waved back. Since we occupied the entire pavement, they would kindly move on to the street itself to pass us, as did those coming up behind, who were moving faster than we were. We took our time. We were in no hurry. Sunday is a day of leisure, after all.

Eight boys. Each of them unique – one of a kind. Each of them precious. It is hard to imagine, now, that I had felt disappointment over four of them – Gordon, Charley, Will and Leo – just because they weren't girls. How silly of me! I could not bear to think now about the possibility of any one of those four not having been born, or having been a girl instead. They were just what the family needed, and their place in the collective was inviolable. I must have been in some kind of delirium – for years! It took a terrible tragedy to wake me up.

And then came Grace. And the twins and Freddy, who complete us. And I do mean that. I won't refer to them as accidents, but they were surprises, and George and I both agree that eight boys and one daughter are enough. There are ways and means of not having children, and *not* having children is our new aim. From now on we will enjoy what we have, stopping just short of ten. Nine is a good number.

So off we went, crossing the street to the pavement – Humphrey, as usual, walking carefully out to the middle of the street, raising his hand to stop the oncoming traffic – and then to the corner, and up Camp Road to the Sea Wall. The Quints of All Boys Town – that's what the older boys still called us all, even though we had long left Albouystown. We left when Grace joined the family; but we seemed still rooted there.

Ma and Pa once again live in their old quarters, having rented out the annexe we built so many years ago. We visit them regularly, and the boys are always delighted to meet again their old friends and convince them that no, we are not now among the high and mighty. We go back every Saturday evening, because that's the evening that George gives his concerts in the church hall. They are invariably packed. George's singing voice has matured along with him and now it holds a deep resonance that always moves listeners to tears. He does not speak much. George has become as steady as an oak. Together we hold this family together, wild though the boys can be.

Sadly, only one of my children – Will – seems so far to have inherited George's musical talent. I do not count Mama and myself among the talented. Yes, we are good – but our talent is *acquired,* whereas George is a natural, as is Will. But music is a vital part of our lives, and we make it every evening. Music, I feel, is the glue that holds us together. Our hearts beat as one when we sing together, and now that Mama has joined us and brought the piano down from Promised Land – well, we are now as good as a choir! The Quint Family Choir – perhaps that should be our next sobriquet. But we will wait till the younger children are old enough to find their own voices. Who knows – perhaps one of them will be a natural, too, like George!

But I ramble. I was about to recount this one Sunday, shortly after Grace's second birthday; a perfectly normal Sunday excursion to the promenade, except for what happened once we got there.

Who did we run into, but Yoyo!

I had not seen her since long before Grace's birth. Once we had reached a truce, it seemed we no longer cared to meet. George and I certainly never return to Promised Land – which in a way saddens me. I would love for the boys, and now Grace, to see where and how I grew up; to know that vast Corentyne sky, and the endless fields of green, sugar cane fronds waving gently in the fresh sea air. To breathe in the intoxicating, unforgettable smell of burnt sugar, to feel the thrill of the seasons of sugar. It is a special place, and their birthright. But we never even speak of making such a trip. Perhaps, deep inside, we both know why.

When Yoyo gave Grace to us, of course; that would have been the time for a thorough reconciliation. Grace is the greatest present of all time, and makes up for all the mistakes of the past. If she were the result – this perfect child – surely one could no longer speak of a *mistake*. Grace *had* to come. There could not be a world without Grace. If Grace had not been born the world would have had a vacuum, a dark hole where she should be. A ridiculous notion, I know, but that's how essential she felt.

Grace's existence has softened me even more towards Yoyo; I wrote her a letter soon after the birth, but she never replied. George worried for a while, saying that we needed an official adoption, but I pooh-poohed that notion. I don't want to deal with lawyers and officialdom. I feel that doing so would put a pall on the miracle of Grace. I love the notion of *trust*. Trust between humans, I feel, is perhaps the highest virtue of all. I trust Yoyo. I am grateful to her. This gift she has given us – well, it has erased all hard feelings. Though I have no urge to meet her, I have forgiven her.

In retrospect, though, after this outing, I have a strange feeling in my belly. So does George.

Chapter Forty-One

George

When I saw Yoyo walking towards us, arm in arm with a tall, blond, sunburnt gentleman, my heart skipped a beat.

It wasn't a good beat.

She was smiling, and not in a good way. She looked up at her companion, back at us, back at him; they exchanged a few words. And then they were in front of us.

Winnie, bless her heart, was as naïve as ever. Ever grateful to Yoyo for the gift of Grace, Winnie had conceived the ridiculous idea that Yoyo would want to know and to see how Grace was developing. She had sent her photos. I tried to stop her but she wouldn't hear of it; she just said, 'Oh *George!* Find some generosity in your heart!'

Winnie in her innocence did not understand one thing: the wounds of the past were deep, and though forgiven, and on the surface healed, I knew how easily the scar could tear. And even the tiniest opening – well, we could do without it.

But this was not to be a tiny opening. Somehow I could sense that. Had had that feeling all along, perhaps from the moment Grace was placed into my hands that Easter Sunday two years ago. And whenever Winnie said we must trust Yoyo, something at the back of my mind screamed no, I don't.

She approached us boldly, smiling. Glancing at Winnie, I saw that she was smiling too, but I know my Winnie and I thought that she was nervous. There was something predatory in Yoyo's smile and Winnie, despite all good intentions, must have felt it. Winnie is naïve, yes, but also extraordinarily sensitive. And sometimes that sensitivity overrides her inborn ability to see the good in others, and to trust. In this case, I felt that flicker of anxiety within her, and squeezed her hand.

'It's all right,' I said under my breath.

'How lovely to see you, Winnie!' gushed Yoyo. Turning to me, she said, 'And you too, George. How are you? A family day, I see!' She spread her arms to include the boys, scattered around the promenade. 'May I introduce my fiancé. Mr Geoffrey Burton.'

Mr Burton shook our hands and nodded, smiling with his lips but not his eyes. His handshake was stiff, and too firm. It crushed my hand.

Yoyo's gaze turned downwards. Grace was walking before us, pulling along Duckie, her yellow wooden duck on wheels; it was her favourite toy. Yoyo fixed her eyes on Grace. I was watching her features like a hawk and I noticed the moment of transformation. The moment the darkness in Yoyo's soul fled, to be replaced with a deep, sweet tenderness. Love. I witnessed that moment. Grace had once again unwittingly worked her magic.

I reached out in that moment and gathered Grace protectively into my arms, picking up Duckie with my free hand. She protested and struggled.

'Walk! Walk with Duckie!' she said, and I handed Duckie to her, but it wasn't enough. 'Walk! I want walk! Put down!'

But I held her tight.

Yoyo's eyes remained fixed on Grace, still wriggling in my arms.

'Shush, Grace, I'll put you down in a moment,' I said.

'Grace, look! Here's a nice aunty wanting to say hello!' said Winnie then, and my heart sank. I longed to be able to say to her, 'Beware, Winnie, beware. Be on your guard! Sharks in the water!'

But Grace heard Winnie's words and turned round and met Yoyo's gaze. She stopped struggling. What did she see in those devouring eyes? What did she feel? Even I, a witness to it all, could feel their power, their hunger, their thirst. Yoyo drank Grace in, pulled her in like a magnet, silenced her, stilled her. I could not see Grace's face but I could imagine those huge dark eyes gazing unerringly back at Yoyo, puzzled, perhaps – who was this lady stranger, why is she looking at me like that – but unable to resist.

At last, Winnie woke up to what was happening and acted.

'Come, Grace, come to Mummy!' she said, reaching out for her daughter. But Yoyo was faster. She reached inside her handbag and removed a little stuffed dog, which she handed to Grace.

'Woof-woof!' said Grace, and Yoyo smiled in delight. She held out her arms. 'Do you want to come to Aunty Yoyo?' she said. Did I detect mockery in that word Aunty, or am I imagining it in retrospect? I cannot tell. I only know it was bad. Because Grace held out her chubby arms to Yoyo and instead of obeying her real mother, Winnie, she almost leapt into Yoyo's arms. Yoyo chuckled in triumph.

'Oh, she likes me!' she said, and there was definitely mockery in *those* words.

By this time Winnie had finally sensed the malevolence in Yoyo's actions. Why, after all, had she been carrying a little toy in her bag? Yes, she had Georgetown friends who were parents, and she probably gave them presents. But if so, why would the toy be in her bag? What was she doing on the promenade on a Sunday afternoon? Georgetown was small and everyone knew everyone else's business. That we come here every Sunday is common knowledge.

This was planned, and it wasn't a good thing. Yoyo was stretching out feelers towards Grace. Feelers, warm to our golden child, cold to us.

The usual empty small talk followed. Winnie asked Yoyo when she was getting married. Yoyo smiled and said, mysteriously, 'soon.' Mr Burton said that he would be returning to his parents' home in Louisiana that week, to 'tie up some loose ends'.

'After that,' he said, 'we'll see. We're in no hurry.'

Yoyo handed Grace back to Winnie. She wore an odd expression on her face.

The conversation, stilted as it was, ran out, and the two of them said their goodbyes. After Yoyo and Mr Burton had gone, Winnie and I looked at each other.

'George – what was that about?' she asked.

'I've no idea. But I don't like it.'

* * *

A few days later Winnie telephoned me at work, a thing I had asked her to do only in dire emergencies. Her voice was shrill with panic.

'George, George, come home! Please come home as soon as you can! She wants Grace back!'

Chapter Forty-Two

Ruth

The lawyer's letter was short, and dripped with honey. It thanked Winnie and George effusively for their willingness to foster Yoyo's daughter Mary during her mother's illness. Yoyo, it claimed, had now recovered sufficiently to care for her daughter, and was naturally most eager to do so. Winnie and George were requested to deliver the child to Margaret Smythe-Collingsworth's home by Friday at 4 p.m. Since it was likely that an affectionate relationship had developed between foster-parents and child, Yoyo was more than willing to negotiate a visitation schedule, whereby either Winnie or George (one at a time, please!) would be welcome to visit Mary at Promised Land occasionally. A sentence confirming Yoyo's deep gratitude for the service rendered.

There was one sentence containing a veiled threat. Should the child not be delivered as requested Yoyo would have no option but to seek a judicial order.

And that was it.

I held a weeping Winnie in my arms as we waited for George to arrive.

'I should have listened to him. I'm such a fool! Why did I trust her? We should have adopted her properly when she was a baby. I'm a fool, Mama, the biggest fool on earth!'

I rubbed her back and said nothing, because there was nothing to say. She was correct. She had acted foolishly, and all in the name of trust. Sometimes Winnie was too kind for her own good, and this was one of those times. Trust Yoyo? Speaking as her own mother, I would rather trust a snake. I had always advised against trusting Yoyo, as had George. But Winnie had insisted that trust was the foundation of all that was meaningful between humans. She wanted to trust her sister. She needed to.

And now this.

George burst through the door.

'Show me the letter!'

Winnie waved it in his direction, her face buried in my shoulder. George grabbed it, scanned it and bounded to the phone.

'Who're you calling?'

'Who do you think? Andrew Stewart, of course. Best lawyer in Georgetown.'

But as it turned out, not even Andrew could save Grace from Yoyo's claws. Winnie and George did not have a leg to stand on. Not even the fact that George was Grace's biological father helped; Clarence's name as the child's father was on the birth certificate – a copy of which was enclosed in the lawyer's letter – and that, it seemed, sufficed. Biology did not count.

'But everyone can *see* that Clarence is not the father!' fumed George. 'Just *look* at her! Everyone *knows* that we…' He glanced at Winnie and left the sentence unfinished.

'It doesn't matter,' said Andrew, who had rushed over the moment he finished work. We were all sitting in the gallery discussing the way forward. Winnie, thank goodness, had managed to calm herself. Grace herself was out in the backyard with the boys. 'Clarence was the legal father, as Yoyo's husband. He didn't contest fatherhood, so there's nothing we can do.'

'But we have raised her for two years!' Winnie wailed. 'Surely that counts for something!'

'As foster-parents. Foster-parents know that they are not the real parents and must sooner or later return the child. That's what fostering means.'

'But she gave Grace to us! Gave, not lent! Mama knows – Mama is the one who tried to persuade Yoyo to keep her!'

'It's true,' I said. 'I didn't like the idea from the start. I begged Yoyo to reconsider, to wait a few days. But Yoyo insisted. "Give her to George," she said.'

'It's your word against hers,' said Andrew. 'Yoyo will argue that "give her to George" meant a temporary arrangement. And since nothing is in writing—'

'But we have a witness! Nurse Prema was there – she heard everything. She saw that Yoyo rejected the child.'

'That was then. The fact of the birth certificate remains. I cannot argue against that. There's nothing I can do, unfortunately.'

'I'm not handing her over. I'm not.'

And Winnie didn't. It was a declaration of war, and Yoyo responded swiftly with a slash of the sword: early on Saturday morning, someone knocked on the front door.

Humphrey ran to open it and called out: 'Ma, it's the police!'

We were sitting at the breakfast table; immediately, all the adults leapt to their feet. We hurried towards the front door. Humphrey had already let them in: two police officers, one with a paper in his hand. He looked at George.

'Court order, sir. We have come to collect the child Mary Smedley-Cox.'

'Well, you can't have her!' cried Winnie. She turned on her heel and rushed back to the dining table, where she scooped Grace from her high-chair and ran towards the back door.

The next minutes were dreadful, among the worst of my entire life. The staid and thickset policemen proved more agile than they looked. They ran in pursuit of Winnie and cornered her. One of them held her, gently but firmly, and while she writhed and struggled the other pried a shrieking Grace from her clasped arms.

Winnie screamed. George yelled. The boys all cried out their protest; Gordon flung himself against the officer who was gradually winning the fight for Grace and pummelled his back. Will climbed the back of the other officer as if he were a tree. The other boys hopped and yelled and screamed. Even the baby, Freddy, in his downstairs cot next to the table, wailed in terror. As for me – I was the only one not screaming, the only one trying, at least, although failing, to remove the boys from the commotion. I managed to grab the twins, one with each hand, and took them into the kitchen. This was not a thing they should be witnessing. I closed the door and went back for Will and Leo. By this time Grace was in the officer's arms and he was heading for the door with his colleague, Winnie behind him screaming and tearing at his clothes. All in vain.

George, finally, was the one to admit defeat. He pulled Winnie back, held her in his arms, where she broke down in the most heart-rending sobs I have ever heard. Worse than at the loss of Gabriella Rose. Worse than my own sobs at the loss of Edward John.

The boys said nothing; they only stared. I shepherded them away. George simply held Winnie and let her cry, stroking her back.

The last thing I heard as I herded the boys into the kitchen was Winnie's anguished cry: 'I hate her! Oh, I hate her! I'll *kill* her! I'll *kill* her, I'll *kill* her!'

Chapter Forty-Three

George

How we all got through that week, I'll never know. Grace's absence left a space in our family that immediately filled with a grief so sharp it was almost as if she had died. The more sensitive boys – Humphrey and Will – cried openly every hour or so, while the others palpably held back their tears, trying to be manly, and ended up as stiff ghosts of themselves. Even the twins seemed to feel, if not understand, the tragedy, crying twice as much as usual. Freddy, who hardly ever cried, now did so constantly. Winnie, of course, was the worst affected. She went through the motions of her duties, an empty robot, her tears dried but her soul atrophied. She who had run this household as if she had eight arms and kept it going like clockwork suddenly complained of exhaustion, and retired to bed each day after lunch (this I learned from a concerned Mama). She who literally wouldn't hurt a fly – I had never seen her with a fly-swat in her hand – and never raised a finger against our children, slapped Gordon for one of his many little transgressions; the first time ever, shocking everyone.

To relieve the situation we engaged a children's nurse, a maid and a kitchen-girl. I worried that Winnie had reached her breaking point; that she would never recover, never be her old self again. As for me, my agony was almost more than I could bear. But life went on, and I moved through the week, albeit as if pulled by puppet strings. Thank goodness for Ruth, who moved to Winnie's place at the core of the family and held us all together.

The following Saturday, a week after Grace's departure, I awoke to find the space beside me empty. This in itself was not a problem; Winnie always rose before me. The problem was the note on the pillow. Only three words, followed by a large W: *I'm so sorry*.

I leapt from my bed and raced down the stairs. It was still dark but outside the kiskadees were already heralding the break of dawn. The house itself was as still as death; nobody had stirred. On a normal Saturday Winnie would be up, bustling in the kitchen, preparing the dough for the breakfast bakes, peeling mangoes for some delicious pudding, grating coconuts – all the things she loved to do for us, and more, because it was Saturday and we would spend the day together. Today, though, the kitchen was dead.

Dread filled my being. What exactly was she sorry for? Where could she have gone so early in the day? I ran down the front stairs to the yard – and immediately I knew. The car was gone. And then I remembered the dream. In it I had been preparing to go on a long journey. I did not know where to. 'Crank the car for me,' I said to Gordon, because he loved cranking. And he had cranked and cranked. 'That's enough,' I said, but Gordon kept on cranking, and the noise in the dream had been so loud it had almost woken me up, but not quite, and I had gone back to sleep.

The cranking had been real.

* * *

I knew instinctively where she had gone. The grief that had been eating into my soul all week turned to black dread, a yawning cave in my innards. I raced back up the stairs, up to Mama's room. Banged on her door, yelled for her. A moment later the door opened and Mama stood on the threshold in her green nightie, rubbing the sleep from her eyes.

'What's the matter, George?'

I was out of breath from my panicked race upstairs, but I managed to pant: 'Winnie's gone. She's taken the car.'

Mama was immediately wide awake, her voice sharp, urgent.

'What? No! Where's she gone to?'

'Where do you think!'

'No, no, no, she couldn't – she can't drive all that way!'

'Of course she can. Mama, we have to stop her! She might do – anything!'

Winnie's desperate cries last week, as Grace was torn from her arms, echoed within me. What if – what if… But no. Not Winnie. Winnie wouldn't hurt a fly, much less… Winnie was the quintessence of calm and sensibility. She was highly emotional, true, but she knew how to tame those emotions for the greater good of the family. With Winnie, head and heart were in perfect balance. She wouldn't do anything to jeopardise our lives. She wouldn't. She wouldn't go so far.

Would she?

Was there, perhaps, a wild beast lurking in the recesses of Winnie's soul, a beast, which, when provoked, would lunge forward and do the impossible? Had it been provoked to that extent? Mother animals, when their young are threatened, will fight to the death. Mother-power when provoked is manpower multiplied by infinity.

Could Winnie kill? Her own *sister*? I pushed the thought away before it was even fully formed.

'I have to go,' I cried to Ruth. 'I have to stop her, bring her back, before, before…'

Before it's too late, I wanted to say, but I couldn't. I would not let myself imagine the worst. Logic tried to argue with my panic. It was all right. Winnie may have driven to Promised Land but she had no outrageous plan to do – to do something terrible. I couldn't even think the words. Not thinking them meant it couldn't happen.

'Yes, you'd better go,' said Mama. 'How will you get there?' Her voice was calm, sensible, not panicked. I needed that. I took some deep breaths and tried to think, to plan.

'I'll ring Andrew. Ask to borrow his car.'

Slowly, rational thought began to claw away the panic. Winnie, it told me, would have planned this thing carefully. She would have aimed to reach the first ferry to Berbice, which was at 6 a.m. It was now just past that time. Probably she was on the ferry right now, the car in the ship's belly, she near the bow gazing at the lightening of the horizon as the sun made its way upwards. I could almost feel into her. Feel the passion driving her forwards, the dastardly sense of revenge and sheer hatred having overtaken all that was good in her soul. Now, being honest with myself, I knew that I had felt it all week.

Provoked enough, Winnie could kill. She would; as a tiger mother would kill to protect her cubs, so could Winnie kill anyone who took a baby from her.

How quickly could I get there? Could I prevent the worst? Was there some way of warning Yoyo?

There wasn't. Telephone lines had not yet reached Berbice. As for telegraphy – well, that was my forte, my domain. We closed at night, but as head of the department I could easily get into the office and send a telegram myself.

But it was no use, because the telegraph office in New Amsterdam would still be closed. It would only open at eight, like the one in Georgetown, and by then it would be too late.

I could drive there myself, but I, too, would arrive too late.

There was nothing I could do except drive after Winnie. Whatever Winnie had planned would take its course. All I could do was arrive after the fact, into whatever mess she had caused.

'You'll stay, won't you, and look after things here?' I said to Ruth.

'Yes, yes of course. You just go.'

I turned and walked to the phone, dialled Andrew's number.

I managed, somehow, falling over the words, to get the story told.

'Of course,' said Andrew. 'Of course you can have the car. Better yet – I'll drive you.'

Chapter Forty-Four

Ruth

I wasn't a witness. This is the story as told to me by others, first Andrew and then Jim.

George and Andrew raced as fast as the car could go to Rosignol, arriving just in time for the nine o'clock ferry. On the other side, they stopped to refill the petrol tank and continued up the coast towards Promised Land. Only about fifteen minutes later, however, they noticed a car parked at the side of the road. It was George's Ford. Andrew stopped and they got out to inspect it.

By now the sun had risen and the day was bright. Peering through the windows of the car, George saw a figure huddled on the back seat. He tried the door, but it was locked, so he knocked on the window. The figure slowly righted itself; it was Winnie. She sat there, forlorn and alone, her face stained with dried tears. When she saw it was George fresh tears pooled in her eyes and trickled down her cheeks.

I can only imagine the sigh of relief that George must have let out. Winnie rubbed her eyes and slowly reached for the door handle. When the door opened George plunged into the back seat and pulled Winnie to him, hugging her and crying.

'I can't do, it George. I can't!'

'Of course you can't.'

'I was going to do it but the car ran out of petrol – I forgot to fill up at New Amsterdam. And then I thought that was a sign. I thought it was a message, not to do it. From God. Or a guardian angel. Or my conscience. Something.'

'Yes, darling, yes!'

'Oh George! I don't know what to do!'

'Let's go home, darling. Let's go home. Andrew will go and get some petrol.' He leaned out of the car, signalled to Andrew and gave him instructions. Andrew nodded, returned to his own car, turned it round and drove off.

'I can't go home, George. I can't go yet. I have to see her. I need to see my daughter! I need to go to Promised Land. I'll *die* if I don't see her!'

'Oh, darling!'

'Please, George, let's go and see her. We've come this far.'

'Darling – it's not so easy. Yoyo—'

'To *hell* with Yoyo! I only want to see my daughter!'

'But she's with Yoyo now. It's not a good idea to go there now, darling. Please! Let's just go home.'

They argued for a while, and Winnie won. Winnie could always wrap George round her little finger. She persuaded George to drive her to Promised Land. George made her promise not to make demands, though: 'You know what Yoyo's like,' he pointed out. 'The more you confront her, the more confrontational she gets. You have to be calm, darling. *Request* a meeting with Grace. Allow Yoyo to think she is being kind and gracious. She did promise visitation rights. That's how to approach this.'

Grace promised to curtail her anger and murderous thoughts, and try for a civil conversation. When Andrew returned with the petrol and they continued on, though, she argued with George again.

'Let her think she is doing you a favour,' he counselled her.

'But she *stole* Grace!'

'No. Grace is her daughter. All she did was break a promise, destroy your trust.'

'That's as bad as stealing.'

'You may be right. But it doesn't matter who's right here. What matters is *strategy*. You want to see Grace – well, you need to play according to Yoyo's rules. All right?'

'All right,' Winnie finally conceded.

So that's what they did. I heard this much from Andrew; he drove back to Georgetown and he reported to me everything that had happened to that point. Needless to say I was relieved, having feared the very worst – some tragedy, brought about by a raging Winnie literally out of her mind with grief. Grief can bring out the darkest impulses in a human – I know that from my own past. In my case, it brought about years of depression. In Winnie it might be violence; I couldn't tell.

Since Winnie was a complete mess – she had slept in her clothes, it turned out, and her face was smudged with dust and tears – they decided to first pay a visit to Jim, so as to clean her up, have some breakfast and generally replenish their inner resources. Jim had always been a touchstone of good sense and advice for both of them, and that was the right decision. Winnie was still very much out of sorts, and it was a good idea for her to regain her composure before she faced Yoyo. Water, rest, food and Jim's company would do the trick.

But even the best-laid plans go awry. As usual, Jim's house was teeming with visitors, among them Arthur Grant, a friend who lived on the main village street. Arthur arrived while Winnie and George were having breakfast. When he heard who they were and where they were going, he shook his head.

'Mistress Cox not home this morning,' he said. 'I see she when I was leaving the house. Driving through the village street, fast-fast. One-a these days she gon' kill somebody, the way she does drive.'

'So she's out? Darn!' said George. George was no doubt eager to get this over with and return to Georgetown.

'But that means Grace will be alone at home! With her nurse-maid!' Winnie's voice was shrill with excitement and new hope. 'George! This is the perfect time to go, if Yoyo's out! Let's just go and grab Grace! Bring her home!'

George sighed, and squeezed Winnie's hand.

'That's nonsense and you know it. They'll just send round the police again. Do you want to go through that agony again? And think about Grace, darling. We can't put her through that. Think how confusing it must be for her!'

Winnie's face fell. 'You're right, I suppose. But if Yoyo's not home we could at least go and visit her.'

Arthur, who had been trying to get a word in edgewise, spoke up then.

'Mistress Cox take the baby with she. I see the nursemaid in the passenger seat, holding the baby.'

'Well, that settles that,' said George, relieved.

'Where could she have gone? How long will she be?' asked Winnie.

'Probably gone to show off her baby to all her friends,' said Jim. 'She's got friends all over the place. New Amsterdam, Planta-tion Glasgow, Plantation Dieu Merci.'

'Really? Even though the baby obviously isn't Clarence's?'

Jim threw back his head and laughed. 'You really don't know your sister! You think Yoyo gives one damn about propriety? The moment she decided to take back that baby – that moment she decided to hell with the scandal. Everyone already knows she slept with George. Might as well be hung for a sheep as a lamb – that's how Yoyo reasons.'

Jim really did know Yoyo better than Winnie did. In spite of her rancour and her rage, Winnie was still inclined to ascribe her own morals and codes of behaviour to her sister – the very way of thinking that had brought about this disaster. A fatal mistake. Winnie was trustworthy and she assumed the same of Yoyo. Had she been as distrustful as I was – as I had warned her to be – she would have insisted on an adoption. She didn't, and now we had this.

'Tell you what,' said Jim. 'Arthur, when you go home keep an eye on the road. When Yoyo comes back home, send a message, or come back and tell us. Meanwhile, Winnie and George can spend some time with me. I haven't seen you-all for years – we'll take time to catch up! How's that for a good plan?'

Winnie was silent. George accepted eagerly. And that's exactly what they did. They were there all day.

* * *

George and Jim tried to spend as normal a day as possible; George kept a close eye on Winnie, spoiled her, buzzed around her to keep her happy, which of course she wasn't. She ate no breakfast and only nibbled at her lunch; she said her stomach was churning, and could she lie down. She made herself comfortable in the downstairs hammock, where she could keep an eye on the front gate. As the day dragged on and neither Arthur nor his emissary reappeared, she grew steadily more nervous, pacing the yard, coming upstairs asking for a glass of water, staring out of the window. George worried, but tried not show it.

'Are you sure they're not back yet?' she kept asking.

'Arthur gon' watch like a hawk. He gon' tell the whole street to watch out, all the neighbours. You know how village people does be! Don't worry. She probably gone to spend the day with friends.'

Winnie would probably have preferred to go and sit on the main street herself, waiting. Once, she suggested going to Promised Land and waiting there.

'I've got the front door key!' she said. 'We can just go in and make ourselves at home and wait.'

'Winnie, Winnie. We can't do that. It's *Yoyo's* home now, not yours. You can't just go in there and wait. That's like breaking and entering!'

three stairs at a time. Smoke, presumably from an open doorway further down the landing, billowed behind him.

'Good God!' cried Jim. George, reaching the foot of the stairs, collapsed into his arms. Holding him aloft with one arm, Jim took the wriggling, screaming bundle from him and flung it to Yoyo, who caught it deftly and ran to the gallery, Winnie in close pursuit, crying, 'Is she all right? Is she all right?'

George collapsed into Jim's arms.

The maid ran from the kitchen with a slopping-over pail of water, the red fire pail always held in readiness in these wooden houses. She headed for the stairs, but Jim raised a hand.

'No!' he said. 'No use. We can't fight the fire. Everybody – downstairs. Outside. Quick!'

Yoyo and her bundle, Winnie and the maid ran for the still-open front door. Jim hoisted the collapsed George over his shoulder, then he too ran for the door. In a trice they were all out of the house, on the front drive.

'We need to get to hospital,' said Winnie, in an instant transformed into a figure of calm. The Winnie of old was back, the crazed beast laid to rest. She laid an arm round Yoyo, who was weeping over the bundled shape of Grace.

'Sssh,' said Winnie to Yoyo. 'She's all right. Hear her crying! That means she's all right.'

'The candle!' Yoyo wailed. 'I must have knocked over the candle! It was on the windowsill! It's all my fault!'

'We need to get her and George to hospital,' Winnie repeated, turning to Jim. But Jim was already at George's car, opening the back door, shoving George into the back seat. He ran round to the front, removed the crank, shoved it into place.

'Take the other car! No room for you both in this one,' he cried to Winnie as he cranked the car. George's car was an almost-new one. The engine turned just once, and began to purr. Jim strode to the driver's door and got in. He turned to Winnie.

'Yoyo's hysterical. You need to go with her and hold the baby. Or drive yourself. Can you manage?'

Winnie took a deep breath to calm her panic. 'But George! I need to be with George!'

'You need to be with Yoyo and the baby,' said Jim, and Winnie nodded.

The watchman appeared out of the darkness.

'Crank the mistress's car!' yelled Jim out of the window as he drove off, wheels crunching on the gravel.

The watchman obeyed, ran to Yoyo's car. The car coughed and spluttered, shuddered and groaned, the lazy old motor reluctant to start. Winnie opened the driver's door.

'Yoyo. Can you drive? Or shall I?'

'I can't! I can't! I have to hold my baby!' wailed Yoyo.

'All right then. I'll drive,' said Winnie nervously.

The watchman cranked at the bonnet. The car juddered, but nothing happened.

'Come on!' wept Yoyo. 'Start! Start! Start!'

Winnie turned to the maid.

'You come too – get in the back. What's your name?'

'Mabel, miss!'

'Good. Sit next to the mistress and try to calm her down.'

Mabel got into the back seat just as the motor turned over, coughed and finally growled into action. The watchman backed away. Already George's car was out of sight. Yoyo's much older car shuddered, almost stopped, coughed again in protest as Winnie turned it to face the gate. She wasn't an experienced driver and had never driven fast. That was Yoyo's forte. But Yoyo was a bawling, spluttering mess, clinging to the equally bawling baby she held in her arms. Winnie said a silent prayer and pressed her foot down on the accelerator, as far as it would go. The car protested, but crept forward, after Jim.

It took two hours to reach the New Amsterdam hospital. George's car was parked outside, empty. The three women, Yoyo still weeping and holding the baby, rushed into the emergency entrance, where they were met by an attendant in white who was waiting for them. He prised Grace from Yoyo's arms, laid her on a bare rusty gurney and wheeled her away, two nurses running beside him, Yoyo at the rear. Winnie closed her eyes and prayed again. She took a deep breath. A nurse approached her and placed a hand on her back.

'Are you all right, madam? Were you injured?'

'No – no, I'm fine. but – my husband. George. Where is he?'

'Oh – the man they brought in earlier. He's got a burn on his arm. And smoke poisoning. They took him to the Burn Unit, madam.'

'Where's the Burn Unit?'

'Come with me.'

The nurse led her outside, pointed to a wooden building across the courtyard.

'That's the Burn Unit. Lots of fires in this country, madam.'

'Thank you.'

'I hope he'll be all right!' the nurse cried after her. 'I'll pray for him!'

Winnie walked across towards the building the nurse had pointed out. She walked slowly, wearily, as if she dreaded reaching it, as if she sensed the worst. A few paces before she arrived Jim emerged from the door. His face was unfathomable. He was struggling to hold back the tears: tears of relief, or tears of pain? Winnie couldn't tell. He said nothing. He simply opened his arms and Winnie fell into them.

And at last she was able to sob, into Jim's broad chest, his mighty arms round her, holding her, offering a comfort that would never be enough.

As for the final outcome: I'll let Yoyo's letter explain.

Epilogue: Eight months later

Yoyo

Dear Winnie,

I've put off writing you this letter for the longest time – ever since that terrible night, but even before that. Long before that. But the time has come now to write it. Everything happened so quickly, afterwards, and I've never seen you since. You said it wasn't my fault but of course it was.

What I've wanted to say to you all this time, what I tried to say to you that night is: I've changed. I really have. People can change, you know. Yes, you know that. You of all people know that. I need to ask your forgiveness. For everything.

I was so blind, Winnie. It was Mary who turned everything around. The moment I saw that girl something in me melted: something hard and unrelenting and proud and self-obsessed. Selfish! The moment I saw her that day on the Sea Wall: that's when it happened. I had to have her, Winnie. I'm sorry but that's the truth. I knew from that moment on that I had to have her – have her back. I know I was harsh the way I went about it but there was no other way as you would not have given her up willingly – would you? You wouldn't.

I had to have her back because I needed her as you don't. You didn't need to learn the lessons of love – I did. And only Mary could teach me. Only she could teach me that love is the greatest, the strongest, the holiest thing on earth. Only she could heal me. And she did. I don't know if I am completely healed but I'm getting there, Winnie, I am. All that hard miserable mixed-up mess that made me such a horrible person – it's gone, it's going. I'm making progress. Remember what Mama used to say: *we live in order to learn the lessons of love.* That's what I'm learning, and Mary is teaching me. You were a natural for those lessons. I wasn't. But I am now.

That night I was so stupid. So blind. So blind in my own happiness I could not see *you* – not really. I could not see your grief and righteous anger. I honestly thought you had already understood that I had to have Mary and had come to visit her, as a friend and sister. I was so eager to let you know I had changed I did not see *you*. That's what selfishness does. It blinds you to the feelings of others. You care only for yourself. You're like a mule with blinkers. That was me, that night, stupidly chattering away unable to see you were about to explode!

So that's my explanation. Mary has healed me, is healing me. I hope that is reason enough for you to at last forgive me. For everything. But because you are the better of us two, and the stronger, I feel you will. I hope you will. I know you will.

I just wanted to say I'm sorry. Sorry about George, sorry about the pain I caused you.

I'm not sorry that Mary is with me. I can't be sorry about that. I just can't. I am sorry I did it the way I did.

I don't think you'll care about my news, but I'll tell you anyway. Jim has been doing well running Promised Land since my departure. As soon as he got my telegram Geoff booked my passage to America and here I am: we married soon after my arrival. You must have heard that from Mama.

But I do not like it here. That is, I like it well enough but it is not the place for Mary. I am a stranger here; the people I have met, those high-class plantation ladies, look down on me because of Mary and I really have no explanation for her existence that would satisfy their judgement. She is a bastard, of mixed race, and there is no place for her here, as there is in BG. She would grow up here an outcast, a pariah, bullied and excluded. She and I, we do not fit in. Geoff was brave to send for us both, but he should have known better. But men never do, do they? Also, since I am here, I have seen his true nature and I do not like it, Winnie. He reminds me so much of Papa – do you remember how shocked we were, when we saw that particular side of Papa? Geoff is the same. Charming and chivalrous on the outside, but a heart of steel when it comes to those beneath him. So for all these reasons we have decided to part company. It will be an amicable divorce as he too sees that we do not belong together. I suppose I am married to the Corentyne, to Promised Land. I cannot be happy anywhere else, not even in Georgetown.

Promised Land might be just a heap of ashes now, but it shall rise again. I shall build it up, make it great, just as I have always promised myself.

* * *

So I am coming home. We are coming home, Mary and I. I have already booked my passage and will arrive on 4 March. I am hoping that by then you have forgiven me. That you will allow Mary and myself to stay in your home for a while – there are matters in Georgetown I need to attend to.

I will rebuild Promised Land, Winnie. I will. You and the boys will always have a home there. The boys need to know their heritage, know the smell of burnt sugar. Perhaps one of them will be interested in sugar farming. Who knows? Mary is their sister; it will be wonderful for her to have eight brothers.

So this is what I am asking. For your forgiveness, and a place in your heart, and in your home. Let me be the sister I was meant to be, before everything went so very wrong! I write this with tears in my eyes, Winnie, and I beg you from the bottom of my heart. Because Mary may have healed me but it is *your* love that will make me whole. Love me as you used to do. Love me again.

Please give my regards to George. I want to say sorry to him too, in person, but I know he isn't as forgiving as you. Nevertheless: I am sorry. Please tell him that.

In all sincerity,

Your sister Yoyo.

Letter from Sharon

Thank you so much for reading *The Sugar Planter's Daughter*. I do hope you enjoyed it as much as I enjoyed writing it.

I'd love to know how you reacted to this story. Did it make you sad? Did it make you cry? Did it make you think? Did it take you back to the past? To a country that you perhaps did not know before? Which of the characters did you like the best, and which one did you love to hate? Did it make you see history from a new perspective? Did it change you in any way? I'd be delighted to hear your reaction, and the very best way of getting back to me is through a review, even a short one.

Getting feedback from readers is always wonderful, and it also helps to persuade other readers to pick up this, or another one of my books, for the first time.

When I write I am always thinking of you, the reader, and feel somehow connected to you. It's thrilling for me to know that out there you, a perfect stranger, are reading the words I wrote, following a story that came from my heart; somehow, this makes you not a stranger, but a friend. Isn't it wonderful how words, stories, can connect us all?

If this is the first 'Winnie' book you've read, perhaps you'd like to find out how her story began. You can do so in the first book of the Quint trilogy, *The Secret Lie of Winnie Cox*. And if you'd like to know how the story continues – because of course it does! – then stay tuned, as I've more up my sleeve. And here's a big secret – you can take a sneak peek far into the future by jumping a few decades: you'll meet Winnie again as a wise Grandma in my previously published novel, *The Small Fortune of Dorothea Q*. She doesn't play the main role in that book, but she's there all right!

To keep up-to-date with the latest news on my new releases, you can sign up to receive an email whenever a new book comes out by clicking on the link below. I promise to only contact you when I have new book out, and of course I'll never pass your email on to anyone else.

www.bookouture.com/sharonmaas

 @sharon_maas

sharonmaasauthor

www.sharonmaas.com

Acknowledgments

How can I ever thank those who gave me this story? It seems to me that everyone I know from my childhood provided the ingredients, starting with my grandmother, Winifred Westmaas, the primary inspiration. Posthumous thanks to my father David Westmaas, my mother Eileen Cox, my aunts and, especially, my uncles from both sides of the family: all gone, unfortunately; and thanks to cousins and friends and neighbours and all the myriad wonderful people I knew growing up in Guyana, or British Guiana, as it was then known. Special thanks go to my cousin-in-law, Peter Halder, whose wonderful memoir about his own childhood in Albouystown woke memories and provided inspiration.

This story grew out of that unique and unforgettable background. I owe it all to them.

I'd like to thank the collection of experts on the AbsoluteWrite forum who answered many of my niggling questions about cars and custody and fires and clubfeet, in particular Jane Smith and Uncle Jim, aka James MacDonald, author.

And of course I'd like to thank the team at Bookouture who helped to birth this book: Lydia Vassar-Smith, Jacqui Lewis, Natasha Hodgson, Tom Feltham, not to mention Oliver Rhodes and the ever-supportive Kim Nash. Speaking of supportive – thanks to my co-authors at Bookouture, the most encouraging and mutually helpful group of people I've ever known. Hugs to you all!